ASHLEY CHANNAE

I0659889

A COUPLE OF FOREVERS

ASHLEY CHANNAE

ASHLEY CHANNAE
PUBLICATIONS

Cover & Design by: ReBelle Design Studio
Edited by: Jill Duska

ISBN: 978-0692264478

Dedicated to
Don, Tiesha, & Diesha.
You never laughed at my dream, and for that, I thank you.

A COUPLE OF FOREVERS

ACKNOWLEDGEMENTS

First and foremost, I would like to give glory and honor to God. Without Him, I wouldn't have this talent. Only He knows the struggle I went through to get where I am today. And I am forever grateful.

To my parents, Stacey and Duane, the weird child you created never had a normal mind, and you two accepted it...LOL. I love you both.

To my brother, DJ, you can do anything you put your mind to. You and the rest of Famous Fly – Don, Ryan, Devin, are going to go far. I just know it. If I can do it, y'all can do it too. HOD will forever make my playlist.

Thank you to all of my family for always keeping me grounded. Whether it was putting me in my place, or making me laugh until I forgot about all of my problems. Tee, Grandma Virginia, Grandma Smith, and Fat-Fat...I love you all so much. And to my Angels, DaDa & Grandad John, I hope I'm making you proud. You two showed me the essence of what a real man should be. RIH, my loves.

To Rochelle at ReBelle Design Studio, thanks for all of your patience, knowledge, and for always keepin' it real.

Thank you to Boo, Peppy, Auntie Carol and Niecey, Shaun, Uncle Shannon, Jamani, Nicole, Ms. Natasha, Kim and everyone at Unique Total Designs, Jonathan, Jason, Leilani, Keona, & Mr. Leonard.

And last, but definitely, not least, thank you to my friends who have not only been my confidants and support system, but also my inspiration – Y'all so ratchet. Y'all know at least one character resembles you...LOL. Ashley C., you're one of the hardest working women I know. You're going to run major things one day. Gernique, you're going to take the world by storm with all of your many talents. Ashley J., your style and sarcasm make you one of the most unique people I know. Tiesha and Diesha, you're both going to find your way in this world. You still have so much learning to do.

Rekay, we've been best friends for over twelve years, and I've loved every moment of it. You're well on your way to bringing in the big bucks, and I'm so proud of you. To my sister Kiara, you are a beautiful mother, and I never see you complain a day in your life. Even though you're younger, sometimes I look up to you more than you know. Keep working hard, and don't let anyone hold you back. And to Shyla "Tiff" Miles, these stories started as a bet...which I won, btw. Who knew we'd be where we are today? I'm so proud of you and all that you've done. This is just the beginning for us both.

If I forgot anyone, y'all know I have my blonde moments. It wasn't intentional. I love you all.
Kisses - *Muah!*

Please contact me with any questions or feedback.
Email: Ashley.Channae@gmail.com
Twitter & Instagram: @ThatsSoooAshley
Facebook: facebook.com/AshleyChannae

ASHLEY CHANNAE

PROLOGUE

The sun was shining, the birds were chirping, and the warm breeze made this particular day in April that much more special for Kyree Wright. Today was the day that he was getting out of prison. After doing three years for selling drugs, he'd grown an appreciation for the smaller things in life. He was going to miss the friends he'd gained over the years, but if he ever saw them again, he knew for damn sure it wouldn't be in a cell.

As the gates to the prison opened, awaiting Kyree was his longtime friend, Fat Boy. He hadn't even noticed Kyree walk up due to his loud car stereo. Kyree just shook his head and laughed to himself. Fat Boy was always so extra. He was looking down at his phone, sending a text message, and standing in front of an all-black 745 with twenty-four inch rims and speakers that could be heard a mile away. As Kyree got closer, Fat Boy looked up and a mile-wide smile crept across his chunky black face.

"My nigga." Fat Boy quickly dapped him up with a pound and a hug. "A'ight, man, that's enough. You been locked up for three years. Who knows what kind of habits you developed in there." They both laughed.

"Nigga, don't get shit twisted, before I have to fuck yo' fat ass up," Kyree warned him.

"Looks like you ain't missed no meals while you were locked up either," Fat Boy pointed out, noticing the extra pounds that Kyree had put on.

"This is all muscle. Ain't nothing to do in there but play ball and lift weights."

"Whatever you say, fat ass," Fat Boy laughed.

"Man, get yo' corny ass in the car and get me the hell away from this muthafucka."

"Naw, this here for you." Fat Boy handed him the keys. "You know I prefer trucks and shit."

"Naw, that's just the only thing yo' big ass can fit in," Kyree laughed.

"Whatever, man. But you know I'm gon' look out for you until you get back on your feet."

"Yeah, good lookin' on the whip. But my ass is not trying to get caught driving without a license right now. So take me to get my L's first. And for now, you drive."

Kyree didn't want to be anywhere near Riker's Island. He had no business being in New York in the first place. Virginia was his home. His plan had been to make one last drop and then be out of the game for good. But things didn't go as planned. Instead of seeing his usual buyers, he saw a swarm of alphabet boys. NYPD, FBI, and ATF were all awaiting his arrival. They offered him probation with no jail time, if only he'd give up his supplier. But Kyree would never give up Pablo. He'd treated him so well over the years, and besides that, he wasn't a fuckin' snitch. He'd die before he ran his mouth like a bitch.

As they pulled away from the prison, Fat Boy played Akon's "Locked Up," his attempt at being funny. Kyree gave him a look and then just laughed at his foolishness. He gazed out the window and actually started to relate to the song. His family only wanted him to do right, but he could never stay out of trouble. He could count on one hand the people that he cared about and who he knew would always have his back: his mother, Fat Boy, his sister, and his ex-girlfriend. He and his ex had been together forever, and although in his last letter to her he told her to move on with her life, he was ready to get his shit together and get her back. No one but Fat Boy knew he was coming home a year early for good behavior, but everyone was sure to be in for a surprise.

CHAPTER 1

"**J**az!" Monica yelled from the bottom of the stairs. "Come help me finish these place settings for the reception!"

"Do I have to?" Jaz whined.

"Uh...yeah!" Monica gave her a "duh" look.

"If you say so, Mama Mo," Jaz joked as she descended the stairs.

"Don't get smart," Monica warned. Although they were both twenty-five, Monica always felt like she had to be the responsible one - or as Jaz would call her, "somebody's mama". But they'd been best friends forever and accepted each other's flaws.

"I was just putting my godson down for his nap. He falls right to sleep for me. You know he likes me more," Jaz teased.

"My son is only two, he doesn't know any better," Monica laughed.

"Whatever. Let's just finish these place settings so I can go home."

Monica was helping Jaz with the place settings for her wedding. They'd been working on a suitable arrangement all day and had yet to find anything that worked. But Monica, being the organized one, eventually found a plan that both Jaz and her future husband Michael could agree on.

"I don't know what I'd do without you, Mo." Jaz hugged her.

"Probably have a ghetto-ass wedding," Monica said as they both laughed.

They sat and reminisced while watching re-runs of *Love and Hip Hop* over a few glasses of wine. The two could talk for hours about any and everything. But Jaz had to be at work early the next morning, so she decided to head home.

After watching Jaz to her car, Monica closed the door behind her. She sighed when she saw the mess they'd made. *She*

3

would leave without helping me clean up, huh? Monica slightly laughed to herself. She washed the few dishes they'd made and was just about to put away the place settings when the doorbell rang. For a second, she wondered who it could be, but then she saw Jaz's cell phone sitting on the table. Monica picked up the phone and started to chastise Jaz before she even opened the door.

"Girl, you would lose your damn head if it wasn't attached to your body," Monica laughed as she opened the door. Her smile was quickly replaced with a look of shock. "Oh my God!" She covered her mouth with her hands. She just knew her eyes were playing tricks on her.

But then the visitor spoke. "Is that how you greet your big brother?"

"Kyree!" She smiled and hugged him tightly around his neck. "I missed you," she admitted.

"I missed you too, Big Head," he chuckled.

"Come in, boy, let me see you." She ushered him inside and closed the door. She looked him up and down. He was sporting a white V-neck tee, dark blue Levi's, and white and blue Griffey's. She couldn't believe that he was standing right there in front of her. She wanted to cry.

"Damn, you picked up some weight," she joked.

"I wish people would stop saying that shit."

"Boy, boo. When did you get out? Does Ma know? Are you home for good? Are you gonna leave the streets alone this time? How'd you get here?" Monica had so many questions to ask him and she couldn't wait.

"Damn, Mo, slow down. Shit, can a nigga have a seat first?" Kyree laughed at his sister's eagerness. "We could discuss this over a home-cooked meal or something, 'cause a nigga's hungry." He rubbed his stomach.

Monica shook her head. Nothing about her brother had changed. "Alright, I was gonna whip up some spaghetti. Make yourself at home, 'cause we have a lot to talk about."

The sound of a child calling for his mother startled Kyree at first. He'd almost forgotten his sister had a son. Monica's two-year-old son, Kayden, met her halfway at the steps. She picked him up in her arms as he wiped his sleepy eyes. "Kayden, this is your uncle, Kyree," Monica proudly introduced him.

Kyree was in shock at how much the little boy looked like Monica. He had her doe-shaped eyes, milk chocolate skin tone, and dark curly hair. He was beautiful. "Hey, li'l man." Kyree stretched his arms out for Kayden and he went right to his uncle.

Monica was surprised. He didn't really like strangers and usually put up a fight when they tried to hold him.

"Now go cook me and li'l man something to eat, peasant," Kyree joked, and Monica hit him in the arm.

Kyree played with his nephew, whom he fell in love with the moment he held him in his arms. They all sat down to eat while Monica asked him a million and one questions. She couldn't help herself. She loved her big brother and hated that she could only get to New York twice a year to see him. Growing up, he was the only father figure she had. When he got locked up, it crushed her heart.

Kyree was relieved when Kayden fell asleep. It was the only thing that saved him from his sister's interrogating.

"I'm going to put him down for bed, but you better not leave. We still have a lot to talk about."

"Whatever you say, Mama Mo," he joked.

Kyree reached for the TV remote. As he flicked through a few channels, he heard Monica's phone vibrating and found it behind one of the pillows on the couch. The picture of a man he'd never seen before popped across the screen, and the name under it read "My Bae". He nodded his head, thinking he had to get to know this dude his sister was calling Bae. After Kayden's father left her high and dry with a baby to raise on her own, he wasn't gonna let another nigga do that to her. He was about to take the phone upstairs to her, but the ringing of the doorbell stopped him.

"Hey, Ky, get that for me!" Monica yelled downstairs.

Kyree opened the door and the girl behind it had her head down, rummaging through her purse.

"Girl, I don't know where the hell I left my cell phone. I think the last place I saw it was here. But I'm not -" Jaz stopped mid-sentence, startled by Kyree's presence. Her heart was racing and her mind was going into overdrive. She just knew her eyes were deceiving her, and all she could think of was the number of glasses of wine she'd had earlier. It just had to be that. No way could it really be the love of her life, who had not only gone to jail, but also told her to kick rocks because their relationship just "didn't work". Naw, it had to be the wine, because that man wasn't supposed to be out of prison for another year. That man wasn't even supposed to be in the state of Virginia. Naw, really, it had to be the wine.

While Jaz was standing there confused, Kyree was ecstatic. He hadn't planned on seeing her for another week because he wanted to get his shit together, but he would take what he could get. "Jazzy," he called her by the nickname that only he called her.

Damn, it really is him, she confirmed to herself.

Kyree could see the shock on her face, but he took her into his arms anyway. Jaz, still in shock, did not return his advances. She was as stiff as a board. But Kyree, knowing that she was just surprised to see him, only held her tighter. "Damn, I missed you, Jazzy."

Jaz began to loosen up, and before she knew it, she had practically melted in his arms. She felt safe and calm in his presence. But all of those feelings came to a halt when she quickly remembered why she hadn't spoken to him in two years. She wanted to do nothing more than cry her eyes out, but she refused to give him the satisfaction of knowing he still had that effect on her. Pulling away from his embrace, she looked at him, confused.

"I'm back, baby girl." Kyree smiled.

"Okay...and?"

Kyree quickly picked up on her attitude. It wasn't what he was expecting at all. "Damn, Jazzy, wassup? Why you trippin'?"

"Trippin'? Nigga, you know what?" Jaz just shook her head. She wasn't going to go there with Kyree, not tonight.

"I just thought you'd be happy to see a nigga," Kyree admitted.

"Ha!" Jaz sarcastically laughed.

Kyree looked at her like she was crazy just as Monica quickly came down the stairs. In all the excitement, she'd forgotten Jaz might be stopping by for her phone.

"Heeeey, Jaz," Monica awkwardly said.

Jaz gave Monica a look that could kill, and Monica returned her look and said, without saying, *I didn't know.*

"Look, I just came here for my phone. Did I leave it here?" Jaz said with an attitude.

"Yeah, let me go get it." Monica went looking for the phone, leaving Jaz and Kyree standing at the door. Jaz stood with her arms folded and all her weight shifted to one side of her body while she shook her head in disbelief.

"I can't find it. Hold on, Jaz. I know it's here somewhere!" Monica yelled from the living room.

That was not the news Jaz wanted to hear, and Kyree's piercing looks weren't helping matters either. "Fuck it. I'll come back later." She turned on her heels, trying to get away from him as fast as she possibly could.

"Wait, Jazzy!" Kyree called after her.

"What!" she barked.

"Ay yo, watch your tone," Kyree warned.

The nerve of this nigga, Jaz thought to herself as she turned around to face him.

"I thought this was Mo's phone, but I guess it's yours," he said, handing her the now-ringing phone.

Jaz quickly took it from him, surprised to see that her fiancé was calling.

"I guess you've moved on, huh?" Kyree asked, a hint of sadness in his voice.

He seemed defeated, and it was something Jaz had never seen in him before. She wanted to cry - for him, for herself, for their relationship. But what they had was over, and he needed to understand that. "The world can't wait for Kyree," she said as she turned to leave.

Kyree was beyond hurt, but he would never let anyone know it. His demeanor seemed cool and lax, but on the inside, he was steaming. He couldn't see how Jaz could move on without him. Sure, he'd told her to move on, but he never expected her to actually do it. He wanted to know how serious she was about this new dude who kept calling her phone. If they weren't that serious, maybe he still had a chance. He was more than sure Monica would know the answer to his questions.

"Ay yo, Mo!" he called out to her after entering the house. Monica was still looking for the phone. "I found the phone, and I gave it to her already. She's gone." Monica stopped looking around and plopped down on the couch. She knew what her brother was going to ask her, and she'd been dreading it for awhile. "Yo, wassup with her and the dude that was calling her phone?"

Monica took a deep sigh. "What do you want me to say, Ky? Did you expect her to wait for you forever?" Kyree sucked his teeth. "But no, Kyree, don't do that. Jaz is my girl, and you didn't see her after you got locked up. She was a mess. And then after a year of waiting around for you, she went to see you, and just out of the blue, you break it off with her. She cried for months after that shit."

Kyree covered his face with his hands in frustration. He was expecting things to go back to the way they were. He hated to admit that his sister was indeed right. He really did expect the world to wait on him. But deep down he'd always known Jaz would eventually come to the realization that she was too good for him. He just didn't want to believe it.

Monica felt so sorry for her brother. She knew the love he and Jaz once shared for each other. She'd seen Jaz cry over him for nearly a year, and now she was seeing Kyree's pain firsthand. "She moved on, Ky. You should too."

Kyree wasn't trying to hear that. "How serious are they?" he wanted to know.

Monica looked at him, confused. "She didn't tell you?"

"Naw, she ain't tell me shit. Every word that came out of her mouth to me was some shit I wouldn't say in church, if ya know what I mean." He let out a slight chuckle.

Monica took a deep breath. "Well..." She was cut off by the ringing of Kyree's cell phone.

"Hold that thought." Kyree answered his phone. "What up, Fat Boy?"

While he was talking, Monica was trying to figure out how she was going to tell him that Jaz was getting married. She was sure it would kill him. Kyree was talking with Fat Boy when he started flipping through a magazine on the coffee table. "What the fuck?" He picked up a small card off the table and brought it up to examine it closer. "Yo, Fat Boy, I'm gonna have to call you back." He ended his conversation and focused his attention on Monica.

"What?" she asked, wondering why he was ice-grilling her.

He held up the card he'd found on the table. "So she's marrying this muthafucka?"

Realizing that he was holding one of the place settings for the wedding, Monica brought her hand up to her face and covered her mouth. This was not how she wanted him to find out. Kyree had the most disgusted look on his face. He was beyond furious.

"I'm so sorry you had to find out like this, Ky."

"You know what? It's cool." Kyree got up to leave. "That nigga ain't me."

Monica jumped up from her seat. "No, Ky. Don't do anything crazy. She's finally happy. Let her be," she begged him.

Kyree nodded his head in understanding and hugged Monica. "I hear you, baby sis. I'm not gonna do anything crazy."

Neither Monica nor Kyree believed what he said. Kyree didn't care how serious Jaz and her fiancé were. In his eyes, she was his soul mate. The love they shared was meant to last forever. He just had to hear her say it was over for himself.

A COUPLE OF FOREVERS

CHAPTER 2

The next day, Jaz cancelled all of her appointments at the hair salon she and Monica owned. She needed time to think, and she hadn't slept a wink all night. Monica had called her to apologize and Jaz had forgiven her. She knew that Kyree's visit was probably a surprise to everyone.

"Are you sure you don't want me to stay with you today?" Jaz's fiancé Michael asked. She'd made up an excuse and told him she was sick and wasn't going into work today.

"Naw, baby, I'm fine. Go to work," Jaz assured him, straightening his tie.

Michael was the head OB/GYN at Maryview Hospital, and Jaz loved it. He had a safe job that didn't cause her to worry. It also didn't hurt that he was very easy on the eyes. His beautiful caramel skin and his tall and handsome frame made him look like a *GQ* model. But his hazel eyes were what drew him to Jaz like something out of a fairytale. He was the calm after the storm known as Hurricane Kyree. It took a lot for her to give her heart to another man, and she was the happiest she'd been in a long time. And yet, one visit from Kyree and he was invading her dreams and had her questioning her own happiness. For the life of her, she couldn't understand why he always had that effect on her.

"All done," she said after finishing his tie.

Michael kissed her on the forehead as he grabbed his briefcase and she followed him out. He opened the door and then turned around to face Jaz. There was thunder roaring, and rain was definitely near. He pulled her close to him. "Now when I get off, we're going to talk about you moving into my house."

"What's wrong with my place?" Jaz asked, but she knew. They'd been having the talk about her giving up her apartment and moving in with him for months now. But Jaz had been tiptoeing around the subject. Something about giving up her place made everything seem so final. But she knew they couldn't avoid the topic forever. They were set to be married in two months. "I promise we'll talk about it later when you get off. But right now, you need to go. You're going to be late for work." She pushed him out the door and he pulled her outside with him. He grabbed her ass and kissed her forcefully on the lips. She pulled away from his kiss. "Boy, don't start no shit you know damn well you can't finish," she teased.

"Now you know I can finish it." He started to push her back in the house, but she pushed him out.

"Go to work before you're late," she giggled.

Michael bit his bottom lip and smacked her on the butt before heading to his car. Jaz shook her head and laughed at his foolishness. Once he'd pulled off, she decided to go inside and change into her gym clothes. She had to release some steam and she always cleared her head with a good workout. Ten minutes later, she was dressed and searching for her gym shoes.

The doorbell rang, and on her way to open it, she noticed Michael had left his key on the dresser. Jaz smiled to herself, knowing he'd probably called out of work just to spend time with her. "You couldn't stay away from me, huh bae?" She smiled as she opened the door.

Bam! A loud clap of thunder sounded.

"Oh my God!" Jaz gasped, and then quickly shut the door behind her. It was Kyree.

"I just wanna talk, Jazzy. I didn't come to start anything," he said from behind the door. "Just give me ten minutes, please."

Jaz's back was pressed against the other side of the door and her heart was trying to beat its way out of her chest. *Why does he have to be out of jail now?* she asked herself.

"Alright, we can do this now or later. But I'll be back here every damn day until you talk to me," Kyree threatened.

Jaz bit her lip. She was seriously contemplating opening the door. Kyree was relentless, and he definitely would keep coming back until she talked to him. She took a deep breath and slowly turned the knob to open the door. "You have five minutes," she stated firmly.

"Cool, I'll take that," he said as she made a path for him to come in. She did a quick look outside and he chuckled. "Don't worry. I waited for your fiancé to leave before I came in."

"Whatever." She rolled her eyes and closed the door.

"I see you let that nigga smack your ass in public and shit," Kyree smirked, remembering the scene he'd just witnessed.

"Well, he has the right to. He is my man. And it wasn't in public; yo' ass is just a stalker."

Kyree laughed again. "Naw, baby girl, I just didn't want to start no shit with you and ya man, so I waited until he left."

Jaz stood with her arms folded, waiting for him to him to get to the point. But he didn't speak; he just stared at her. He couldn't help himself. The black spandex Nike workout pants and halter she were wearing was just more evidence that a lot had changed over the past three years. She was still the 5'7" brown bombshell he'd fallen in love with all those years ago, but now her body had matured even more. Her hips had grown, and her ass, although a nice size three years ago, had also grown phatter. She'd even cut her hair into a cute bob and added dark orange highlights.

Why is he staring at me? Jaz wondered. She hated to admit it, but she couldn't keep her eyes off of him either. He'd picked up some weight, but there was no doubt about it, it was all muscle on his 6'4" milk chocolate frame. His goatee connected flawlessly on his perfectly chiseled chin. He was sporting a black polo shirt, black Levi jeans, black Jordans, and an all-black Yankee fitted cap. He smelled like Euphoria by Calvin Klein. *Damn, he looks good,* she admitted to herself. This was all getting to be too much for her. "You have four minutes now, so you better use it wisely."

"A'ight, I guess I'll get right to it then." Kyree clasped his hands together. "How serious are you and dude?"

"Are you serious?" Jaz asked, dumbfounded, as she held up her ring finger, showing off her three-karat canary yellow diamond engagement ring.

13

Kyree shook his head. "Naw, that ain't what I meant, and you know it."

"So what the hell did you mean, Kyree?"

"Do you love him?"

Jaz looked him in the eye. "Yes, Kyree. I love him. He treats me good, puts my needs first, and he loves me back. And as far as I know, he's never once cheated on me."

"I never cheated on you, Jazzy." Kyree looked at her like she was crazy.

"Every chance you got, you were with your bitch." Jaz was practically in tears just thinking about it. Kyree still had no clue what the hell she was talking about. In the five years they were together, he had never once cheated on her. "Oh, you don't know?"

"No, I don't. You're talking crazy as hell."

"The streets, Kyree! You loved the streets more than you loved me. She was your main bitch, and I was your side chick. I could never compete with her. So many times I told you to leave that hoe alone, but you just couldn't let her go." The tears she was trying so hard to control were now creeping up at the back of her throat and threatening to pierce her eyelids. "She never had love for you like I did. And then that bitch got you locked up for three years and left you for dead. But I was the one that was suffering most while she went on about her day. As soon as you got locked up, she started fucking with the next nigga." Her tears were now revealing the pain that her heart could no longer keep inside. Kyree got up to tend to her, but she pushed him away with her hands. "No, let me finish," she protested. He hated to see her like this, but he knew she'd been holding a lot of anger and resentment in since he'd been locked up, so he allowed her to finish.

She wiped her face with the back of her hand and continued, "I loved you despite your faults, and when you got locked up, I waited for you like a dumbass. And then you just pushed me away. For what, that bitch?"

Kyree wasn't sure if she wanted him to speak just yet, so he took a few seconds before saying anything. "Look, Jazzy, I never meant for 'that bitch', as you call it," he let out a slight laugh, "to get in the way of us. I loved you more than anything in this world. I was fucking with that bitch to take care of us."

Jaz wiped her face and put her hand up to stop him. "Hold that thought," she said as she walked to her bedroom.

Kyree sat on the couch and waited patiently for her return. He had no idea she felt that way, but he knew she was right. She begged him to stay home every day, but the streets kept calling him. He just couldn't get enough of the fast money. He had originally come there with the intention of telling her about the barbershop he was working on opening. He was finally going to leave the streets alone. Now he was starting to think that maybe she was better off with Michael. But Kyree wasn't going to let her go until he knew for sure. Jaz returned with a huge Nike duffel bag and dropped it at his feet.

"What's this?" he asked as he opened up the bag.

"It's the money you left with that bitch. After you got locked up, I went and collected what was due to you. I spent a little of it when we opened up the shop, but I made sure I put it all back. I figured you'd need it when you got out." She sat on the couch Indian style as he rummaged through the bag.

"Jaz, this has to be like -"

"$20,000," she cut him off. "I figured you'd fucked the bitch enough to earn your keep." They both let out a slight laugh.

Kyree smiled; he always knew she was a rider. "Naw, I can't take this," he said, zipping up the bag.

"And why not?"

"Because it belongs to you. I worked those streets for you."

"Well, I don't want it," she half-heartedly told the truth.

"Well, that's tough, 'cause your stubborn ass is just gonna have to deal. 'Cause I ain't taking it back."

She sucked her teeth. She knew he wouldn't take it; he was so set in his ways sometimes. "Alright then, fine. I guess I'll spend it on my wedding." She shrugged.

Kyree shook his head. That shit was still eating at him.

"Ky, can I ask you something?"

"Anything," he admitted.

"Why did you call it off?" That question had been eating at her for three years now, and she was finally face to face with him to ask.

Kyree took a deep breath and spoke slowly and calmly. "Because I didn't want you to hate me. They were talking about giving my ass ten years for ten keys. The only reason I didn't get ten was because my lawyer found a loophole in the search warrant and I was only charged with gun possession. But thinking about all the time I was supposed to get, I couldn't have you doing that time with me. Eventually you would've started to hate me. Ten years is a long time to ask someone to do, especially when they're out in the free world."

Jaz started to cry again, even harder than before. Kyree wasn't taking no for an answer this time. He pulled her over to him and held her in his arms, tightly. She was saying something, but her muffled speech made it hard for him to understand. But there was one word that stood out to him.

"Pregnant!" he said out loud. He pulled her away to look at her. He got up from his seat and began pacing the floor. "So you're pregnant by this nigga?" Kyree was furious. He wanted her to carry his first child. It wasn't supposed to be like this.

"No!" she jumped up. "I'm not pregnant!" Kyree stopped pacing the floor to look at her. "I'm not pregnant now...but I was." Kyree shook his head, confused. "I found out I was pregnant two days before you went to New York."

"So wait, we have a child?" Kyree asked.

She hesitantly shook her head no. "The day you got locked up, I miscarried," she cried.

Kyree put his face in his hands, trying to wrap his head around what had happened. "Why didn't you tell me?"

"I didn't want you to worry. You had enough on your mind at the time. I didn't tell anyone, not even Mo."

Kyree sat on the couch, his head still in his hands. Without the stress from him running the streets, Jaz could have probably given birth to a healthy baby. They would be together right now and not trying to piece together what happened to their relationship. He couldn't look at her without wanting to cry, but he refused to let himself. He could only imagine how alone she must've felt. Jaz was crying and she didn't care if he saw anymore. He moved in closer to console her and she pushed him away. But he wouldn't budge. She punched him in the chest, and he let her. She punched him again, and again, and again, until finally she just gave in and allowed him to console her. Kyree was beginning to think him showing up there was a mistake, that maybe she was better off without him. He hadn't seemed to bring much good into her life. All he ever did was mess things up for her. Once again, although Jaz hated to admit it, she felt safe in his arms, like everything was right with the world for once.

He rocked her back and forth, and then kissed her forehead. "I'm sorry, Jazzy. I'm so sorry you had to go through that alone," he admitted. He wiped her tears with his thumb and then he kissed her cheek, left, and then right. Wiping her tears with his lips, he graced his lips across hers. Her breathing was heavy. Then he stuck his tongue in her mouth.

"Oh, shit," Jaz moaned between breaths. She knew this wasn't right, but she didn't understand how something so wrong could feel so damn right. His mouth moved from her mouth to the spot on her neck. She was trying to resist his advances, but Kyree wasn't playing fair. He knew what that spot did to her. She tried pushing him away, although she wasn't really giving it much effort. "Aaahhh...Kyree, stop. We can't do this."

"And why not?" He continued to flick his tongue across her neck.

"Because I'm engaged!" She pushed him away with more force this time.

"Damn, Jazzy, why you trippin'?" He was starting to get aggravated.

"Because, Kyree! You can't always have shit when and where you want it. The whole world doesn't revolve around you." She shook her head in frustration. "You know what? Your five minutes are up. Get the fuck out!"

"A'ight, Jazzy, I'll leave. But just answer me this." She looked over at him, waiting for him to ask his question and get the hell out of her life for good. "Do you still love me?"

She looked at him like he was crazy. "What kind of question is that? I'm getting married in two months."

"I didn't ask you about that. I asked if you still loved me. Fuck that other nigga."

"Yes, Kyree, I love him...and I fucking hate you!" she said with malice in her tone.

"Naw, you don't mean that shit." Kyree refused to believe her. He could see right through her lies. They were made for each other, and she knew it. "You might love that nigga, but we both know you're *in* love with me."

"I hate you, Kyree!" she screamed, on the verge of tears.

Kyree saw the pain and hurt in her eyes, and on instinct, he pulled her close. There was no way she believed what she was saying. Jaz missed him, but she wasn't sure she could get past all the hurt.

Kyree wrapped his arm around her neck and just held her. He kissed her on the forehead, and this time she hugged him back. She inhaled his scent and let peace consume her. He kissed her gently, and then greedily. She missed this feeling. He picked her up, and she instinctively wrapped her legs around his back. The last thing on her mind was her fiancé. Now all she could think of was how long it had been since she'd had some good dick. Sure, her fiancé was decent, but he was so mediocre compared to Kyree. Kyree was thicker, bigger, and could make her cum more times in thirty minutes than Michael could in a week. Kyree was also a big freak, and she loved it.

He held their lip lock as he carried her to the bed and laid her down. She quickly removed his shirt, and he hers. She smiled at his well-toned milk chocolate chest. His mouth traced kisses from her mouth to her breasts. He gave every inch of her body the attention it desperately needed. He took her fingers into his mouth one at a time. When he got to her left hand, he removed her engagement ring with his teeth and then spat it across the room. She looked at him like he was crazy, and he grinned.

"You don't need that shit anymore," he said. He forcefully pulled her by her ankles and then removed her pants. He removed her underwear and went to kiss the lips of her pussy.

Jaz didn't just call him Hurricane Kyree for the destruction he left in her life, but also because of his tongue game. Lil Wayne didn't have shit on Kyree. He was the original Pussy Monster, and Jaz was wet before he'd even pulled up the hood. When he started to flick his tongue back and forth, Jaz thought she was going to lose her mind.

"Shitttt...damn...nigga!" She bit her bottom lip. She just knew she'd draw blood if she bit down any harder. He removed his tongue, in and out, and Jaz had a vice grip on his head with her thighs. "Oh my God, Kyree! Please, stop," she begged him. Kyree wasn't stopping though; he wanted her to get hers. "Shittt...aaaggghhhh!" she screamed, cumming all over his face.

Like a dog with a steak in front of him, Kyree lapped up every bit. He loved to see the satisfaction on her face, and the shaking of her legs let him know he'd done a great job. He opened her legs and removed his jeans. Jaz had lost all sense of reality. She'd forgotten what ten inches of dick looked like, and she sure couldn't wait to remember what it felt like.

Kyree sucked on each of her breasts and then entered her slowly. She fit like the missing piece to a puzzle around his dick. He rocked inside her, back and forth. "Shit..." he moaned. The feeling couldn't be compared to anything but bliss for him. It was way better than the sex he was getting from the female guards in prison.

"Oooh," Jaz moaned. She arched her back, allowing him to enter as far as he could go.

Kyree wrapped her legs around his waist and beat her soaking insides like a drum. He was working every inch of her walls and she couldn't take it anymore. His stroke was like a love TKO, and all she could do was tap out. It was over. She clamped her walls around his dick and came, long and hard.

Satisfied that she'd gotten hers but not quite ready to cum yet, Kyree rolled over to switch positions. He wanted her to drive him to his destination. Although she was as limp as a rag doll, Kyree guided her on top, and eventually she had the energy and strength she needed to ride him to his peak. Jaz was working it slow, speeding up at the right moments, nibbling on his chest. Kyree thought he was going to go crazy. His eyes were rolling to the back of his head and he was biting his lip. He could no longer hold it in, so he stopped Jaz from moving just a little bit and he released himself inside of her.

"Gotdamn, girl!" He smacked her on the ass and she fell on top of him.

Kyree was done for. Jaz smiled at her handiwork as she looked up at him. Although the sex they had was great, happiness with him was always only momentary, and she wouldn't allow him to disappoint her again. But she fell asleep on his chest anyway, basking in the moment.

Jaz awoke two hours later to the ringing of her cell phone. The storm had ended, and she tried to adjust her eyes to the sunlight that was peeking through her bedroom window. She looked up at Kyree and slowly got up, as to not disturb him. But he awoke in her absence. She opened her drawer and slid an oversized T-shirt over her head. Her phone vibrated, and she quickly picked it up. It notified her that she had one missed call, a voicemail, and a text message, all from Michael. She opened the text message first.

>>> **11:08 AM, My Bae: Just checking n on u. Hope you're feeling better. Love u.**

After reading his message, an instant feeling of regret, guilt, and disgust came over her. She brought her hands to her face and shook her head. She had never felt so low in her life.

"What's wrong?" Kyree asked, noticing the distressed look on her face.

"I'm sorry, Kyree. This was a mistake." She began to cry.

"A what?" Kyree just knew he'd heard her wrong.

"A mistake, Kyree. I'm engaged. We should've never done this." She wiped her face with the back of her hands.

Kyree couldn't believe what he was hearing. He sat on the bed dumbfounded. There was no way the girl who was talking now was the same one he'd fucked just hours before. It couldn't be the same person, because this person was talking crazy.

"What the fuck you mean a mistake?" The vein on the side of his head was pulsating.

"It means what the fuck it means, Kyree! We have to think realistically. You're never going to change for me, and I can no longer spend my life trying to make you into something you're not."

Kyree was tired of trying to convince her he was going to change. Sure, he'd said it a thousand times before, but this time was different. Three years in prison had helped him to realize that. "Man, fuck this shit," he said as he quickly got up to retrieve his clothes. "You know what, Jazzy?" he said as he put his shirt over his head in one quick motion. "This is some bullshit."

"But I love him, Kyree," she said in between sniffles.

Kyree sucked his teeth. "You can tell that to him, and whoever the hell else, all you want. But the only person losing here is you. You'll never be able to give your all to him because your heart will never be fully in it."

He slid his right foot into his shoe. "I love you, Jazzy, but I'm not gonna wait forever." And with that said, he turned to leave.

As soon as Jaz heard the door shut, she fell into her pillow and cried. She had never been much of a crier, but when Kyree came around, everything about her changed. He had the power to consume her emotions and fuck with her head. It often scared her. He wanted her to make a quick decision, and if that decision wasn't on his behalf, he wasn't happy. He was cocky, arrogant, and selfish, but she hated to admit that was what she fell in love with. But what Kyree didn't understand was that no matter what she decided, someone would get hurt. It was like they were playing tug-of-war with her heart. On one end, she had the man of her dreams sent to sweep her off her feet. And on the other end, she had the man she'd always loved who always seemed to disappoint her. For once in her life, she was going to think with her head *and* her heart. She picked her ring up off the floor, put it on its rightful place, and picked up her phone to return Michael's call.

CHAPTER 3

The next day Jaz was at the salon early to open up. She sat at her desk going over the books and looking over the inventory as Keri Hilson's "Beautiful Mistake" crooned through the speakers, expressing every emotion she felt at that moment. She just had to find a way to clear her head. Being at the salon was something she looked forward to every day. Yesterday was the first day she'd called out since she and Monica had opened Mo' Jaz Salon two years ago. Business had been rough at first, but within months of opening, they had things running smoothly.

The salon was located on High Street in Portsmouth, VA. It attracted clients from all over wanting to get their hair done by the best stylists in the seven cities. They specialized in hair, waxing, makeup, manicures, and pedicures. They employed four other stylists and two manicurists, but they were the head stylists and usually received the most clientele. With Monica's brains and business savvy, and Jaz's brains and creativity, they had one of the hottest salons in the area.

Monica and Jaz had dreamed of opening a salon since they were twelve years old and doing all of the neighborhood girls' heads. Jaz was so proud of how far they had both come. Their salon was her pride and joy. She'd decorated it herself, incorporating all earth tones into the decor, giving it a homey feel. There were five washbowls and hood dryers, two stations set just for manicures and pedicures, and a station in the back for makeup and waxing. Two brown sofas sat in the waiting area with rust-colored throw pillows, and a glass and cherry wood coffee table sat in front of each sofa. Espresso-colored walls, oak wood flooring, and granite counter tops with dark cherry wood cabinets graced the booth of every stylist. But what stood out the most was that there were two stage platforms to the left and the right of the shop, made especially for the two head stylists.

23

A dimly lit spotlight graced Jaz and Monica as they worked their magic on their clients' heads. That was all Jaz's idea. She said, "They need to know who the HBIC's are 'round here." Monica laughed, but she had to agree.

Walking into the shop, Monica was so surprised to see Jaz. Jaz was never the first one to arrive anywhere. Monica would often joke that the only thing she was ever on time for was her period.

"What the hell are you doing here so early?" Monica asked, placing her McDonald's bag down at the front desk.

Jaz hadn't heard her come in, and she was surprised to see her as well. "What you mean early? We open at 9:00 and it's ten minutes till."

"Bitch, I know what time it is. I just didn't think yo' ass knew what the morning time looked like," Monica laughed.

Jaz rolled her eyes and grabbed her McDonald's bag. "What you get me?" Jaz rummaged through the bag.

Monica snatched the bag back. "Shit. I've never known you to be conscious at this hour."

"Please, Mo," Jaz pouted. "Can I at least have half?"

Monica sucked her teeth. "Damn, you act like a baby sometimes," she huffed, giving in and breaking off half of her bacon, egg, and cheese biscuit.

Jaz smiled. "Can I have half of your hash brown too?"

Monica looked at her like she was crazy. "Bitch, don't push your luck."

Jaz laughed as Monica sat down to join her. "So why are you here so early?" Monica asked, taking a bite of her food.

"I was trying to finish this inventory."

"The inventory I usually have to ask you like thirty times to do? Are you feeling well, child?" Monica got up to feel her forehead for a fever.

"Stop, Mo," Jaz laughed. "I just wanted to get a head start."

"Um hmm," Monica eyed her sideways.

"What, you don't believe me?"

"Uh...no," Monica looked at her like she was crazy. "I

know what this is. You still trippin' because Ky came home."

Jaz sucked her teeth and rolled her eyes. "Not even." She took her last bite of her biscuit and got up from her seat.

But Monica wasn't done with her just yet. She finished the rest of her food and was right on Jaz's tail. "Jaz, I'm not playing with you. I don't wanna be Monica to y'all's Ross and Rachel again."

Jaz laughed, but Monica was serious. For years she watched Jaz and Kyree play an emotional game of the hearts, and she'd be stuck in the middle. She was totally against them dating in the beginning. Jaz was her best friend, and Kyree was her brother. The two never even got along at first, and they constantly butted heads. Monica could remember all too well the course of events that led up to the two being more than just her brother and best friend.

7 Years Ago...

Monica and Jaz were freshmen at Norfolk State University and enjoying being away from home. The freedom was a whole new experience for them. With Jaz growing up with a strict father after her mother passed away when she was only twelve and Monica finally getting away from Kyree's short leash, they were having the time of their lives. Monica had just started dating a Navy boy from Texas named Latrell. And Jaz was in an on again/off again relationship with her boyfriend of two years, Devin.

This particular day in February, Monica was out with Latrell and Jaz and her boyfriend Devin were in her dorm room. They were looking like they were going to be off...again.

"Who was that bitch that called my phone, Devin?" Jaz barked at him.

"Jaz, stop trippin'! I told you about that shit!" he countered. They'd been going back and forth for over an hour, and Jaz still couldn't get a straight answer out of Devin. To hear about him fucking around on her was one thing, but to have another girl call her cell phone and describe the apple-shaped birthmark on his ass was a whole 'nother fucking story.

"So you're not gonna tell me?" Jaz sat, dumbfounded.

"Naw, I ain't gon' tell you shit. Ain't shit to tell. The bitch is lying, Jaz."

Jaz looked at him like he had two heads. "You must take me for some kinda fool."

"Fuck it then! Don't believe me."

"I know how I'll get my answer," Jaz said, getting up to reach for his cell phone that was on the dresser.

"Bitch, are you crazy?" Devin barked, snatching the phone from her grasp.

"Give me back the phone, Devin!" Jaz pushed him into the wall, and before she knew it...

Smack! Devin's backhand came barreling across her face. Jaz went stumbling backwards as she quickly reached for her throbbing eye. "Ahhh!" she screamed, realizing what had just happened.

"I told you to put my fuckin' phone down," Devin said as he scrolled through his phone as if nothing happened.

Jaz was stunned for a minute. She couldn't decide what hurt more: the pain from the smack, or the fact that she'd allowed some man to put his hands on her. Her father had raised her better than that. This nigga had her all the way fucked up. She regained her composure and rose to her feet.

Bam! Devin never saw the lamp coming for his head. It instantly knocked him to the floor. "You stupid muthafucka!" Jaz yelled. Before he could regain his composure and charge at her, security was breaking down the room door.

"Stupid bitch!" Devin screamed as security took him away, blood trickling down his face.

Security took a statement from Jaz, and she said that she didn't want to press charges, seeing as though she did hit him with the lamp. She just wanted him out of her life - forever. The nosy-ass dorm mates were too much for Jaz. She just wanted Monica to come home so that she could tell her everything. She had major trust issues, and everyone in the dorm didn't need to know her business. After giving them all short answers, they eventually left, and Jaz was left to clean up the mess she had made. As she swept up the last of the broken lamp pieces, a familiar voice caught her attention.

"Damn, Big Foot! What the fuck you do, kick the door down?"

"I don't have time for your shit today, Kyree." Jaz and Kyree usually went at it like Pam and Martin, but Jaz was just not in the mood tonight.

"I just came to check on Mo, Killjoy, so calm the fuck down." Walking into the room, Kyree looked around, confused. It looked as though a WWE brawl had taken place. He looked at Jaz, but she avoided looking in his direction. As she bent down to pick up a chair, he noticed the bruise on her face. He quickly grabbed her chin and made her face him. "Who the fuck did this to your face?"

Jaz pushed his hand away. She couldn't stand to be that close to him. It was like admitting to herself that their bickering was nothing more than pent-up frustrations from a love she had harbored deep down inside for Kyree since she was a child. "Let me go, Kyree. It's nothing. I fell," she lied.

"Jazzy, tell me anything," he said, not once believing her.

"Didn't I tell you not to call me that shit?" She actually hated to admit that she loved when he called her that. He was the only one in the world who ignored her hate for the name.

A passerby yelled, "Ay yo, Jaz, I heard you hit that nigga with a lamp! Yo' ass is crazy, girl," the boy laughed as he walked by.

Kyree's gaze shifted to Jaz. "So it was that nigga Devin, huh?"

"Damn, I gotta get my door fixed," Jaz said, just above a whisper. "It's nothing, Ky. It's over with."

"Naw, fuck that!" Kyree was pacing around the room. He was infuriated. The vein on the side of his head was pulsating, and he had the look of death in his eyes.

Jaz knew that look. "Please let it go, Kyree," she pleaded.

"Stay here, Jazzy, I'll be back," he said as he turned to leave.

Jaz followed him all the way to the car and begged him not to do anything stupid, but her attempts fell on deaf ears. Kyree was ready to body a nigga. Jaz had no idea the pain Kyree felt in his heart when he saw her face. To him, she was more than his sister's friend. He'd harbored feelings for her as well, but he hid them behind insults like a child. But there was no way he was going to let some bitch-ass nigga put his hands on her and get away with it.

Two hours had passed and Kyree had yet to return any of Jaz's calls. She had no idea what was going on, and it was killing her. Monica still wasn't back yet, and she didn't want her to worry until she knew for sure what Kyree was planning on doing. Fed up with waiting, she got in her car and headed for Kyree's apartment. She was relieved to see his car out front. She knocked on the door and he opened it wearing nothing but a bath towel. She was thrown off by his perfectly toned body, which was covered in street wounds and tattoos that each told its own story, his physique comparable to Michelangelo's *David*. She snapped out of her trance and quickly remembered why she was there in the first place.

"Can I come in?" she asked.

Kyree obliged, moving to the side so that she could enter. He shut the door behind her. Jaz had always loved Kyree's apartment. He kept it neat, but it was still definitely a bachelor's pad. In his living room sat a black leather sofa, a fish tank against the wall, a huge flat screen TV with surround sound, and every game system there was.

"What up?" he asked like nothing was wrong.

"Um, nigga, are you that slow? You know why I came over here. What the fuck did you do to Devin?"

Kyree sucked his teeth and walked away toward the kitchen. He opened up the freezer and took out a bag of frozen peas. "Here." He handed her the peas. She looked at him like he was crazy. "Put the damn peas on your face before you look like a damn blueberry."

Jaz sucked her teeth and snatched the bag from his hands. He walked to the back room and returned wearing balling shorts and a wife beater.

"What did you do to Devin, Kyree?" Jaz asked him again. This time she was calmer.

"What the fuck you care for? That nigga fucked you up, and you're concerned about him?" Kyree asked in disbelief.

"I don't!"

"Sounds to me like you do care."

"Well, I don't. I just don't want you to get in any trouble because of me," she admitted.

It warmed his heart to know that she was more concerned about him than Devin. "Well, it's cool. I left ya man breathing. He'll survive the ass whoopin' I gave his stupid ass." Kyree plopped down on the couch and she sat down beside him.

"After that shit, he's no longer my man. No nigga puts his hands on me and thinks everything is all good. He got the game all the way fucked up." She snatched the remote control from his hands and started to flick through the channels.

Kyree slowly shook his head. "You're a trip, you know that?"

Jaz shrugged her shoulders. "Well, I no longer have a door in my room, and I want to watch TV."

"Naw, not that. I mean, you keep fuckin' with these li'l boys and that's exactly what's gonna happen. They're gonna beat your ass 'cause they don't have any sense."

Jaz rolled her eyes. She didn't need a lecture; she could get that from her father. "Well, when a real man approaches me, I'll be sure to let you know."

"You wouldn't know a real man if he was standing right in front of you, defending you, and letting you watch his damn TV."

"What?" Jaz asked.

"Man, nothing." Kyree had no idea where that came from, and he wanted to let it go. Jaz was confused as well. She just knew he couldn't have been talking about her. He hated her. She had to be over-thinking things. Besides, Kyree was a major hoe, and he had a different girl for everyday of the week. No matter how much she wanted him, too many circumstances prevented it.

They sat back in silence and watched TV together, and before they knew it, they'd both fallen asleep. Jaz wasn't sure how she'd managed to fall asleep on his chest, but damn if it didn't feel good. She looked up at his face. It was perfect in her eyes. But he was her best friend's brother, which meant he was off limits.

Kyree awoke to her staring at him. He took his thumb and grazed the bruise on her eye. He kissed her bruise and they continued to stare into each other's eyes. Before he knew it, he couldn't control his urge to kiss her lips, and he did. It made him feel better when she returned his advances by sliding her tongue in his mouth. Jaz had no idea what to expect. She'd dreamed about this for years. His lips were so soft. She just wanted to enjoy the moment forever.

Present...

Monica snapped back to reality. That was seven years ago. After Jaz told her, she was grossed out at first, but she knew about the deep feelings the two had for each other. They thought they hid it well, but they couldn't hide anything from the one who knew them best. The faraway look Jaz had on her face now was an all-too-familiar look. Monica always felt like she was stuck in the middle, torn between her best friend and her brother. But now Jaz was engaged, and she couldn't have her backtracking. It wasn't good for her.

"Look, Jaz, I know you loved Kyree at one point. But you're happy with Michael now. He has a good job, he treats you well, and he's willing to marry your crazy ass." Monica let out a slight laugh. "Don't let Ky sell you a dream."

Jaz looked at Monica. There was no way she was going to tell her about yesterday now. She was sure Monica would be disappointed in her. "Listen, Mama Mo." Jaz laughed at her, and Monica rolled her eyes. "I'm not going back to Ky. Sure I loved him once, but now I'm in love with Mike. Ky and I talked so that there wouldn't be any bad blood between us, and we've worked it out. He understands, and we're both cool with that. Besides, we both know you don't wanna re-do those damn place settings." They both laughed.

"Um hmm." Monica looked at her sideways. Something was off, and she just couldn't put her finger on it. But before she could probe Jaz with any more questions, the shop door opened, and in walked Ms. Ray.

"Hello, beautiful bitches!" he announced as he made his grand entrance.

The girls all laughed. Flamboyant and adventurous, Ms. Ray was always the center of attention. He was born Raymond Anderson, but the name Raymond didn't fit a queen such as himself. Butt injections had given him Beyoncé's ass, and he was well on his way to having Pam Anderson's breasts. He walked in wearing blue leggings, a sparkly silver shirt, and six-inch silver pumps. But what set his outfit off even more was the royal blue bob wig he was wearing. He was truly a character.

"Boy, what the hell are you wearing?" Monica just had to ask.

He sauntered over to them. "You like?"

Monica and Jaz both laughed. "You look like Blue's Clues trampled over a damn disco ball," Monica laughed.

"Oh, I see y'all are some haters." Ms. Ray turned up his nose at them.

"Not true, boo," Jaz corrected him. "I think you look triple F: fierce, fun, and fab." Jaz and Ms. Ray snapped their fingers simultaneously.

"Y'all hoes are crazy." Monica shook her head. "I swear I'm going to initiate a dress code up in this muthafucka."

"Whatever, hater!" Ms. Ray snarled. "So," he said, focusing all of his attention on Jaz, "what brings you to work today? And at what time?" He checked the clock on the wall. "9:00? In the morning?" Ms. Ray started to feel Jaz's forehead.

"Boy, stop," she giggled, smacking his hand away.

"I'm serious. You don't come in yesterday - the first time

I've ever seen, by the way. You're early today, also a first. And you're glowing like you just got dicked down. And I know that ain't what's poppin' dot com, because you and Michael have been waiting for like three months for y'all's wedding night. For what, I have no clue, because it ain't like y'all ain't already fucked. So give us the tea, bitch? What the hell is going on with you?"

Ms. Ray was definitely putting her on the spot. It was true that she and Michael had decided to wait until they were married until they had sex again. It was her idea, mostly, but he reluctantly agreed. She just thought it would make their wedding night that much more special if they had something to look forward to. But now she had spoiled that moment with Kyree. If only it didn't feel so good while it was happening, and so bad after, she wouldn't feel so guilty explaining herself. "Nothing." Jaz rolled her eyes in annoyance.

"That's what ya dick suckers say," Ms. Ray countered. He was looking at her, trying to figure her out, and so was Monica.

Jaz definitely didn't need this kind of heat. The only person working at the salon, besides Monica, who knew about her and Kyree, was Ms. Ray. He always called them Ross and Rachel, and said that whenever they realized it, they were going to be together. Jaz was worried about her secret, but knew that Kyree wouldn't tell Monica. He always kept his personal life private, and he didn't like a lot people in his business. But Monica could always tell when something was wrong with her, and she was like a CSI detective when she wanted to really know something.

"She won't tell me either, Ms. Ray," Monica said.

"Y'all so damn nosy." Jaz walked back to her booth.

"Oooh, Mo," Ms. Ray said in a childlike tone. "I know what it is." He grabbed Mo by the arm and they both stood in front of Jaz and ice-grilled her.

Jaz was as nervous a hooker in church. She just knew they'd figured out her secret. *Damn*, she said to herself.

"Yo' ass went against your plan and let Michael slide up in through ya good stuff, huh?"

Jaz took a silent sigh of relief; she thought they'd figured her out. She knew they wouldn't be satisfied with her saying nothing was wrong, so she decided to tell them what they wanted to hear. She smiled. "Damn, y'all some detectives. I know y'all gon' let me. He is my fiancé."

"So you called out of work for a freak session? Eww, y'all nasty," Ms. Ray teased.

"Now I know yo' hoe ass ain't talking," Jaz laughed.

"Hey, ain't no shame in my hoe games." Ms. Ray gave Jaz a high-five.

"Y'all are crazy," Monica shook her head and laughed at their silliness. "I have work to do." Monica walked away as her first client walked through the door.

A COUPLE OF FOREVERS

CHAPTER 4

The salon was in full effect, and by lunchtime, Jaz had already had four clients out the door and one in the chair. Working was really keeping her mind off of Kyree. It helped that Michael called to check on her and also brought her lunch. He was always so attentive. Her decision to be with him should have been an easy one. She had no idea why she was making things so complicated.

Jaz was sitting her client, Deja, down in her chair after being under the hood dryer when she heard her say, "Gotdamn, who is that sexy-ass nigga that just walked in? I might have to steal somebody's husband tonight, girl."

Jaz laughed, only to look up and see Kyree holding Kayden. Her heart dropped to the pit of her stomach. They were both dressed in V-neck white T-shirts, all-black jeans, and black and white LeBron shoes. Every woman in the salon was looking at Kyree like he was a piece of meat, especially Asia. Jaz couldn't stand that bitch. Kyree spoke to them all as he made his way to greet Monica.

"So you can't speak to nobody, Ky?" Ms. Ray said.

Kyree turned around to look at him, and at first glance, had no idea who he was. Ms. Ray had always been flamboyant, and very much gay, but surgery had changed him in the last three years. Kyree wasn't used to seeing him like this. Although his lifestyle disgusted him, Kyree was always cordial. "Damn, my bad, Ray. I ain't know that was you. Wassup, man?"

"Oh, nothing, I'm just doing me, being fabulous." He batted his long fake eyelashes.

Kyree just shook his head and focused his attention back on Monica. He couldn't tolerate too much of Ms. Ray and his over-the-top attitude.

"Mommy!" Kayden screamed.

"Boy, I know you don't have my son dressed like you. Got him looking like a little thug." Monica laughed as her son

35

reached out to hug and kiss her.

"We good, Mo. Just chill," Kyree assured her.

"Um hmm. So what y'all gettin' into?" Monica asked.

"Me and li'l man about to go handle some grown folks business." Kyree laughed, as Jaz ear hustled from the other side of the salon. He had yet to acknowledge her, and she wondered if he even would. He was pissed with her after leaving yesterday, and she felt wrong for what she'd done. There was no way she could face him after that. She pretended to be busy with Deja's hair and not notice him, but Kayden had other plans. He tapped Kyree on the chest as his hand reached out for Jaz.

"Josh," he called her by the nickname he'd given her since he couldn't pronounce Jaz correctly.

Kyree turned to see who he was talking about, and he was surprised to see it was Jaz. He'd seen her when he walked in, but he tried to not to make eye contact. He didn't know how to act around her. Knowing he couldn't have her was just too much for him. She was adamant about their place in each other's lives, and it killed him to know how she felt. But Kayden was so persistent, and he kept tapping Kyree's shoulder for him to take him to her. Kyree tried letting him go, but for some odd reason, he wouldn't allow Kyree to put him down. Monica was watching them both, trying to see their reactions toward each other. Kyree, knowing how his sister was, quickly put his pride aside, and brought Kayden to Jaz's booth.

Jaz nearly burned Deja's head when she saw him approaching her. "So you're Josh?" Kyree laughed as he passed Kayden to Jaz. When their hands touched, they both hid the feeling of nervousness that shot through their bodies.

"Yeah, he never could say Jaz, could you Kay-Man?" She blew kiss bubbles on his cheek and tickled his stomach. Kayden laughed, showing his one dimple on his left cheek, just like his mother. Kyree watched in awe as she held Kayden. For a second, he thought back to the child they could've had together. He was sure Jaz would've been a great mother. "What auntie's Kay-Man want, huh?"

"Candy!" he proudly yelled, knowing he could get

whatever he wanted from his auntie Jaz.

"No he does not!" Mo spoke up as soon as she heard the word "candy".

"You're right, he wants an apple, huh, Kay-Man?" He shook his head no, and Jaz whispered something in his ear, and he quickly nodded his head yes. "See? Now let's go get that apple." Jaz winked at him.

Jaz excused herself from her client for a moment. She was too busy checking out Kyree to even notice she was gone. Kyree was making small talk with Deja, who asked him about his shoes, when the nail tech spilled her fake nail tin all over the floor.

"Shit!" she yelled as she scrambled to pick up the all the nails.

Kyree saw her and quickly approached to help her. "I got you, ma," he said as he used one of her business cards to scoop up the nails for her. He dumped the nails on her table and stood up to brush off his pants.

"Thank you." She smiled, showing off a set of pearly whites.

Kyree finally got a chance to really look at her. He couldn't help but be mesmerized by her smile. It was somewhat exotic. He could tell that she was mixed with something, he just couldn't tell what.

"You're welcome—"

"Asia," she cut him off. She held out her hand and he shook it.

"Well, I'm Ky, Asia." He smiled back at her. They continued to talk, just as Jaz was coming from the back room.

Jaz was holding Kayden in the air, making him laugh, when she spotted Kyree getting acquainted with Asia. An instant feeling of anger came over her. She hated Asia, and often considered firing her on more than one occasion. But she was the best nail tech in the area. She did nails like it was nobody's business. It was really just her attitude that sucked. Asia thought she walked on toilet tissue because she was the shit. Mixed with Black and Asian, she was sort of like the best of both worlds for most men. Most people said she almost looked like Nicki Minaj. But she was the true definition of a gold digger, and she could quickly spot a broke nigga from a rich nigga. Jaz could see her putting on her sweet, innocent act for Kyree, and it made her sick to her stomach. *That bitch is so fake,* Jaz said to herself.

Ms. Ray walked up to Jaz and whispered in her ear, "Oh, Rachel, this is just like the episode when you found out Ross was messing with that French girl." He paused and pretended to cry.

"Boy, shut up! He ain't my man. He's free to mess with whatever piece of trash he wants to."

"Um hmm. Well someone seems a bit jealous, if you ask me."

"Not even," Jaz waved him off. "I have a fiancé, remember?"

"Whatever." Ms. Ray walked away, not believing a word of what Jaz was saying. Even a blind man could see that she was lying to herself.

Monica could also see it, but she refused to say anything. She had convinced herself she was going to stay out of it this time, and she meant it, although seeing her brother talk to Asia wasn't too pleasant either. She didn't like or trust the bitch. She was on her way to break up their little encounter when she saw Jaz put a little extra switch in her walk with Kayden in her arms. *This bitch thinks she's slick!* Monica laughed to herself as she styled her client's hair.

Jaz walked over to them and handed Kayden to Kyree. "He's all yours." She smiled. "I got him all sugared up for you too. Ain't that right, Kay-Man?" She tickled him. "Just don't tell yo' mama about that candy in your pocket." She put her hands up to her lips, signaling for him to keep quiet, and Kayden giggled as he did the same. He and Jaz had already discussed it in the back.

"Damn, Jaz, you tryna make my day hard, huh?" Kyree smiled as she fixed Kayden's shirt.

"You'll be fine." She smiled back at him as she turned around to leave. Not once had she even acknowledged Asia's presence. She walked away with a new pep in her step. She knew she still had him when she felt his eyes roam to her ass from behind.

But then she heard him say, "A'ight, Asia, I have your card. I'll give you a call later. Say bye to Mommy, Kayden."

"Bye Mommy! Bye Josh! Bye everybody!" he yelled.

All of the patrons couldn't help but say, "Aw!"

Jaz waved goodbye to Kayden, but she felt defeated. She had no idea why though. She wasn't supposed to feel like this towards Kyree. She shook her head and continued styling Deja's hair, reasoning with herself that Kyree was free to see whomever he wanted.

"Monica, girllllll," Asia said, fanning herself with her hand. "Yo' brother is fine as hell!" Monica looked at her like she was crazy. "We gon' be sisters, girl," she boasted.

Monica thought to herself, *Bitch, over my dead body and yours.* But she caught herself and simply laughed her off. She glanced over at Jaz, and she seemed to be unfazed. Monica just hoped it was real.

The rest of the day at the salon went by smoothly, and by 10:00, the only ones there were Monica, Jaz, and Asia. Monica was cleaning up, Jaz was counting the drawer, and Asia was giggling at her phone. Jaz was just finishing up when she received a text message on her phone. Her heart dropped when she saw the message was from Kyree.

>>> **10:03 PM, 757-555-0126: Yo, this Ky. I'm going 2 respect your wishes. But we do have 2 b around each other because of Mo. So let's just squash it.**

She didn't know what to say, but she knew he was right. There was no need for them to keep up the awkward charade. His maturity with everything was actually a relief. She sent him a quick response.

<<< **10:06 PM: Ur right. We're both adults. Let's just b friends.**

>>> **10:07 PM, 757-555-0126: Coo. I was thinking about giving Mo a surprise party 4 her bday next month.**

<<< **10:10 PM: That sounds good. I'll help out as much**

as possible.

    >>> 10:13 PM, 757-555-0126: Coo. I'll b n touch. One.

Jaz felt better about their relationship after that message. She was happy they could try to be friends and remain cordial for the sake of Monica. She'd been wondering what she was going to do for Monica's birthday for a while now, and she was glad to have some help. She saw a car pull up outside, and a giddy Asia walked to the door.

"That's my ride, y'all." Asia smiled as she grabbed her purse.

"Alright, girl, see you tomorrow." Jaz waved her off and watched her ride away.

Monica came from the back room and sat down beside Jaz. "So how'd we make out?"

"We did well," Jaz said, putting the money in a bank bag.

"I'm so tired," Monica confessed.

"Me too. And I'm hungry," Jaz admitted.

"When aren't you hungry?" Monica shook her head and laughed as Jaz rolled her eyes.

"Whatever. You wanna go to the bar? Get some food and drinks? My treat," Jaz offered.

"You ain't said nothin' but a word." Monica hopped up, amped. A good drink was just what she needed to help her get over the busy day she'd had.

Jaz felt the same way. She couldn't stop thinking about her infidelity. It was eating at her that she'd done such a thing to Michael. He didn't deserve that. But she loved him too much to ever tell him.

When they arrived at the bar, it was packed to the max. It was ladies night, and all of the drinks for women were marked half off. Monica and Jaz found a table in the back and ordered a basket of wings and fries. Monica wasn't that hungry, but the Long Island iced tea was just what she needed. Jaz sipped on her amaretto sour as she enjoyed the DJ and waited for her food. She and Monica were deep in a conversation when they saw Asia walk in, and not too far behind her was Kyree. They were both shocked, to say the least.

"What the fuck is he doing here with her?" Monica asked, disgust evident on her face.

"I don't know, but we should invite them over," Jaz said as she waved her arm in the air, trying to get their attention.

Monica looked at Jaz like she was crazy as hell. Not only was Jaz inviting her enemy over to their table, she was also inviting her ex, and they were there together. Monica felt like she was in the twilight zone. Her girl was definitely sipping on more than the amaretto in her glass.

"Look, Ky." Asia tapped him and directed his attention to Jaz and Monica.

When Kyree turned around and saw Jaz and Monica, he was also surprised. After picking up Asia from the salon, they went to catch a movie, and now they were about to enjoy drinks. But with his sister and Jaz there, Kyree couldn't be more uncomfortable. To make matters worse, Jaz was waving them down to come to their table.

"Let's go sit with them," Asia said. "There aren't any other places to sit anyway." She looked around at the crowded bar.

Kyree would've rather sat in the bathroom than sit next to his ex and his sister while he was on a date. He figured Asia obviously didn't know their history, or else she would've also taken a seat next to the porcelain bowl.

But little did Kyree know, Asia knew more than she'd let on. She was well aware of who Kyree was the moment he walked in the salon. She knew the nigga used to carry more weight than Lifetime Fitness. He'd been in jail for the past three years. He was Monica's brother, and most importantly, Jaz's ex. She secretly hated Jaz and was extremely jealous of her. She didn't understand why Jaz got everything. To Asia, Jaz had it all: the doctor fiancé, her own salon, a nice-ass whip, good looks, and everyone loved her. She wanted to be just like her. When Jaz cut her hair and everyone in the salon raved about how good she looked, a week later, Asia had the same cut. Asia only pretended to be friendly with Jaz. Her ulterior motives were hidden behind fake smiles and laughs. When Asia saw the look on Jaz's face when Kyree walked in, she was sure that she still had feelings for him, and Asia was going to do everything in her power to make sure the two were never reunited.

"Hey y'all." Jaz smiled as they approached their table.

"Wassup?" Kyree said.

"Hey," Monica spoke dryly.

"Scoot down some, Mo. Let them sit down," Jaz said.

Monica reluctantly obliged, but before Kyree could fully sit down, Asia spoke up. "Naw, we just came in for a quick drink, and then we're headed home. We just wanted to stop by and say hi. You ladies enjoy yourselves. Come on, Kyree," Asia said. Her work was accomplished. She just wanted Jaz to see her with Kyree. But Jaz wore a poker face and refused to let Asia get the satisfaction.

"Okay, bye y'all." Jaz smiled as they walked away. She took a sip from her drink as Monica gave her the side eye. "What?" Jaz asked.

Monica didn't say anything; she just shook her head. Jaz was tripping and she was sure she was putting on a front for Asia. Everyone knew the two didn't like each other.

"Whatever." Jaz rolled her eyes at Monica as she took a bite from her chicken wing. "So have you talked to Latrell's lying ass?" Jaz asked.

Monica rolled her eyes in disgust. "Nope." It was no secret that Kayden's father was full of shit. He had taken her through so much over the years that if the saying was true that whatever didn't kill you made you stronger, she probably could one-up Superman in the strength department - except her kryptonite would be his dick.

"Fuck him, Mo!" Jaz said. "Kayden doesn't need his no-good ass in his life anyway," Jaz reasoned.

Monica nodded her head in agreement, but it was much more than that to her. She wanted Kayden to have something she never had: a father. "I know you're right, J, but why should Kayden have to go without a father because I made a lousy choice in choosing the right one for him?"

Jaz had no idea what to say. She'd been there through it

all, and she saw the effect Latrell's absence was having on Monica. She may not have wanted anything to do with him, but she wanted the world for Kayden. Since college, Latrell had been nothing but trouble for Monica. She fell head over heels in love with him and he broke her heart time and time again. Him being a boat boy and leaving every couple of months only made it that much easier for him to cheat on Monica, leave until shit blew over, then return when the heat died down. And Monica would gladly take him back with open arms. Jaz hated him, and Kyree had threatened his life more than a few times.

It wasn't until Kyree was locked up and Monica was pregnant with Kayden that things really started to go bad for them. One night Monica received a call from a Texas area code. She was reluctant to answer it at first, but she did. To this day, she still regretted it. The call came from a woman claiming to be Latrell's wife and the mother of his two children. Monica would've preferred hearing a pretty lie over the ugly truth that day.

When she confronted Latrell about it, he admitted it, but claimed to still love Monica. She called it off with him and he went back home to his family in Texas. After being together for four years, she never once thought he'd forget about their son. He paid his child support on a regular, but it still wasn't enough to cure the absence of a father. He'd only seen Kayden twice in his whole life, and it was when he stopped through on business. It was pretty much evident that Latrell just wasn't shit, and probably was never going to be shit.

"It's okay, Monica. I swear Kayden's going to grow up to be fine. And if Latrell doesn't give a damn now, he sure will when my Kay-Man makes it to the NBA." Jaz pretended to shoot a basketball in the hoop.

Monica couldn't help but laugh.

"He's gonna be just like LeBron and his no-good daddy. And Kay-Man gonna thank his Auntie Josh for teaching him everything he knows, watch."

Monica was dying laughing at Jaz's foolishness. She could always count on hanging with her girl Jaz and letting whatever problems she had go. "You are so slow." She shook her head. "Damn," she sighed.

"What?" Jaz asked.

"I just don't know what kept me blinded all those years," Monica wondered.

Jaz gave her a look and said, "Bitch, you know."

"What?" Monica asked, taking a sip from her drink.

"That dick, bitch!" Jaz boasted.

Monica burst out laughing, spitting her drink out across the table.

"Eww, Mo, you spit on my damn wings," Jaz whined.

"Girl, you'll be alright. I bet you still eat 'em too."

"Ya damn right," Jaz said, picking up a wing and biting it. "Hell, you ain't had no dick in so long, I'm pretty sure your mouth is clean enough." Jaz laughed, and Monica playfully pushed her.

"Fuck you!" Monica laughed.

"Bitch, I'm flattered, but I ain't gay. You better go buy yourself a toy." Jaz turned up her nose.

Monica couldn't help but laugh uncontrollably as Jaz made wise cracks to lighten the mood. "Oh my gosh, I hate you!" Monica shook her head.

"I love you too." Jaz smiled, holding up her glass, signaling for Monica to toast with her.

CHAPTER 5

Kyree was relieved that Asia was ready to leave the bar. He wasn't too fond of her speaking for him though. She seemed like a cool girl, but she had the game fucked up if she thought she was running shit. Kyree dictated his own moves, and Asia's forwardness was new to him. He didn't really like it, but since he was just getting to know her, he let it slide. Besides, he wasn't being completely honest with her anyway. He saw her as nothing more than someone to kill the time with. Years on the streets had opened his mind to the different women in the world, and he was more than sure Asia was a paper chaser. He wasn't mad at her though; she could get it how she lived it. But he was for damn sure it wouldn't be on his dime. There was one thing Kyree wasn't, and that was a sucker-ass nigga.

Leaving the bar and opening her car door, Kyree bit his bottom lip and shook his head at her ass. It definitely was a thing of beauty, and the black leggings she wore only enhanced her curvaceous frame. He hopped in the driver's side and pulled off into the night.

Asia practically melted in the warm leather seats of his black 745. The power she felt was comparable to nothing she'd ever felt before. Sure, she'd been with niggas with money, but none possessed the key to life like Kyree. He had money, power, and respect. She craved the attention. She had no idea Kyree had plans to leave the game alone for good. He was really trying to go legit. When he first got out of jail, he wanted to go straight for Jaz, but now that she was moving on with her life, his desire to do the right thing was lagging. The barbershop he planned on opening wasn't going as planned, and fast money seemed like the only way to keep his pockets stacked.

For the longest time, nothing but the sounds of Jay-Z and Rick Ross's hit "Fuck With Me You Know I Got It" filled the car until Asia said, "You're welcome."

Kyree looked at her crazy; he couldn't have heard her

45

right. Why the hell would he be thanking her? "What?" he asked, turning the music down.

"I said, you're welcome," Asia said with confidence.

"What for? Should I be grateful to you for something?" He eyed her, confused.

"Yeah. I got you out of that awkward situation."

Kyree looked at her while still trying to keep his eyes on the road.

"I know you and Jaz used to be real tight before you got locked up."

Kyree had no idea she knew. "How did you -"

"Please, Ky." She leaned her head back on the headrest and spoke with her eyes closed. "I know who you were before you got locked up. Everyone does. But I'm not concerned with all of that."

"You're not?" Kyree smirked, pulling up to the salon and stopping in front of Asia's candy apple red 2011 Range Rover. "Then what are you concerned with?" Kyree asked, becoming intrigued by her forwardness and confidence.

Asia lifted her head up and looked him in the eye. Her catlike eyes were hypnotizing, sexy, and almost scary. Kyree had to blink a few times just so he wouldn't get dizzy. "I'll be honest with you, Ky. The only things I'm concerned with are me, you, and him." She licked her lips seductively.

"Him?" Kyree asked, confused.

Asia smirked as she looked down at his crotch and bit the side of her lip. Kyree shook his head and let out a slight laugh as she reached over his lap and lowered his seat back. His dick immediately started to get hard as she started to unbuckle his pants. He stopped her so that he could take his .9 out of his waistband and put it on the floor. Being the paranoid type, he put it within arm's reach and hit the lock button on the car doors. He knew for sure bitches were always trying to set niggas up, and he wasn't going to literally be the one caught slipping with his pants down.

Kyree had been with many women and had seen pretty much everything. Asia was going to have to do something more spectacular than suck his dick to impress him. She popped an Altoid into her mouth and he looked down at her with a cocky smirk as if to say, *I'm not impressed*. Asia was known around town for her head game, which made most men think she was a brain surgeon and not a nail tech. Asia was confident in her skills and she paid no attention to his lack of interest as she eased his boxers down as well. The hole in his boxers wasn't big enough for the tricks Asia had in mind. Her mouth watered at the sight of his dick standing at attention. Never before had she seen a ten-inch dick, but she was more than up for the challenge.

She placed his dick in her delicate hands and then lowered her head to meet with the awesome sight before her. She took her tongue slowly across the tip while massaging his balls, working her way down to the base and back up again until she found the vein she was looking for. She took the tip of her tongue and moved it rapidly over the large vein on his penis. Kyree thought his head was going to explode. She was simultaneously blowing both of his brains, and she hadn't even taken him into her mouth yet. He grabbed on the car door handle for support and grasped it tightly. Asia secretly smiled to herself, knowing she was doing a good job. If only he knew, she was just getting started. She worked her tongue down to the base of his dick, back up, and then in one quick motion, she took him inside her mouth.

"Gotdayum, girl," Kyree hissed, taken aback. The cooling sensation from the Altoid mixed with the vacuum-like suction she created around his penis was unlike anything he'd ever felt before.

Asia bobbed her head up and down. His girth was nothing for her; she had no gag reflex. *Damn, does this bitch even have tonsils?* Kyree thought as he held on to her head, guiding her up and down. He was hitting the back of her throat, and she had yet to gag once. He felt his load building up, and he was trying to hold off for as long as possible. But the slurping noises she was making, mixed with the fact that she had more than six inches of his dick inside her mouth, made it that much harder to do. He bit his bottom lip, his eyes rolled to the back of his head, and he could no longer hold it anymore. He tried to pull her head up, but she resisted. "Shit!"

Asia was going to finish the job she started. She continued to bob her head up and down, doing tricks with her tongue, until she felt his children touch the back of her throat. Kyree's heart was racing as he groaned. Asia waited until he was looking at her, and then she opened her mouth, showing him his cum on her tongue. She proceeded to close her mouth, and then she swallowed. Kyree felt like he was in another world. She lowered her head back down again and licked up the remaining juices left on his dick.

Asia got back up and gave him a devilish grin. Kyree just shook his head and gave a slight smile as he watched her fix her face in mirror. Asia looked over at Kyree. He was definitely spent. She had put in some of her best work. "So, did I impress you?"

Kyree didn't respond. He couldn't stop shaking his head, and it was just the validation she needed to commend herself on a job well done. Asia let out a slight chuckle as she blew a kiss to Kyree. "I take it I'll be hearing from you?" He didn't respond. She kissed his dick, "Oh yeah, I'll be hearing from you." She laughed as she got out of his car and into her own.

"Damn," Kyree said out loud to himself as he pulled up his boxers and jeans. *Homegirl's definitely a hoe. But shit, I'll keep her around for a minute*, he thought to himself. *Hoe's need love too.* He laughed as he started the ignition and pulled off from the parking lot.

Meanwhile, Asia sat in her car, silently kissing it goodbye. She just knew her head game had upgraded her to the 2014 model Range - hell, maybe even a Benz. She was securing her place in Kyree's life. Jaz would definitely be feeling like shit after she saw Asia on the arm of the man who was once the love of her life. Although she told Kyree her concerns, she failed to mention her two biggest concerns of all: Kyree's money, and making Jaz as unhappy as possible. Asia pulled away from the parking lot, feeling on top of the world. But she had no idea how hard making Kyree forget about Jaz would be. Unbeknownst to her, the whole time she was blowing his top, he was picturing Jaz's face in his mind.

But that didn't stop Asia from being on her high horse at the salon. Asia never thought she'd admit it to herself, but she was actually falling hard for Kyree. She was always the fuck 'em then leave 'em type. As soon as she got what she wanted from a man, he was of no use to her anymore. But Kyree was different than any man she'd ever been with. He was more of a challenge to her, and she loved it. Men always gave her what she wanted, especially after she put down her head game, but Kyree treated her like a woman should be treated. He courted her, befriended her, and treated her with respect. Although he was a man of few words, they always had fun together. She no longer saw herself trading in her Range Rover for another top of the line luxury vehicle. Kyree would never give her money. He'd spend money on her, but it would never touch her hands.

Kyree was a gentleman, but he wasn't a sucker. To him, Asia wasn't his girl; they were just kickin' it. He could never give his heart to another. Jaz had the key, and she was refusing to give it back. So while Jaz was off planning her wedding, Kyree was off enjoying the single life. Each night Kyree enjoyed the company of a different woman to pass the time. Asia was just one of many, and Kyree made it no secret to her. She didn't like it at all; she was used to being number one. But she accepted it nonetheless. She didn't really have a choice in the matter. Either she had to accept it, or Kyree was kicking her to the curb without even the slightest afterthought. And the dick was just too good for her to let him go. But admitting to anyone her real position would just make her seem irrelevant. She could never let that happen, especially around Jaz.

One day, while Jaz sat in the back of the salon waiting for Michael to pick her up for dinner, she sent a confirmation text to Kyree. After weeks, they'd finally decided on a place to have Monica's surprise birthday party. They never spoke about anything more than Monica's party, and Jaz was happy that they could remain friends. But his messages were always so short, and she always felt like they were forced. It was so awkward. She would have rather gone back to the days when they were younger and hated each other than to have to deal with the awkwardness. It didn't help matters that he was dating Asia either. She didn't want Kyree, but she also didn't want to see him with Asia. She was so scandalous. For weeks after her and Kyree's rendezvous in his car, she went on about how much she really liked him. Jaz usually ignored Asia when she spoke about Kyree. If Asia wanted to put on a show, Jaz wasn't going to buy a ticket. When Jaz saw Asia coming to the back with the broom, she pretended to busy herself with her phone, randomly scrolling through it, checking old text messages, the salon's Facebook status, whatever she could do to avoid any conversation with Asia. But Asia saw an opportunity and she took it. While sweeping around Jaz, she said, "I hope we can still be cool?"

Jaz looked up from her phone. "What?"

"I know you and Ky used to have a *li'l* thing back in the day," Asia said, putting emphasis on the word li'l, letting Jaz know that it meant nothing to her.

Jaz was appalled. What she and Kyree had was way more than anything he and Asia could ever have. She had to remind herself that Asia was just hungry for attention and she shouldn't feed her. She stood up from her seat and spoke slowly as she tried to bite her tongue. "Asia, sweetie," Jaz let out a slight chuckle, "it's cool. Kyree and I had a 'li'l thing'", she used the finger quotes, "that lasted four years, three years ago."

"Oh, I just didn't want it to ruin our friendship," Asia lied. Truth was, she could care less.

Jaz almost laughed. *Bitch, please, we've never been friends. We just tolerate each other.* "Girl, please, we still girls." Jaz almost threw up from the lie she told.

"You sure?"

Asia was really trying to get a reaction out of Jaz, but Jaz held a straight face. "Yeah, sweetie," Jaz said in a condescending tone. She looked up just as Michael walked through the door.

"Hey, how're you doing..." He paused as he tried to remember Asia's name, "Asia, right?"

Asia turned up her nose, but no one noticed, so she quickly forced a smile. "Yeah, that's right. Mike?" She pretended not to know Michael's name as he nodded. "I'm good, and you?" she asked, making small talk.

"I can't complain. Hungry as hell though. Waiting on Jaz to hurry up so we can go to dinner." He eyed Jaz like only a man in love would.

Jaz smiled back at him. He was so handsome in his tan slacks and brown polo shirt. She walked over to him, feeling a bit victorious as she looked back at Asia and said, "Oh, I'm more than sure."

Asia stood there feeling defeated as Jaz and Michael left. But Asia was convinced that it was just a matter of time before jealousy reared its ugly head and Jaz lost her cool. She was going to make sure of it.

A COUPLE OF FOREVERS

CHAPTER 6

Jaz sat across from Michael as he told her a funny story while they waited on their food at PF Chang's - or at least, Jaz thought it must've been funny because Michael kept laughing. It wasn't that she didn't love his sense of humor; it was that her mind was elsewhere. All she could think about was how much she didn't deserve him. He was too good for her. Since the day they'd met, he'd been nothing but loving and patient. She could still recall walking into his office and meeting him a year and a half ago.

Jaz was nervous as hell as she sat in the waiting room of the new doctor's office. Her old gynecologist had referred her to him. She was just starting to get used to her old doctor when he told her he was moving to DC. She wanted to follow him to DC just for her yearly exams. She didn't like everyone getting a free peek and feel of her goodies. It just felt so wrong. But she'd heard about this new doctor, and her previous doctor assured her that Dr. Jacobs was the best in the business - next to him, of course. So Jaz decided to give him a chance. She'd just finished telling what felt like her whole life story on the new patient entry forms when the nurse said the doctor was ready to see her.

Following the nurse to the back, Jaz was escorted into the room where she was to be examined. The nurse issued her a gown and left the room as Jaz proceeded to remove her clothes. "Damn, I shouldn't have worn these tight-ass jeans," she said aloud as she tried to get out of her curve-hugging Seven jeans. She knew it was going to be a battle trying to put them back on. She slipped on the gown, which covered less than nothing, and proceeded to look around the office. It wasn't like her old doctor's office. It had a much more comforting feeling. She felt like she was at home and not about to get her goodies poked and prodded. The walls were painted light blue, there was hardwood flooring, and smooth jazz played throughout. Plaques adorned the walls, all with nothing but rave things to say about Dr. Jacobs. He had a Bachelor's in Science from Virginia Tech and a Master's and PhD in Medicine from Johns Hopkins. Dr. Jacobs's records were definitely remarkable. But it would take more than a few plaques from high profile schools to impress Jaz. Ever since her mother went into a hospital when Jaz was just twelve years old and never came out, Jaz hated hospitals and doctors.

The nurse came in to give a basic once over and then told her the doctor would be in shortly. Jaz patiently waited as her feet dangled from the table. She took a deep breath as she heard the doorknob turn, and in walked the most handsome man she'd ever laid eyes on. Dressed in an all-white lab coat and green tie, he stood about 6'2" with skin the color of caramel and the most kissable pink lips. *Gotdamn, he looks good,* Jaz said to herself. He reminded her of the actor Shemar Moore.

"Alright, Ms. Elliott, please put your feet up in the stirrups," he said, still having yet to look up from his clipboard.

Jaz did as she was told. She really did hate this part; she couldn't wait to get it over with. Dr. Jacobs placed his clipboard on the counter, and then turned around, seeing Jaz's face for the first time. She was breathtaking. Jaz made eye contact with him and caught a glimpse of his catlike hazel eyes. They were hypnotizing. He was making her feel nervous. He shook his head, trying to snap out of his daydream. He pulled his chair around to her front as Jaz nervously twiddled her fingers on her stomach and looked up at the ceiling.

He pulled her gown down, and turned his head. "Can you close your legs, Ms. Elliott?"

Jaz removed her legs from the stirrups, confused. "Is there something wrong, Doctor?" Jaz was baffled. She couldn't figure out what his problem was.

"Yes, there is a problem," Dr. Jacobs said, scribbling something on his clipboard.

Jaz had no idea what the hell was wrong. She knew her shit was tight. It was fresh, cleanly shaven, and just the sight of it drove most men crazy. She didn't know what the hell the doctor's problem was. "What's the problem then?"

"I just can't do this."

"And why the fuck not?" Jaz asked, getting defensive.

"Because it wouldn't be ethical, that's why."

"Why wouldn't it be? Don't you get paid to look at pussies all day?" Jaz asked, her tone raising an octave. She was beyond pissed, but *she had to take a stand.*

Dr. Jacobs couldn't help but laugh.

"What the fuck are you laughing at?" Dr. Jacobs chuckled even harder this time. Jaz was fed up with the bullshit. She hurriedly grabbed her clothes and began to quickly put them on as Dr. Jacobs stood there and continued to write on his clipboard. "This is some bullshit!" Jaz barked as she jumped up and down, trying to fit her ass in her jeans. Why did I wear these fucking jeans? Jaz chastised herself, angry that her dramatic exit would be fucked up because of her phat ass. It really was a gift and curse. She put on her red suede pumps while mumbling obscenities under her breath. "What the fuck kind of doctor are you anyway?" Jaz just had to ask.

Dr. Jacobs looked up from his clipboard and stepped into her personal space. Jaz's chest was heaving from anger, and his piercing stare was making her feel uncomfortable. She put her head down, unable to look him in the eye. He lifted her head with his finger so that she was facing him and said, "The kind of man who likes to chase his pussy." Jaz's mouth dropped in shock. He was so cocky and straightforward. She found it sexy and intriguing.

"I look at pussy all day. But I don't want to see yours just yet. I'm going to earn that right."

Jaz loosened up a bit. She hadn't been with a man since Kyree had gotten locked up over a year ago, but the man in front of her was making her feel like she was well overdue for a dick down. Feeling more comfortable, she let out a cocky laugh and said, "And what makes you so sure about that?"

Dr. Jacobs licked his bottom lip as he eyed Jaz up and down. "Oh, I will," he said, as he turned to leave. "I'll refer you to another doctor. A female one. We'll be in touch." And just like that, he was gone.

Jaz thought he was the most arrogant son of a bitch she'd ever met - next to Kyree of course. But she loved his cocky, yet confident attitude. He challenged her. "I knew my shit was tight," Jaz laughed to herself as she picked up her purse to leave.

Jaz found it hard to believe that was a year and a half ago. Sitting there, she wondered if she should tell him the truth. Her infidelity was killing her. She felt like she wasn't being true to herself. But she wondered if telling him would only cure her own guilt while still leaving him hurt in the process. She had no idea what she should do. She didn't want to lose him. She really did love and care for him.

"Babe?" Michael said, waving his hand in her face. "Jaz?"

Jaz snapped out of her trance and realized he was talking to her. "Huh? Yeah? What's up?"

"You've just been in another world all night. Are you alright?" he asked, concern evident on his face.

Jaz gave him a reassuring smile. "Yeah, I'm alright."

"Are you sure?"

"I'm good, Mike. I'm just a little stressed out about the wedding and all. There's still so much left to do," she lied.

"Well, you know my mom said she'd help out with as much as possible if you're feeling overwhelmed."

"No, it's okay. Mo's been helping me," Jaz quickly said. Truth was, she couldn't stand Michael's mother, and she probably wouldn't spit on the uppity bitch if she were on fire. She knew the feeling was probably mutual. She went into meeting his mother with an open mind; she was actually excited. But as soon as Michael introduced them, Mrs. Jacobs made it known that she didn't like Jaz: the way she dressed, her choice of career, the way she talked, everything. Mr. Jacobs was a retired OB/GYN, and Mrs. Jacobs was content with the woman being at home, barefoot and pregnant, with her man's dinner ready and on the table when he came home. But Jaz made it clear that she was not giving up her salon after they were married. Her salon was her baby, and she loved doing hair. She needed a sense of purpose. Her father had instilled good values in her, and Jaz was headstrong. Even though his mother didn't, Michael said he understood. He actually liked and respected Jaz's drive and ambition.

"She said she called you today to go over the wedding and you didn't answer," Michael said, taking a sip of his water.

"Who did?" Jaz said, trying to buy herself some time to think of a good lie.

"My mother." Michael looked at her like she was crazy.

"Oh, I haven't even looked at my phone all day. It was so

busy at the shop. You know Easter is coming up," Jaz lied. Truth was, she'd seen his mother's name roll across her phone's screen several times, but she couldn't stand to answer it. She knew that she just wanted to bark orders at her about her wedding. Jaz wanted so desperately to tell her to mind her own damn business. Everything Jaz wanted for the wedding was always wrong, and everything Mrs. Jacobs wanted was always right. The two were like oil and water; they just didn't mix.

"I know you two don't get along, but we're all going to be a family. So y'all are going to have to find some common ground," Michael reasoned.

Jaz looked at him like he was crazy. She never once said anything disrespectful to his mother. It was always Mrs. Jacobs with a smart comment, and on a bad day, Jaz always had an even smarter response. It bothered Jaz that he was so blind to his mother's dislike and blatant disrespect for her. Just as Jaz was about to tell him off about his "y'all" comment, the waitress returned with their food. Michael was only saved by Jaz's hunger. The orange chicken, mixed vegetables, and white rice on the plate before her was a sight for Jaz's sore eyes.

"Thank you," Jaz said to the waitress. "Can you bring some extra duck sauce?"

"Sure thing," the waitress said.

"Um, this looks good," Jaz practically moaned as she mixed in all of her food.

"Sure does," Michael agreed as he mixed around his beef and broccoli.

They bowed their heads and said grace, and as Jaz lifted her head, the waitress was back with her duck sauce. Jaz poured it over everything. Michael looked on in shock as Jaz practically drowned her food with it.

"Damn, babe," Michael laughed.

"What?"

"Don't you think you're going overboard with the duck sauce?"

Jaz shrugged her shoulders and put the duck sauce down. "Damn, I didn't know I had to ask you how much sauce I could put on my damn plate." She rolled her eyes with an attitude.

"What the hell is your problem?" Michael was taken aback. He had no idea where her sudden attitude came from. "Fine then, I won't say anything else to you tonight. Shit," Michael said, digging into his food.

Jaz immediately felt bad. She was taking her anger and guilt with herself out on him. She just had so much on her mind, so many secrets she was keeping inside. She took a deep sigh. "I'm sorry I took my frustrations out on you, baby. I just have a lot of stuff on my plate," she admitted.

"Yeah, I see you have a lot on your plate - which you just drowned in fucking duck sauce." They both laughed. "But really, Jaz, anything you have going on, just let me know. That's what I'm here for."

Jaz contemplated telling him. If she didn't say something, she would surely snap at any minute. "Well," Jaz swallowed hard, "do you remember my ex that I told you about before you?"

"Yeah," Michael nodded his head.

Jaz's heart felt like it wanted to pound its way out of her chest. "He's out of jail now," Jaz finally said.

"Is that all?" Michael asked.

"Well, actually, no," Jaz admitted.

Michael dropped his fork and shook his head, preparing for news he just knew couldn't have been good.

"Well, I told him I'm engaged. But you know he's Monica's brother, so it's hard for me to avoid him." Jaz looked down, and played with the food on her plate. There was no way she could look him in the eye. "And he wants me to help him plan Monica a surprise party."

Michael took a huge sigh of relief. "Is that all?" He smiled.

Jaz shook her head yeah and gave him a quizzical look. "What'd you think I was going to say?"

Michael shook his head and picked up his fork as he let out a light chuckle. "Nothing, Jaz," he lied. He really thought she was going to tell him that she was back fucking with her ex. The truth was, Jaz contemplated it. But living with her guilt would have to suffice. She couldn't bear to see the hurt on his face. She loved him too much to ever devastate him just to relinquish her own feelings of guilt.

"So you're cool with us planning Mo's party?" she asked, just to be sure, even though she'd been planning it with him for a month now.

"Of course. It's cool with me." He looked up from his food to look her in the eye. "Jaz I love you. You're going to be my wife in less than two months. That nigga was smart enough to let you go three years ago so that I could be dumb enough to be having dinner with you today. Hell, I want to throw that nigga a party to thank him," Michael laughed. Jaz smiled back at him. He was always saying the right things. But truth was, it was secretly eating him up inside. He just wanted her to know that he trusted her. "Do you love me, Jaz?"

"Of course I love you," Jaz admitted.

"Then that's all that matters. I trust you, Jaz. I know you wouldn't do anything to jeopardize what we have." Michael gave her a reassuring smile, and Jaz weakly returned his smile as she picked up her fork to place a huge chunk of chicken in her mouth. She immediately felt like shit. She was so repulsed with herself. Here she had a good man that was willing to give her the world, and she had almost jeopardized it for one night of passion with her ex. Michael's confidence and trust in their love was amazing. *I gotta get my shit together*, she thought to herself.

Jaz cleaned her plate while Michael still had some left. The waiter boxed it up for him, and then asked them if they wanted dessert. They said yes and had a much-needed talk while the waiter went to retrieve their food.

"So have you talked to your landlord about getting out of your lease?" Michael asked.

"Yeah, actually I talked to him yesterday. He said it wouldn't be a problem," Jaz said, taking a sip of her lemonade. Truth was, she still had yet to get to it. She really wasn't in a rush to give up her place. It was her first apartment, and the whole idea was so scary. Moving into a new place with her soon-to-be husband should have been a joyous occasion, but for Jaz, it was the scariest time in her life. She loved Michael, but she was more afraid of what she'd do to him than what he would do to her. She always had a way of messing up whatever was good in her life.

"That's what's up," Michael said, slightly distracted by his ringing cell phone. He ran his hand over his face in frustration as he read over a text message.

"Is everything alright?" Jaz asked him.

"Yeah. It's just that Mrs. Taylor is expecting her twins, and... You know what? Forget it. I'm having dinner with my fiancée, someone else can handle it." He put his phone on silent and placed it back on the table.

Jaz placed her hand on top of his. "It's cool, Michael. I don't mind. Business before pleasure."

"Are you sure?" he asked.

"Of course I'm sure. But she's been waiting nine months, so ten more minutes won't hurt her. Shit, I want my dessert."

Michael laughed at her silliness. "I don't deserve you, girl."

Jaz smiled on the outside, but thought to herself, *If only you knew how much you really didn't deserve me.*

CHAPTER 7

Stepping out of her all-black convertible top Camaro, Jaz ascended the walkway to the small one story ranch-style brick home in downtown Portsmouth. As soon as her Adidas touched the pavement, she immediately felt a sense of comfort. Comfortably dressed in a pink and white Adidas short set with the matching shoes, Jaz picked up the newspaper that lay on the porch. She rang the doorbell, and when she got no answer, she tried turning the knob. The door opened right up and Jaz walked inside.

With all of the drama going on lately, she had been neglecting the most important man in her life. Before there was ever anyone else, there was always him. "Daddy!" Jaz yelled throughout her father's house. She knew he was home because his red Toyota Tundra sat outside in the driveway. "Daddy!" she yelled again.

"I'm back here, baby girl!" he yelled back.

Jaz followed his voice to the backyard. She opened the screen door and walked outside, but she didn't see her father anywhere. "Daddy?" she called out to him.

"Up here, Jazmine."

Jaz turned around and looked up. Seeing her father up on the roof sent instant panic through her heart. "Daddy! Get down from there," she chastised him.

The distressed look on his daughter's face was all Calvin needed to come down from the roof. He was only cleaning the gutters, something he did every year around this time. But he hated to stress her; she worried about him so much. He laughed to himself as she carefully held the ladder while he climbed down. "Daddy, why did you leave the front door open? Anybody could've come in the house," Jaz said, more like she was the parent and he was her child.

"Not if they know what's good for 'em. You know I still keeps my Glock locked and loaded, ready for whatever," he stated firmly.

Jaz shook her head and laughed, knowing that he was dead-ass serious. He dropped the gutter cleaners in his hand on the ground and embraced his daughter.

"How've you been, baby girl?" Jaz's dad Calvin said as he gave her a peck on the cheek.

"You know me, always staying busy. Have you been taking your pills?" Jaz quickly redirected the question, always concerned about her father's high blood pressure.

"Yes, I've been taking my pills. But that's not what I asked you. How have YOU been, Jazmine?" He called her by her full name; she hated that.

"I've been good, Daddy. Just going to work and planning the wedding."

Calvin slowly shook his head as he took a seat on one of the lawn chairs. "Baby girl, guess who I saw yesterday?" He quickly changed the subject.

Jaz followed suit, and also took a seat. "Who'd you see yesterday?"

"My main man Ky," Calvin boasted.

Jaz rolled her eyes.

"Did you roll your eyes at me, girl?"

"No sir," Jaz shook her head. But she knew how her dad felt about Kyree. He could do no wrong in his eyes.

"Yeah, he told me he got out a month ago. Told me he's trying to open up a barber shop."

"Well, that's good for him," Jaz stated, annoyed with where this conversation was going.

"So have you spoken to him?"

"Yeah, we talked."

"Well, when are y'all going to squash the bullshit and get back together?"

Jaz looked at him like he was crazy. "Daddy!"

"What?" Calvin asked, dumbfounded.

"I'm getting married. You know, to Michael, my fiancé, the one with drive, goals, ambition, and a legal job?" Jaz spoke to him like he was slow.

Her father just shook his head. Unlike Michael's mother, he didn't disrespect Michael or show his dislike for him. He actually tried to find something in common with him. But keeping up a fake conversation was something he couldn't do, so he was always short and to the point with Michael. He didn't doubt that Michael was a good guy; there were just some things about him that didn't sit right with him.

"What don't you like about Michael?" Jaz asked in frustration.

"I just don't think he can be trusted, baby girl. What kind of man can sit and look at women's..." He paused, trying to think of a decent word to use in front of his daughter. "Private business and not get a little curious?"

"Daddy, he's a professional. It would be unethical of him to do anything like that."

"'Cause I know if it was me, I'd be—"

"Daddy!" Jaz cut him off. She would rather not hear about her father and his many women. He was forty-five years old, tall, with skin the color of smooth dark chocolate and a thick black beard with little specks of gray throughout his face and head. He could pull almost any woman he wanted, but his heart died when Jaz's mother Simone lost her life to cancer thirteen years ago. But that didn't stop him from playing his hand at a few women. He never got too close to them, and Jaz was more than fine with that. She loved being the only girl in his life. She was kind of selfish when it came to her father. Jaz was the only child, and although her dad tried to discipline her, he always ended up giving in. He spoiled her rotten, put fear in the heart of every guy she'd ever dated, and he always put her first.

But of all the guys she'd ever dated, Calvin always held a soft spot for Kyree. When Kyree was younger and first moved to the neighborhood, Calvin was like a father figure to him. He taught him how to cut hair, warned him about the streets, and always told him to have a legal hustle. Kyree listened to everything Calvin said as if it were one of the Ten Commandments. He got odd jobs around the neighborhood mowing lawns, cutting hair, walking dogs, whatever he could find. But it wasn't long before Kyree noticed that mowing lawns wasn't bringing in as much money as selling drugs. When Calvin found out, he was disappointed, but he didn't judge him. He just told him to be careful. He too had started off selling heroin. But Simone's death had given him a little girl to look after, so he got a real job as a plumber. He started off working for someone else, and now had his own business. He was a hardworking man who didn't believe anything should be handed to him, and for that reason, he hated the fact that Michael's family was rich.

"Jaz, I just want you to be happy, that's all," Calvin said with all sincerity.

"And I am, Daddy. I love Michael, and I want you to be happy for me," Jaz said, practically in tears. She wanted the two men in her life to love each other just as much as she loved them.

Although Calvin had his doubts about Michael, there was nothing he wanted more than to see his daughter happy. "A'ight then, baby girl. If you like him, then I love him." He gave her a reassuring smile and Jaz got up to hug him.

"Did you eat today?" Jaz pulled away from their hug to look at him.

"I had some beef jerky earlier."

"Daddy," Jaz sighed in a chastising tone.

"What? That's food. And it's good too."

Jaz shook her head and laughed. "Come on, Daddy, I'm going to find you some real food."

Jaz made her father lasagna and stayed to talk with him while it cooked. They sat and watched the NBA playoffs together while arguing over whose team was going to make it to the finals. They rarely got to spend any time together, and Jaz appreciated it when they did. She left without eating the lasagna after Calvin told her about his friend Jodie that was coming over. Besides the fact that Jaz didn't want to meet his new lady friend, she had other plans later that night.

Michael had called earlier to cancel on their plans to go the movies, so she was supposed to be going with Monica. Last night wasn't the first time Michael had to end one of their dates, but she understood he had a very demanding career and she would have to get used to it if she was going to be his wife. It often bothered her, but he always made up for it the next day by showering her with attention. But Monica would definitely make up for her not being able to spend time with Michael. She was sure to release whatever stress was going on in her life by sharing a few laughs with her best friend since middle school.

The smell of jasmine teased her nostrils as she walked into her house. She loved the smell and so did her mother, hence her name. She knew it was going to be bittersweet giving up her apartment. Her cell phone rang before she could set her bag down. Instantly knowing who the caller was from the Beyoncé "Flawless" ringtone, Jaz answered, "What up, trick?"

"You are so rude," Monica said.

"Whatever. I already know why you're calling. I'm already dressed and ready, just waiting for your slow ass," Jaz said, knowing Monica was always on time and she was not.

"Well, actually..." Monica said, as if she were stalling.

"What, Mo?"

"I was calling to ask you if we could reschedule." Monica bit her lip, hoping Jaz would be okay with her cancelling at the last minute.

Jaz sucked her teeth. "Why?"

Mo sighed heavily. "Because Mario finally asked me out again."

"Oh hell naw! I know yo' ass ain't cancelling on me for some dick?"

"It's not even like that, J; we're just going to dinner."

"Um hmm, tell me anything, Mo." Jaz rolled her eyes.

"Bitch, don't act like that. You know you'd do the same if you were me," Monica reasoned.

"Whatever, Mo. Just go and have fun," Jaz said, disappointed.

"I will. But there's one more thing." Mo winced on the other end of the phone because she knew Jaz was going to have a fit when she told her.

"Oh my gosh, what, Mo?" Jaz asked, slightly aggravated.

"Well, my mom has bingo tonight and Kyree has plans too, and you know my mom was supposed to watch Kayden. I was wondering if -"

"Aw, hell naw, Mo! You cancel on me, and then you want me to stay home and babysit?" Jaz shook her head. "Bye, Mo." She hung up the phone, frustrated. She immediately regretted hanging up on Mo because she realized she was being selfish. But she was pissed that she was going to be spending Saturday night in the house by herself. Everyone seemed to be doing something but her. Her phone rang a minute later, the ringtone informing her it was Monica again.

She sucked her teeth. "Yeah, Monica."

"I go to you house, Josh?" Kayden asked in his broken speech.

Jaz shook her head and smiled. There was no way she could say no to that. Kayden melted her heart every time he called her Josh. *Damn, Mo know she ain't right for this.* She loved her godson and there was nothing she wouldn't do for him. "Of course auntie's Kay-Man can come over."

"Okay." Jaz heard ruffling in the background and then she heard Kayden say, "Her say yeah, Mommy."

"Hello?" Monica got back on the phone.

"I hate you, Mo!" Jaz couldn't help but laugh.

"What?" Monica laughed too.

Monica and Jaz could never stay mad at each other for very long. They'd been around each other long enough to know the right buttons to push. Whenever they got mad at one another, one of them would eventually call and give in, picking up wherever they left off.

"So what're you wearing to your freak session?" Jaz asked, plopping down on her couch.

"It's not a freak session. But if you must know, since it's kind of cool outside, I was thinking about wearing my white MK blazer, yellow skinny jeans, and yellow wedge peep toe heels."

"Naw, Mo, wear the white wedge peep toe heels," Jaz said, knowing everything in Monica's closet.

"You think so?" Monica asked as she searched through her closet for the shoes.

"I know so."

"Oh, I found them. You were right, they do look better."

"I'm always right. Remember that, and I promise you'll go far."

Monica rolled her eyes. "Whatever."

"So I know you ain't had dick since T.I. went to jail the first time, and –"

"Jaz!" Monica yelled, shocked.

"Bitch, please, you know it's been a while." Jaz laughed, and Monica joined her.

Monica had to admit, it had been a while. But since Latrell broke her heart, she was skeptical about who she allowed in her life and between her legs. "Well, I guess you can call me Luigi tonight," Jaz said.

"What the hell are you talking about?" Monica asked, confused.

"'Cause I'm helping you out while you find out if Mario's mushroom is super enough to fill your peach." Jaz smirked.

Monica burst out laughing, "Oh my gosh, Jaz!"

A COUPLE OF FOREVERS

CHAPTER 8

Jaz prepared her house for Kayden's arrival. She was going to make the best of their Saturday night together. She had planned on ordering a pizza, pigging out on candy, and playing the Xbox One until they passed out. Monica would probably kill Jaz if she knew, but Jaz didn't care. She was the fun aunt, and the only rule at her house was that there were no rules. Spending time with Kayden always made her feel good, and she couldn't wait for him to get there. Monica said her mother Jackie was bringing him around 7:00, and it was already 7:10.

She was setting up the Xbox to the big screen TV in the living room when she heard the doorbell ring. Flinging the door open without looking through the peephole, she was immediately taken aback. Kayden was on the other end, but she didn't expect Kyree to be holding him. She hadn't actually seen him since their run-in at the bar nearly a month ago. They had only been communicating through text messaging, and even then, it was only about Monica's party. Jaz stood their speechless. He was sporting a navy blue Crooks and Castles cardigan, Crooks and Castles blue jeans, and a pair of blue and white Nike Dunks graced his feet, along with a blue and white Yankee fitted on his head. Jaz had no idea how she should approach him. It was the first time the two had been alone together since the day she had her moment of weakness.

"Hey, Jaz," Kyree broke the silence.

"Wassup, Kyree," Jaz spoke. "Hey, Kay-Man." She tickled Kayden while he was still in Kyree's arms and he squirmed and giggled.

"You better stop. Li'l man was just saying how bad he had to go to the bathroom. I wouldn't want him to piss on himself and you have to clean it up." Kyree let out a slight chuckle.

Jaz quickly pulled her hands back. She surely didn't want to clean up that mess. "Do you have to go to the bathroom,

Kayden?" she asked him.

"I gotta go pot," Kayden said, tugging at the crotch of his pants. Jaz reached out her hands and Kayden went right to her.

"Hell, I gotta go pot too," Kyree laughed.

Jaz shook her head and laughed as she made a path for him to come in. She took Kayden to the bathroom in her bedroom while Kyree went to the one in the hallway. When she thought she heard Kayden was finished, she asked, "All done?"

He vigorously shook his head no. "I gotta make stink," he said, almost as if he were straining. Jaz couldn't help but laugh. He was so cute with his little legs dangling from the oversized toilet.

"Okay. I'll be right out here. Yell for me when you're ready." Kayden nodded his head yes and Jaz cracked the door behind her. When she walked into the hallway, she was laughing so hard that she nearly bumped into Kyree who was walking out of the bathroom.

"My bad, Jaz," he apologized.

"You good," Jaz said, walking behind him. "Hey, I thought Ms. Jackie was going to bring him."

"She didn't want to be late for bingo. You know how that goes."

Jaz nodded her head in understanding. For as long as she could remember, Jackie had been going to bingo every chance she could. When they were younger and Jackie hit big, Jaz and Monica were guaranteed to go on a shopping spree of some sort. "Yeah, Ms. Jackie don't miss bingo for nobody," Jaz laughed.

"Naw, she sure as hell don't," Kyree agreed. There was a brief silence between them, then Kyree said, "Hey, I talked to my homeboy who runs Club House, and Mo's birthday is all set."

"That's sounds great. And I already told everybody at the shop. I have a plan to get her out that night, and I don't think she suspects a thing. Monica is going to be so surprised." Jaz smiled.

"I know, right?" Kyree said, caught off guard by his ringing cell phone. "Hold on a second, Jaz." She nodded her head in agreement, as he proceeded with his conversation on

70

the phone. "What!" Kyree barked into the phone. "I don't give a fuck how you get the shit done, just get it done!" he barked, quickly ending the call.

Jaz could only hear one end of the conversation, but from the end she was on, it didn't sound good. "Is everything alright?" she asked him.

"Yeah, everything's all good," he lied.

Jaz sucked her teeth. "Come on, Kyree, this is me you're talking to."

Kyree knew Jaz knew something was up with him. She had a way of looking him in the eyes and getting the truth out of him no matter what it was. They were more than just ex-lovers; they were once each other's best friend. For a second, he contemplated letting her inside his head, but he glanced down at her hand, noticing the constant reminder that she could no longer be his confidant. "Naw, it's good, Jaz. But check it; I gotta go handle some business right quick, so I'll holla at you later."

Jaz shook her head in disappointment. "Deja fucking vu," she said, remembering past times in their relationship. Kyree saying he had to handle some business was always his way of saying, without actually saying, that he was going to run the streets. Jaz truly felt like a mistress to the streets throughout their relationship. But now she didn't understand why she even cared. It was no longer her concern.

"What?"

"Nothing, Kyree," Jaz dismissed the issue. "You don't owe me an explanation."

Kyree looked at the all too familiar look on Jaz's face. It was definitely one she used whenever she was frustrated with him. He hated the fact that she was always right though. He was actually on the phone with one of his workers, who said they couldn't make a drop because their car was broken down. To Kyree, this was totally unacceptable. If his money was involved, no excuse was acceptable. He didn't give a fuck if his worker had to make a P. Diddy cheesecake walk as long as he got his money. But he could never tell that to Jaz. And she was right. He wasn't indebted to her, but he didn't like seeing her disappointed in him.

"You know what, Jaz, you're right, I don't owe you shit. But, if you must know, that was one of the contractors for the barber shop saying he was going to need more time to put in the hardwood floors," Kyree half told the truth. Actually, the contractors had called to say that, but that definitely wasn't them on the phone just now.

As much as she wanted to, Jaz just couldn't believe him. While everyone around her believed Kyree was changing, she couldn't help but revert back to the old Kyree, who always said he was going to leave the streets alone. His promises of change fell on deaf ears when it came to Jaz. She just shook her head. "Tell me anything, Kyree."

"You don't believe me?"

Jaz wanted to say, *Hell no*, but it really wasn't her concern anymore. She truly did care about his wellbeing, but it was no longer her job to worry herself with thoughts of Kyree's whereabouts. She was engaged to a man she loved unconditionally. She was finally moving on with her life. "What does it matter anyway?"

Kyree couldn't give her the satisfaction of being right about him this time. "You know what? Fuck it! Don't believe me. I can show you better than I can tell you." He was beyond frustrated as he picked up Kayden's book bag from off the floor and threw it over his shoulder.

"What the hell are you talking about?" Jaz asked, confused.

"Josh!" Kayden yelled from the bathroom.

"I'll be there in just a minute, baby!" Jaz yelled back at him, and then she turned to Kyree for an explanation.

"Go wipe his ass, get your purse, and meet me in the damn car," Kyree said authoritatively.

"And what the hell for? You must be out yo' damn mind, Kyree. You got me fucked up if you think I'm going anywhere with yo' crazy ass," Jaz stated firmly with her arms crossed and all of her weight shifted to one side of her body.

"This is not up for discussion. Meet me in the damn car.

You have five minutes," Kyree stated while opening the door. "Don't make me have to come back in here after yo' ass, Jaz." He shut the door behind him and Jaz stood there speechless.

Jaz had no idea if she was more appalled that he had come at her the way he did, or that she was actually on her way to wipe Kayden's ass and be at Kyree's car in less than five minutes. No one in the world had the power to bark orders at her without being laughed at, told to go fuck themselves, and given her ass to kiss. No one except Kyree, that is. She hated that he still had the clout to make her oblige to even the rudest of requests.

"Arrogant son of a bitch," Jaz grumbled, locking her door behind her with Kayden in her arms. She opened the back door of Kyree's car, buckled Kayden in his car seat, and climbed in on the other side of the backseat.

Kyree looked at her through the rearview mirror. "Get yo' ass in the front seat. Do I look like a damn chauffeur?"

Jaz sucked her teeth. She did not want to be that close to him, but she unwillingly gave in. Sitting on the passenger's side, she buckled her seatbelt and turned to Kyree. "You happy now?" she snarled with her arms folded tight.

"I'm good," Kyree smirked, pulling off from her apartment building.

"Where the hell are we going anyway?" Jaz asked.

"Just sit back. You'll know when we get there."

Jaz rolled her eyes, bit her bottom lip, and shook her head. Kyree knew she was mad, but he couldn't tell her just yet. He ignored the looks she was giving him by turning up Drake's song, "All Me," which was playing on the CD player. They rode with nothing but the music to drown out the silence between the two of them. Jaz kept her gaze out the window. She was afraid she might mash Kyree's head into the window if she even glanced at him. *Why the fuck did I come?* she argued with herself.

****

While Jaz was beating herself up, on the other side of town, Monica was rejoicing. So far, her date with Mario had been going great. They had just finished seeing the new Tyler Perry movie and were now enjoying each other's company over dinner at Captain George's Seafood. She just knew Jaz was going to have her head on a silver platter, because that was everything they were supposed to do together. But Jaz would just have to get over it. Monica hadn't been on a date in a long time. Between work and Kayden, her schedule never really allotted her the time to do much of anything, which is why, after a hundred times of asking her out, she finally said yes to Mario.

She really liked Mario. He was a mechanic at the Lexus dealership where she got her Lexus IS serviced. He was about 6' feet tall with neat dreads, a thick dark beard, and skin the color of smooth peanut butter. Mario was undeniably attractive, and he always made her laugh.

"How's your food?" Mario asked her.

"This shit right here, nigga," Monica pointed her fork at her steamed vegetables, potatoes, and fried scallops, "this shit right here, this shit is heavenly." Monica and Mario both laughed at Monica's Katt Williams reference.

"I should've got what you got," Mario said, not liking the taste of his salmon. "Let me taste." Mario tried putting his fork near Monica's plate, but to no avail. Monica blocked his hand.

"Boy, unless you want to pull back a nub, I suggest you go get your own," she threatened. Mario laughed at her forwardness.

"Damn, so a nigga can't have a taste?" he asked.

"Uhhh...no!" Monica gave him a "duh" look.

"I bet you let me taste something before the night's over." He slowly licked his lips and Monica blushed.

"Boy, you crazy," she laughed. But her mind wondered about his long tongue and the things it could possibly do to her.

"Um hmm, we gon' see how crazy later." He got up from the table. "I'm 'bout to go get me some scallops since you won't give me a taste," he smirked.

Monica shook her head. Curiosity was killing her cat, and if he played his cards right, satisfaction would definitely bring it back. She smiled to herself while taking a sip from her sangria, then she heard a voice from behind say, "Hey Monica." She turned around to see who it was and nearly spit out her drink. She opened her mouth to speak, only no words came out.

"How you been?"

She shook her head, trying to snap back to reality. "What are you doing here?"

"I just came here with a couple of my boys off the boat. You ain't happy to see a nigga?"

Monica turned up her nose. Standing before her was the man she thought could win a Tyrese lookalike contest, but yet still made her sick to her stomach. Known to most of his friends as La, she only called him by one name. "Hell no, Latrell!" she barked, looking around to make sure Mario wasn't in earshot.

He gave her a sinister smirk. "A'ight, I can take a hint," he said, walking away. When Latrell was out of sight, Monica's breathing became even heavier. He always managed to show up at the worst times. He couldn't even spend time with his own damn son, but yet he found a time to drop in town whenever he felt like it.

"Unfuckingbelievable." Monica shook her head in disgust.

"Monica," she heard a deep voice say.

She jumped at the sound of the voice, only this time it was Mario. She held her chest. "Boy, you scared the shit out of me."

"You a'ight?" he asked, noticing the flushed look on her face.

"Yeah, I'm fine. This sangria just has me tripping," she lied.

"Don't tell me you can't hold your liquor," he laughed. "I might have to take advantage of you tonight," he joked.

Monica smirked at him. "Whatever, Mario. Will you excuse me while I go the ladies room?" He obliged her request by standing up when she did. "Oh, a gentleman, I see."

"Mama ain't raise no heathen." They both laughed as Monica made her way to the restroom.

She was happy to see the bathroom was empty because she needed time to clear her head. Her breathing was becoming heavy again and she thought she was on the verge of a panic attack. Grabbing a paper towel, she dampened it with water and dabbed at her face so as not to mess up her makeup. She glanced at her reflection in the mirror. Monica stood at 5'3", 125 pounds of nothing but body. She was thick in all the right places, with skin the color of warm cocoa, one deep dimple on the side of her cheek, and thick, long black hair. She was undeniably beautiful. But whenever Latrell came around, he made her feel weak and stupid. Her mere existence would be reduced to a small puddle with just the sound of his voice. For years, he had managed to lie about their entire relationship. He was living a double life with a wife and kids, and Monica was none the wiser. Every time she thought about it, she only got angrier. There were so many questions that went unanswered.

Taking a deep breath, Monica tried to pull herself together. She straightened her hair with her fingers and applied an extra coat of lip-gloss before taking one last look in the mirror. Satisfied with her appearance, she opened the bathroom door, not willing to allow Latrell to fuck up her date. But just like always, he managed to cross her path at the most inopportune time. She bit her bottom lip as he slowly approached her in the hallway of the restrooms. She rolled her eyes and tried to walk past him, but he grabbed her arm.

"Let go of my fucking arm, Latrell!" she snapped, pulling her arm away.

Latrell held his hands up in surrender. "I'm not trying to hurt you, Monica. I just wanted to talk."

"What the fuck do we have to talk about?"

"Well, first off, how you been? You look good as hell." He slowly licked his lips, eyeing her up and down.

Monica shook her head. "Like I thought, we don't have shit to talk about. Goodbye, Latrell." She turned to leave again, and he grabbed her arms. She gave him a look that could kill, and he quickly released her.

"Could you just give me a minute? I really just want to

talk."

"About what?" Monica was beyond annoyed.

"About our son!" Latrell looked around to make sure none of the other patrons in the restaurant heard him getting loud.

"What the fuck is wrong with you?" Monica couldn't believe him. For years, she'd been trying to get him to be a part of Kayden's life. He had never made any effort, and now all of a sudden he was ready to be a father.

"Look, Monica, this isn't about us. It's about Kayden, and whether you like it or not, I am his father. I know I haven't been there for him in the past, but I'm ready to step up now. I see you here with ol' boy, but there's a lot more I have to tell you. So can we talk after you leave here?"

Monica didn't want to have shit to do with him, but her son was a soft spot. She wanted him to have his father in his life. This went bigger than the mistakes she and Latrell made; this was about Kayden. Taking an unsure sigh, she said, "We'll see."

Latrell nodded his head. "Bet. I'll call you."

Monica didn't respond; she just turned to walk away. When she got back to her table, Mario stood up and sat down after her. "Damn, you a'ight? I thought you fell in or something." He smiled.

Monica returned his smile, but she was actually in another world.

Noticing her distance, Mario asked, "You okay?"

"Actually, I'm feeling a little queasy." Monica grabbed at her stomach.

"You want to leave?" Mario asked, concern evident in his voice.

"Yeah, if you don't mind."

"No problem, let me just take care of this bill."

Monica nodded her head. She really liked Mario, but like so many times before, Latrell always found a way to mess up her happiness. She wanted to believe everything he was saying, but his constant lies in the past had made it impossible. All she could do was hope that he was being genuine about wanting a relationship with Kayden. She was not allowing him around her son until he proved himself worthy. No one hurt her baby - not if they valued their life.

CHAPTER 9

Jaz was beyond relieved when Kyree finally stopped the car. The ride was only fifteen minutes long, but it felt like an eternity. Every stop light seemed a little bit longer, and the silence was deafening. Sure, there was music playing, but the awkwardness made for a huge elephant in the car. Jaz looked out her window to see where they were and immediately recognized the place. Kyree saw the expression on her face and gave a sly grin.

Jaz slowly exited the car as Kyree retrieved Kayden from the backseat. "So you finally did it, huh?" she asked him as she looked up at the marquee that read "The Barbershop".

"I always said I would. I'm a man of my word," Kyree reminded her as he opened her door.

Jaz remembered for years how Kyree always said he wanted to open up his own barbershop in this very location. She encouraged him to do it, but she never thought he would. He could never sit still long enough to ever get it up and running. Kyree's dream was always to incorporate the two things that relaxed him and make it one. Jaz was not surprised to see two doors to The Barbershop. One side was a barbershop and the other side was a music studio.

Jaz walked through the actual barbershop first. Upon entering, she could see that it was still under construction. "You see the damn floors?" Kyree pointed out.

Jaz simply rolled her eyes. She couldn't give him credit just yet. She was sure he was still hiding something. Her eyes perused the area. It was actually quite spacious, and there was definitely a lot of potential within the shop.

"This is going to be the spot; I can see it now." Jaz closed her eyes and briefly envisioned the shop full of male clients talking shit, watching sports, and waiting to get their hair cut.

Kyree smiled to himself. He loved to see the look of admiration on her face.

"I want to see the studio now." Jaz excitedly turned on her heels, headed for the door.

Unlike the barbershop, the studio was almost complete. Burgundy-colored walls filled the halls while hardwood maple covered the floors. There were two smaller studio rooms, which Kyree explained would be for smaller artists. When Jaz entered the third, larger studio, she was surprised to see that the occupied sign was lit up. Kyree gave her the go ahead to enter. Jaz was greeted by a familiar face she rarely ever saw.

"Oh my God!" Jaz ran and embraced her longtime friend. "Slim!" she yelled, wrapping her arms around Fat Boy's not-so-slim neck.

Fat Boy smiled and embraced her back. "Girl, where you been at?"

"Here and there, you know me. I see you lost a few pounds." She poked at his stomach. He hadn't lost much of anything really, but Jaz always boosted his ego by saying he'd lost weight and she always called him Slim.

"Yeah, I lost some pounds and my man Ky found 'em." They both burst into laughter.

"Don't let Jaz see you get yo' ass fat ass kicked," Kyree joked.

Fat Boy waved him off. He truly was happy to see Jaz. He disagreed with Kyree's choice to break up with her in the first place. When Kyree first went to jail, he made Fat Boy promise to look after Mo and Jaz, emotionally and financially. But when Kyree called off their relationship, Jaz was so angry that she told Fat Boy to stop coming around if he was just doing it for Kyree. So, to Jaz's knowledge, Fat Boy kept his distance. Little did she know he was the reason the salon's contractors charged them so little, how furniture and fixtures just sort of came to them at ridiculously low rates, and why they were able to buy the space at such a great price. With orders from Kyree, Fat Boy made it happen.

Fat Boy admired Kyree's love for her. He knew how the two felt about each other, which was why upon hearing of her nuptials, he neglected to inform Kyree. The walls of the prison were not a place to hear about that kind of bad news.

"What you doin' with this nigga anyway?" Fat Boy asked.

"He kidnapped me." Jaz shrugged.

Fat Boy looked at Kyree, who simply sucked his teeth. "Don't believe her crazy ass...in the car pouting like a baby and shit." Jaz rolled her eyes. "Let me holla at you for a minute." Kyree motioned with his head for Fat Boy to follow him out into the hall.

"A'ight. It was good seeing you, girl." Fat Boy hugged her again.

"A'ight, Slim." Jaz smiled.

Fat Boy grabbed Kayden's nose on his way out the door and he giggled.

"Come on, Kay-Man, we're about to go in the booth," Jaz said. She picked him up and opened the door to the studio. She brought him toward the microphone and put the headphones on her head. "Sing yo' song, Kay-Man."

"OG Bobby Johnson...OG Bobby Johnson," Kayden sang close to the microphone.

Jaz was in tears with laughter as he bobbed his head and sang his favorite song by Que. Jaz couldn't help but notice his fun and join in as well. She hadn't even noticed Kyree walk in and press the record button. Kyree was dying laughing as well.

He pressed the button to cut into her headphones and said, "Y'all look crazy as hell."

Jaz nearly jumped out of her skin, startled by the sudden interference. Jaz grabbed at her chest. "Boy, you scared the hell out of me!"

When Jaz walked out, Kyree was laughing so hard that he could barely breathe. She put Kayden down and playfully hit Kyree in the arm. "Shut up, it's not that funny."

"Ay, go back in there and sing something. For real this time," Kyree said.

"Why? So you can laugh? I think not." Jaz rolled her

eyes.

"Naw, I'm serious. If I remember correctly, you can hold a li'l tune."

Jaz blushed, but flattery wouldn't work this time. Kyree whispered in Kayden's ear and then Kayden said, "Sing, Auntie Josh! Peez!"

Jaz couldn't say no to those long eyelashes. They got her every time. She entered the booth and proceeded to put the headphones on. She had no idea what to sing until she heard the instrumental to Monica's "Angel of Mine" playing through the headphones. Jaz looked up at Kyree through the glass that separated them. To her surprise, he remembered her favorite song. Kyree smiled as she bolted out a beautiful rendition to the song. Her voice may not have been Grammy-worthy, but Kyree thought it was sweet and angelic.

Jaz's eyes were closed the whole time she was singing, and halfway through the song, she opened them, only to realize the person she saw with her eyes closed was the same person she saw with her eyes open. It frightened her to the point she stopped singing.

"Why'd you stop?" Kyree cut into the headphones. "You were doing so well."

"It's getting kind of late and Kayden still hasn't eaten yet."

Kyree knew that was probably her way of saying she had to get back to her fiancé. He simply obliged her request by nodding his head. He locked up the studio and drove in the opposite direction of Jaz's house. "Where are you going?"

"Just sit back."

"Oh my God, you really are kidnapping me."

Kyree simply looked at her and she turned her head toward the window. She figured she should probably just be quiet until they got to their destination, wherever that might be. Ten minutes later, Kyree was pulling into the parking lot of a Chinese buffet restaurant.

"Don't look at me like that," Kyree said. "You know you're hungry. I heard your stomach growl a few times while we were in the studio."

Jaz pushed him in the arm and he laughed. He got Kayden from the backseat and Jaz reluctantly followed behind him into the restaurant. He knew about her love for Chinese food, and she had to admit, she was hungry as hell. She was more worried than anything that someone would see her with Kyree. It was never a good look for an engaged woman to be seen with her ex, no matter how friendly or casual the occasion. How would she explain this to anyone? Kyree, noticing her obvious looks of being her own lookout, laughed at her. She sucked her teeth at him as the hostess seated them at a table. Jaz took Kayden by the hand and proceeded to the buffet to make their plates. When they sat down and Jaz relaxed more, she was able to enjoy herself.

Jaz and Kyree laughed like old times. She remembered back in the day when they would both sit at home and watch movies and eat Chinese food all day.

"When'd you start liking duck sauce, girl?" Kyree noticed the mounds of sauce drowning her plate. Jaz shrugged her shoulders. He recalled a time when she was more partial to soy sauce while he couldn't dare have Chinese food without duck sauce. "I guess a lot has changed, huh?"

Jaz didn't answer. She just continued feeding Kayden his food. "I'm proud of you," she said, just above a whisper, not bothering to face him.

Kyree looked up from his plate to make sure he'd heard her right. "What?"

Jaz looked at him this time. "You actually got out and did the things you said you would. I know you're going to be mad successful. You've been cutting hair since you were fifteen, and your ear for good music is impeccable." Jaz smiled. "So yeah, Kyree, I'm proud of you."

"Thanks. That really means a lot to me," Kyree said with all sincerity. He looked at his watch. "Wow, it is getting late. Let me let you get home to your fiancé." Kyree had to cut their dinner short. Knowing how Jaz felt was all too real for him. His only intention when he got out of jail was to make her proud. To hear her say it out loud warmed his heart. He suddenly wanted to make this next move, his last move in the game. Even if he couldn't have Jaz to himself, her opinion mattered more than anyone's to him. Kyree never wanted to disappoint her again. He was twenty-eight years old, and he was more than aware his luck was going to wear off if he didn't go legit soon.

On the drive home, Kyree stopped at the gas station. "You want anything out of here?" he asked Jaz.

"Naw, I'm good," Jaz said, fiddling with his stereo system.

When Kyree closed the door, Jaz heard Kayden sneeze and she looked back only to find him fast asleep. She was more than elated about that. Monica had already sent her a text message while she was at the restaurant asking if she could keep him overnight, and Jaz more than happily agreed.

Hearing her phone vibrate, Jaz reached for it, only to find out it wasn't hers. She looked down in the cup holder and saw that it was Kyree's. She wasn't trying to be nosy, but she couldn't help but see Asia's picture pop across the screen. Jaz was immediately taken aback. She never took Asia's relationship with Kyree seriously. She was sure their liaison was strictly physical, but she also knew Kyree didn't keep jump-offs around for longer than a week, and Asia had already been around almost a month. But Jaz was sure Asia was nothing more than eye candy. No man wanted to take her to the family cookout; they wanted her on their arm at the club.

Jaz brushed the call off until she saw a text message pop up. It wasn't hard for her to see the message. Kyree never kept a lock on his phone. He was so honest and it always felt like he had nothing to hide. Besides, if it were incriminating evidence, rest assured it wouldn't be information one could find on his cell phone. Kyree was way too smart for that. She looked back to make sure Kyree wasn't coming and did a quick look at the message. Jaz still didn't want him to know she looked, so she positioned her body to read the message without actually moving the phone. Her mouth dropped when she read the message.

>>> **10:15 PM, Asia: Can't wait 2 c u tonight. My mouth is watering 4 the dick. :-P**

Jaz turned up her mouth in disgust. The two were free to do whatever they wanted. Jaz just couldn't figure out why it bothered her so much. *I just know that hoe is up to no good,* she reasoned with herself.

Kyree was back at the car now, filling up the tank with gas. She made up her mind that she was going to play it cool and pretend as if she never saw the message. *If he wants to fuck with Asia, that's his problem. He's a grown-ass man.* She shrugged it off.

Kyree got back in the car and looked back at Kayden. "We wore li'l man out, huh?"

"I guess so."

He picked up his phone and smirked at the text. Jaz noticed him from the corner of her eye and just shook her head. He called Asia back and Jaz tried to drown out the radio while she ear hustled.

"What up?" he said into the phone. Kyree tried to keep his phone conversation short out of respect. He didn't want to give her any indication of who he was talking to. For all she knew, it could've been one of his homeboys. But little did he know, Jaz was very well aware that it was Asia. "Yeah, I got the message. That's wassup. So you gon' handle that for me?" His face was stern as he spoke.

Jaz rolled her eyes. Hearing this conversation was making her sick to her stomach.

"Word. So I'm gon' get up with you in about an hour. One." Kyree ended the call.

Jaz was so relieved to see him hang up. She was sure if she heard another word she would regurgitate the Chinese food she'd just eaten.

"Jaz, guess who I saw in the gas station."

"Who, Kyree?" Jaz asked, her tone obviously short.

"Remember Pete from the old neighborhood? He asked about you too. That nigga got like eight kids and shit." Kyree laughed, but Jaz didn't.

"That's wassup," Jaz said, her gaze focused out the window.

"You a'ight?" he asked, noticing her detachment.

She bit the inside of her jaw. "Yeah, I'm good."

Kyree knew she wasn't being honest with him. She always bit her jaw when she was tight about something. He had no idea what it could've been that caused her sudden attitude. "Naw, for real, what's good, Jaz?"

She abruptly turned to face him. "Didn't I tell you I was fine? Shit!"

Kyree wasn't going to give her any attention this time. He was more than accustomed to Jaz's temper tantrums, but he wasn't going to feed into it tonight. "A'ight, you trippin'. I'm gon' hurry up and get you home."

"Do that then," Jaz said under her breath. For the first time in a long time, Jaz noticed that Kyree hadn't called her Jazzy since the day he left her apartment. She actually hated the name, but it was what he always called her. She couldn't recall a time when Kyree ever called her Jaz. Maybe this time he really was over her and ready to move on with his life. He was right about not waiting forever. Even though she was moving on with her life, it still hurt to see him also moving on with his.

CHAPTER 10

Pulling up in front of Jaz's apartment building, Kyree proceeded to get Kayden from the backseat. "I got him," she stopped him. She couldn't stand to see him for another second.

"This boy is heavy. Fall back and grab his bag," Kyree demanded, picking Kayden up.

Jaz had to admit he was right. She grabbed the bag and headed to her apartment to open the door. Kyree walked Kayden to Jaz's bedroom and laid him down. Jaz was waiting for him by the door.

"Did I do something to you?" Kyree just had to ask her.

Jaz crossed her arms and sucked her teeth. "Look, I'm good. Go fuck one of your little hoes. Don't worry about me."

Kyree was beyond shocked. Jaz claimed to not care about him or anything he did, but here she was with an attitude about him seeing other women. "What the hell is your problem?"

"Nothing, Kyree. Bye!" She tried to close the door on him, but he stopped her with his foot.

Kyree was obviously much stronger and she couldn't hold the door anymore, so she had no choice but to let it go. "Look, you're gonna stop acting like a damn child. You keep spewing this bullshit about your perfect-ass fiancé and how you've moved on with your life, but yet you're worried about who the hell I'm fucking?"

"I'm not! Don't flatter yourself, nigga." Jaz waved him off.

"What the hell do you want?" Kyree was beyond frustrated.

"From you?" Jaz looked at him like he was crazy. "Not a damn thing."

Kyree sucked his teeth and shook his head. "A'ight, Jaz. Whatever." He gave her one last look before finally walking away.

She closed the door as Kyree walked away to do God knows what with Asia. She didn't even want to think about the disgusting things Kyree and Asia were about to get into. Jaz placed her hands over her face in distress. She couldn't believe she allowed herself to get out of character. That was something she just didn't do. She tried to let it go as she went to remove Kayden's shoes and jacket. She slipped on his pajamas with him being none the wiser. He really was worn out for the night, but that usually didn't stop him from waking her up in the morning for breakfast. Smiling at the thought, she decided to leave him in her bed. He looked so peaceful.

After a hot shower, Jaz tried to relax her mind and clear her head. She pulled out her Kindle and proceeded to read *Broken Promises* by Shyla Miles. She was knee deep into the book when she heard a key enter the lock. Jaz looked over at the clock, which read 11:30. She could recollect a time when her man coming home past 10:00 worried her sick, but Michael usually came home at the same time every night, if not sooner. Jaz listened intently as the door opened and closed. He removed his shoes at the front door, dropped his keys on the counter, went to the refrigerator, put something in the microwave, and then proceeded towards her room. Opening her door, Michael turned on the light, surprised to find her up reading.

"I didn't know you were up," Michael said.

Jaz smiled at him. "I wanted to wait for you to get home."

He walked over to her, bending down to plant a gentle kiss on her lips. "You know most guys would go postal if they came home and found another man in their bed," he joked, looking at Kayden.

Jaz tried to control her laughter without waking Kayden. She got up from the bed to hug Michael. The scent of his cologne tickled her nostrils. His strong arms wrapped around her gave her a sense of wellbeing and purpose. The love he had for her showed in everything he did, including a simple hug. She pulled away from their hug to look at him. "So what're you cooking?"

"Just a Hot Pocket. Something quick."

Jaz nodded her head as he removed his shirt and tie. He was wearing only a wife beater, and Jaz couldn't help but admire how good he looked. She followed him into the kitchen, where he retrieved his Hot Pocket from the microwave. She made him a glass of lemonade to go with his food.

"Gotdammit!" Michael yelled.

Jaz quickly turned around to see that he had bit into the piping hot Hot Pocket, without letting it cool first. Jaz started laughing as Michael proceeded to curse. "Damn, Jaz, that shit ain't funny," he winced. "I burned my damn tongue."

"Aww, come here." Jaz grabbed his face into her hands. "Let me make it better." She pulled his face close to hers and kissed him, taking his tongue into her mouth. As Jaz sucked on his tongue, she could feel the swell in slacks growing with each passing second. Michael grabbed at her ass and forcefully pushed her against the counter. To Michael's knowledge, they hadn't had sex in almost four months and he was fiending. He was going to get her to end her "no sex 'til after the wedding" pact, even if it killed him. He moved his hand up her shirt and unsnapped her bra.

His hand was massaging her breasts, but all Jaz could think about was her unfaithful day with Kyree. Every time she tried to enjoy his touch, visions of Michael's face while she rode Kyree popped into her head. The hurt on his face was unbearable. She had no idea how she could be so stupid. It was really fucking with her. Jaz pulled away from their kiss. "No, Michael, we promised," she said, trying to get out of the situation.

Michael pulled her in close so that the bulge in his pants was resting on her thigh. "I know, baby, but damn. We already fucked and you are going to be my wife anyway, so this pact makes no sense to me." He hungrily kissed her neck. He started licking her spot, and Jaz couldn't help but to bite her bottom lip. She started thinking back to the first day she and Michael explored each other's bodies.

Jaz couldn't believe that after only four dates, she was the one cooking for Michael. She really liked his cockiness and confidence. After letting him win in a game of spades, she agreed to cook him dinner. It was really just an excuse. She hadn't been fucked in over a year and Michael had her curious the moment she walked into his office. He was the perfect remedy for getting over Kyree. Tonight she was preparing shrimp alfredo and a homemade strawberry cake for dessert. Michael rang the doorbell just as she was finishing up the food. He greeted her with a kiss and a dozen pink roses.

"Damn, that smells good," he boasted.

"Wait 'til you see how it tastes," she bragged.

Michael looked her up and down. "Oh, I can't wait to see how it tastes." He licked his lips slowly.

Jaz laughed at his slick comment, but Michael really was amazed. His mother had always told him working girls didn't know how to cook, but Jaz had completely proved his mother wrong. Her food was outstanding, and her homemade cake was the best strawberry cake he'd ever had. He wouldn't find out until later in their relationship that Jaz couldn't bake if her life depended on it and the cake was actually made by Monica.

"Damn, girl, you got down on that meal." Michael wiped his mouth with his napkin.

"I know I did." Jaz smiled proudly.

She got up to grab his plate, and he pulled her down onto his lap. He forcefully kissed her and Jaz placed her hands around his neck. He massaged her thigh with one hand while the other hand eased its way up her ruched miniskirt. Jaz hadn't been touched like this in a long time and she was beyond nervous. She pulled away from their lip lock, and Michael immediately regretted his forwardness.

"Damn, Jaz. I'm sorry," he said as she stood up. "I didn't mean to move so fast. I'll take it down a notch."

Jaz didn't say anything. She just walked over to her surround sound stereo, found a suitable playlist on her iPod, and walked backwards toward her room, beckoning him closer with her finger as Tanks's "Can I" played in the background. Michael rubbed his hands together in anticipation. He followed her to her room, wrapping his arms around her waist as they fell onto the bed. Michael removed his shoes with his feet. He removed Jaz's blouse with one hand while the other hand massaged her breasts. Jaz didn't want to let go of their kiss as she also quickly removed his clothing. She unbuckled his pants and he reached into his pockets for a condom. The black and gold wrapper gave Jaz confirmation that he was indeed working with a nice size.

She lifted her butt off the bed as he tried to ease her skirt down over her hips. Unsnapping her bra, he began to massage her breasts then sucked each one diligently. Jaz was in pure ecstasy and so was Michael. He brought his mouth up to her face and began to suck on her bottom lip. The wetness brewing in Jaz's underwear from pure anticipation was electrifying. Michael was always so cocky, and she was eager to see if it was all talk or if he could really back it up. Michael had something to prove to Jaz. He had spent his whole life learning the female anatomy, and he wanted to show her the tricks he had up his sleeve.

While he sucked on her bottom lip, he moved her underwear to the side and placed two fingers inside her warm slit. Jaz's eyes opened from surprise. When he started moving his finger in a circular motion, Jaz was in total bliss. Never before had a finger fuck felt so good. She started to work her hips with the movement of his fingers as he dipped them in and out of her honey pot. His precision with his two fingers was something only a doctor could master. What he did next caused Jaz to lose all sense of reality. "Ahhhhhhhhh!" Jaz screamed at the top of her lungs as he found her G-spot with just his two fingers. Her legs started to shake, her breathing lapsed, and her juices flowed out of her like a water fountain.

Jaz was spent, but Michael wasn't done just yet. He still had a point to prove, and he wasn't going to rest until he did just that. He looked up at her and greedily licked her fingers. Jaz knew what was next, and if his tongue game was anything like his finger game, she couldn't wait to find out.

Michael licked from her belly button down to her throbbing clit. He used the tip of his tongue to tease her as Jaz grabbed hold of his head. She couldn't take the taunting; she thought she was going to lose her damn mind. She moaned as he dove in deep with his tongue, touching the spot that so few men had found.

92

"Ah shit, boy!" Jaz let out a loud scream as she came down from her second orgasm in almost a year.

Seeing Jaz look almost incapacitated, Michael was pleased with his work. He gave a cocky smirk. "I'm not done with you just yet. You're going to cum one more time for him." Michael looked down at his erect penis, and so did Jaz. She was satisfied to see that he was working with almost eight inches, and although she'd had bigger, he was still decent. "You think you're ready for another round?" he asked.

Jaz only looked at him. He really had no idea who he was fucking with. She and Kyree would go for hours, doing the freakiest things imaginable. But she was going to go slow with Michael. She couldn't show him all of her tricks on the first night.

Her playlist had just switched to Chris Brown's "Wet the Bed". Michael began sucking on her collarbone while only inserting the tip of his dick.

"Ahh," Jaz let out a slight moan.

"You want me to put it in?" He continued to pull in and out of her dripping wet slit, not giving her the full effect.

Jaz was on the verge of going delirious. She had to have all of him. "Yessss," she moaned with her eyes closed.

"Naw, I don't think you're ready for him yet," he bragged.

Jaz had enough of the teasing and Michael needed to know that if he thought he was going to keep up this little game, he had another thing coming. It didn't take much for her to lose interest, and he was most certainly fucking up what Jaz hoped to be her third nut. She was ready for the major penetration that her body had been craving for so long. Looking up at him, she grabbed ahold of his ass and pushed him all the way in. Michael smiled at her forwardness. He was moving his hips in a circular motion, Jaz, being the control freak that she was, grabbed hold of his hips and made his rhythm match the song. She too worked her hips to match his motion. Michael was hitting all of her walls while sucking on each of her breasts and trying his best not to cum just yet. But Jaz was so wet, and his dick kept sliding out. He was trying his best to stay focused when Jaz rolled him over onto his back, the whole time keeping his dick still inside of her. She rode him like a horse, never once going to fast or too slow.

"Shit...girl...damn," Michael said, in between breaths.

"You can't hang?" Jaz gave him a wicked smirk while nibbling at his earlobes. She loved the feeling of being in charge.

"Wait, Jaz." He grabbed hold of her hips, trying to stop her movement. *"Right there, don't move."* Jaz stopped moving and Michael held on tightly to her hips. *"Ahhh, shit, Jaz!"* he yelled out as he released a gut-wrenching orgasm. Never before had he cum so fast. But the hold Jaz had on his dick was comparable to no other female he'd ever been with before. He lay there, done for, as he pulled Jaz in close to him, placing kisses all over her neck and back.*

Jaz just wished she could've been as satisfied with his dick as he was with the ride she just gave him. There were just spots he wasn't hitting that she so desperately needed him to hit. She reasoned with herself that he'd eventually figure it out. She really liked him and just hoped that he could be the missing piece in her life. Sexually, he definitely wasn't a Kyree, but mentally, he definitely wasn't a Kyree either, which made her decision to keep him around, despite a few flaws, that much easier.

A year and a half later, Michael still didn't give her the penetration she so desperately needed. He stimulated her and made her cum in other ways, but not once with his penis. But the man ate her pussy like it was his only means of survival, so it didn't surprise her when he said, "Come on, baby. Eating ain't cheating." He sucked on her neck and Jaz burst out laughing.

"Boy, you're a trip!" She gently pushed him off of her. "Michael, it's only one more month. Can you wait just a little longer?"

Michael dropped his head in defeat. "Man, okay. But it's not going to be easy, especially not if you're going to keep wearing these tight-ass sweat pants." He smacked her ass and Jaz grabbed at it.

"Ouch, nigga, that hurt!" She playfully punched him in the arm.

"Can't hurt worse than these fucking blue balls." He sucked his teeth and Jaz laughed as he walked away with his Hot Pocket in his hand. "I'll be in the guest room, watching Cinemax."

Jaz laughed again. "You need some lotion?"

"Real fucking funny, Jaz," he said, shutting the door to the guest room behind him.

Jaz laughed. It was actually kind of sad. She had never planned on sticking with her no sex before the wedding rule this long and she hated to deny him the pussy. But her tryst with Kyree was really messing with her head. Their sex had always been magical, and he always fulfilled her needs. His dick touched places inside her that Michael never had and probably never would. And sure, Michael could make her cum, but not the way that Kyree could. Now she was questioning if she and Michael could really last if she wasn't completely satisfied in the bedroom. Walking back to her room, she stopped at the guest room to check in on Michael.

"Okay, cool," she heard him say as he ended a call on his cell phone.

"Who was that?" Jaz quizzed, startling him.

"Just the hospital. I was just making sure Mrs. Donahue didn't go into early labor."

"Oh." Jaz brushed it off, entering the room and lying down on the bed beside him. He pulled her in close so that she was resting on his chest. Jaz listened as his heart beat at an irregular pace. "You okay, baby?" she asked him.

"Yeah, I'm fine. I just can't wait until we have our own kids. I bet they won't be lying in our bed all night like ya boy in there," he smirked.

Jaz playfully hit him in the chest. "Shut up. He's fine. I'm gonna go back in there in a minute. But for right now, I just wanna lay here with you and watch TV." Jaz and Michael dozed off briefly before Jaz was awakened by the vibrating of her cell phone. Looking at the clock on the nightstand, she realized it was two in the morning. Wondering who it was, she eased herself from under Michael and picked up the phone, only to realize it was Michael's phone. There was a text message that read:

>>> **2:03AM, The Hospital: It's time!**

Jaz, taking a deep sigh, tapped Michael to wake him from

his slumber, only he didn't budge, so she nudged him a little harder. "Mike, wake up. The hospital just texted you."

Michael blinked his eyes repeatedly, trying to awaken himself. What time is it?" he asked, propping himself up on his elbows.

"2:00," Jaz said, handing him his cell phone. "Here, I thought it was mine."

"Damn," Michael said, reading the text message. "I'm sorry baby, but—"

"You gotta go. I know," Jaz cut him off.

"Yeah, Mrs. Donahue is having her baby and she's been having a lot of complications."

"It's cool, Mike," Jaz said, getting up from the bed.

Michael could tell that she was upset. He hated to leave with her mad at him. Pulling her down onto his lap, he kissed her neck. "I'm sorry, baby. Do you forgive me?"

Jaz turned her head and he began to tickle her. She couldn't help but laugh uncontrollably. "Okay...okay," she gave in.

"Okay then. Now go in there and get some sleep. I'll be home before you know it," he said, standing her up. He smacked her ass as she was walking out.

"Ouch! Keep playing," she warned him.

He smiled back at her as he retrieved his clothes to take a quick shower. Jaz shook her head at the way Kayden was laying on her bed. She could've sworn when she left he was on the left side of the bed, and now he was sprawled out in the middle. She repositioned him so that she could lie on her rightful side. As she lay in bed, she listened to the sound of the shower running and wondered if this was to be her life from here on out. This was beginning to be another Kyree situation. Michael coming and going at odd times during the day was an all too familiar feeling. She reasoned with herself that this was a totally different scenario, because unlike Kyree, Michael wasn't out risking his life; he was saving them.

ASHLEY CHANNAE

CHAPTER 11

After Mario dropped her off at home, Monica found solace in a hot bath. She could see the disappointment on his face when she ended their date, and although she hated to do it, she had no other choice. It wouldn't have been fair to Mario if she was physically on the date, but not mentally. He was actually very funny and interesting, and she was seriously contemplating letting him be the man to end her drought. But those plans were put to rest the moment she saw Latrell. It didn't help matters that he walked around with such a smug attitude, as if he didn't have a care in the world, which shouldn't have been the case, considering the fact that he had a two-year-old son that he didn't even know.

There was a time when she was head over heels in love with him. No one could tell her anything about Latrell without her shutting them down immediately. On more than a few occasions, Kyree expressed his negative opinion about him, but whenever Monica would ask him why, he would simply say, "There's something about dude, Mo. I don't know what it is, but it's something." That was never a reasonable explanation for Monica to leave him completely alone. Besides, Kyree was always overprotective. Even Jaz never fully trusted Latrell. Monica could still hear Jaz's voice in her head saying, "I don't know, Mo. He's gone too much; he may be hiding something." And sure enough, they were both right. Latrell was hiding a whole family back in Texas.

When the woman called saying she was Latrell's wife, Monica's heart stopped. She couldn't believe her ears. But what threw her back even more was the fact that the woman called like it was Monica's fault, as if Monica was the home wrecker and not Latrell's lying ass. No stranger to confrontation herself, Monica let the bitch have it. When she hung up the phone, everything inside of her wanted to take her man's word over some random chick, but there were some things she said that

Monica just couldn't let go. Too many dates coincided with missed holidays, there were too many quick trips out of town when he was stationed in Virginia, and too many secret bathroom phone calls in the middle of the night. She refused to believe her woman's intuition, and now she was left with the remnants of not going with her gut. When she confronted Latrell about it, his face looked as though he'd seen a ghost. He tried to explain himself, but all the apologizing in the world couldn't fix it. Monica wasn't trying to hear shit he had to say.

To make matters worse, a week later, Kyree got locked up and she found out she was six weeks pregnant. She told Latrell, and he denied it being his. Monica was more than happy to give him a DNA test as soon as Kayden was born. She never thought he would force her to take him to court just to get a DNA test. But all the court hearing did was prove that Kayden was, in fact, Latrell's son, and it ordered that he pay child support. She never wanted his money; all she wanted was his presence - not for her, but for Kayden. He never once showed interest in wanting to work out a custody agreement. In fact, the only time he'd seen his son was when he showed up to the courtroom when Kayden was only a few months old, and that was only at a glance.

Monica could've killed him when she saw him walk through the courthouse lobby with his wife and two kids. Giving the fake-ass happy family a quick once-over, Monica could clearly see that Latrell was taking a step up by dating her. His wife, although pretty, couldn't hold a candle to Monica. She was petite, but her cuteness was covered up with the red bumps that adorned her face that she tried to hide with an excessive amount of makeup. Latrell's two daughters had the biggest heads she'd ever seen. She said a silent thank you to God that she didn't have any girls by him to be cursed with that head.

Monica's glance was discreet, but Latrell's wife couldn't have been more obvious. The looks she gave Monica showed nothing but pure hate and jealousy. She turned up her nose at Monica and rolled her eyes, but Jaz was on it before Monica could even say anything. She defused the situation by suggesting to Latrell that he get rid of his wife while the court proceedings were going on. That was really putting it lightly, considering she actually told him, "Get that bitch out of here before I beat her ass, and then send Kyree's boys to fuck you up. And that's just if I don't handle your bitch ass myself." Latrell knew Kyree's goons didn't play games and he didn't want that kind of heat, so he told his wife and kids to wait for him at the hotel. Monica was on the brink of depression after that whole fiasco, but her mother and Jaz refused to allow her to be. She was so grateful to them both. She didn't know where she'd be in life if it weren't for them.

Now that she'd actually seen Latrell in town, it was messing with her head. As she reveled in her bubble bath, Teairra Mari's song "'Til You Cry" emitted from her surround sound. The words to the song conveyed every emotion she felt at that moment. There were so many things left unsaid, so many questions she never got to ask, and so much hurt that she suffered because of his lies. As she continued listening to the melodic sounds coming from her speakers, something she promised herself she'd never do again happened. A single tear escaped from her eyes. Monica promised herself the day after the court proceedings, when Latrell made no effort at seeing her son, that she would never shed another tear for him. She quickly wiped the tear away and released the water from the tub.

After drying off her body, she applied her favorite Victoria's Secret body lotion, Love Spell. Just as she was putting the finishing touches on, her cell phone vibrated. She had no idea who it could've been; it was damn near one in the morning. It immediately hit her. It had to be Jaz. She was the only one who didn't give a damn what time she called. Shaking her head, she put her phone on speaker, trying not to get lotion on it.

"What up, hoe?" she answered.

"Uh, hello? Monica?" the caller answered.

Monica nearly jumped out of her skin at the sound of the voice on the other end. She wanted to say something, anything, but all she could manage was, "Huh?"

"Yo, Monica, this La." Latrell waited for her response.

"Uhhh," she said, unable to get anything else out.

"Look, I know it's late. But I really do need to talk to you. Can I come over?"

That snapped Monica out of her trance. "My house?" she asked.

"Yeah," he chuckled lightly.

"Naw, I don't think that's such a good idea."

"Look, I just need a minute. I'm outside now. Open the door. I have a lot I need to say."

"Naw, you may as well turn your black ass back around, 'cause you ain't coming up in here," Monica stated firmly.

"Look, I have answers. And I know you have questions."

Monica contemplated letting him in for a moment. He was right. She did have a lot of questions that only he could answer. Taking a deep sigh, she said, "A'ight, but you have five minutes. No more, no less."

"Word, I'm at the door now," he said hanging up the phone.

Monica quickly retrieved her purple terrycloth bathrobe and tied it tightly around her waist. Once again, Latrell had all the power. He had made the call, driven to her house, insisted she open the door, and fucked up her zone. But Monica wouldn't allow that to happen this time. Going into the safe in her closet, she retrieved the small handgun Kyree had given her for protection. She always hated guns, but Kyree was unrelenting in teaching her and Jaz how to use them. She didn't think Latrell was crazy enough to try anything, but she needed to have the upper hand for once. He wasn't to be trusted, and Monica wasn't going to allow him into her space again without some form of security. Making sure the gun was on safety, she slid it into the pocket of her bathrobe.

With her hand on the doorknob, she took a deep breath before slowly opening it. There he stood, Latrell Stapleton, all 6' feet of him, dressed in a pair of dark blue jeans, all white Nike Dunks, and a white Polo shirt, his bald head glowing in the moonlight. The man was indeed sexy and looked so much like her son that it was almost frightening. But no matter how good he looked on the outside, behind the mask was an ugly liar. She opened the door wide enough for him to come in.

Looking over her townhouse, he nodded his head in approval. "I like what you've done to the place."

"You've never even been here before. How the hell you know where I live anyway?"

"I do send a check here every month," he reminded her.

"We don't need it. We're fine without."

"Where li'l man at anyway?" he questioned, looking around.

"His name is Kayden, in case you didn't know. And he's not here right now," she snapped.

"I know my son's name, Monica."

She sucked her teeth. "What do you want anyway? Your five minutes are quickly running out."

"Look, I know it might be too late for an explanation, but I really want to make things right."

"You got a lot of fuckin' nerve." Monica shook her head.

"Could you just hear me out for a second?"

Taking a seat on her couch, Monica crossed her legs, ready for him to answer her questions after all of these years. Pulling the gun from out of her pocket, she placed it down on the coffee table in front of her.

Latrell's eyes grew as big as saucers. "What you gon' do? Shoot me?"

"If you say some shit I don't like, I just might. You got four minutes. Now talk, nigga!" she stated confidently.

Latrell shook his head and gave a sly smirk. She was still as feisty as the day he'd met her. "A'ight, cool. This is your house, I guess I have to respect that," he said, taking a seat on the bar stool across from her. "I just want you to know that my feelings for you were real," he said. Monica simply rolled her eyes. "They were, really. But I got married right out of high school to a girl I went to school with. We were both really young, but I was going into the Navy, and you know you get more money if you're married. So that's what we did. Going into the marriage, she'd already had two twin girls." Monica pretended as if she didn't give a damn, but it did slightly piqué her interest. "I never loved her, and when I got stationed here in VA, I met and fell in love with you."

Monica looked at him like he was crazy. "And you're telling me this because?"

"Because I want to be with you. And our son."

Monica bit the inside of her jaw to stop herself from going completely postal and picking up the gun. She wanted to shoot him right in his lying face. "Do you know how it fucking felt to get that phone call from that bitch? Huh, nigga? Do you know how I felt?" She looked at him like he was crazy and she thought she could slightly see the guilt on his face. "I felt like shit! The man I loved, took up for when everyone said he wasn't shit, and trusted with all my heart, had a wife and two kids that I knew NOTHING ABOUT!"

"I didn't plan on falling in love with you, Monica," he admitted.

"Is that supposed to make me feel some type of way? 'Cause it doesn't!" Monica could feel the tears threatening to pierce her eyelids and stain her face, but she refused to let them. She still had a lot of shit she so desperately needed to get off her chest, and Latrell was going to hear it. "And then I tell you I'm pregnant, and you deny our son? What kind of shit is that?" she said, standing up and getting in his face.

"My wife told me it probably wasn't mine."

"Your wife?" Monica looked at him like he was stupid. She couldn't take it anymore. She took her right hand, mushed his face with all of her might, and said, "You stupid muthafucka!" Latrell nearly fell backwards in the chair. He had to restrain himself from acting on instinct, and he allowed her to walk back to her seat on the couch.

"I deserved that," he admitted.

"Naw, nigga, you deserve way worse." Placing her head in her hands, she took a deep breath. "If I was the one you loved, Latrell, then you should've taken my word over hers. No one else should have mattered."

"I know, Monica, and I'm sorry."

"Latrell, you're the sorriest muthafucka I have ever met in my life! Besides, none of that matters anyway. Hell, everything you're telling me right now could be a lie, for all I know."

He walked over and started to sit closer to her on the couch, but the look she gave him suggested otherwise, so he opted for sitting on the other end of the couch. "I swear on my mama's grave I'm telling you the truth right now."

"Let me ask you something." Monica had to look him in the eye to be sure he was being honest when he answered her next question. "When you found out Kayden was in fact yours, why didn't you at least make an effort to see him?"

"I was scared, Monica. I wasn't sure how things between us would be. I knew you hated me."

"But that has nothing to do with your son. I wouldn't have him suffer just because I was angry with you. You're his father, Latrell, and yet you acted like he didn't even exist, like he was just a check to you."

"And I'm sorry for that. That's why I'm here now. My wife and I got a divorce. I just got stationed back in VA. And I know I can't make up for time lost, but I'm willing to try to make time now."

Monica was beating herself up. This was all she'd ever wanted, but she couldn't trust Latrell. He was good at making promises he couldn't keep. Monica was grown and could deal with his lies, but her son didn't need that disappointment in his life. She didn't want Kayden to grow up hating his father like she and Kyree did. She wanted him to have the relationship with Latrell like Jaz had with her dad. She admired it; it was such a rarity where they came from. "I don't know, Latrell. I need time to think about this."

"A'ight, bet," Latrell nodded his head in excitement. "But I got one more question." Monica looked at him, waiting for his question. "You and me. Is there a possibility that we could—"

"Hell the fuck no!" Monica stood up, furious. "Nigga, are you out of your fucking mind?"

"Damn, calm down, Mo. You don't have to get loud." He tried to calm her down with his hands.

"Apparently I do! 'Cause yo' ass can't seem to comprehend the fact that I wouldn't fuck with you like that if Jesus himself came down and told me to."

"Stop with the theatrics, shawty." He waved her off his thick southern accent showing through.

She stood in front of him again while he looked up at her from the couch. "For years I asked myself why. Why me? Why my son? Why her? Why'd you lie? I blamed you for so much shit wrong in my life. But the day Kayden was born, you were the least of my concerns." Monica could no longer hold it in anymore. She was in a battle with her tears, and her tears won. "I fucking hated you!" She pointed her finger in his face. "But you gave me one of the most precious gifts in the world, so I had to stop hating you and move on with my life. And now you're saying you want back in?" She looked at him like he was delusional.

Seeing the pain on Monica's face hurt Latrell to his core. He knew he had hurt her, but knowing how badly, he just couldn't take it. Standing up, he did the only thing he could think of to stop her tears. He embraced her. Monica pushed him off of her. Pounding his chest, he said, "Hit me again."

At first, Monica just looked at him, and then she took him up on his offer. She pushed him again, but he continued to pound on his chest. Monica made a fist and struck him in the chest.

"Harder!" he challenged her.

Monica hit him harder in his chest, again, and again, and again, until finally she was out of breath. It felt so good to hit him. She'd wanted to punch him for so long now. Every emotion she ever had was built up into her punches. Latrell rubbed his chest. He was seriously in deep pain. The first couple of punches didn't hurt, but after a while, Monica developed mammoth strength. But Latrell would never show exactly how much pain he was in. "Damn, girl. You hit like a dude." He let out a slight laugh and so did she. "You feel better now?"

"Not really. I'm still angry with you. We used to be better than this, Latrell. What happened? Why'd you lie to me?" Monica pleaded, losing another battle with her tears.

"I was stupid. And I'm sorry. I can't express that enough," he stated sincerely. She was crying, and Latrell couldn't help himself. He pulled her in close, and held her tight. She couldn't move even if she wanted to, and as much as she hated him, she had to admit his embrace was somewhat comforting.

"Damn, La, I hate you!" she sniffled into his shirt.

He pulled her back to look at her. "La? Since when did you start calling me La?"

"Since you went from acting like the Latrell that used to make me feel good to the La that made me feel like shit," she admitted.

Wiping her tears away with his thumb, he could see the sadness in her eyes. She looked as though she'd been dealing with a world of hurt, and even though he was the disease that caused it, he wanted to be the cure. He gently kissed her on the forehead. Monica didn't resist. He kissed each cheek, each eye, her chin, and then her lips. Monica always had the softest lips and he loved to suck on them. She loved his kisses as well, which was why she didn't put up a fight when he stuck his tongue in her mouth. Caressing her body, he started tracing her neck with the tip of his tongue.

"Ahh," she let out a soft moan. After the second moan, she realized how wrong this was. "Stop...ahh!" she whimpered as he slipped his hand inside her robe and started to massage her exposed breasts.

"You really want me to stop?" he asked in between sucking on her breasts.

"Yessss..." she moaned.

"Naw, I don't think you do." He nibbled at her nipples.

Her mind knew that she should probably stop him, but the wetness between her legs said otherwise. She hadn't been touched in a long time. There was only one man she'd been with after Latrell, and although he was a nice guy, he was awful in bed. But if there was one thing Latrell could do besides fuck up her life, it was fuck her right.

Latrell was in heaven. He'd dreamed about going back to the place he longed for between Monica's legs, smelling her scent, hearing sounds of her sweet breath moaning in his ear. His now ex-wife would never compare to the essence that was Monica. He really was still in love with her, and even though she hated him, he wanted her to remember how good they once were.

"I used to make you feel good, Mo," he said as he untied her robe. Placing his hand in between her legs and inserting two fingers into her canal, he said, "I can still make you feel good." He played with her clit while placing hickeys all over her stomach.

"Oh my God," Monica moaned, damn near delirious.

"I'm so sorry, Monica."

"Ugh!" Monica sucked her teeth. She was fed up with his weak-ass apologies. Pushing his head down forcefully, she said, "Shut the fuck up before you ruin the mood."

He looked up at her and smiled. She had pushed him into perfect position with the dripping wetness between her legs. That was right where they both wanted him to be. Picking her up by her thighs, he rested each of her legs on his shoulder. Monica was up so high in the air she thought her head was going to hit the ceiling. With her kitty planted right at his mouth, he went to town with his tongue. He enjoyed the taste of her sweet juices as they trickled down his chin. Monica was getting dizzy. He was working her insides with his tongue like she was a car, and he had the Midas touch. Holding onto his head for dear life, she nearly bit a hole through her lip. "Put me...down...Latrell. I'm gonna...fall," she managed to get out.

Latrell loved the helpless position he had her in, but he had to admit, her thighs had him in a headlock and he needed a breather. He gently placed her down on the couch and went back to his task at hand. He sucked, licked, and flicked until Monica's body couldn't take it anymore. She grabbed hold of one of her couch pillows and had her first stomach-clenching orgasm in years. Her body was so weak; she couldn't do anything but lay there and shake for a moment. Latrell looked on in satisfaction as he began to remove his shoes. Monica looked at him like he was crazy.

"What the hell are you doing?" she asked, nearly out of breath.

"Getting ready to give you this anaconda you been missing, that's what," he laughed.

"No the hell you're not! Your five minutes are up," she stated.

He looked at her like she was crazy. "Are you serious?"

She reached her arm out and retrieved the gun off the coffee table. Aiming it at him, she said, "Dead serious!"

He was pissed. Monica had gotten hers, but she wouldn't even allow him the same satisfaction. "Man, that's not fair. My dick harder than Chinese math and shit." He attempted a laugh, but quickly stopped when she didn't join in his laughter. "What kind of nigga would I be if I left after some shit like this?"

Monica looked at the gun and then looked at him like he was stupid. "A smart one."

Latrell quickly put his shoes back on. He was beyond heated. "Man, Monica, this is fucked up. What kinda nigga do you think I am?"

Monica didn't lose focus as she had the gun still aimed at him. "Well, Latrell, you are what you eat." She gave him a sinister smirk.

Latrell shook his head and gave a defeated chuckle. He had to admit, Monica did have one up on him. He would allow it and take the L. He probably could've easily taken the gun from her, but she was a woman scorned and he wasn't aware of the strengths she possessed. "A'ight, Monica, you win this time," he said, walking toward the door. She followed him, her gun still directly pointed at him. "But I was serious about seeing my son. When can I see him?" he questioned, now fully outside.

Monica snickered. "NEVER!"

"Wha—"

She slammed the door in his face before he could finish speaking.

Monica thought having one up on Latrell would make herself feel good, but it only made her feel low. With her back pressed against the door, she slid down to the floor. What she did may have been wrong, but she wanted him to hurt just as much as she had over the years. And sure the only thing that was hurt of his was his pride, and maybe his blue balls, but it still felt good. If only for a second, she would relish in the moment and not go back to the harsh reality that Latrell was in fact back in town and there to stay.

"Shit, I should've let him eat me twice," she laughed to herself.

CHAPTER 12

It was Saturday afternoon and Monica stood in the mirror teasing her hair. The day before, Jaz had given her fresh tight spiral curls with golden highlights to spice it up. Wearing a white crop top with a graphic New York City scene in the background, ripped gray high waisted jeans, and a pair of black Madden Girl pumps, Monica was ready to roll out. It was her 26th birthday, and she and Jaz were going to have lunch and do a little shopping. They were supposed to leave at twelve, but it was already one o'clock. Jaz had called fifteen minutes ago saying she was around the corner, but Monica knew that she was probably just getting in the car, so she took her time getting ready.

Looking at her face, she applied a little MAC concealer under each of her weary eyes. It had been a week since she'd seen Latrell, and she still had no idea what to do about letting him see Kayden. She wanted him to show how serious he was, and until he did that, she wasn't going to allow her son to be in the company of a stranger.

Hearing Jaz's booming speakers before quickly hearing her lying on the horn, Monica rolled her eyes. Placing her black D&G shades over her eyes, she grabbed her keys, threw her black Michael Kors bag over her shoulder, and was out the door. As she was walking towards Jaz's car, Jaz was walking towards her house.

With her arms out stretched, Jaz reached for a hug. Monica tried to dodge her, but Jaz wouldn't allow it. "Happy Birthday, mama." Jaz hugged her tight.

"Let me go, Jaz," Monica laughed.

Releasing her, Jaz looked her up and down. "You looking very rocker chic today, girl."

"You're not looking too bad yourself. But that shirt?" Monica just shook her head.

"What?" Jaz was wearing a pair of ripped pink jeans,

white Alexander McQueen sneakers, and a white Married To The Mob T-shirt with pink writing that read "Do I Look Like I Give A Fuck".

"Really, Jaz? Really?" Monica asked, and Jaz just shrugged. "You better not let Mike's uppity-ass family see you with that."

Jaz looked at her like she was crazy, then simply pointed to the words on her shirt one by one.

"Well, you better give a fuck. Mike gon' beat that ass."

Jaz rolled her eyes and continued toward the house. "Where the hell are you going? We were supposed to leave an hour ago."

"I gotta pee. Come open the door."

Monica sucked her teeth. She should've known. Jaz did this every time before they went out. Five minutes later, they were finally leaving.

"So why are you *really* wearing that shirt?" Monica asked her. She didn't believe for one second that Jaz just didn't give a fuck. Jaz sometimes had a hard time expressing how she felt, and she knew the shirt was a silent cry for help.

Jaz took a deep sigh while keeping her eyes on the road. "Because, Mo, I just don't anymore."

Noticing the sadness in her friend's voice, Monica quizzed, "What's wrong?"

"Mo, Michael's mother is getting on my last nerve. She keeps trying to control everything about the wedding. I swear if she says one more thing to me, I'm going to take a needle and pop her balloon-looking face," Jaz threatened.

Monica couldn't help but laugh. She'd met Mike's mother before, and she was indeed on the portly side. "Well, Jaz, you'll be married in a month, and she won't have shit to control." Monica tried to find the silver lining in what was obviously a fucked-up situation for Jaz.

"It's not just that, Mo, it's..." She paused.

"What?" Mo asked, concerned.

Jaz debated on whether or not to tell Monica about her new feelings and insecurities about marrying Michael, but after careful consideration, she decided against it. She knew that if she told her about that, Monica would ask her why and Jaz would have to tell her about her fling with Kyree. It was Monica's birthday, and she didn't want to stress her out with that kind of news. "It's nothing. I guess you're right."

"I'm always right."

Jaz laughed her off. Caught off guard by the ringing of her cell phone, she looked at the number that was on her navigation screen. She didn't recognize it. Deciding to answer it anyway, she hit the answer button on her steering wheel to activate her Bluetooth and allowing the call to be heard throughout the car. She quickly regretted it, hoping that it wasn't a call from someone calling to ask questions about Monica's surprise party. "Hello?" she answered hesitantly.

"Hi, Ms. Elliot, this is Jane from Tiffany's Bridal calling to let you know that your dress is in and we've already made the adjustments that you requested. We just need you to come in to make sure everything's in order."

Glad that it wasn't a party guest calling, Jaz took a sigh of relief. "I'm sorry, Jane, but I am just too busy today to—" She was cut off by Monica nudging her in the arm.

"Go. We can go eat after."

Jaz looked at Monica to make sure it was okay and then she returned to her phone call. "On second thought, Jane, I'll be there in twenty minutes."

Twenty minutes later, Jaz and Mo were in the fitting room of the bridal store. Mo was sitting down reading a magazine and Jaz was taking forever to come out. "Damn, you're not done yet?"

"Shut up, Monica!" Jaz yelled, struggling with putting the dress on.

"You alright in there?"

"No," Jaz solemnly said.

It sounded to Monica like her girl was on the verge of tears. "I'm coming in."

When Monica opened the door, Jaz was sitting down with the most pathetic look on her face, while Jane looked a little frustrated. "What the hell is wrong with you?"

"I think they did the measurements wrong," Jaz whined. "I can't get it over my hips."

Jaz looked so pitiful. There she sat, in only her undergarments, with her beautiful vintage ivory-colored dress stuck mid-thigh. Monica couldn't help herself; she burst out laughing. "Shut the fuck up, Mo!" Jaz snapped.

"Hey, don't get mad at me because you put on some weight since your last fitting. I told you to stop eating all that bullshit so you can still fit in that dress." Monica was laughing so hard she had a headache. It was no secret that Jaz usually ate like every meal was her last meal, but now she was definitely suffering the consequences.

"It's not funny, Mo. I've just been under a lot of stress," Jaz said, eyeing the sales associate for some backup.

Jane vigorously nodded her head. "Yes, this happens to a lot of our brides." It really did happen a lot, but she hated being the one to have to fix an already stressed bride's dress. But it was her sale and she was going to make a huge commission off the $7000 dress.

"See, Mo!" Jaz reasoned. But Mo wasn't hearing her; she was laughing too hard. "Fuck you, Mo! Get out!" Jaz tried to push her out of the dressing room.

"Okay, I'm sorry." Monica calmed down. "Do you need anything?" Jaz shook her head no. "You sure? 'Cause I got some Vaseline in my purse. We can put that on your fat ass and slide that dress right on up." Monica burst into tears again. Even Jane let out a small chuckle. Jaz jumped up and pushed Monica outside of her dressing room and slammed the door behind her.

The lady at the bridal store took Jaz's new measurements and Jaz and Monica were off to finish celebrating Monica's birthday. Monica was on Cloud 9 enjoying the full body massage Jaz had treated her to. After getting a full mani and pedi, they both lay on their stomachs as a masseuse worked out kinks in their necks they never knew existed.

"Thanks, Jaz. But you know Asia or one of the other girls at our shop could've done our nails and feet for free."

Jaz rolled her eyes at the sound of Asia's name. All week since coming across her text message to Kyree, she'd been avoiding her. "Yeah, true. But I just thought this would be fun."

"You seem stress. You have the tension right here," the Asian man spoke in broken English to Monica as he kneaded her neck. "I fix that," he said.

"Damn that feels good," Monica said.

"So don't think I forgot, hoe," Jaz said.

"Forgot what?"

"Forgot to ask you about your date last weekend."

Monica was hoping she would never ask about that. She didn't want to have to explain that Latrell showed up. She and Jaz never kept secrets from each other, and if Jaz knew what happened with Latrell, she would surely flip. She wanted to enjoy the rest of her birthday without the mention of Latrell.

"Was Mario a perfect gentleman?" Jaz asked.

"Yeah. He was funny and sweet," Monica said, hoping she wouldn't ask any further questions.

"Oh, that's good. Sooo, did you get your juice box ate until you couldn't breathe?"

"Jaz!" Monica blushed, embarrassed.

"What? They don't know what the hell we talkin' 'bout." Monica shook her head at Jaz. "So did you?"

Having a slight flashback of last weekend, Monica bit her bottom lip. "Girlllll," Monica said, realizing she could actually tell Jaz what happened without telling her who it was. "That nigga ate the box so good, I coulda shot his ass," she laughed at her own inside joke.

"Damn! That's what the fuck I'm talking 'bout. Get it, Mo!" Jaz boasted.

Monica wished she could tell Jaz more, but she couldn't. She didn't want to bring any added stress in Jaz's life, so she continued to let Jaz believe it was Mario. Besides, they still had so much planned for her birthday.

After the spa, she and Jaz went to the mall to do some shopping. Monica had plans of going to the Hibachi grill with about ten of her closest friends, but after they all cancelled on her at the last minute, she cancelled her reservation. Although an intimate evening with her friends was what she wanted, that was a no go. Jaz tried to convince her that going out to the club would be fun. After much persuasion and Jaz agreeing to buy her outfit for the night, Monica reluctantly agreed. Besides, her mother had Kayden for the weekend, so she really didn't have any plans.

Worn out from shopping, the girls caught a movie at the Cinebistro. Monica always loved it there. It was the perfect place to catch a movie while eating dinner at the same time. She said a silent thank you to God that the new Madea movie was sold out. Jaz wanted to see it, and she'd hate to have to tell her that she'd already seen it with Mario. So instead, Monica suggested they go see the new Kevin Hart film. Jaz was reluctant at first, but after gobbling down a whole pizza and laughing until she cried, she was pretty much over the Madea movie.

When the girls got back to Monica's house, they were beat. Stepping out of her five inch heels, Monica darted for the bathroom. She really had to pee. Knocking on the door, Jaz said, "Wake me up in an hour."

When Monica came out of the bathroom, she was pissed. Not only had Jaz gone to sleep, but she was sprawled across her bed, and not in the guest room. "Jaz! Go in the other room!" Monica barked, trying to pull the covers. She tried to at least move her to the side so that she too could fit, but Jaz didn't move, and Monica eventually took the hint that she wasn't going to. Realizing that she was going to have to go into the guest room of her own house, she took a long annoyed sigh. "Well give me my damn pillow. You drool!" Monica snatched the pillow from under Jaz's head. Jaz's head fell to the bed. She popped up, and Monica made a run for the guest room.

"You better run!" Jaz barked.

Monica awoke an hour later and she tried to wake Jaz, but she wouldn't budge, so she took her shower first and made another attempt at awaking Jaz after. Still with no luck, Monica grabbed a cup of water and poured it over Jaz's face.

"Ahhh!" Jaz jumped up, pissed.

"Get yo' ass up now!"

"If I wasn't so tired, I'd kick yo' short ass!"

"You ain't gon' do shit," Monica stated surely.

"What time is it?" Jaz yawned.

"8:30."

Jaz jumped up and darted for the bathroom. "I told you to wake me up in an hour."

"I did, but your ass wouldn't move."

Jaz couldn't believe she'd slept so late. She was supposed to be ready and out the door by 9:30, and she knew that it was going to take longer than that for her to finish getting dressed. She'd promised Kyree that she'd have Monica at the club by 10:00. She knew she'd have to move fast to make up for it.

By 9:45, Jaz had pretty much made up for the time she'd lost. Giving each other a quick onceover before leaving, they were both equally satisfied. Jaz wore the red asymmetrical BCBG dress she'd just bought only a few hours ago with her favorite pair of black Jimmy Choo open-toed pumps. They were her favorite pair of shoes as well as the most expensive pair she owned. She opted for no makeup tonight, only choosing to apply her favorite MAC lip-gloss to her full lips. Her hair had grown in the past month and now touched the middle of her neck. Cut into layers, her burnt orange highlights neatly rested every other layer in a wrap as smooth as silk.

Not to be outdone, Monica wore a purple sequined BCBG dress with the back cut out, courtesy of Jaz, with black BCBG peep toe booties. Glittery purple eye shadow rested on her eyelids while pink lip-gloss adorned her lips. She and Jaz both showed their identical rose tattoos located on their leg. After snapping a few pictures with their phones, the girls were ready to go. Grabbing her clutch bag filled with both her and Jaz's belongings, Monica and Jaz were out the door and headed to Club House.

ASHLEY CHANNAE

CHAPTER 13

Jaz whipped her Camaro into the front of the club and handed the valet her keys. The club was packed to the brim with people and the line was wrapped around the building. Monica immediately regretted coming out. There was no way she was standing in that long-ass line all night. But Jaz surprised her by bypassing the patrons who stood in line, trying to make the free before eleven special, and walking straight up to the bouncer. She smiled and whispered something in his ear. He returned her smile, and before they knew it, he was removing the rope to allow them entrance. They didn't have to show ID, be checked by security, or even pay. Monica could hear the hating bitches gawking because they were still waiting in line and the thirsty niggas trying to holla as they walked by. Monica was impressed with Jaz's skills, and she just had to ask.

"What the fuck did you tell him?" she eagerly inquired.

"I gave him your number and told him you wanted some birthday dick when the club let out." Jaz gave a sinister grin.

"Fuck you, Jazmine!" Monica pushed her.

Jaz just laughed as they walked inside the club. The scene was definitely live. Club House was definitely the place to be. The loft-like appeal and comfortable setting gave the club its name – House. There were beautiful white and black couches throughout, two bars on each floor, and a stage big enough to host some of the hottest artists that came to town. Three floors separated the haves from the have-nots. The higher up you were, the bigger your pockets were. The DJ was playing all of the latest tracks, men and women were dressed in their flyest gear, and it was packed to the max. Actually, it was too packed for Monica's own comfort. She could barely move throughout the crowded club. She hated crowds. She always had it in her mind that if something was to ever go down, too many people would cause too many casualties, and she would be caught in the mix somehow. This was not the type of party she was looking for, and she was ready to go home.

"Jaz, this is too much." Monica shook her head.

Jaz knew how set in her ways Monica was. She just knew she was going to want to leave next, so she had to move quickly. She smiled and turned to Monica. "I have an idea. Let's go to VIP," Jaz boasted.

"Bitch, please. And how are we going to get in there?"

"Bitch, look at us. This wouldn't be the first time we did this," Jaz reminded her. And it truly wasn't. Anytime Monica and Jaz went clubbing, they were always invited to VIP, but never at a club such as House, so Monica was still very unsure. She didn't want to get her bubble burst. "Come on, girl, trust me," Jaz assured, grabbing her hand and leading the way.

Jaz flirted with the VIP bouncer, whispering in his ear, and he released the rope with no problem. Monica was shocked, to say the least. Things were going more smoothly than she thought, especially when they bypassed the second floor and went straight for the third.

"How the hell did you pull that off?" Monica just had to know.

Jaz didn't answer her; she just walked toward the back and into a private room. Monica just knew Jaz was feeling herself now. There was no way she was getting them into VIP private corridors as upscale as this. But, nevertheless, she enjoyed watching her work the scene. As Jaz flirted with the final bouncer, she walked into the dark private room with Monica right behind her.

The room was so dark that Monica instinctively grabbed ahold of Jaz's arm. "Shit, Jaz, what the fuck is this?"

But Jaz didn't say anything, and Monica was unsure of what kind of weird shit Jaz had brought her to.

Then, out of nowhere, the lights suddenly came on and a crowd full of people yelled, "Surprise!"

Monica covered her face with her hands in shock. She was speechless. Before her stood a host of her closest friends and family, dressed to the nines, surrounded by gifts, food, and bottles galore. All of the stylists from the shop, a few of her clients, Kyree's friends, and a lot of people she didn't even know were all in attendance. She was so excited; she thought she was going to cry.

"So did we have you fooled?" Jaz broke the silence.

"Damn right!" Monica grabbed at her rapidly beating chest and everyone laughed. "Thanks y'all!" Monica smiled, unable to control the tears. Monica looked through the crowd of smiling faces and found Kyree. He was dressed in a black and gray striped Lacoste cardigan, black Levi's, gray Sperry boat shoes, and a custom-made black ZShock watch with black diamonds encrusted into the bezel.

He approached her with a cocky smile and pulled her in close by the neck. "Happy birthday, Big Head."

He kissed her cheek and all of the guests said, "Aww!"

"Thanks, Ky." Monica hugged him.

"Don't just thank me. Jaz helped too." He looked over at Jaz.

"Thanks, J." Monica hugged her tightly.

"Anything for you, girl." Jaz smiled.

Monica didn't know who was taking pictures, but she saw the flashes from every direction. She felt like a celebrity.

"Alright, everybody, it's my sis's birthday, so we're gonna keep the bottles coming. Y'all just make sure you have yourselves a good time. Ay, DJ, turn that shit back up!" Kyree toasted his glass in the air.

Everyone cheered him on with thunderous applause. There was nothing they loved more than free drinks and good music. And there was nothing Kyree loved more than making the ones he loved happy. He was blowing a good penny on Monica's party, but the look on her face when she walked in made it all worthwhile. He had missed out on a lot while he was locked up, and he had a lot to make up for. There weren't that many people in the world he cared about, so he often splurged on the ones he loved.

Hugging Monica one more time, he said, "A'ight, Mo, mingle with your guests and have fun."

"I will. And thanks again."

Jaz couldn't wait to steal Monica away from Kyree. She had a few surprises for her too. "Girlllll, wait until you see who's all here," Jaz said, grabbing her by the arm.

"Happy Birthday, Lover!" Ms. Ray greeted Monica with a hug and a kiss to each cheek. "You're looking fab," he said.

Monica looked him up and down. "And you're looking...um..." She had no idea what to say. She was sure Kyree had to pull some strings to get him in there like that, considering that it was a no-go for men to dress like that inside the club. Ms. Ray was wearing hot pink sparkly leggings, six-inch white pumps, and a white see through blouse. But what set the outfit off even more was the fact that Ms. Ray had the nerve to be wearing a pink bra underneath. "Boy, why in the hell do you have on a bra?"

"Honaaaay, hate does NOT look good on you," Ms. Ray said as they all laughed.

"Heeeeey, Mo!" her homegirl said, her arms outstretched for a hug.

"Hey, Kori!"

"You are wearing that dress, girl," Kori complimented.

"Thanks, girl. But don't let Tremell catch you in that fuck 'em dress."

Kori instantly rolled her eyes at the mention of her boyfriend's name.

"Where my girl Bri at?" Monica asked, knowing that if Kori was present, her best friend, Bri, couldn't be too far behind.

"She over there." Kori pointed over her shoulder to Bri, who was getting herself a glass of Ace of Spades. Monica waved at her and Bri signaled she'd be over in a second. Moments later Bri was approaching them, trying to balance five glasses in two hands.

"You know the birthday girl can't be walking around without a drink in her hand." Bri handed them all glasses.

"Thanks, girl," Monica said, hugging her.

"You're welcome. Now isn't this way more fun than going to some damn Hibachi Grill?"

"Yeah, I guess. But I was about to kick all of y'all's asses for cancelling on me too," Monica said as they all laughed. The girls conversed for a while until Sage The Gemini's song "Red Nose" came on.

"Oh naw, that's my shit!" Ms. Ray exclaimed.

"Mine too," Bri said, dancing and popping her booty with him. They were on their second glass and definitely feeling a buzz.

"Come on, y'all, let's go to the dance floor," Ms. Ray said.

"We'll catch up with y'all," Jaz said, pulling Monica away. She still had a surprise for her.

As they tried to make their way through the crowd, Monica was stopped by everyone. Jaz thought she'd never get to show her what she had in store for her. Finally getting through the crowd of people, Jaz found the one person she was looking for. "Look who I invited," Jaz said to Monica.

Monica looked at her suspiciously, and then Jaz moved to the side, revealing Mario, who was talking to a few of his boys. The second he saw her, a huge smile spread across his face. Wearing a light blue polo shirt, dark blue jeans, and a pair of white Prada shoes with his long dreads braided to the back, he looked damn good. He reached his arms out and pulled her in close. Taking a whiff of his sweet cologne, Monica enjoyed being in his embrace. She hadn't seen or spoken to him since last week. It wasn't like he hadn't called; she just wasn't answering. With so much going on in her life, she just wasn't ready to deal with him. But now they were face to face, and she had nowhere to hide.

He whispered in her ear, "Don't think I forgot that shit you did." Monica looked at him, confused. "Getting my dick hard and then fleeing on a nigga," he stated boldly.

Monica's mouth opened in shock. She couldn't help but to laugh.

Noticing Monica was having a good time, Jaz whispered in her ear, "You can thank me later."

"We good over here?" Kyree interrupted their conversation, a look of venom in his eyes.

Monica rolled her eyes. "Yes, Ky. This is my friend Mario.

Mario, this is my big head nosy-ass brother, Ky."

"What up, my man?" Mario said, his hand out for some dap.

Kyree looked at Mario and then at his hand as if it was infected with a contagious disease. Jaz knew she was going to have to run interference. He was always so overprotective of his sister.

"Kyree and I are going to get a drink. You two have fun," Jaz said, practically pulling Kyree away. Once they were a far enough distance away, Jaz released his arm. "Leave them alone, Kyree."

"Whatever." Kyree waved her off, taking a sip from his glass of Hennessy.

Jaz rolled her eyes at him. They both stood leaning over the railing, looking down at the club-goers on the dance floor.

"So where yo' fiancé, Mitch, at?" Kyree asked, not bothering to look at her.

Jaz looked at him. He had to be feeling himself from that drink. "His name is Mike, and he should be on his way," she said, taking a look at her phone to see the time. "Where's Korea?" Jaz smirked.

Kyree couldn't help but chuckle. He was starting to see how much Asia got under Jaz's skin. He wasn't the one for playing games, but he liked getting a rise out of Jaz. It didn't take long for him to realize she'd seen his phone last weekend when Asia texted him. Seeing the perfect opportunity to piss Jaz off, Kyree said, "Here come my baby right now."

Jaz turned to see Asia walking up the stairs. She wore a blue dress barely covering anything with her hair neatly layered, just as Jaz's was. *I swear this bitch wanna be me,* Jaz said to herself.

Asia smiled upon seeing Kyree. "Hey Jaz, girl," Asia said.

"What up, Asia?" Jaz responded.

"Hey baby." Asia hugged Kyree tightly around his neck.

Jaz could've thrown up in her mouth at the sight before her. She really thought she was going to lose it when she saw Kyree grab her ass. Rolling her eyes, she focused her attention back downstairs. Truth was, she'd been waiting on Michael to text her back all day. He promised her he'd show, and she really wanted him there by her side, especially if she was going to have to sit and look at Kyree and his hoe all night. Her prayers were answered when she saw Michael approaching the stairs through the crowd. Smiling and meeting him before he reached the steps, she jumped in his arms. Boldly kissing him on the lips, she couldn't have been happier to see him.

"Damn, baby," Michael laughed. "What was that for?"

"I just missed you," she admitted. Taking a look at him, Jaz frowned up her face. He was still leisurely dressed in his work slacks, a shirt, and tie. He looked like a car salesman, not someone out to have a good time. Jaz didn't understand why he was still wearing his work clothes, considering the fact that she'd ironed his clothes and had them lying on the bed for him.

"I didn't have time to go home and change," he admitted.

"Forget it," Jaz huffed, fixing his clothes, trying to give him some sort of swag. Removing his shirt from his pants, Jaz unbuttoned it so that his wife beater was visible and she united his tie and let it hang freely around his neck. "I guess this will do," she reasoned.

"Why does it matter?" Michael asked.

Jaz didn't respond. She was acting weird, and Michael was confused as to why. This wasn't like her at all. She usually liked seeing him in his shirt and tie. But now it bothered her. He had no idea why she was tripping over something as simple as what he was wearing.

Following behind her up the stairs, Jaz took his hand. Walking up to Kyree with her heart beating at a hurried pace, Jaz said, "Kyree, there is someone I'd like you to meet." Kyree looked up at the guy standing behind Jaz and his stomach instantly started to churn. "Kyree, this is Mike. Mike, this is Kyree."

There they stood, the two men that held her heart, face to face for the first time. Jaz was surprised as hell when she saw Kyree reach out his hand first to shake Michael's hand.

"It's nice to finally meet you," Kyree said as he and Michael shook hands firmly.

"And you as well. I've heard a lot about you," Michael said.

"All good, I hope," Kyree grinned.

"Of course." Michael smiled, hugging Jaz from behind. "Hi, Asia," Michael said, remembering her name this time.

So now this uppity muthafucka remembers my name. "Hey Mike." Asia gave a fake smile.

Downing the rest of his drink, Kyree said, "Well, if you'll excuse me. It was nice meeting you, Mike." He walked back over to the party with Asia trailing right behind him.

Kyree was on fire inside. Sure, he knew that Jaz had moved on. But now he was meeting the dude for the first time, and he was hugging Jaz like he used to - like he was supposed to. Like no one else was supposed to. He wanted nothing more than to toss Michael over the balcony, but he decided to remove himself from the situation instead. And yes, he had Asia, but that was momentarily. What Jaz had with Michael was supposed to be forever.

Jaz watched as Kyree walked away. To the world, he may have seemed unfazed, but she knew that was just a show. Kyree never initiated a handshake with a perfect stranger. She hadn't meant to hurt him; she just wanted to finally make a formal introduction as to draw out any suspicion. Turning back around to face Michael, she smiled at him.

"So that's your ex, huh?" he asked.

She nodded her head. "Yep."

"I should've thanked him for letting you go," he said, hugging her.

Jaz smiled. Wanting to change the subject, she said, "Let's go get a drink."

Ushering him through the party near the fully stocked bar, Jaz thought she was going to be sick again. In the corner, hugged up on the couch, sat Kyree and Asia. Asia was massaging Kyree's thigh and whispering into his ear. Rolling her eyes, she turned her focus back to Michael. With his Ciroc and lemonade in hand, he and Jaz found a seat.

Seeing Monica approach her giddily, Jaz smiled, happy she was enjoying herself. "Hey Mike," Monica greeted him.

"Hey to you. Happy birthday." Michael hugged her.

"Thanks." She smiled. "Hey J, I'm 'bout to go take this nigga out on the dance floor and twerk sum'in'." She boasted while shaking her butt.

"A'ight now. I ain't mad at'cha," Jaz laughed.

"Y'all coming?"

Looking back at Michael and then back at Monica, Jaz decided against it. "Naw, maybe later."

Monica shrugged and walked away, holding Mario's hand behind her.

"You sure you don't want to go out there?" Michael asked, knowing how much Jaz loved to dance.

"No, I just wanna sit here with you." She smiled, nudging his arm. Truth was, she knew how Michael felt about a lot of rap music. It wasn't that he didn't like it; he just didn't know a lot of it. They were opposites in so many ways, which was why Jaz was attracted to him. She turned him on to a new world, and so he did the same for her. They were always teaching each other new things. Every day was a new beginning with a different ending.

Wrapping his arm around her, Michael took a swig of his drink. "So you're not on call tonight?" Jaz asked, noticing him tossing back his drink.

"Nope."

"Good, 'cause I want you all to myself," she admitted.

Michael kissed her on the cheek. Unbeknownst to them, Kyree was watching from afar. Asia was whispering in his ear, but Kyree wasn't hearing her. All he saw was some other man's arm around Jaz, some other man making her laugh, kissing her, and he didn't want to even think about what they did when no one was around. Deep down he knew this was the type of man that Jaz deserved, but he just couldn't picture her with anyone that wasn't him.

Asia could see that Kyree's focus was on Jaz, but there was no doubt in her mind that she could change that. Moving

126

her hand to his crotch, she inched her way toward the large tool inside his pants. Kyree immediately turned to look at her. Without saying anything, he took the rest of his glass of Paul Mason back, stood up, and pulled Asia to her feet. She had no idea what he was planning on doing. She was slightly confused and turned on at the same time. Pulling her in front of him, he walked while hugging her from behind. Asia could feel his hard-on pressed against her butt. Smiling from ear to ear, she relished the fact that she could feel Jaz's eyes on them as they walked. She was elated when Kyree smacked her ass without warning. She was sure Jaz was probably losing her mind.

And she couldn't have been more right. Jaz was sitting down, watching from the corner of her eye. Noticing her staring, Michael grew heated. There was no way she could be staring at Kyree so blatantly with him sitting right beside her. He was convinced that she was still trying to prove something to Kyree. She couldn't still be feeling him, not after he put in so much work repairing her heart that Kyree broke. Taking another look from Kyree to Jaz and noticing Jaz biting the inside of her jaw, Michael's suspicions were confirmed.

"What the fuck?" Michael said.

"What?" Jaz asked, not quite sure if she'd heard him right.

"Jaz, why the fuck are you staring so hard at that man?" he barked.

Caught off guard by his accusation and his tone, Jaz asked, "Excuse me?"

"You heard me, Jaz. You haven't been able to keep your eyes off of that man, who seems to be minding his own damn business, all fucking night."

Looking around to make sure no one could hear them, Jaz said, "You trippin'. Ain't nobody looking at his ass." She rolled her eyes.

Michael just nodded his head in frustration. "Okay, Jaz. Cool."

Jaz looked at him like he was crazy. How dare he come at her like that? She wasn't one to just stand around and take such disrespect without defending herself. She couldn't allow him to end the conversation, especially with something as simple as "cool".

"You got some nerve! I'm surprised you can see me looking any damn where when you're constantly looking at your phone every second. I thought you weren't on call today," Jaz challenged him. She was right though. Michael had been looking at his phone nonstop since he got there. It was annoying as hell. She couldn't figure out what could be so important if he wasn't on call.

"I'm not on call!"

"Then why the fuck you keep looking at your damn phone? You waiting on your bitch to call?" Jaz couldn't believe she'd said what she said and neither could Michael. She just wanted him to know how it felt to be accused of something. Even though she regretted what she said, it was already done and she couldn't take it back. She wasn't even sure she wanted to if she could. So she kept her poker face as they stared each other down.

"What? What kind of shit is that? Don't try to flip this shit, Jaz."

"I'm not trying to flip shit! I told you I wasn't looking at that nigga, and I meant it. But yet, you can't even tell me who you're expecting to call you."

"This shit is crazy. I'm not expecting a call from no bitch!"

Jaz sucked her teeth. "Whatever, Mike. I'm going out on the dance floor. Fuck this shit."

Jaz got up and headed toward the dance floor, leaving Michael sitting there dumbfounded. He had no idea how shit went from bad to worse within a split second. In no time at all, Jaz had managed to flip the entire script and redirect all the attention from her peeping her ex to him conversing with another woman. But in actuality, he never stood a chance. Jaz could be a master at manipulation when she needed to be.

In need of another drink, Jaz headed to the bar downstairs instead of the fully stocked private bar they had in

VIP. She'd stand in the long lines with the rowdy club-goers just so that she wouldn't have to go back in VIP and face Michael. Patiently waiting for the bartender to come back with her shot of Patron, she started to think about what Michael was saying. She knew he was right. She was watching Kyree and Asia like a hawk. It angered her tremendously. She reasoned with herself that it was more so the fact that he was with Asia that angered her, but she knew that wasn't the case. It infuriated her seeing Kyree with anyone that wasn't her. She was aggravated beyond belief. She had no idea how she could feel this way when she was in love with Michael. Her emotions were wreaking havoc on her brain. Finally, having her drink in hand, Jaz took the liquid down, hoping it would ease her mind.

Looking around at what should've been a joyous occasion, Jaz noticed Mario walking toward the bathroom. She wondered where Monica could be, so she went searching for her. She saw Ms. Ray, Kori, and Bri, but they said they hadn't seen her. Jaz made her way through the crowd until she saw her in the distance. Monica was standing against the wall with her head down, focused on her phone. She was obviously a little tipsy, because she kept swaying, and with all of her attention diverted on her phone, she didn't notice who was approaching her. But Jaz did. Deciding to approach him before he made his way over to Monica, Jaz walked right by Monica, who didn't notice a thing because she was on her phone, and held him at bay.

"Damn, Jaz. Good to see you too," he smirked.

"Listen, La, this is Monica's birthday. Don't come at her with that bullshit tonight. Fall back," Jaz warned him.

Licking his lips, Latrell said, "And if I don't?"

Jaz looked at him like he was crazy. He really knew better than to challenge her. He had to be drunk. "Well, Kyree's here. So if you want to find out, try me," Jaz dared him.

Latrell contemplated it for a moment and then decided against it. "A'ight. It's yo' world, Jaz." He backed away with his hands up in surrender.

Jaz didn't like the sarcasm in his tone at all. Something told her that he wasn't going to let up. Her threat to get Kyree was only going to hold him off for a little while. There was no doubt in her mind that Monica could hold her own, but she was noticeably intoxicated and she really didn't need any of that drama on her birthday. Finding one of the stylists from the shop, Tameka, Jaz made sure she stayed to keep an eye on Monica while she went to look for Kyree.

.

CHAPTER 14

After ten minutes of looking high and low, pushing through people, and asking everyone she knew if they had seen him, Jaz still had no luck finding Kyree. She was exhausted. Her feet were definitely on shoeicide watch as she tried to prevent what she knew was going to be a huge blow up. Finally giving up, Jaz figured she'd just get Monica upstairs to the VIP so that she wouldn't see Latrell. Walking back to where she'd left Monica, Jaz was stopped dead in her tracks. The sight before her had her feet glued to the floor. She couldn't move even if she wanted to. Her head began to spin and she swore she saw complete red for a split second. Walking back inside the club was Kyree and Asia. Asia's dress was twisted, her hair disheveled, and her makeup was smeared. Kyree, on the other hand, looked cool and relaxed. But Jaz knew better. She was sure they'd snuck away from the party to have a private fuck session somewhere.

And she was right. Kyree had just finished letting Asia ride his dick in the front seat of his car. After seeing Jaz with Michael, he was in need of a stress reliever, and Asia was practically begging him to fuck her brains out. But seeing the look on Jaz's face made him feel guilty - for what reason, he did not know. And although they stood at least fifty feet away from each other, their eyes locked, time stopped, and everyone else in the club seemed to disappear. It was as if she'd stopped the music in the club and telepathically asked him, "Why?" and as if he too entered her mind and replied, "Why not?" Even though no words were spoken between the two of them verbally, Jaz knew she'd pushed him directly into the arms of Asia. She had no one to blame but herself.

Bumped out of her trance by a guy trying to pass her, Jaz couldn't bear to look at Kyree for another second. She almost turned to leave, but quickly remembered why she was looking for him in the first place. Sucking up her pride and walking over to him, she looked from him to Asia, then back to him. "We need to talk."

"About what?" he asked.

Jaz looked at Asia and then looked at Kyree. Asia could see Jaz was tight and knew she wanted to talk to Kyree in private, but she wouldn't dare give her the satisfaction of being the one to make her leave. She looked at Jaz, rolled her eyes, and then looked back at Kyree.

Kyree was stuck between a rock and a hard place. He was going to piss someone off with whatever decision he decided to make. Jaz and Asia were both standing with their arms folded, with all of their weight shifted to one side, ice grilling him. Kyree looked to Asia, and she instantly grew heated. She knew that was his way of asking her to give them a moment in private.

Asia was infuriated, but she would never show it. Kyree was always picking Jaz over her, but the difference between the two of them was that Asia never gave him any attitude. She figured she'd just be opposite of whatever Jaz was, and if that included putting up with playing second fiddle, she would just have to deal for now. She was sure that with Jaz's attitude, she wouldn't be second best for too long. Using her finger to turn Kyree's head so that he was facing her, Asia kissed him greedily on the lips. She sneered, wiping his mouth with her hand.

"It's cool, Ky. Y'all talk. I have to go to the bathroom to fix my makeup anyway." She made sure she looked Jaz up and down before walking away.

Did that bitch just grit on me? Jaz asked herself. Asia was already walking toward the bathroom when Jaz turned around with the intention of snatching her bald.

"Jaz!" Kyree stopped her. Taking a deep breath, Jaz tried to calm herself down. Deciding to let it go, she diverted her attention back toward Kyree. "What was so important?"

"La's here."

"What?" Kyree asked to make sure he'd heard her right.

"La, nigga! Latrell! Your sister's ain't-shit-ass baby daddy!" Jaz said with an attitude as if he were slow.

"Where he at?" Kyree demanded to know.

Jaz put her hand up to his chest to stop his path. "No, Kyree. Don't do anything stupid." Jaz could see the look of venom in his eyes. It was an all too familiar look. She knew that Kyree had it out for Latrell since he found out Monica was pregnant and Latrell wasn't doing shit for her. Latrell had disrespected his sister, and niggas had died for way less. The only reason why the nigga was still breathing was on the strength of Kayden. He couldn't dead his nephew's father.

Looking down at Jaz's pleading eyes, Kyree said, "Cool. I got this." Then he pushed her out of his way.

Jaz grabbed his shirt and tried to stop him. "What are you going to do?" She begged to know.

"Chill out, Jaz, and go keep an eye on Monica. Make sure she don't see that nigga." Kyree pulled his arm from her grasp and walked away, throwing his hand up over his head to let her know the conversation was over.

Jaz regretted telling him. She had no idea what he was going to do, but she knew she had to find Monica before shit got too crazy. Walking to the place where she'd left her, Jaz cursed herself for leaving her. It was too late. Latrell was already in her face, and the conversation they were having didn't look good from where she was standing. Quickly making her way over to them, her suspicions were confirmed. Monica was drunk, but it was true what they said, because a drunken mind did indeed speak a sober heart. And Monica was living proof.

"Fuck you, Latrell! You will never see my fucking son!" Monica screamed at him. They were starting to draw a crowd as Jaz approached them.

"Bitch, don't come at me with that shit! When the judge sees these fucking text messages you sent me, I bet yo' ass will be the one crying to see him."

Monica looked at him like he was crazy and Jaz held her back. "Muthafucka, over my dead body!" she retorted back. But her drunken mind didn't realize the severity of the text messages she'd sent to him. She had no idea he was in the club when she sent the many text messages. She'd called him everything from a stupid son of a bitch to a crooked dick muthafucka. Within each message, she'd also told him that she'd never allow him to see Kayden.

"Fall back, Monica. Only thing you was good for was riding the crook in my dick." He got in her face.

Monica's eyes grew big and she charged at him. Jaz stepped in front of them while Tameka tried to hold Monica back. It was obvious that they were both drunk and not of sound body and mind.

Latrell continued to smirk, confident that Monica wouldn't touch him. "Bitch, ain't nobody scared of you!"

"What about me, muthafucka?"

Latrell turned around to see Kyree, and if looks could kill, he was sure to be lying six feet deep. Kyree stood with confidence, not saying much of anything, only glaring at Latrell. Latrell wasn't a punk, but Kyree's name held major weight around the city. He wasn't stupid; he didn't want beef.

"My bad, Ky, man. It's just me and your sister got some unfinished business, my dude. That's all."

"Well, it's gonna have to stay unfinished, 'cause you gotta roll," Kyree stated firmly.

Latrell looked at him skeptically. "No disrespect, my dude, I'll leave Mo alone for now, but you can't make me leave the club."

Instead of sending Latrell to the hospital with multiple contusions, Kyree simply took a deep breath and signaled with his hand. In seconds flat, two burly security guards came on each side of Latrell and scooped him off the ground. Latrell tried to release himself from their grasp, but he couldn't. The whole way out, he was yelling and screaming, "This is some bullshit!"

Kyree walked over to a hysterical Monica and placed one hand on her shoulder. She was breathing heavily and on the brink of tears. "You a'ight, Mo? You wanna go home?"

She tried to control her breathing and keep her tears at bay. She looked up at Kyree and shook her head no. "I'm good, Ky." She wasn't going to allow Latrell to fuck up her birthday like he fucked up everything else in her life.

135

"You sure?" Kyree asked.

"Hell yeah! Let's go back to VIP!" She smiled with a new burst of energy.

That was all Kyree needed to hear. He smirked and escorted her back to VIP in a playful headlock. Before they reached the steps, they were bombarded with an inquiring Ms. Ray, Kori, and Bri.

"Girllllll...I just knew I was gonna have to go kraza on a bitch," Ms. Ray said.

"Boy, what the fuck is kraza?" Monica asked.

"It's karate, with a razor!" Ms. Ray did a slight karate kick and pretended to whip out a razor. They all burst into laughter.

Kyree shook his head and released Monica from the headlock he had on her. She was with her friends now. He was fine, as long as she was having a good time. He walked up the steps with Jaz tailing him. He was so smooth with calling over the security guards, and she just had to know how he pulled it off. He leaned against the bar, his drink still in hand, slowly sipping. Looking over at her, he asked, "What?"

"How you pull that shit off?"

"I told you I got connections," he simply said.

Jaz nodded her head. She had completely forgotten that he did know the owner. He'd neglected to tell her that he was also a silent partner in the club. She didn't need to know everything. There was a time when he would tell her just about anything, but now he felt as if he had to keep his distance.

Remembering a time where Kyree would have busted Latrell's skull open for testing him, Jaz smiled to herself. She was proud of him for keeping his cool and handling the situation like a mature adult. "Thanks for being the bigger person tonight," she looked at him and said.

He didn't return her look; he simply nodded his head and gazed ahead.

"You can't look at me now?" Jaz asked, caught off guard by his standoffish attitude.

"Yeah. But you might wanna go. You got company."

Kyree slightly aimed his glass in the direction Jaz needed to direct her attention to. Jaz turned to see Michael standing across from them. He had a look on his face Jaz had never seen before. She couldn't read him. His brow was furrowed and his lips were pursed. Briskly walking over to them, he grabbed her arm and pulled her to the side. Jaz snatched her arm away.

"What the fuck is your problem?" Jaz asked, surprised by his sudden demeanor.

"My problem? Jaz, you walked away from me when we were arguing about that nigga, and now I find you in his face. Again!"

"We were just talking. Damn, Mike!"

Michael nodded his head as if he'd just had a moment of clarity. "I don't have to put up with this shit, Jaz. I'm gone." Michael couldn't even look at her as he turned around to leave.

"That's the best thing you've said all night. Bye, nigga!" Jaz yelled back at him. But she couldn't believe that he'd actually left so abruptly. She just couldn't be put on blast in front of everyone. Seeing her friends headed her way, Jaz prepared herself for what she knew was going to be the third degree.

"Damn, you too, Jaz? Everybody got man problems tonight." Ms. Ray shook his head.

"Man, I don't know why he's trippin'," Jaz lied.

"Girl, y'all making me not even wanna go home to Tre's ass tonight. He might blow up too. I think it's a full moon or something," Kori said.

"He needs to, with that little-ass dress you wearing." Ms. Ray tugged at the bottom of her dress. She smacked his hand away and they all laughed.

"Fuck these niggas! Y'all know what we need?" Bri asked.

They all answered one after the other.

"New niggas?" Kori said.

"Some good dick?" Ms. Ray said.

"Some sleep?" a tired Jaz yawned.

Bri just shook her head.

"Spit it out!" Monica said.

"We need another drink, bitches!" an already-inebriated Bri announced.

"I'll drink to that!" Monica sang.

"Aw, hell naw, who taking these hoes home?" Ms. Ray asked.

They all laughed and Jaz glanced over her shoulder at Kyree. Asia was slow grinding on him to Sizzla and Rihanna's hit "Give Me a Try". Bri was right; she did need a drink - and something strong if she was going to have to look at that shit for the rest of the night.

"Well what the fuck we waiting on? It's a celebration. Let's celebrate!" Jaz shouted.

By the end of the night, the girls were beyond fucked up. Ms. Ray, Bri, and Kori had all rode with Tameka. They all loved when she went somewhere with them. She could and would drive any and everywhere. She didn't drink, smoke, or do that much partying for the matter. Married with two kids, Tameka was just grateful for the time away from home.

"Well, let me get these drunk hoes home," Tameka announced to Jaz.

"I ain't drunk," Bri slurred.

"I wanna go to IHOP," Kori said.

"Me too!" Ms. Ray exclaimed.

Tameka rolled her eyes. "These drunk hoes are going home!" she stated firmly.

"Y'all be safe," Jaz laughed.

The club had let out fifteen minutes ago. After taking back four shots of Ciroc, dancing with Mario until she could no longer stand, and nearly falling a couple of times, Monica was completely fucked up. She lay lightly snoring on Jaz's lap.

Unlike Monica, Jaz only had two shots and a half glass of champagne the whole night. She was tipsy, but she wasn't completely drunk. Usually she was six shots in before she was even feeling light-headed. But tonight her game was all fucked up. Her blow-up with Michael had completely thrown her off her square.

A drunken Monica started stirring in her sleep and Jaz knew what was next. She quickly grabbed the bucket under the table and aimed Monica's head inside of it. Monica hurled into the bucket while Jaz held her hair. She knew it was coming. Passing her a napkin, Monica wiped her mouth and rested her head on Jaz's shoulder. Jaz wasn't surprised at all when Monica started to cry.

"It's okay, Mo. Let it out," Jaz rocked her back and forth.

"Fuck that nigga, J. He ain't gon' get my baby," Monica slurred.

"I know, I know," Jaz comforted her.

Kyree walked over and asked, "She good?"

Jaz nodded her head.

As if on cue, Asia was right behind him. "Damn, Mo, you a'ight?" Asia laughed.

"She fine, bitch, get out her fuckin' face!" Jaz barked.

Everyone was completely taken aback except for Monica, who had fallen asleep again and was none the wiser.

"Bitch?" Asia repeated to make sure she'd heard her right. "I know you're drunk, so I'm going to charge that to the reason why you're acting so stank," Asia said.

Jaz rolled her eyes. She really didn't want to take it there with Asia tonight. She was tired, slightly tipsy, and she just wanted to go home. Looking up at Kyree, she said, "Look, can you take her home?"

"Why can't she go home with you?" he asked, confused.

"Because, Kyree, she wants to go home," Jaz lied. The real reason Jaz didn't want Monica to come home with her was because she didn't know if Michael was going to be at her house, and she was sure they were going to have a heated argument when she arrived. Normally, Jaz probably would have gone home with Monica until the heat died down, but she figured the longer she and Michael left things unsaid, the worse it would get.

Kyree could look at her and tell she was only telling him the half-truth. Figuring she probably needed to work things out with her man, he agreed to take Monica home. Jaz handed him

Monica's house key from out of her purse. "A'ight, cool. Who's taking you home?"

Jaz looked at him stupidly. "I am. I drove here, remember?"

Kyree shook his head. "Naw, I don't trust you driving home. You've been drinking."

"I'm fine, Kyree," she assured him, standing up and stumbling.

"Hell naw, fuck that! Ay, Fat Boy!" Kyree called over his shoulder.

"What up?" Fat Boy asked.

"I need you take Jaz home for me," Kyree said.

"I'm not leaving my car here!" Jaz spoke up.

"Well, then Fat Boy will drive your car home, and I'll come get him later."

"Naw, I can't do that Ky. Jaz got that little-ass Camaro. My big ass can't fit in that shit," he chuckled.

Kyree was frustrated with the whole thing and so was Jaz as she headed for the door. "I'll be fine!" she yelled over her shoulder.

Kyree was slowly losing his patience with Jaz. She could be such a brat sometimes, and he knew it. But he would never allow her to drive home drunk. He always thought the worst, and he would never forgive himself if something were to happen to her. Sucking his teeth, he asked Fat Boy if he could take Monica home. He agreed without the slightest hesitation. Kyree took the steps two at a time, with Asia right on his heels, in an attempt to catch Jaz before she left.

"Here's your vehicle, ma'am." The attendant held Jaz's keys in the air. She reached into Monica's clutch bag, searching for a tip to give him. Finally finding a five-dollar bill, Jaz smiled and handed it to him. "Thank you." He smiled, handing her the keys.

Before Jaz could grasp the keys, a hand came from out of nowhere, taking the keys from the valet's hands. "What the fuck?" Jaz turned around to see who was so eager to grab her keys and rolled her eyes. "Kyree, give me my keys!"

140

"Look, I'm not letting you drive home drunk." He turned around to Asia. "You mind driving Jaz's car home for me?"

"Over my dead fucking body!" Jaz retorted. She couldn't believe the nerve of Kyree. There was no way his hoe was taking her home.

Asia turned up her face at Jaz and then looked back at Kyree. "I would love to do this for you, but she's obviously drunk and trippin' right now, so I don't think that would be a good idea."

Jaz thought about it for a second before realizing this would be the day she'd let Asia have it. For too long she'd tolerated Asia, but she was tired of it now. Normally Jaz would continue to do her and not pay Asia any attention, but seeing her with Kyree tonight was the last straw. It was almost as if Asia was throwing it in her face and taunting her. The alcohol in her system was playing with her emotions and clouding her judgment. So with liquid courage, and reckless abandon, she said, "Bitch, I ain't drunk! I just don't like yo' wannabe ass!"

"Bitch, I don't like your ass either!"

"I can't tell. You wanna be me so bad. You'll never ride in my shit!"

Asia gave her a sinister smirk. She'd been waiting on Jaz to snap, and it looked like she was really getting under her skin now. But Asia needed to add more fire to the flames that were brewing from Jaz's head. She had one more thing to say. "I might not ride your whip, but I sure as hell ride ya boy's dick!"

"Ugh!" Jaz had no idea what came over her as she went charging at Asia. Before she could fully reach her, Kyree had scooped her up off the ground. She kicked and screamed while yelling obscenities the whole time. "You thirsty trick bitch!" Jaz yelled.

The majority of the club-goers were gone, but the valet sure got an earful. Security was about to step in, but Kyree assured them he had the situation under control. Tossing Jaz in the front seat of the car and then slamming the door, he hit the lock button from her remote. Frantically trying to open her door, Jaz caused the alarm to go off. "Ahh!" she screamed covering her ears with her hands.

Kyree bent down at the window. "If I turn the alarm off, are you going to act like you got some damn sense?"

"Fuck you, Kyree!" she screamed at him.

"A'ight then, cool," he said, walking away.

Unable to handle the noise any longer, Jaz called out to him. "Okay, Ky! Shit!"

"That's what I thought," he said, hitting the button to silence the alarm.

Jaz sat in the front seat stuck. She couldn't move if she wanted to. If she tried to open the door, the alarm would sound again. Busting the window out with her Jimmy Choo crossed her mind a couple of times, but she eventually decided against it. Feeling defeated, she crossed her arms tightly, cursing Kyree the whole time.

Kyree walked over to an amped-up Asia. She was pacing back and forth, calling Jaz every name in the book. "Yo, why did you say that shit?" Kyree questioned her.

Asia couldn't believe he was getting on her case when it was Jaz's fault to begin with. "How are you going to take her side when she started this shit?"

"I'm not taking anyone's side. But why the fuck you say that shit?" Kyree just had to know. There were some lines you didn't cross, and she'd crossed it.

Asia realized she was getting beside herself, seeing as though Kyree had a low tolerance for bullshit. Staring down at the ground, she tried to seem apologetic. "I'm sorry. She just got to me. I had to say something back."

Kyree knew that Jaz was wrong for what she said. Anyone probably would've reacted the way Asia had in that situation. He couldn't blame her for wanting to have the upper hand in the matter. "Look, y'all are two grown-ass women. Y'all can work this out under different circumstances, I'm sure." Kyree wasn't sure he even believed that. Jaz could be so headstrong sometimes, and if she said something, she usually meant it - drunk or not. "How'd you get here?" he asked.

"I rode here with my homegirl. You told me to,

remember?"

Kyree thought back to earlier that day when he told her she was going home with him. The look on her face now was so sad and disappointed. He felt wrong for having to leave her. Against his better judgment, he reached into his pocket, pulled out his house keys, and gave them to her. "Take my car to my house. I'll get Fat Boy to bring me home."

"Are you sure?"

He pulled her in close and whispered in her ear, "When I get home, I want you waiting under the covers with nothing on but a smile."

She looked up at him and gleefully took the keys. She sashayed away as the valet was just pulling up with Kyree's car.

"Don't fuck up my shit!" he called out to her just as she slammed the door.

Kyree took a deep breath, taking in the fact that he'd prevented two major confrontations in one night. But quickly sighing, he realized that he still had to deal with Jaz until he got her home. The few drinks he had barely gave him a buzz. Unlike some people, he could handle his liquor. Jaz and Monica, on the other hand, were major emotional drunks. Whereas Monica usually laughed and cried, Jaz would get angry and honest. They were both creatures of habit. Hopping into the front seat of Jaz's car, Kyree looked at her and let out a slight chuckle as he adjusted the seat to his fitting.

"What?" she snapped.

"Nothing, man." He started up the car and pulled away from the club. Any high he had before was definitely fucked up by the night's events. And the night was hardly over.

CHAPTER 15

The ride home was a quiet one. Nothing but the smooth sounds of the after dark radio station elevated the speakers until Jaz decided to break the silence. "So where yo' hoe at?"

Turning down the music to hear her more clearly, Kyree replied, "What?"

"You heard me. Did you send her home, Kyree?"

Kyree briefly looked away from the road and glanced at Jaz. "You're drunk."

"I ain't drunk! Just answer the question."

"I ain't gotta answer shit!" he retorted back, picking up his cell phone and dialing Fat Boy's number.

"A'ight, whatever. You better not tell that bitch where I live either or else I'm gon' fuck both y'all up," Jaz said, turning her gaze out the window.

Kyree was about to cuss her out, but Fat Boy answered the call just in time. "Yo, I need you to come get me from Jaz's house."

"I thought Asia was gonna trail you," Fat Boy said.

"Man, it's a long story. You drop Mo off yet?"

"Naw. Me, Monica, Tink, Diamond, and Jason at IHOP. Mo got a second wind and wanted to get something to eat," Fat Boy chuckled.

Kyree sucked his teeth. "A'ight, man. Just roll through to come get me as soon as you leave."

"I got you," Fat Boy assured him before ending the call.

"Mo a'ight?" Jaz asked with concern.

"Yeah, she good. She went to IHOP with Fat Boy and a couple other people from the crew."

"Damn, I should've went with them," she moped.

"Naw, you need to get home to yo' man." Kyree let out a slight laugh, remembering the show they'd put on at the club earlier.

Jaz rolled her eyes at him as her cell phone vibrated from an incoming text message. It was from Michael.

>>> 2:39 AM, My Bae: We both need time to sober up. I'm going home. We'll talk later. STILL love u.

Jaz turned her phone over, annoyed. They needed to talk, and later wasn't going to make things right NOW. She was slightly intoxicated, but the effort would make it all worthwhile. They'd never had such a serious fight before, and she didn't want their first one to be over something as minuscule as this. Sighing heavily, she kept her gaze out the window. "Do you like her, Kyree?"

He glanced at her briefly. "What you want me to say, Jaz? Huh? Yeah, I like her. She cool peoples," Kyree admitted, pulling up to Jaz's apartment.

Jaz turned to look at him. "Did you fuck her?"

Kyree stopped on the brakes abruptly, causing them both to jerk forward. Drunk or not, Jaz was really trying him. Putting the car in park, he decided to give her the ugly truth she so desperately wanted. "In every fucking way imaginable. Literally!" Kyree snapped. "Yeah, I fucked her. I'm a single-ass man. I can do what the fuck I want. Don't you fuck that gump-ass nigga you with every night?"

Jaz looked at him as though she was seeing him for the first time, and the person she was seeing, she didn't like at all. "Fuck you, Kyree!" she seethed, getting out of the car and slamming the door behind her.

Kyree wasn't about to let her just walk out on him like that. He quickly got out of the car. "Naw, fuck that!" He grabbed her arm and turned her around so that she was facing him. "How you gon' ask for the truth if you can't handle it? You gave me the truth. You moved on. So I am too."

Jaz yanked her arm away. "Leave me alone, Kyree." She walked away briskly. Her feet were killing her, but Kyree's words were killing her worse. He was right. She really couldn't handle hearing him openly say he was fucking other girls and moving on with his life.

But Kyree wasn't done. He wanted her to feel the same

hurt he had when she told him she was getting married. Following close behind her, he said, "What? You can't talk now?"

Trying to ignore him, Jaz quickly took to the steps, falling before she reached the third one. "Ah, shit," she whimpered.

Immediately growing concerned, Kyree rushed to her aide. "You a'ight?"

"Move the fuck away from me!" She smacked his hand away.

"Fuck it then," Kyree threw his hands up, walking away. "I'll wait for Fat Boy in the car."

Trying to get up, but failing horribly, Jaz said, "Wait!"

"Tell that gump-ass nigga to come downstairs and help you!" Kyree yelled at her.

"He's not here, he's at his place. Shit!" Jaz struggled to pull herself up.

Stopping in his tracks, he looked up at the sky and shook his head. He turned around and saw her struggling to get up. Jogging over, he tried to help her.

"No, don't help me now. Let me call my gump-ass nigga," she said with an attitude.

"Man, cut it out," he dismissed her smart comment. "Let me see it."

Reluctantly, Jaz turned to face him so that he could see her knee.

"It's just a little blood. You'll be a'ight with some peroxide and some bandages. Come on." He placed her arm around his neck and tried to help her up the stairs.

"Ow. Ky, stop." Jaz had to stop because it hurt to walk.

Kyree placed her arm back around his neck and then lifted both of her legs off the ground, cradling her in his arms. "Give me the keys. I got you, ma," he assured her.

Jaz looked him in the eye and found comfort in his arms. She was sure he wouldn't allow her to fall. She handed him the key and wrapped her other arm around his neck as well. Kyree opened the door and carried her to the bathroom. Sitting her

146

down on the toilet, he searched through her cabinets for something to clean her wound with. Pouring alcohol on a few cotton balls, he bent down and reached for her knee. Jaz snatched her leg away.

"Uh uh, Kyree. That's gon' burn."

"Well, Jaz, you don't have any peroxide. Do you want it to get infected?" She shook her head no. "A'ight then, hold still. I told you I got you."

Jaz did as she was told and winced as he dabbed her knee with the cotton ball. "Shit," she grimaced.

"Stop being a baby," he said, placing a Band-Aid on her knee. "I'm done."

"Thanks," she said. He nodded his head, putting everything back in its rightful place. "Look, I'm sor—"

"It's cool, Jaz. You don't have to apologize to me. I know you're drunk."

"I'm not dru—" The words weren't even clean out of her mouth before she was turning over and spewing all of her stomach's contents into the toilet. "Arghhhhh!" she bellowed.

Kyree shook his head as he left her hovering over the toilet. Returning with a bottle of water and a warm washcloth, he dabbed her forehead, and held her head up so that she could drink.

Regaining her composure, Jaz sat with her back propped up against the tub. "Can you give me a minute alone? You can wait for Fat Boy in the living room if you want. No one's coming home tonight."

Kyree obliged her request, shutting the door on his way out. Finding a spot on her couch, Kyree reached for the remote off the coffee table. It wasn't long before he heard the sound of running water from Jaz's shower. He wasn't sure if Michael was coming home or not, so he kept his gun at his waist, ready if the nigga wanted to act stupid. Michael didn't look like the type, but he could never be too sure.

Looking all around, Kyree could recall when he and Jaz got their first place together. She had spent weeks decorating. She loved every minute of it. She was good at it too. Her place

147

now spoke wonders about her impeccable taste. Her living room was a combination of greens, browns, and blues. African art adorned her walls while pictures of family and friends rested on every table. Noticing that some of the art was on the floor instead of on the walls, Kyree did some investigating. It didn't take him long to realize that Jaz was moving. He figured she would eventually be living with Michael, but he didn't think that would be right now.

Placing his hands over his face in frustration, Kyree decided he needed a stress reliever. Going into his pocket, he pulled out a vanilla cigarillo along with a bag of the finest purp in Hampton Roads. He wasn't really much of a smoker, but it always worked at relieving whatever stress he was going through at the moment. Grabbing a magazine from off the table, he split the cigarillo, released the guts onto the magazine, and replaced it with the purp. After perfectly rolling it into a blunt, he retrieved his lighter from his pocket to dry it and then headed outside to the balcony.

Jaz slipped on a blue PINK by Victoria's Secret wife beater with the matching striped boxer shorts. Walking out into her living room, she thought Kyree had left, but quickly realized differently when she felt the draft from her open balcony door. Stepping out on the terrace, she saw him sitting on her patio chair, smoking a blunt. He looked as though he was dealing with something heavy. She went and stood in front of him. "What's wrong with you?" Jaz asked sincerely, knowing he only smoked when he was stressed.

"Shit," he said, taking a toke from the blunt. Jaz rolled her eyes and snatched the blunt from between his fingers. "What the fuck, Jaz!" Kyree barked.

"Calm down," she said, taking the blunt between her thumb and forefinger and bringing it to her full lips. Taking a pull from the blunt, Jaz thought back to the last time she partook in the herbal pleasure. She and Monica were seniors in college and Jaz was stressed about Kyree's reckless lifestyle. There was a time when she worried about him more than she did herself. Looking down at him, she moved in closer and sat on his lap. Straddling him with her thighs, she tried to lock eyes with him, but he refused to face her.

"Man, g'on head, Jaz. You're drunk." He turned his head.

Jaz took another pull from the blunt, and grabbed his chin so that he was facing her. Holding the smoke in her mouth, she inched closer to his face and blew the smoke at his nose. Taking the shotgun like a pro, Kyree inhaled the smoke and released it through his mouth. Jaz moved toward his ear, and with her lips pressed against it, she blew another cloud of smoke through his ears, and then turned to face him as he exhaled the smoke through his nostrils. Facing him again, she took another pull, held the smoke in her mouth, locked eyes with him, and with their lips just inches apart, released the smoke towards his mouth. Kyree held the smoke in his lungs and released it out in smoke rings. Jaz burst into laughter, and Kyree couldn't help but join her. They'd been practicing those tricks for years.

"You wild as hell, yo. And you're fucked up," he laughed her off.

Jaz rolled her eyes. "Why do you keep calling me Jaz?" she slurred with a glazed over look in her eyes.

He looked at her skeptically. "What you mean? That's your name."

"But you NEVER used to call me Jaz. I used to be your Jazzy," she pouted.

Kyree thought for a minute. He couldn't recall when he had last called her Jazzy, but he knew why he stopped. She was very much inebriated, but she had asked, and he was going to tell her. "'Cause you're not my Jazzy anymore; you're just someone else's Jaz," he said with all sincerity.

Jaz was beyond hurt, but the reality of the situation was that he was right. Nuzzling her nose into the crook of his neck, Jaz inhaled his scent. The buzz from the drinks and the purp had her completely fucked up. But she'd never admit it to anyone - not even herself. She kissed him on the neck, and he cocked his head to the side.

"Jaz, you're drunk," Kyree said.

"No...I'm...not..." she said between kisses on each side of his neck. Finding her place on his face, she greedily kissed his lips.

Kyree didn't want to take advantage of her, but the shit felt so right. Her breath tasted of the mouthwash she'd just used, her breasts sat up perfectly in her tank top, and her thighs and ass were begging to be squeezed and caressed. His dick was practically about to rip through his jeans. But as Jaz eased her hands up his shirt, the ring on her left finger grazed his back, and he was once again reminded of her upcoming nuptials. Visions of Jaz and Michael, packed boxes, and wedding bells popped into his head. Opening his eyes, he grabbed a hold of Jaz's wrists and pulled her off of him.

Jaz was confused. Quickly getting up, she ran inside the house in a race for the bathroom. Once again, she was throwing up. Kyree got up from his spot on the porch and went to check on her.

"You a'ight?" he asked.

"No! Get the fuck out!" she screamed, embarrassed, her head still over the toilet. She couldn't believe that she'd allowed herself to get played like that. She had practically thrown herself at him, and he turned her down. He'd never turned her down before.

"Hell naw! I'm sick of this shit. You moved on, and I'm trying to. So why don't we both try to stay the fuck away from each other?" he said, looking at his ringing cell phone. "A'ight, I'll be down in a second," he ended the call. "But like I was saying, I'm done with this. 'Cause all we ever do is hurt one another, and I can't keep doing that to you. It's not healthy for either one of us."

"Whatever, Kyree. Do what you do best. Leave me! Bye!" she said, malice in her tone.

She had no idea how hard that was for Kyree to hear. He never meant to leave her for three years, and had he listened to her, he never would've had to. But now shit was different, and he just had to do what was best for him. Protecting his heart from the only one who had ever managed to penetrate it was the best move he could make.

Giving her one last look, he said, "Bye, Jaz."

Hearing the door shut behind Kyree, Jaz slumped down over the toilet. She felt like such a fool. He was right. The odds were stacked against them and they were doomed to fail. She hated that she was so conflicted. Her mind and her heart were playing an emotional game of truth or dare. Hiding from the truth she didn't want to hear or face, she dared herself to love. As she hugged the toilet, praying to the Porcelain Gods, letting go of everything she'd eaten in the past few days, she wondered what she was going to do with her life. According to Kyree, he was never going to speak to her again, and although Michael still loved her, he wasn't speaking to her at the moment either. Beyond tired, she managed to lift herself off the floor. She brushed her teeth, placed the trashcan by her bedside, and fell asleep to the soulful sounds of Bridget Kelly's song "In the Morning". The song fit her mood perfectly as she drifted off to sleep, dreading the awful hangover that was sure to kick her ass in the morning.

CHAPTER 16

Jaz awoke the next morning to the sound of her ringing cell phone. Without even looking, she reached her arm out on her nightstand, but her phone wasn't in its usual spot. Propping herself up on her elbows, she did a glance around her room. The ringing of her phone had stopped, but the ringing in her ears was still present. Her head was spinning out of control as she rubbed her eyes, trying desperately to remember the other night's events. And then it hit her. It was as if she were watching a movie, only it was real. She lay back and put her hands over her head in frustration as she watched the drama series known as *Her Life* replay in her head. She remembered having a good time with her friends, getting into it with Michael and him leaving, Latrell and his confrontation with Monica, almost beating Asia's ass, and then Kyree basically saying he didn't want shit to do with her anymore. And as if on cue, she flung the covers over her body and made a mad dash for the bathroom.

"Arrgghh!" she barfed into the toilet. "What the fuck...arrgghh...did I...arrgghh...drink?" she asked herself. She couldn't understand what could have given her the worst hangover in her life. Sure, she'd had hangovers before, but none this extreme.

Thinking back to every drink she'd consumed the night before, Jaz was confused. She was sure she'd only had a half glass of champagne and two shots that she never even finished. She'd been drinking since she was seventeen. Two shots didn't do anything for her these days. Figuring it must have been the purp, she shook her head and flushed the toilet. "Fuck this shit. I'm never drinking or smoking again," she promised herself.

After brushing her teeth and washing her face, her phone started to ring again, but this time she saw it sitting on top of the toilet. Picking it up and not recognizing the number, she wondered whether or not she should answer it. Shrugging her shoulders, Jaz thought, *To hell with it.* "Hello?" she said in a low raspy voice.

"Bitch, it's just me." Monica laughed at the male voice Jaz tried to imitate.

"Oh." Jaz sucked her teeth and climbed into the safe haven of her bed. "Whose phone are you calling from?"

"I'm at the soul food place in downtown Portsmouth. I was calling to see if you wanted something to eat, but I can't find my phone. Please tell me you have it," Monica prayed.

"Yeah, I got it," Jaz said, remembering why she'd taken it with her in the first place.

"Thank God. I'm on my way to come get it now. We need to talk anyway."

"Naw, Mo. I just wanna go back to sleep," Jaz whined.

"I'm not taking no for an answer. Besides, it's twelve o'clock. I'll be there in fifteen minutes. You want anything?"

Rolling her eyes to the ceiling, Jaz said, "Naw, I'm good."

"Don't be tryna eat my food when I get there, 'cause I ain't sharing shit. So I'm gonna ask you again. Do you want anything, Jaz?"

Even though Jaz didn't have much of an appetite now, she was sure that seeing Monica's food would indeed entice her taste buds. "Yeah, get me the usual. And use your key, 'cause I'm going back to sleep." Jaz hung up the phone. Looking at the screen, she saw that she actually had five missed calls and two text messages, all from Michael. The text messages were just informing her that they needed to talk later, but first he had to help out at the hospital because they were short staffed.

Plugging her phone into the charger and placing it in its rightful place on the nightstand, Jaz tossed the covers over her head. She wished last night hadn't happened. Michael didn't deserve the attitude she gave him. But she was just so vulnerable and emotional, and unfortunately for Michael, she took out all of her pent-up frustrations out on him - and on Asia as well, but that was one she could live with. She wasn't happy with herself for getting out of character, but she knew they were sure to butt heads eventually. There was always something about Asia that Jaz didn't like, and her comments about Kyree last night only sent her over the edge even more.

Twenty minutes into a deep sleep, Jaz was awakened by Monica plopping down on her bed. Jaz didn't say anything; she only rolled her eyes and turned back over to go to sleep. Grabbing the remote from off the nightstand, Monica turned on the TV. Finding an episode of *Love and Hip Hop* on Jaz's DVR she'd never seen, she spread out her food in front of her on Jaz's bed and ate her pepper steak and rice. After the show went off, Monica couldn't take it any longer. She had to know exactly what happened last night, and Jaz was the only person who could piece things together for her. It was going on 2:00. Jaz had slept enough, in her eyes.

"Wake up, Jaz!" Monica shook Jaz's shoulder.

"Noooo," Jaz griped, throwing the pillow over her head.

"Don't make me get the water," Monica threatened.

Wanting more sleep, but knowing Monica was dead-ass serious, Jaz groaned and sucked her teeth. Wiping her eyes, she looked at Monica and shook her head. "What do you want, Monica?"

"I want you tell me what happened last night. But first I want you to go brush your teeth." Monica held her nose.

Jaz propped herself up. "Hell naw, you wanted me up! Now I'm up. I'm not doing shit. What you see is what you get!" Jaz blew her breath in Monica's face and Monica damn near fell off the bed.

"Eww, Jaz!"

Jaz laughed as she got up to go the bathroom and once again brushed her teeth. She kind of felt like she'd used her toothbrush more in the last few hours than she had all week. Returning to her room, Jaz saw her food sitting on the dresser. Picking it up, she took it to her bed. "Can you bring me something to drink?" Monica looked at her like she was crazy. "If you don't, you'll never know what happened last night." Jaz smiled, knowing she had all the leverage. Monica rolled her eyes as she got up to retrieve Jaz a bottle of lemonade from the refrigerator. "And some duck sauce packets!" Jaz yelled from the other room.

"Here!" Monica slammed the drink down on the dresser and tossed the duck sauce packets at Jaz.

"Thank you." Jaz gave a sinister grin.

"Whatever. Who puts duck sauce on fried chicken anyway?" Monica turned up her nose, and Jaz simply shrugged. "Just tell me what happened," Monica said.

Pouring all of the duck sauce packets over her fried chicken, Jaz paused for a split second before bringing the food to her mouth. The fried chicken, collard greens, candy yams, and cornbread, may have looked good to some, but Jaz was hesitant to eat it. She was so afraid she wouldn't be able to hold the food down. Deciding that it was best she eat something, she shrugged it off and took a bite full of her favorite meal in the world up to her mouth. Chewing slowly and not feeling as though she was going to have a visit with Uncle Earl, she began to chew normally. Looking up at Monica, Jaz noticed her impatience. Exhaling heavily, Jaz began to tell her as much as she could remember about the previous night's events.

Bringing her hands up to her face, Monica looked to be in shock. "Oh my gosh, Jaz! The last thing I remember was dancing with Mario on the dance floor. Right after that, he went to the bathroom and Bri gave me another shot - of what, I couldn't tell you. I just know it's the reason for my current amnesia." Monica saw her phone sitting on the dresser and raced to retrieve it. She went through the messages that she'd sent to Latrell and couldn't believe her eyes. She couldn't believe she'd said those things. What was more surprising than anything was the accuracy and truthfulness in every last text message. They all expressed exactly how she felt, but she didn't need to give him any ammunition to think she was an unfit mother. Shaking her head in disappointment, Monica started to cry. "What am I going to do, Jaz? They're going to take my baby away if they see this shit!"

"No the hell they're not, Monica," Jaz assured her, getting up to retrieve her clutch bag off her dresser.

"And how can you be so sure?"

"Because," Jaz said, tossing something on the bed.

Monica picked it up and noticed it was a phone. It wasn't one she'd ever seen before. It wasn't hers or Jaz's. "Whose phone is this?" Monica examined the iPhone.

"That nigga La's phone," Jaz said, sitting back on the bed. "I took it from him when he got into the scuffle with the security guard."

Monica's eyes grew big with excitement. "Jaz, I could kiss you right now!" She grabbed her around the neck and hugged her tightly.

"Look now, I told you about that gay shit. I told you I'm strictly dickly, bitch," Jaz joked.

"Shut up," Monica laughed and pushed her. "I really am grateful though."

"Don't be. I'm not going to allow that bitch-ass nigga to hurt you. What right does he have anyway, coming into town and not telling you and shit?" Jaz was pissed off. She hated Latrell and the smug air he breathed. Monica bit her lip as Jaz went on her "We Hate La" tirade. Stopping and taking a look at Monica, Jaz knew there was more to the story than she was letting on. "Wait. What aren't you telling me, Mo?"

"Wellllll..." Monica twisted her fingers in guilt.

"Aw, hell naw, Mo! You fucked him, didn't you?" Jaz shook her head, knowing Latrell could always win Monica back with his sex game.

"No I didn't!" Monica spoke up.

Jaz exhaled deeply. "I was 'bout to say."

Monica bit her bottom lip. "Well, technically, I just let him eat me." Jaz looked at her with her mouth agape. "But we didn't fuck though," Monica quickly said. Jaz looked as though she didn't believe her. "I'm serious, Jaz. I kicked him out after he ate me."

"So how'd this all happen?" Jaz wanted to know.

Monica broke down and told Jaz the whole story, from seeing him at the restaurant to him showing up at her house and telling her about his wife, to him eating her out.

"Damn. So what are you going to do? You gon' let him see Kayden?"

"Honestly, Jaz, I don't know. I've never wanted to keep him away from his son. He's going to have to show me he's genuine. I can no longer just take Latrell's word. It's been proven to not be good for shit." Monica let out an exasperated breath. "But I do know I don't want the courts involved. I just hope we can work this out in a civilized manner, like adults."

Jaz nodded her head in agreement. "I'm sure y'all can," she admitted, letting the words sink in for a second. But there was still one question Jaz just had to ask. "Ay Mo, how did you get that nigga out the house without giving him none?"

Monica shook her head in embarrassment. "Girllll, I used that gun Kyree gave me. I told the nigga he was what he ate, and considering he just ate my pussy, I held the gun on him until he left."

By the end of the story, Jaz was in tears with laughter. She couldn't believe her ears. "Bitch, you really aimed a gun at this nigga?"

Monica shrugged. "I don't know why I did it. I just know I was mad and I allowed my emotions to get the best of me. You know what I mean?"

Jaz stopped laughing only to shake her head, thinking about her encounter with Asia the previous night. "Don't I know it."

Noticing her best friend's sudden change in behavior, Monica knew something was wrong. "What's up, Jaz?"

"Well, you weren't the only one who did some fucked up shit last night," Jaz said as Monica looked on in anticipation. "You can't remember shit, and I wish I could forget all the shit I did."

"What did you do?"

"Well, Michael showed up, and things were going a'ight until he started trippin' and we got into it. It was petty as hell, Mo. So he got up and left. And then while I was dealing with that bullshit, I asked Kyree if he could take you home for me, and that bitch Asia said something to me and I popped off."

Monica sucked her teeth. "What you do, Jaz?"

"Nothing. Why do you automatically assume it was my fault?" Monica gave her a look that said it all. Jaz did have a tendency to let small things get to her, especially when she kept shit bottled in for too long. "Look, I didn't do shit. Kyree broke it up before I swung that bitch around the parking lot like a rag doll."

Monica let out a slight chuckle. "Well, it was bound to happen sooner or later. She does have a snotty-ass attitude sometimes. What'd she say anyway?"

Jaz contemplated telling Monica. There was so much she had kept from her lately, and she knew Monica was going to be disappointed and hurt. Jaz just had to tell someone how she was feeling. With all that was going on in her life, she needed to talk to her best friend. She and Monica never kept secrets from each other. But Jaz didn't want her to worry, so she had neglected telling her everything. Now was her moment of truth. Taking a deep breath, Jaz looked away.

"She said some shit about fucking Kyree and I just snapped," Jaz shrugged.

Monica brought her head back and just looked at Jaz. "And why do you care?"

Jaz sucked her teeth. Monica was never going to take her side on this. "I don't, Monica. I was just drunk and I think I just needed a reason to hit that bitch."

Monica looked at her sideways. She knew Jaz wasn't telling her everything and she was just waiting for her to finally be honest.

"I'm serious, Mo. I think I was just mad at Mike. I guess the liquid courage got the best of me. I've been throwing up all—" Jaz couldn't finish her words before she was making a run for the bathroom. She jumped up so fast that Monica barely had enough time to react.

Walking to the bathroom, Monica figured Jaz must've had a hangover. Her head was bent over the toilet, getting rid of the chicken she'd just eaten. "Damn." Monica shook her head, holding Jaz's hair back. "Bri got yo' ass too, huh?"

Jaz started laughing as she lifted her head. "That's the thing, Mo," Jaz said, trying to stand up, but not without a hand from Monica. "I only had two shots and a little champagne," Jaz said, reaching for her toothbrush.

Monica thought that was kind of weird. Jaz was usually six shots in before she was even tipsy. She had been a professional at holding her liquor since before they were even old enough to legally consume the substance. Monica tried to think back to the last time she'd seen Jaz throw up from a hangover, and she couldn't. Not once had she ever been the one holding Jaz's hair. Jaz had always been the one holding Monica's hair, soothing her, and then laughing at her drunken stupidity the next day. This wasn't like her best friend. Monica stared at her skeptically.

Jaz looked up at Monica, eyes wide and toothpaste dripping from her mouth, and said, "What?"

"Nothing," Monica said suspiciously.

"Well, fine then," Jaz said, annoyed, turning off the water. "I'm going back to sleep," she said, crawling under her covers.

"Whatever, Jaz." Monica grabbed her purse.

"Lock my door on your way out."

Finally hearing the door shut, Jaz took a sigh of relief. Dozing off into a deep sleep, she was awakened twenty minutes later by a thud hitting her in the rear. "What the ..." Jaz quickly turned over to see what had hit her in the ass. She reached over to pick up the blue box and adjusted her eyes to read it. "Clearblue...pregnancy test?" she read aloud.

"Yeah, bitch!" she heard Monica yell from the kitchen. "I went to get you one, 'cause I believe your ass is pregnant." Monica walked back into her room and handed her a bottled water.

"I have to change my locks. Your ass is crazy." Jaz looked at her with disbelief.

"Don't waste your money. You know I'll get a key anyway. Now drink this water so you can take that test."

"Bitch, are you still drunk?" Monica shook her head matter-of-factly. "Then why the hell would you think I'm pregnant?"

"Because I know you, Jaz, and you haven't been acting the same lately."

"I've just been stressed. I'm getting married in a month, and it's just getting to me. That's all, Mo," Jaz assured her.

Monica picked up the box and handed it to Jaz. "Then put my mind at ease and take this test. Please," Monica practically begged her.

Jaz knew Monica worried a lot. It was one of the main reasons she held off on telling her imperative information. They were equally overprotective of each other, but Monica was always the more emotional one. Jaz usually guarded Monica from the truth, hoping to spare her feelings. Taking a deep breath, Jaz decided to put Monica's mind at ease. Getting up off the bed, Jaz snatched the box from Monica. "And after I take this test, and it proves you wrong, we're going to get your head examined," Jaz said. She was dead serious. Monica was surely losing her mind.

"And that's fine." Monica threw her hands up in surrender. "You need the water?"

Jaz gave her the hand, informing her that she didn't need the water. Luckily, for her, she already had to pee, and the sooner she did that, the sooner she'd be rid of Monica. Reading the back of the box for clarification, Jaz thought back to the last time she sat on a toilet, pissing on a stick. At the time, she was worried sick and happy all at the same time. She wasn't sure how she should feel, but couldn't wait to tell Kyree. He was supposed to be coming back from a trip to New York the day she found out. When he didn't return her calls or her texts, she instantly grew angry. She left crazy messages on his voicemail, cursed herself out for being pregnant by him, and was seconds away from cutting up every piece of clothing he owned.

And then as time passed she grew worried, and then angry again. After twelve hours without hearing from him, she was back to worrying. It wasn't until the next day that Jaz received a call from Ms. Jackie informing her of Kyree's arrest. She told her to be expecting a call from him later that day. Jaz sat impatiently awaiting his call by the phone. It seemed to take forever. When she finally heard from him, she tried her best to hold it together. But when she asked him how long he was going to be away, he simply told her he loved her, and Jaz knew that was his way of saying shit was fucked up. Jaz broke down and cried. When she got off the phone with him, the sharp pain in her side let her know that something was wrong with the baby. Remembering the long and painful drive to the hospital alone, Jaz shook her head, trying to erase the dreadful memory from her consciousness. Flushing the toilet, she placed the stick on a paper towel and proceeded to wash her hands.

"You about done in there?" Monica yelled out to her.

Jaz turned off the light to the bathroom and limped out into her bedroom to an impatiently waiting Monica.

Monica looked at her funny. It was the first time she'd noticed it. "Why the hell you limping?"

Jaz waved her off, remembering her trip up the stairs. "Long story."

Monica shrugged her shoulders. "Soooo, you finished, bitch?"

Jaz pushed the open pregnancy test in Monica's face and she flipped out. "Eww, Jaz! What the fuck is wrong with you? You pissed on that and then you rub it on my face?" Monica wiped her face repeatedly as Jaz set back and laughed. "That shit ain't funny!"

Jaz continued laughing. "I'm just fucking with you, Mo. That's the extra one they give you in the box. Calm down."

Monica looked at Jaz like she wanted to slap her. "You play too damn much." She pushed her.

"Whatever." Jaz flopped down onto her bed. "Gimme my remote." She snatched it from Monica's grasp. Monica looked at Jaz, waiting on her to give her some kind of answer as to what went down with the test. "What?"

"What happened?"

"Shit, I don't know. I left it for your crazy ass. I told you I ain't pregnant. Michael and I ain't fucked in months, and I'm still on the pill just in case. So go get your confirmation and get yo' ass out my house," Jaz said as she continued to flick through channels.

Monica rolled her eyes and walked to the bathroom. She flicked on the light and looked at the test sitting on the sink. She could barely read it, and she didn't want to touch it, so she lifted the paper towel with box to the test.

"Now can we go to Maryview to get your head examined?" Jaz yelled from the other room.

Monica came back with a depressed look on her face. She looked almost defeated. "I guess we can go to Maryview." Monica took a huge sigh.

Jaz laughed. "I told yo' crazy ass."

"But we won't be at Maryview for me. We'll be getting your prenatal vitamins girl." Monica jumped on the bed, excited.

Jaz stopped laughing to look at her. Monica was good for playing jokes, but this was one joke Jaz just didn't think was funny. She jumped up from her seat and raced to the bathroom. She closed her eyes tightly and said a silent prayer to God that Monica was just being her usual asshole self. But when she opened her eyes, the digital pregnancy test couldn't have been clearer. The test read: PREGNANT. Jaz's heart was beating a mile a minute, her head was spinning, and she thought that at any second she would pass out. It didn't help that Monica kept yelling, "I told you so!"

Jaz quickly remembered that those home pregnancy tests could be wrong sometimes, and that's why they usually gave you two in one box. Running to her bedroom, Jaz picked up the extra pregnancy test she'd used to play the trick on Monica. Racing back to the bathroom, she sat on the toilet and tried to pee again, but to no avail. "Shit!" she yelled aloud. She made another mad dash for her bedroom and retrieved the bottled water Monica had tried to give her.

Monica continued to laugh as a frantic Jaz ran around her room like a chicken with its head cut off, trying to guzzle the whole bottle of water. "Shut the fuck up, Mo!" Jaz snapped.

"Why are you so antsy? What, you didn't want to have a baby out of wedlock? Get over it, Jaz. This is the twenty-first century. Shit happens. You're getting married in a few weeks. It won't matter anyway. You and Mike are going to make wonderful parents."

Jaz stopped pacing at the mention of Michael's name, and that's when reality set in. There was no way in hell she could be carrying Michael's baby. They hadn't had sex in almost five months. But Jaz was on the pill, and she didn't really think about it. She continued to take the pill just in case she and Michael ever had a moment of weakness. She just wasn't expecting that moment of weakness to be with Kyree. But it was the only thing that made sense. Lately, she'd been eating nothing but duck sauce. She actually hated it, but it was one of Kyree's favorite condiments. She'd been putting on weight, her breasts were getting bigger, and she had been tired and irritable as hell lately. Realizing the severity of the situation she was in, Jaz sat on her bed, her head in her hands, and she began to cry. Noticing her best friend crying, Monica immediately rushed over.

"What's wrong, J? I thought you'd be happy about this. You always talked about having kids with Mike."

"That's just it, Mo." Jaz shook her head.

"What, Jaz?" Monica looked concerned as she sat in anticipation of whatever bomb Jaz had to drop.

Jaz looked at Monica and knew she had to tell her. She'd held in too much for too long. The weight on her shoulders was too much for her to carry on her own. It was time she stopped protecting Monica from the truth. It was inevitable, and she'd rather Monica found out now rather than later. "Mo, there's no way I can be pregnant with Michael's baby. I fucked up, Mo. I fucked up." Jaz tried to wipe her face with the back of her hand.

"Well then who—" Monica began. And then it hit her. She looked at Jaz, and the look on her face said it all. "Kyree?"

Monica leaped up. Jaz just continued to shake her head. She couldn't believe it herself. Seeing the pitiful look on her face, Monica was sure Jaz was going through some shit. Instead of lecturing her, she needed to be there for her girl, but it was just so hard. She had so many questions.

Jaz knew she did, so instead of holding up the walls, Jaz decided to knock them all down. She took a deep breath and told Monica everything. She told her about the baby she lost when Kyree was locked up, about how they talked things out the day after he was released, and about her moment of weakness. Jaz made sure she left nothing out this time. By the time she finished telling Monica everything, she felt 100 pounds lighter, and Monica's mouth needed help off the ground. She was beyond shocked. She wanted to be mad at Jaz for keeping so much from her for so long, but she didn't want to cause her any more worry. She simply consoled her and asked her the only question that truly mattered. "Do you still love Kyree?"

"But I'm engaged, Mo." Jaz looked at her desperately, almost as if she were searching for an answer that she couldn't figure out herself.

"That's not what I asked you, Jaz. You've kept a lot of shit from me, and we don't do that. So remember, before you answer this, this is me you're talking to."

Jaz thought for what seemed like forever. She couldn't for the life of her figure out why this was so hard. She really didn't want to hurt anyone, but the only person she was hurting was herself. The stress of it all was killing her. Every day she tried to come off as strong, but every night she went to sleep crying. Fed up and tired of lying like nothing was wrong, Jaz decided to speak with her heart and not her mind for once.

"Yes, Mo." She let out an exasperated breath. "I still love Kyree, and it kills me every day. I can't eat, I can't think, I can't sleep, I just can't be me without him. It just feels like a part of my soul is missing, like I walked around feeling like I was a whole person my whole life, only to realize when I lost him, I lost half of me. Mo, I've been in love with Kyree since I was twelve years old, only I just didn't know it. Every time I see him with another girl, I wanna beat that bitch's ass and cuss him out in every way imaginable." Jaz let out a slight chuckle through her tears.

But Mo was having a fight for her life trying to keep her tears at bay. She wanted to remain calm for Jaz, but she'd never heard her speak so intensely about anyone. She knew Jaz and Kyree had a crazy love before, but she always thought that if Jaz got rid of Kyree, she could be happier. She'd be less stressed and less worried. But now she was seeing, for the first time, that Jaz was going to be worried and stressed with or without him. At least with him, she'd be happy as well.

"And I know everyone thinks Michael is the one for me, and I love him Mo, I do. But I'm *in* love with Kyree. He makes me so mad, but yet, he makes me so happy too. I can't see my life without him, Mo. And now that I'm sure I'm carrying his baby, I don't know what I'm going to do. He's with Asia now," Jaz sniffled. "And he made it perfectly clear last night he didn't want shit to do with me anymore."

"Bullshit," Monica confidently said. "You know what this means, right?"

Jaz looked up confused. "No, what?"

"It means we have a nail tech to fire, and another one to hire." Monica and Jaz both let out a long overdue laugh. "And it also means you're going to have to talk to Kyree and tell him everything you just told me."

Jaz looked down at the floor. "What if he really doesn't want shit to do with me?"

"Girl, please. You two may not have known it, but I've known since the day you locked eyes on each other and immediately started throwing insults that you two were in love. I just don't know why I pushed you to be with Mike. Maybe I just wanted you to be happy, and I thought Mike could make you happy. I see now that I was seriously tripping. I'm sorry, Jaz. I should have been a better friend to you."

"What?" Jaz asked surprised. "I should be the one apologizing. I kept so much shit from you. I'm sorry. No more secrets?" Jaz said, her pinky out.

Monica shook her head but grasped on to her pinky anyway. "No more secrets," they swore with a pinky promise. "You're corny as hell," Monica laughed. Jaz shrugged. "But for real, y'all gotta work this shit out quick, 'cause I refuse to have my li'l' niece or nephew be somebody's bastard seed and my best friend be just another baby momma. I will carry both y'all asses on Maury, and if he ain't the daddy, I'm kicking out your two front teeth." They both let a boisterous laugh.

"Fuck you, Mo!" Jaz playfully snapped.

"First you fuck my bro, now you wanna fuck me too? Eww, Jaz!" Monica backed away from her.

Jaz couldn't help but laugh. She needed this - anything to keep her mind off of her current situation. One thing was for sure: she wasn't looking forward to it all. But the decision she was making just felt right. She just hoped Kyree felt the same way.

CHAPTER 17

Kyree lay in bed, his hands behind his head, staring up at the ceiling. He was deep in thought. He'd meant what he said to Jaz the other day about it being over and him finally being through with all the bullshit. It hurt him being away from her, but it hurt him even more being so close to her and still not being able to have her to himself. He was selfish when it came to Jaz, and that night, he finally came to the realization that there was no going back. He had to move on with his life, just as she had. She infuriated him with her teasing. He would've fucked her every which way on that balcony, but he couldn't get past the fact that she would once again fuck him and then go back to planning her wedding as if he didn't matter. Kyree wasn't an emotional nigga, but he felt as though she neglected his feelings way too often. He was certain now more than ever that she was no longer in love with him. Jaz was going to marry Michael, and the fire that once burned for him was blown out the day he told her to move on with her life. He blamed himself more than anyone. Jaz had done nothing but exactly what he said: "move on".

The words played over in his head like a broken record as a delicate hand caressed his chest. "So what's the plan for today?"

Kyree looked down at a stirring Asia. She'd just awoken from getting her back broken out. They'd spent all weekend together having animalistic sex, only leaving the house for food. Today was Tuesday, and she wasn't in a rush to get back to a job she was sure she no longer had. But Kyree had business to tend to. Their time together was fun while it lasted, but it definitely had to be cut short.

"Sorry, shorty, I gotta take care of some business," Kyree said.

"Well, then what am I supposed to do?" She gave him a disappointed look.

Kyree licked his lips as if he were deep in thought.

"Ugh," Asia huffed, quickly getting up. "Well can you at least take me home? You know I haven't had my car with me since I've been here."

Kyree thought for a moment. He really didn't have time to take her home. His silence told Asia all she needed to know. She sucked her teeth, giving him a disgusted look.

"I should've known you wouldn't give a fuck." She stomped toward the bathroom.

Kyree watched from the bed as she put on a show. He hated dealing with women and their emotions, but he hated being the bad guy even more. He had promised her they'd spend all week together. He blamed himself for her being out of a job. If it wasn't for all of his drama, she'd probably still be cool with Jaz and wouldn't feel so uncomfortable around the salon. He got up from the bed, grabbed his keys, and as Asia was coming out of the bathroom, she walked into his bare chest.

"Get out of my way." She tried to push him, but to no avail.

"Calm down and listen," Kyree said. Asia rolled her eyes, but did as she was told. "Look, I'm riding with Fat Boy. Take my car, go home, change your clothes, and I'll have Fat Boy bring me by there so I can take you out tonight."

Asia smiled and hugged him tightly around his neck. They usually never went out, and the fact that he was letting her use his car again showed her that he really did care somewhat about her. The first time she just knew it was all because he felt sorry for her because he had to take Jaz home, but now Jaz wasn't even around. No one could tell Asia that she wasn't winning as she took the keys and pulled away from Kyree's house in his 745. Kyree really didn't trust her, or too many people for that matter, but he figured it would calm her down for the time being. Besides, he didn't mind letting her put a few miles on his whip. He was in the process of getting a new toy anyway.

Dressed and out of the shower, Kyree sat down on his couch to play a game of 2K14 on his PS4 until Fat Boy arrived.

He was knee deep into a heated game with The Pacers and The Heat when he heard a knock at the door. He looked at the clock on his cable box and noticed Fat Boy was kind of early. *Good, I can whoop this nigga on the game real quick before we leave*, Kyree laughed to himself. Putting his game on pause, he got up to answer the door. When he took a glance through the peephole to make sure it was him, Kyree took a step back. It most definitely wasn't Fat Boy at the door. He had to do a double take to make sure his mind wasn't playing tricks on him. But he was right the first time; it was definitely Jaz.

He couldn't for the life of him figure out what she wanted. He was sure they had both made it very clear that they probably should never see each other again. He really had too much shit going on for him to worry himself with Jaz at the moment. Figuring that maybe she would leave, he watched her from the peephole. Comfortably dressed in a gray PINK by Victoria's Secret workout suit with a pair of black Nike running shoes, she appeared to be nervous and fidgety, taking numerous deep breaths. When he saw her reach for her cell phone, he darted for his. But he couldn't find the shit, and by the time he did, it was already ringing very loudly. He immediately silenced it, walked back to the peephole, and saw Jaz with her ear pressed against the door. She looked back and rolled her neck, and this time she knocked even harder now that she was sure he was home.

"Kyree, don't play with me. I didn't come to start no shit. I just came to talk to you. I know you're in there. I'm not leaving until you talk to me," she continued to knock.

Taking a deep breath, Kyree decided to give in. He swung the door open, causing Jaz to jump. She wasn't sure if it was from surprise or if it was from the scowl that was plastered on his face. For the first time ever, he looked as though he hated her. He was noticeably annoyed and livid.

And she was right; Kyree was pissed. He was tired of the back and forth between the two of them. It was getting old and he wasn't trying to hear shit she had to say. But Jaz really didn't care. She had a lot to get off her chest, and Kyree was going to hear her out whether he wanted to or not.

"Can I come in?" she hesitantly asked.

He looked her up and down and then walked away, leaving the door open for her to enter. Jaz turned up her lip at him and shut the door behind her. She could've slapped him when she heard him say, "You got five minutes," and smirk. It was like déjà vu. Knowing he was still probably pissed with her from the other night, she dismissed it. Kyree plopped back down on the couch and turned his game back on. He wouldn't even acknowledge her presence.

"I know you're still pissed with me, but I have something important I need to talk to you about."

"I hear you. Talk," he said, more focused on the TV than anything.

Jaz sucked her teeth. She knew she was probably playing with fire, but she had to get his attention. She walked over to the TV and turned it off. Kyree jumped up and gave Jaz a look that could kill.

"What the fuck is wrong with you, Jaz?" he barked, heated.

"I had to get your attention. I'm trying to talk to you, Kyree." She pleaded with her eyes for him to give her his undivided attention, but he still refused to look at her.

"Then talk, Jaz." He walked right past her into the kitchen.

"Could you at least sit down for a second?"

"Naw, I'm good." He grabbed a bottled water out of the refrigerator.

Jaz took a deep breath and rolled her eyes. She was starting to think this was a bad idea. But she'd been trying to work up the nerve to talk to him for two days, and she needed him to listen.

"Your time is running out, Jaz. I got shit to do," he stated.

The coldness in his tone had finally gotten to her, and she lost her nerve. "Forget it." She turned to leave.

Kyree grabbed her arm and stopped her. "Don't do this shit again, Jaz. This is why I didn't wanna go through this shit with you today. I'm tired of this back and forth, cat and mouse shit. I'm moving on, ma. Just go on with your life and let me do the same."

"But I can't, Kyree." She looked down at the floor.

"And why the fuck can't you?"

"Because..." she started, on the verge of tears.

"See, this that bullshit I'm talking about, Jaz. Because what, Jaz, huh? Why the fuck did you come over here? What the fuck was so important?" He pulled up her face by her chin, forcing her to look at him.

"I'm pregnant, Kyree!" She smacked his hand away from her face and let out a long overdue breath.

Kyree backed away from her as if she'd just been diagnosed with the black plague. "I don't believe this shit," he said, shaking his head in frustration. Her words not only pierced his eardrums, but they also pierced his heart.

"I wanted to tell you as soon as I found out, but I wanted to be sure. I just left the doctor, and he confirmed it."

"Well congratu-fucking-lations, Jaz." He gave her a condescending clap and let out a slight laugh. "I hope you and the doc live happily ever after."

"Excuse you?" Jaz was taken aback. "You think I would come to you if it was his?"

Kyree's eyes grew big. "I know you not tryna say that it's mine."

She got into his face and started pointing her finger at him. "I'm not TRYING to say anything. I'm TELLING you. I'm PREGNANT...with YOUR child."

"Go 'head, ma. You expect me to believe that bullshit? We fucked once. You probably fuck that nigga every night. Miss me with all that, Jaz." He waved her off.

"Kyree, I haven't fucked him in months. I'm telling you the truth!" she cried. "I don't even want to be with him anymore, Kyree."

He continued to shake his head disapprovingly. This was an all-time low for Jaz. He never thought she'd go this far. And over what? Jealousy? "This is about Asia, huh?" he said.

Jaz looked at him like he had two heads. "Nigga, you must be crazy. I don't give a fuck about that hoe."

"As soon as you saw me with her, you couldn't help yourself. You just had to one-up her. But what I don't understand is, if you're so happy with the quack, why the fuck you making up lies to keep me around, huh?" He got into her personal space and backed her up against the wall. Jaz tried to turn her head so that she couldn't see the fire in his eyes, but it was inevitable. His palms were pressed against the wall and his arms were blocking her from going anywhere. "What, that nigga ain't hittin' it right and you want the death stroke back? Is that it?" he whispered in her ear. Jaz closed her eyes tightly. She had never seen him so angry. He was like a madman.

"Fuck you, Kyree! I hate you!" she screamed at him.

Kyree stepped back and gave a sinister laugh. "You hate me so much you made up some bullshit-ass lie to get me back? Yeah, right."

"So basically, you're calling me a lying-ass hoe? Is that what you're trying to say, Kyree? Huh?" Jaz prayed desperately that he'd say no. She didn't want to have to slap the taste out of his mouth.

"I mean, hey," he said, throwing his hands up. "That's how you're acting right now."

Jaz brought her hand back to smack him across his face, but he caught her hand just in time. "Hell naw." He shook his head. "It ain't going down like that." He grabbed her arm and pushed her towards the door.

"But I'm telling you the truth, Kyree. I am pregnant. Ask Mo," she continued to cry.

"Oh, I don't doubt that you're pregnant. I just know it ain't mine," he said, opening the door.

"It is yours!"

"Now how would the doc like it if I paid him a visit today and told him that you were trying to pawn his child off on me?"

Jaz stood there stunned. "You wouldn't!" she dared him, not really sure if he would or not.

Kyree shrugged.

"Fuck you, Kyree!"

"Bye, Jaz!" he said right before slamming the door in her face.

Jaz stood there in shock for a moment before making a brisk walk to her car. Once in the safe haven of her car, she sat in the parking lot of Kyree's apartment and cried. This wasn't the Kyree she knew. She'd never expected him to be so heartless.

But little did she know, a few yards away, Kyree was in his house experiencing the worst heartache ever. He was still convinced that the woman he loved was carrying another man's child. It took everything in him not to comfort her when she cried. He hated to see her cry, but he just wasn't buying her tears today. He wouldn't be the nigga he was if he believed some shit like that. With his forehead and hands pressed against the wall, Kyree tried to steady his breathing, but it was hard for him to get past the hurt. His mind drifted from the huge blow Jaz had just delivered to him, to the lie she tried to tell, and finally to the fact that there would be no hope for them now, and he just snapped.

BOOM! Kyree hit the wall with so much force that he put a hole through it. "Fuck!" he yelled, more from his emotional state, than from the blood trickling down his knuckles. He was angry at the world and he wanted to do nothing more than to get away from the bullshit. And almost as if he could read his mind, Fat Boy called and said he was outside. "Give me five minutes," Kyree said before ending the call.

Rinsing the blood off his hand, Kyree made himself a homemade bandage with a towel. Jaz was really fucking with his head, but he had to stay focused. He was on his way to go handle a major move with Fat Boy. If this deal with his connect went through, he was sure to retire a millionaire in under a year. Any doubt he had in his mind about his safety was put to rest as soon as Jaz told him about her pregnancy. Although his mother and sister may have said otherwise, he really saw nothing else he had to live for. But first, he had some unfinished business he had to take care of. There were some people in his life he had to get rid of for good, and he didn't have time to waste.

While Kyree pondered his future, Jaz drove around aimlessly for hours, just riding around Hampton Roads. She had a full tank of gas when she left Kyree's house, but now she had less than a half a tank. Monica and a few others blew her phone up, but Jaz didn't bother to check to see who it was. After three missed calls and a couple unread text messages from Monica, Jaz decided to turn her phone off. She needed some time to herself. Her day had gone from sketchy to downright shitty.

After leaving the doctor's office and him telling her that she was indeed pregnant - and six weeks, at that - Jaz knew she had to tell Kyree. She had no idea how he was going to react, but she knew she didn't want to waste even a second this time. Last time she neglected telling him, she had a miscarriage, and she didn't end up saying anything until three years later. She regretted it to this day, and she refused to let that happen again. When she went to his apartment she was uncertain of how things would end, but she wasn't expecting him to be so callous and cruel.

But despite all of his harsh words, she still loved him more than anyone she'd ever loved, which was why she was on her way to Michael's house to end things with him, once and for all. She couldn't continue to hurt him. He deserved someone who was going to love him for the great person that he was. He needed someone who could return his love, and Jaz just wasn't that someone. No matter how hard she tried to fight it, her heart still ached for the gangster asshole that probably wasn't shit to most, but was the shit to Jaz. She swore to God when she saw him again that she was going to slap him so hard, he was sure to briefly go deaf. It pissed her off just thinking about him basically calling her a lying hoe. She gripped the steering wheel until her knuckles turned white, she was so angry with him. But she'd worry about that later. She had more pressing issues at the moment.

174

With her iPod on random, Jaz could've thrown it out the window when she heard it play Jazmine Sullivan's "In Love with another Man". "What the fuck?" she said aloud. That song was just too personal at the moment, and it was the last song she wanted to hear. She reached for her iPod to change the song, but it fell in between the seat. She tried to reach for it while driving, but she couldn't fit her hand down far enough to reach it. Finally getting fed up with the whole thing, Jaz simply said, "Fuck it," and turned off the radio completely, riding the rest of the way in silence.

Pulling up to Michael's mini mansion in Virginia Beach, Jaz thought she had to be the biggest fool on the planet. Any woman would kill to live in that house with the fine-ass doctor and make beautiful babies. But Jaz was always fighting the norm. They were set to be married in a month, and here she was about to break his heart into two. She couldn't help but ask herself, "For what?" A nigga who, if she saw him at any second, she would punch him in his face? Shaking her head, trying to think, she had no idea what she was going to say to him, but she knew she wasn't going to tell him of her deceit. It would only add to the hurt she was already going to cause him.

Jaz checked her face in the mirror before exiting the car. She'd been crying off and on since leaving Kyree's house, but she wanted to look presentable when she broke the news to Michael. Taking a deep breath, Jaz exited the car and ascended the long driveway to his doorstep. She always did love his humongous wraparound driveway. There was enough room for at least eight cars. Three alone belonged to Michael. He had a blue Range Rover, a black Dodge Challenger, and a silver 750. The man loved his cars.

Looking around at all of his cars, Jaz noticed one that she'd never seen before. Well, actually, she had seen it before, just never in Michael's driveway. With her brow furrowed, Jaz said, "He wouldn't." Her heart raced a mile a minute as all different thoughts ran through her head. She dropped her keys in a rush to get inside the house. She was barely through the door when she heard the commotion upstairs. Taking the steps

175

two at a time, Jaz got to the top step and followed the sounds to the guest bedroom. She knew there were definitely some punches being thrown because she could hear stuff falling and someone being pushed against the wall.

"Oh my God! No, Kyree!" Jaz burst through the door, expecting to see Kyree and Michael fighting, but what she saw was ten times worse. Her heart stopped, her body grew hot, and her head started to spin. For a split second, everything around her went black. She thought she was going to pass out. Finally regaining her vision, Jaz could only muster up three words. "WHAT THE FUCK!"

"Oh my God, Jaz!" Michael screamed, quickly grabbing a sheet from off the bed to cover his naked body.

Jaz couldn't believe her eyes. He was standing there, naked, with an erection that was dwindling at the sight of Jaz. But what got Jaz even more riled up was who he was fucking. Walking into her man's house and seeing his naked ass fucking someone was one thing, but when he moved and she saw who he was fucking, Jaz thought she could surely kill them both.

"It's not what it looks like," Michael tried to explain as he quickly grabbed his boxers, trying to put them on and stumbling to the floor.

"Then what the fuck is it, Mike?"

"I can explain, Jaz," Michael tried to reason, still failing at pulling up his shorts.

"You don't have to explain shit, Mike. This bitch act like she didn't know. She knew," Asia said, calmly putting on one of Michael's shirts and a pair of his shorts.

"Shut the fuck up!" he shushed her.

Jaz tried to control her breathing. She had to bend over to keep herself from collapsing. Michael ran over to her aide. "Baby, you alright?" he asked, placing one hand over her back.

"Get your fucking hands off of me!" Jaz smacked his hand away and he tried to comfort her again, but she quickly kneed him in the groin.

"Ah shit!" he screamed, going down with the quickness, grabbing at his throbbing crotch.

Jaz ran her hands threw her hair in frustration. This could not be happening. She needed to get away from this situation before she killed them both. "I can't take this shit right now!" she screamed. She turned to leave, but Asia just had to throw salt on the wound.

"That's right, bitch. I got both yo' men," Asia smirked, following behind her into the hallway. "I just got one question." Jaz stopped dead in her tracks. She wanted to hear what the bitch had to say. "How my pussy taste, bitch?"

Asia had finally crossed the line, and something inside of Jaz snapped. Jaz turned around with the quickness and sent a mean right hook to the side of Asia's face. Asia never even saw it coming as she fell to the floor. Jaz could've left it at that, but she didn't want to. Asia had been asking for this ass whoopin' for a long time, and Jaz was going to give her what she wanted.

"Stand up, bitch! I don't want you to say I sucker punched you. Stand yo' ass up!" Jaz egged her on. Asia backed away on her hands, trying hard to pull herself up, but her lip was swelling up fast and it was hard for her to gain her balance. "I said get up!"

Asia had been waiting to whoop Jaz's ass as well. She hated that Jaz got everything she wanted, and today was her day to show her just how much she hated her. With a new burst of energy, she used the wall to balance herself. She looked over at Michael, who was no help, still moaning and rolling on the floor about his shattered jewels. Reaching onto the table, Asia quickly grabbed a flower vase and flung it at Jaz's head.

Jaz ducked just in time, and now she was even more heated. She charged at Asia, pushing her down on her back. Jaz continued to sit on top of her, throwing blow after blow, wherever she saw fit. "I give yo' ass a chance to fight fair...and you wanna come at me like that? Fuck you, bitch!" Jaz had completely blacked out. She looked like a madwoman. All Asia could do was scream and grab a hold of Jaz's hair. "Let go of my hair, you stupid bitch!" Jaz punched her one last time in the eye, causing her head to hit the floor.

Asia let go of Jaz's hair to grab at her throbbing head. Jaz was about to send another blow to her face when Asia's crying snapped her out of her trance. She looked down at a weeping Asia, and that's when Jaz saw the blood that covered not only Asia's face, but also Jaz's hands. Her breathing was heavy as she realized what she had done. She didn't regret it for one second, but she couldn't believe she'd blacked out like that. Getting up from off the floor, Jaz looked down at Asia and then over to Michael. Sure, she had done her dirt, so could she really blame him? *Hell yeah, I can!* Jaz reasoned with herself.

Jaz walked over to Michael and knelt down towards his ear so that he could hear her clearly. "In case you hadn't noticed, the wedding is OFF!" Jaz got back up, looked at him, and said, "Oh yeah, I'm pregnant. But it ain't yours, limp dick muthafucka!" She kicked him one last time in the groin.

"Ahhh!" he shrieked.

Jaz then walked over, and knelt down beside an almost unconscious Asia. "I told you I was going to kick your ass. Fuck with me again if you want to," she warned her. "Now ask the good doc to fix your sorry ass up," Jaz said, getting up to leave. She looked at both of them in disgust. They both had tried her, and both had committed an epic fail. She shook her head as she turned to leave.

Jaz walked outside with everything that went on during her day weighing heavy on her brain. In no time, her day had managed to go from bad to worse. She couldn't believe what she'd just seen. Her mind was wrecked with endless questions. The whole time she was feeling guilty about sleeping with Kyree, she wondered how long Michael was sleeping with Asia. She couldn't for the life of her figure out why Asia hated her so much. She'd never been nothing but nice to her. That wasn't to say she trusted her, but until recently, she'd never disrespected her. Jaz looked down at her hands. The pain in her knuckles was starting to kick in.

"Ouch!" Jaz hissed, but not from the pain from her hand. Jaz had to stop walking for a minute to grab at the pain on her side. The aching lasted all of ten seconds and then quickly subsided. Taking a deep breath, Jaz figured it must've been a cramp or something. She hadn't been to the gym in a while, and the beat down she put on Asia had caused her to work up a sweat. She walked to her car and started it up, but before she could put the car into drive, the discomfort returned. This time, it was way worse than before, and instead of lasting ten seconds, it lasted twenty.

"Oh my God!" Jaz screamed, recognizing the all too familiar pain instantly.

Jaz thought she was having a nightmare. Powering her phone back on, she waited until the pain subsided and redialed that last number she'd called. But after two rings, she was sent to voicemail. "I fucking hate that muthafucka!" she screamed, pressing the end button. Feeling lightheaded, Jaz dialed Monica's number and she instantly picked up.

"Girl, where have you been? I've been calling you all day!" Monica chewed into her.

"Listen, Mo, I'm not feeling too well. Something's wrong," Jaz droned.

Immediately hearing the panic and anxiety in her voice, Monica grew worried. "What's wrong, Jaz? You okay?"

"I don't know, I just...ahhh!" Jaz screamed.

Monica's heart began to beat rapidly. "Jaz, where are you?" Monica said, promptly grabbing her keys, ready to go see about her friend. "Jaz!" Monica screamed at her when she didn't get an answer.

Once again, the pain was gone, and Jaz was able to speak clearly. "I'm at Mike's house now, but I think I can make it to Sentara. It's only a few minutes away."

"Okay, I'm on my way," Monica said, instructing with her finger for Ms. Ray to finish her client's head. "Jaz, stay on the phone with me while you drive." Monica hit the unlock button on her cars' remote.

"Okay," Jaz whined.

Monica tried to make small talk with Jaz as they both made their way to Sentara, but Jaz's groaning every so often was making it hard for Monica to concentrate. When Jaz said that she was at the emergency room, Monica still refused to get off the phone. Jaz convinced her she was okay to check in, so Monica reluctantly agreed, assuring her she'd be there in ten minutes.

Jaz proceeded to the front desk to check in. "Hello, my name is Jazmine Elliott. I'm six weeks pregnant and I'm experiencing major pains on my side. I think I'm having a miscarriage," she stated as calmly as possible.

At the mention of her being pregnant, the lady behind the desk grew more alert and immediately picked up the phone. "Ma'am, I'm calling the doctor down now," she said.

"Okay, thank...ahhhhh!" Jaz screamed again, bent over in pain. "God, please don't let me lose my baby!" she said aloud.

The nurse ran from behind the desk just in time to catch Jaz before she passed out. The last thing she saw before losing consciousness was her mother. She had a beautiful calming light surrounding her smiling face.

CHAPTER 18

J az awoke twelve hours later to a beeping sound. Looking all around, she tried to make a guess as to where she was. To her right, she noticed a sleeping Monica curled up in a chair. Quickly darting her eyes down and noticing the tubes in her arms, panic set in and the beeping monitor grew rapid as it hit her where she was and why she was there. Jaz reached down to touch her stomach and felt a sharp pain in her lower abdomen. Frantically turning to her right, she tried to call out to Monica, but her throat felt as though she'd swallowed sandpaper. Jaz tried to muster up as much spit as she could. Never before had it been so hard to say Monica's name, but Jaz managed to shakily get out. "Mo."

Monica blinked her eyes and quickly shot up from her spot on the chair. "Jaz!" Monica ran over to her side. Noticing Jaz struggle to speak, she grabbed a cup and filled it with water. She brought the straw up to Jaz's mouth and watched as she drank up every bit. "Is that better?"

Jaz nodded her head yes.

"Okay, I'll be right back, Jaz. Don't go anywhere."

Jaz gave Monica a look that said, *Where the hell am I supposed to go, bitch?*

Noticing how dumb her comment was, Monica had to laugh at herself as she turned to leave. She walked over to the nurses' station and they paged the doctor. Monica looked up at the end of the hallway and saw Calvin walking toward her, carrying the Frappuccino he bought her along with his large coffee and a bag filled with scones and other goodies. Her smile was all the confirmation he needed.

"She's awake?"

Monica nodded her head yes and Calvin quickly proceeded to her room. Placing the food he'd brought down on the counter, Calvin almost cried when he heard Jaz say, "Hi,

Daddy." Her voice was barely above a whisper, but it was comforting all the same.

For twelve hours, Calvin had been running himself ragged with worry. When Monica called him and told him Jaz was in the hospital, he got there as fast as he could. What shocked him even more was when Monica told him that the doctors thought she was having a miscarriage. He had no idea his baby girl was even pregnant, and he wanted to know why she would keep such a thing from him. But he couldn't question her secrets at this moment. All he wanted to do was hold and comfort her.

"Hey, baby girl." He hugged her and kissed her forehead. Jaz gave him a warm smile.

"You scared the hell out of us, girl," Monica said, frantically trying to stop the tears that wouldn't stop falling from her eyes.

"You feeling alright, baby girl?" Calvin asked.

Jaz somberly nodded her head. But she needed answers. She was sure she'd lost her baby, but she needed to hear the doctor say it for sure. "Daddy, what happened?" Jaz asked, her words shaking as she too started to cry.

Calvin had no idea what to tell her. Luckily, for him, the doctor walked in just in time to save him.

"I see you're up, Ms. Elliott. I'm Dr. Emerson," the tall and handsome doctor said. He was a 6'2" tall Italian with boyish good looks and deep blue eyes.

Jaz watched impatiently as he looked at her chart and checked the monitors. It seemed to take him forever and she was losing her sanity. She wanted him to just spit it out. The gloomy looks on Monica's and her dad's faces were killing her.

"Doctor Emerson," Jaz got his attention. "What happened?"

Dr. Emerson looked from Calvin to Monica, then back at Jaz again. "I'm sorry, Ms. Elliott, I thought they would have told you." He took a deep breath. "Well, Ms. Elliott," he continued.

"Call me Jaz, please," Jaz cut him off. The informalities weren't very comforting at all.

Dr. Emerson gave her a warm quick smile before taking another deep breath. "Well, Jaz, we had to immediately operate on you as soon as you came in. An emergency laparoscopic appendectomy was needed to save your life. Your father gave the consent, and we proceeded to operate." Looking at the confused and worried look on Jaz's face, Dr. Emerson went on to explain in more detail. "Basically, your appendix ruptured, which caused the severe abdominal pains in your lower right side you were experiencing. The surgery went very well, if I might add."

Jaz propped herself up on her elbows so that she was sitting up. It hurt, but Monica was right there to adjust her pillows. She wanted to sit up to make sure she understood him correctly. "So doc, what you're telling me is that I had appendicitis?" Jaz looked on for confirmation.

"Yes ma'am," he nodded.

"And..." Jaz started, beginning to cry again. "My baby? Is my baby okay?" she pleaded.

"Your baby is fine, Jaz." He gave her the most reassuring smile he could gather.

Jaz brought her hands to her face and let out a joyous cry. Never before had she heard such good news in her life. Her hands were shaking, her heart was pounding, and tears of joy flowed freely from her eyes. Monica was there with a soothing hand on her back, as she too was overjoyed.

"You have a very strong baby, Jaz. A rupture, such as the one you suffered, can leave behind many deadly and toxic fluids. He or she is truly a fighter and came through unscathed from the whole incident. I will tell you that your blood pressure is extremely high, and I do want to monitor it overnight. But after that, you're free to go home." He beamed again, and Jaz thought she could just melt from his smile alone.

"Thanks, Dr. Emerson." She gave him a cunning smirk in return. "Hey, Dr. E," Jaz said, getting formal with him as well.

He blushed. "Yes, Jaz?"

"Have you met my sister Monica?" Jaz looked over at Monica.

He smiled again, and Jaz thought she could just die. "I don't think we've been formally introduced, no." He brought his hand out to shake Monica's hand. "Hi Monica, I'm Robert, but my friends call me Bobby."

Monica blushed as she too shook his hands. "It's nice to meet you, Bobby."

Taking a glance at his watch, he said, "I'm scheduled to go to lunch now. Would you like to join me in the cafeteria?"

"Uhh—" Monica began.

"She'd love to," Jaz cut her off.

Monica thought she could slap Jaz. But the doctor was extremely handsome, so she looked up and said, "I'd love to. Just give me a minute."

"Great. I'll be just outside the door," he nodded his head. "Nice meeting all of you. Just give me a buzz if you need me."

"Will do," Jaz said, waving goodbye. When he was out of sight, Monica quickly replaced her smile with a scowl, directed at Jaz. She playfully punched her in the arm. "Ow!" Jaz grabbed her arm. "I'm in the hospital, remember?" She poked out her lip.

"Girl, please. You're going to be in the infirmary you keep playing with me," Monica warned. Calvin shook his head and laughed at their foolishness.

Jaz had almost forgotten he was even there, and when she turned to face him, the look he gave her said it all. He looked hurt, like he wanted answers as well. Jaz looked at Monica and Monica quickly got the hint.

"I'll be in the cafeteria. Call me if you need me." Monica gave her a hug. "Don't you ever scare me like that again," she warned her. Whispering in her ear, she said, "You die on me, bitch I'll kill you. Hear me, bitch?"

"A'ight, Ike." Jaz tried to control her laughter, since it hurt her side. *What's Love Got to do With It* was one of their favorite movies, and Jaz knew that line like the back of her hand. "Bye, crazy," Jaz shook her head. When Monica was out of sight she took a deep breath, prepared for the millions of questions she knew were to follow her dad's disappointed eyes. "I can explain, Daddy," she began.

"All I want to know is where that no-good fiancé of yours is. How can he not be here when his soon-to-be wife is in the hospital? And you're pregnant? When I see that bitch nigga, I'm going to crack his skull."

Jaz's eyes grew wide. Her dad was from the old school, and she was sure that what he was making wasn't at all a threat, but a promise. Her dad had never broken a promise to her. But as much as she hated Michael, she just wanted to let everything go. Before her dad went to jail for assault, and possibly murder, Jaz broke down and told him everything - well, almost everything. She left out the part about her finding Michael in bed with her former employee and fixed it up by saying he was unfaithful. She also told him that Kyree was indeed the father of her child, and not Michael.

The look on his face, after she revealed everything, made Jaz want to cry. "I'm sorry, Daddy. Are you mad?" She looked down at her lap. She was so ashamed.

Calvin shook his head no. He wasn't at all mad. Disappointed? Yes. But not mad. He and Jaz usually talked about everything. He hated that she would keep such a thing as serious as this from him. But he couldn't say he didn't see it coming. From the day that Jaz introduced him to Michael, Calvin knew he wasn't the man for her. He admitted favoritism toward Kyree, but that was only because he admired his ambition. He reminded him so much of himself, and he felt as though his daughter was safe with Kyree. But he couldn't tell Jaz anything about Michael; she had to find that out on her own. He was just glad that she found out what he saw the day he laid eyes on him, now, and not later when they were already married and it was too late. He was just waiting for Jaz to make her own mistakes and hopefully learn from them. But now knowing the truth, Calvin had one more question. "So does Kyree know?"

Jaz pursed her lips and shook her head no. She couldn't tell her father Kyree disowned their baby. It would crush him. It was bad enough it was killing her. "I haven't had a chance to tell him. I just found out the other day."

"Well, when are you going to tell him?"

"Soon," Jaz sighed, wanting desperately to end this conversation

"Well, good, 'cause all this foolishness has got to stop. I knew you two belonged together since day one. Now y'all need to get your shit together and take care of my grandbaby before I slap you both upside the head."

"You're crazy," Jaz laughed. "But you might have to. I don't think Kyree wants anything to do with me."

"Naw, baby girl, that's where you're wrong. I know the look of a man when he's madly in love with someone. And if it's true and real, like I'm sure it is, then you two have nothing to worry about."

Jaz smiled at her father. He was always so confident and assuring. She just wished she could share in his optimism. She really didn't see things as such. Kyree had expressed to her his feelings, and it had hurt Jaz to her core. She didn't think she could take any more rejection from him. If her doctor knew the amount of stress she was under, high blood pressure would be the least of his concerns. He would probably put her on suicide watch. She didn't even want to think about Michael, but there were still so many unanswered questions she had for him. She was sure she hadn't heard the last from him, especially not after dropping a major bomb and then abruptly leaving. Jaz needed to talk to someone, so when Monica returned, Jaz sent her father to get her a change of clothes from her house. As soon as he left, Jaz told Monica about her horrible day.

Monica couldn't believe it. She knew Asia could be a bitch, but she never thought she would stoop so low. But what pissed her off the most wasn't even Michael; it was her brother. She couldn't believe Kyree would say those things to Jaz. He was definitely out of line. "I can't even breathe right now I'm so mad at his ass," Monica seethed.

186

"No, Mo. It's not worth it. He was mad, and it's understandable. I'm sure he'll come around eventually," Jaz said, more to convince herself than anyone.

Monica shook her head, and just as she looked up, she made an immediate snarl. "Speak of the damn devil!" Monica turned up her lip at Kyree.

"Well, hey to you too, Mo." Kyree figured Jaz must've told her what happened, and from the look on her face, he was definitely sure it was before she had actually called him. When Monica called to tell him Jaz was in the hospital, he cut his trip to Charlotte short and raced home, getting two speeding tickets in the process. He was angry with Jaz for lying to him, but he would never be able to live with himself if something were to happen to her and he was too stubborn to go check on her.

"And what the hell are you doing here?" Monica got into his face, her arms folded, on the attack.

"It's cool, Mo," Jaz assured her. "Could you give us a moment alone, please?"

Monica grabbed her purse and purposely bumped Kyree on the way out.

They were finally alone, and Kyree couldn't help but notice the needle in Jaz's arm. It was only an IV, but coming out of her arm, it looked way worse to him. He hated everything about hospitals, from the smells, to the sadness, to the feel of death. It was all so eerie for him. "How you feeling?"

"It was just appendicitis. I'm feeling better, just a little tired."

Kyree nodded his head. He had never had a more awkward conversation with Jaz. He had questions, but he didn't want to bring up the baby, especially since he'd already made up in his mind that it wasn't his anyway. Jaz patiently waited, as he said nothing else. She rolled her eyes to the ceiling.

"So your, um," he stammered for the right words, "baby a'ight and shit?"

Jaz brought her head back, shocked. "OUR," she emphasized the word, "baby is doing fine. Thanks for asking."

Kyree sucked his teeth. He wasn't trying to hear this bullshit today. He came to see her because he was concerned. He really wasn't in the mood to argue. "Look, Jaz, I just came by to check on you. But since I see you're okay, I'm gonna roll out." He turned to leave, placing a get well soon teddy bear on the counter next to her bed.

Jaz's eyes grew big; she was taken aback. This could not be happening again. "So wait," she stopped him from walking. "You still don't believe me?" she asked him dumbfounded.

Kyree gave her a look that pretty much said it all. Jaz was boiling. She picked up the teddy bear off the counter and flung it hard at his head. She winced in pain, quickly being reminded of the appendix she'd just had removed. "You know what? Fuck you, Kyree! You don't have to believe me. I don't need you for shit. I did fine without you these last couple years, and my child and I will be fine without you now!"

Kyree turned around and gave her a sinister smirk. "Asia told me how you fought her because you were jealous, and how you were probably making this whole thing up to get me back."

"What?" Jaz was shocked to say the least. "Did she tell you the whole story? I'm sure she didn't."

"She didn't have to. I know how you love to control shit. Always want what you can't have. But just stop it, Jaz."

Jaz thought her head was going to explode she was so mad. "So let me get this straight..." She had to gather her thoughts before she threw something else, something not as soft as the teddy bear, at his head. "You took that bitch's word...over mine?" Jaz pointed at her chest.

"I'm just saying the shit don't add up."

Jaz nodded her head slowly as if she were finally coming to grips with something. "You know what, Kyree? It's cool." She threw her hands up in surrender. "Go live your life. I won't bother you anymore. Just know this." Kyree waited for her response. "I'm done. There is no going back. I NEVER want to see you again. Just stay the fuck out of my life, and I'll stay the fuck out of yours."

She said it so calmly and with such finality, that it almost scared Kyree. He gave her one last look, picked up the bear and put it back on the counter, and then turned to leave. This was not where he was expecting things to go, but Jaz just wouldn't let the baby shit die.

Seeing Kyree leave this time was like a wakeup call for Jaz. With one hand on her stomach, she thought about the baby growing inside of her and the high blood pressure she'd been recently warned about. She didn't want to risk losing her baby for anyone. God gave her a second chance, and she was going to use it wisely. When she passed out and saw her mother's face, she took it as a sign. Her child was a blessing, not a curse, and Kyree really didn't have to care. She knew he was mad, but this was a little extreme. The ultimate blow for her was when he took Asia's word over hers. It was like a punch to her already-bruised abdomen. Kyree had managed to make her feel lower than low. She hated him for the power he always seemed to have over her. Feeling the tears approaching, Jaz forced herself not to cry. She refused to ever shed another tear over him. Crying had gotten her nowhere. She was beyond fed up and finally at her breaking point. Her one and only concern now was her unborn child. "It's just me and you, kid," Jaz said, looking down at her stomach.

While Jaz sat contemplating her life, Kyree made a brisk walk to the elevator, repeatedly pressing the down button, hoping it would speed up the process. Seeing Monica approach him, he sucked his teeth. "I ain't got time for this shit, Mo. G'on somewhere."

"Whoa!" Monica threw her hands up, surprised by his attitude. "I just came to ask you where you were going."

"That's none of your business," he said frankly.

"It is my business when my best friend is lying in a hospital! Pregnant! With your child!" She poked him hard in his chest.

"Ha!" Kyree laughed. "She better go holla at her fiancé. Jaz trippin' fighting Asia and shit." Kyree couldn't stop shaking his head. He couldn't believe Jaz lately.

"Nigga, you trippin'. I bet Asia didn't tell you the reason why Jaz beat her ass was because she caught her fucking Mike when she went to break up with him so she could be with your dumb ass." Kyree looked as though he were considering the possibilities. "Ask yourself this," Monica began. "Has Jaz EVER lied to you? In all of the years you've known her, has she ever told you a lie? Do you think she would bring some shit like this up to you if she wasn't 110% sure?" Monica was losing her patience with Kyree. "I'm gonna let yo' stupid ass think about that for a minute. Now you go cool off and be here to take her home tomorrow!" she ordered.

Monica didn't even wait for his response as she turned to leave. Her words resonated heavy on his brain. Kyree thought for a long time, and not once had Jaz ever lied to him. She would never do anything so cold as to lie about a child either, especially not after they'd already lost one. He thought long and hard before he made his next move. As he stepped off the elevator, and headed outside to Fat Boy's truck, he knew where his next move was most certainly going to be. Kyree needed answers, and there was someone he needed to visit to get those answers.

Kyree dropped off Fat Boy at some chick's house, and he agreed to let him use his truck. Asia still had Kyree's car and he wasn't ready to get it from her just yet. He had some business to tend to. Stepping out of the truck and into the parking lot, Kyree made his approach.

"Oh shit!" Michael held his chest.

"Calm down, my dude," Kyree calmly stated. "I just wanna talk to you."

Michael was skeptical. He'd heard nothing but bad things about Kyree's reputation. Jaz hadn't told him much, but he'd done his research. But Kyree honestly did just want to talk. He'd come to Michael's job with nothing but the mere intention of him answering a few questions. It was three in the morning, and it could have just as easily waited until later, but Kyree needed answers now.

Michael tried to steady his breathing as he fixed his posture. "Well, what do you want to talk about?"

"You and Jaz. What's up with y'all right now?"

"Well, she caught me in a pretty compromising position and called off the wedding." Michael looked away, ashamed. "I've been trying to talk to her, but she's not at home and she won't return any of my phone calls. I miss her, and I'm sorry. I hope she can forgive me. I love her, I just–"

Kyree placed his hand up, signaling for Michael to stop. He didn't want him going any further with his apologies and confessions of undying love for Jaz. That was not why he came there. "Did she really catch you and Asia fucking?" Kyree cut straight to it.

Michael sighed heavily. "Yeah, unfortunately she did. But I see she shouldn't be too bent up about it, seeing as though you two are about to have a baby." Michael bit his jaw.

"What makes you so sure the baby ain't yours?" Kyree just had to know.

"Jaz made up some rule about no sex before the wedding after I proposed. We haven't had sex in almost five months," Michael explained. As much as it pained him to see Jaz go, he knew that she was never fully committed to their relationship.

Kyree put his hand over his mouth and slowly grabbed at his face. He couldn't believe it. "Word. A'ight, cool." Kyree turned to leave.

"But ay, man," Michael called out to him. Kyree turned around. "Watch out for Asia. I was her doctor first, and she's not the most stable person."

Kyree nodded his head as he got into the truck. Michael's words were still replaying over in his head as he knocked on Asia's door. He wasn't sure what he meant by unstable, but he for damn sure wasn't going to stick around to find out. After he got his keys, he was done with her for good. He was just about to knock again when Asia opened the door.

Kyree jumped back slightly at the sight of Asia's face. He wasn't expecting to see her looking so fucked up. Jaz had really done a number on her. Her lip was busted, her cheeks were bruised, and both of her eyes were black and blue. When he talked to her on the phone earlier, she told him that she and Jaz fought, but she failed to mention that the only fighting back she did was with her own face.

But even with a busted lip, Asia still managed to smile at him. She opened the door for him to come inside and hugged him around his neck, but Kyree didn't return her advances.

"What's wrong? Is it because of the way I look?" Asia covered her face in embarrassment.

Kyree had to stop himself from laughing. Her face really was fucked up. "Naw, it ain't that."

"Then what is it?" Asia asked, worry plastered on her face.

Kyree looked away. He hated this part. "Look, what we had was fun and all, but we gotta end this shit."

"What? Why?"

"Because this shit ain't gonna work."

"Why? Because of Jaz?" Kyree didn't say anything, and Asia just nodded her head. "I knew it. You don't even have to say it." Asia shook her head. "You know that baby ain't yours, right? She's probably not even pregnant."

"She is pregnant. And it is mine. I talked to Mike." Asia looked away. She wasn't sure how much he knew. "Why you fuck Jaz fiancé, yo?" Kyree just had to know why she would do something so malicious. Asia stood with her arms folded, tapping her foot, and biting the inside of her jaw. "Asia!" Kyree spoke up.

"What? Shit!" she barked.

"Did you hear me? Why you fuck Mike?" Kyree asked, agitated.

"Because!"

"Because what?"

"Because I'm sick of everybody thinking that bitch is the shit. She ain't shit. Got all you niggas fooled, kissing the ground that she walks on." Asia continued tapping her foot. "I can't stand that hoe. She caught me with a sucker punch. I should press charges for what she did to me."

"Don't do that," he said.

"And why not?" Asia rolled her neck.

"Because I said so, that's why!" Kyree fumed.

"Nigga, please!" Asia waved him off. "Goodbye!"

Kyree did not feel like taking it there with Asia tonight. As far as he was concerned, what they had was over. He shook his head and turned to leave, but not before grabbing his keys off the table.

Asia walked behind him as he made his way to the door, taunting him the whole time. "Oh, and tell your bitch when I see her..." Kyree stopped in his tracks to listen to her. "I'm gonna drop kick her dead in her stomach." She was deep into a sinister laugh when she felt the life being choked out of her.

Instantly, upon hearing Asia talk so recklessly about harming Jaz, Kyree snapped and proceeded to choke her. He had her up against the wall with both of his hands gripped firmly around her neck. "What the fuck you say? Huh?"

But Asia couldn't talk if she wanted to. She clawed at his hands, but to no avail. Kyree wasn't in a right state of mind. When she started to turn blue, Kyree grew scared and released her. He had never before put his hands on a woman. He felt ashamed as he watched Asia gasp for air, and as she regained her color, he wondered how someone so beautiful could be so ugly.

Bending down so that she could hear him clearly, he said, "Don't fuck with me, ma. The police won't be able to save yo' ass if you try me."

Kyree was starting to think he'd been locked up too long, because either people forgot or they just didn't know who the fuck he was. Niggas were truly testing his gangster and he couldn't have that. But knowing that money talked to most hoes, he went into his pocket, pulled out a big wad of money, peeled off two stacks, and set them beside her. "This should cover the damages. Now, I ain't gon' tell you but once. STAY THE FUCK AWAY FROM JAZ!" Kyree picked up his keys that he'd dropped on the floor and then stood up. He hated that he had to

193

resort to this, but he was starting to think there were a few screws loose in her head or something.

As soon as he was gone, Asia jumped up and locked her door. Reaching for her purse, she dug inside it, still trying to steady her breathing. Finally finding what she was looking for, she pulled out the orange tube and tried desperately to pull the white cap off. Her hands were shaking, and when she finally got it opened, white pellets fell to the floor. Hurriedly trying to pick them up, she grew frustrated. "Fuck this shit!" she screamed, throwing the orange tube across the room. Nervously running her hands through her hair, she scooped the tablets off the floor and poured them all down the sink. "I don't need this shit anymore! I don't need anyone!" she yelled, flicking the switch on the wall.

"Hahaha!" Asia gave a sinister laugh as the garbage disposal sounded, signaling the end to all of her Abilify pills. The only thing on Asia's mind now was getting rid of all the things in her life that she felt held her back.

CHAPTER 19

The next day the doctor said it was okay for Jaz to go home. He was still concerned about her high blood pressure, but he said he'd do a follow up in a week when he removed the sutures from the appendix removal. With all of her belongings packed, Jaz sat and watched TV until Monica arrived to pick her up. She assured everyone she could drive on her own, but the doctors wouldn't allow it. *Ring Ring!* She turned to answer the ringing hospital phone.

"Hello?" she answered.

"Jaz, it's Mo. I've been calling your cell phone all day, what's up?"

Jaz rolled her eyes. "Oh, I turned that shit off. Michael was getting on my damn nerves. I'm not trying to hear shit he has to say."

"That nigga..." Monica just shook her head.

"Yeah, fuck him. But anyways...what the hell is taking you so long? I'm hungry, I'm tired, and I'm ready to go. And I seriously think my female nurse is trying to fuck me."

Monica burst out laughing. "What the hell?"

"Girl, I'm serious. Three times this hoe has asked me did I want a sponge bath. And each time, I told that hoe I can wash my own ass." Monica was still laughing, but Jaz was serious. "I'm dead ass, Mo. This shit ain't funny. Now hurry the hell up before I beat that bitch into the ICU."

Monica stopped laughing to get serious for a minute. "See, about that—" Monica began.

"Mo! What the hell?"

"Well, if you would've had your phone on, you would know that I can't make it. Shit is hectic at the salon. But I got someone coming to get you."

"Who? My daddy?"

"Naw," Monica said.

"Then who, bitch? 'Cause I'm ready to go."

"Calm down, J. Kyree will be there to pick you up in a half hour."

"What!" Jaz just knew she'd heard her wrong.

"He talked to Mike, and he believes you now, Jaz. He's been calling you all morning," Monica pleaded her brother's case.

"So wait, he had to talk to Mike to believe me?" Jaz huffed. "He couldn't just take my word for it?"

"Jaz, don't do that. He's really sorry."

"He's sorry, alright!" Jaz nodded her head and bit her lip.

"Jaz!" Monica scolded. "Don't be like that."

"Whatever, Monica. I'll talk to you later."

"Jaz, wait—"

Click.

Jaz hung up the phone before Monica could even finish. She didn't want to hear shit else Monica had to say. It seemed like everyone in her life was on Kyree's side. No one gave a damn about how he made her feel with the harsh things he said to her. With the way she was feeling right now, if she never saw him again, it would be too soon. Kyree had said and done things that she didn't think she could ever forgive him for. She didn't think she could make it in a car ride with him without killing him, but she really didn't have a choice in the matter. Someone had to sign her out before she could leave. She couldn't drive anyway; Monica had taken her keys.

Scrambling to come up with a plan, Jaz was drawing a blank. Looking out the window, she saw that her room wasn't too far from the ground. "Hmmm..." she thought. "Oops," she quickly remembered, staring down at her stomach. "Mommy's a little slow, I know, baby," she giggled, rubbing her stomach. Glancing out the window again, she could see her car just outside. She felt like she was so close to freedom, but she couldn't quite grasp it. And then, out of nowhere, it hit her.

Quickly grabbing her purse, she reached into the back pocket and found her spare key. She'd never needed it - until now that is. "And Monica said I was dumb for leaving my spare in my purse. I'll show her ass." Jaz gave a sly smirk. Peering out into the hall, she noticed the nurse's station was packed with every nurse in the building. "Shit," she cursed, knowing she'd have to get one of them to buzz her out. Just as she was about to give up hope, she saw a young girl who looked to be about sixteen. She was a cute petite girl, light-skinned, with long, sandy brown hair. Jaz saw her chance and she was going to take it. "Hey!" The girl turned around toward Jaz. "You wanna make fifty bucks?"

An hour later, Jaz was dropping her keys on the coffee table of her room at The Towne Place Suites in Virginia Beach. After seventeen-year-old Latrice discharged Jaz from the hospital, Jaz thanked her and gave her fifty dollars as promised. She then got in her car with no idea as to where she was going. She was sure that if she went home, Kyree would follow her there. She didn't feel like dealing with him just yet. She needed time alone, so she put in her prescription at the drug store, and as soon as it was ready, she checked into a hotel.

The suite had all of the amenities so she didn't have to leave. There was a full refrigerator, a stove, microwave, and a big screen TV. But most importantly, there was peace and quiet. After taking the pills the doctor gave her, Jaz showered and then curled up in the big king-sized bed, praying to God for answers on what to do with her life. She knew she couldn't hide forever, but for the time being, the hotel would suffice as her safe haven.

Drifting off into a deep sleep, Jaz awoke ten hours later feeling like a new life was breathed into her. Extending her arms to the ceiling, she smiled. She couldn't remember the last time she'd slept so peacefully. Flicking on the TV, she grabbed the toothbrush she'd just recently purchased and waited for her phone to power on. She figured she might as well let someone know that she was okay before they sent out a search party. Her phone wasn't on a good five seconds before it was buzzing with alerts. Her first instinct was to turn it off; she didn't need the drama. But her second instinct told her that her family was probably worried sick.

Rinsing her mouth out, Jaz took a deep sigh as she retrieved her phone and began to scroll through the messages. In total, she had sixty-three text messages, forty-seven missed calls, and twenty-two voicemails. She hadn't turned her phone on in almost two days, so she was expecting a lot of messages, but damn, this was ridiculous! The first fifteen text messages were all from the night she was rushed to the hospital. She couldn't believe Michael had tried to apologize and justify his cheating. "He has got to be the stupidest doctor in the world!" Jaz continued to shake her head. Scrolling past Michael's name, she proceeded to check her other messages. She smiled at all of the get well texts she'd received from all of her friends. She felt so loved and appreciated. Her brief happiness was put on hold when she came across the messages from Kyree. In every message, he'd apologized for his actions as of late, but Jaz wasn't trying to hear it. No amount of apologizing could make up for him hurting her. She loved Kyree with all of her heart. He was the only man to ever capture it, and he'd probably be the last. She just couldn't allow him that right again.

Listening to her voicemails, Jaz decided to save all of them. She and Monica would have a great laugh at Michael's expense later on. When she got to Kyree's voicemails, she had to laugh at herself for pulling off and leaving the hospital with everyone being none the wiser. Kyree seemed to be stressed with worry and so did Monica. Her father was the same, but she decided to call Monica first.

"Jaz!" Monica didn't even bother with the pleasantries. She was just so happy to hear from her.

"Yes, Mo." Jaz picked up the remote and started flicking through the channels.

"Don't 'yes Mo' me! Where have you been? Are you okay?"

"Calm down, Mom," Jaz laughed, knowing Monica hated that.

"Don't get cute, Jaz." Monica rolled her eyes. It wasn't her fault that she worried a lot. She blamed the people around her for causing her to worry. They had the problem, not her.

"Ugh," Jaz huffed.

"But where have you been, for real?" Monica wondered.

"I'm okay, Mo. I just couldn't face Kyree just yet. He really hurt me with a lot of the shit he said. I feel so tired. I just needed some time alone."

"Shit," Monica said. "Now I feel like shit for sending him up there. My bad, Jaz."

"It's cool, Mo. I'm over it."

There was a brief silence before Monica asked, "So where are you?"

"Don't worry about it. Just know I'm safe."

"So you're not going to tell me where you are?" Monica asked, dumbfounded.

"Nope," Jaz simply said. For all she knew, Monica could be sitting right next to Kyree. She didn't think Monica would intentionally do something like that, but she had to take extra precautions. Monica's silence told Jaz that her feelings were hurt, so she had to make up for it. "Look, Mo, I know you're feeling some type of way, but I really do just need some time alone. The doctor said I needed rest, so I'm getting it."

Monica sucked her teeth. "Well, I guess. But when are you coming back to work?"

"Next week."

"Okay. Well let me call everyone and tell them you're alive before they have the whole hood looking for you."

Jaz laughed, knowing she was right. "Alright. Call you tomorrow. Kiss my Kay-Man for me."

"Will do." Monica ended the call, and then turned around

"So what she say? Where the hell she at?" Kyree grilled her.

"I don't know, boy, shit!" Monica was so frustrated with him. He'd been nagging her all day about Jaz.

"What the fuck you mean you don't know? She didn't tell you?" Monica shook her head no, but she really didn't think she would even tell him if she knew where Jaz was. Hearing the tired and dreary tone in Jaz's voice, she was starting to think she really did need the time alone.

"Look, she's doing fine. Just give her some time."

Kyree wasn't trying to hear that though. Upon hearing that Jaz was carrying his child, he wanted to do nothing in the world but take care of them both. All he ever wanted to do was be with Jaz. Now that they were bonded together by this child, Kyree just wanted her to know how much he loved her. She could be so stubborn sometimes, and he knew he was probably going to have to do a lot more apologizing and ass kissing to get her back.

But Jaz wasn't sure what she wanted from Kyree at this point. She wasn't even off the phone five minutes with Monica before Kyree sent her a text message.

>>> **11:13 PM, Kyree: Mo told me ur ok. I just wanna talk 2 u. Call me.**

Jaz rolled her eyes and turned her phone off. She still needed more time. In the past few months, her world had been completely flipped upside down. She'd gone from being a bride-to-be, to a girl lost and confused, carrying her ex's child and regretting every decision she'd ever made. Loving Kyree just wasn't going to cut it anymore. With Michael, she had security. With Kyree, there was uncertainty. Sighing heavily, Jaz picked up the phone and stared at it intensely before deciding to power it on again. She went to dial Kyree's number, but immediately decided against it and dialed the number to the nearest pizza place. When her pizza arrived, Jaz curled up in the bed with her iPad and watched movies on Netflix until she fell asleep.

The next morning, Jaz awoke to more missed calls and texts from Kyree. Last night he was more calm and relaxed, but today, he was tense and irritated. She laughed to herself because she was sure he was losing his mind. "That's what he get!" She rolled her eyes. Deciding to go to the mall for some retail therapy, she got up to shower and brush her teeth. Noticing she had a missed call from Monica, she dialed her back and put the phone on speaker. When the phone stopped ringing and Jaz didn't hear anyone, she said, "Hello?"

"Oh, so you can answer the phone for Mo, but you can't answer the shit for me?"

Jaz was mid-gargle when she heard Kyree's deep voice over the phone. She nearly choked trying to get her thoughts together.

"It's cool. You ain't gotta say shit." He licked his lips and shook his head. "But yo, you will hear me out." Jaz didn't say anything. She couldn't even if she wanted to. She was too busy trying to recover from the mouthwash that had gone up her nose from choking. "Look, I'm sorry for the way I acted. I ain't mean that shit I said. A nigga just didn't know. What'd you expect me to think, Jaz, huh?" He waited for her to say something, but she just stood there staring at her phone. "I know you're mad at me, but I talked to yo' boy and I know the baby's mine now."

"So you had to get confirmation from some nigga you don't even know?" Jaz spoke up. "You couldn't just take my word for it?"

"Nah, I didn't mean it like—"

"Well then what the fuck did you mean, Kyree? 'Cause I'm lost." She tapped her foot to calm her already-plucked nerves.

"Fuck, Jaz! Why you always gotta do this shit?" He rubbed his temples. "Look, I'll keep it one hunnid since you asked for it. You know no nigga in his right mind would've believed the story you told me. I just needed to get all the facts first. But I do still love you, and I really want to make this work."

"Well, with an apology like that, how could I not be thrilled?" Jaz sarcastically laughed.

"Yo, stop being a brat. What else do you want from me? Shit!"

"Nothing, Kyree. You just want everyone to follow your lead and I can't do it anymore. Too many times, I've let you put me second when I should've been, without a doubt, first. Too many times, I've taken your word, whereas you have to second-guess mine. And way too many times have you made it look so easy to walk away while I've begged you to stay. But you know what?" Jaz gave a slight chuckle. "I'm tired of it. If you want to see your child, I don't have a problem with that. I know you'll make a great father. But a relationship between the two of us will NEVER work. Goodbye, Kyree."

"Wait, what—"

Click! Jaz hung up on him mid-sentence.

Kyree sat looking at the phone. *What the fuck just happened?* he asked himself, not sure where things had gone left.

But Jaz felt rejuvenated. She held her on, spoke her piece, and got the last word, all without shedding a tear. Yeah, some retail therapy was definitely what she needed. Shopping was always the cure she needed to make herself feel good. While at the mall, Jaz saw that the salon was calling her. She wasn't sure if it was Kyree or not, so she answered it and waited for the caller to speak.

"Hello? Jaz?" Monica yelled, annoyed.

"Oh, my bad. I wasn't sure if it was you or your arrogant-ass brother." Jaz rolled her eyes.

"Why would he be calling you from the shop phone?"

"I don't know, Monica. You tell me," Jaz said, getting on the defensive.

"What the hell is that supposed to mean?"

"He called me earlier from your cell phone. I thought it was you, so I called it back."

"Jaz, I haven't had my phone all day. I thought I left it at home, but I haven't had time to go back and get it. You think I would give him my phone knowing you said you needed some time alone?"

Jaz thought for a moment. "Damn, I'm sorry, Mo. I'm just a little on edge is all. I know you wouldn't do no shit like that."

"Well you better act like you know before I have to beat some sense into yo' ass." Monica warned. Jaz laughed. "So what did my brother have to say?"

"I'd rather not make myself mad while I'm in this mall," Jaz shook her head.

"It's cool. Don't let him stress you. Just enjoy your time alone."

"I am. Believe me. But enough about me. Have you talked to La since the weekend at the club?"

"Yeah. We're supposed to meet up next week," Monica stated.

"I hope it's in a public place this time. I don't wanna hear you going from saying, "fuck YOU La,' to you saying, 'fuck ME, La'."

Monica couldn't help but laugh at Jaz. "Ugh, I hate you, Jaz."

"Love you too." Jaz smiled.

The girls talked the whole time Jaz was at the mall. By the time she was done shopping, she had racked up on clothes. The next day she went shoe shopping, and then the day after that she went toy shopping for Kayden. This was the most expensive time alone she'd ever spent. She only left to go shopping, but while she was in her room, she did a lot of reflecting. Her Kindle was filled with new books she'd purchased and read in no time, the salon's books were done for the month, and she'd watched every movie she wanted to see but didn't have the time for before.

She tried to busy herself so as not to think about Kyree, but it was so hard, since he kept calling and sending her text messages. She had to block his number just to get some rest. But that didn't stop him from once again invading her dreams and taking over her every thought. He was like a disease she couldn't rid herself of. The more she tried to stop thinking about him, the more she actually did. She came to the realization that once she thought she was over him, she never really was. The moment she said, "Yes, I'll marry you" to Michael, flashbacks of her and Kyree played in her head. She lied to herself so many times that she'd actually started to believe the bullshit.

Jaz wondered just how mad she could actually be at Michael. She'd done nothing since they'd gotten together but push him away. She didn't want to live with him, she lagged in the wedding plans, and she was never truly honest with him. If she were, she wouldn't have led him on. But Jaz couldn't get over catching him in the act of fucking another chick, especially since it was Asia. She felt like a fool for not seeing it sooner.

But who could she blame? Had she been fully committed, he would've never had the opportunity to go astray - at least not without her knowledge. Had it been Kyree who always said he had to go to work at odd hours of the night, Jaz would've gone with him. But now that she thought about it, Michael could've been sleeping with Asia, and whomever else, for months. She'd done her dirt, and she accepted it. But catching Michael in the act was a totally different scenario. It was all too real. She'd never trusted Asia in the first place, but at least now she knew it was for good reason. Everyone said she was trippin', but Jaz knew Asia's phony disposition was all a front. She was just glad she found out now rather than later.

Everything was all starting to sink in, and after almost a week at the hotel, Jaz was finally ready to go home. She'd just left her doctor, who had removed her stitches, and said that she was good to go back to work the next day. It was Monday, and the salon was closed, so she didn't have to return to work until Tuesday. Her clients were so happy to hear that she was back that she was actually booked for the whole week. She hadn't even told anyone she was returning home. She knew she had a long week ahead of her, and all she wanted to do was take a nice long hot bath and go to sleep in her own bed.

Placing her key into the lock, Jaz opened the door to her apartment, tossed her suitcase inside, and reached for her other bags. She thought she could take them all in one trip, but she'd clearly underestimated her shopping abilities. "Shit, I'll get the rest tomorrow," she said, tossing another bag into her house. Locking the door behind her, she turned around, "Ahhhhhh!" she screamed, grabbing at her chest.

Sitting there on her living room couch was Kyree. He sat tranquil and unfazed by her screams. Whereas he was calm, Jaz was about to shit bricks. She had no idea he would be at her house. She thought she'd have time to prepare for their encounter. He was never even supposed to know she was home - hell, no one knew she was home.

"Boy you scared the shit out of me!" Jaz stated, still grabbing at her chest. "Are you trying to send me into early labor?" Kyree didn't say anything; he just looked at her and shook his head. "How in the hell you get in here anyway?"

"Don't worry 'bout all that." He stood up and walked over to her. Jaz felt two feet tall as his 6'4" frame stood in front of her, staring her down, not saying a word.

"What?" She looked away, annoyed.

"Jaz, don't give me that shit. I've been calling your ass for a week and you haven't answered for me once. You wouldn't even tell me where the hell you were."

"I didn't have to. You ain't my damn daddy, Kyree." Jaz walked past him.

"Ay," he grabbed her arm and stood in front of her. She looked him up and down as though he'd lost his damn mind. He released her arm. "Cut it out," he said, not at all phased by the look she gave him.

"Kyree, don't start with me today. Please just go home," she tiredly stated.

"I'm not going nowhere. You're carrying my child, and I'm going to be here every step of the way," he stated sincerely.

Jaz wasn't trying to hear him. Quite frankly, she was tired of the same old bullshit and truly couldn't care less. "Ha!" she sarcastically chuckled.

"I'm serious, Jaz! I love you, and I know you still love me." He pulled her in close and she pulled away.

"Kyree, please!" Jaz held up her hands in front of him.

Kyree was confused. He tried being tolerant with Jaz, but she knew more than anyone that he really didn't have much tolerance for petty shit. "Look, Jaz," his voice raised an octave. "I'm tryna fucking apologize to yo' crazy ass. You've been gone for damn near a week; you ain't called or even sent a nigga a fuckin' text message. I'm sorry, shit!"

Jaz stood expressionless. "Are you finished?"

"What?" Kyree's eyebrows drew inward.

Jaz brought her hands together, and clapped after each syllable. "Are...you...fin...ished...Ky...ree?"

Kyree just stood there. He had to remember who she was, because for a second, he saw himself backhanding her across the room. But he really didn't have anything else to say. Jaz's new attitude had him speechless.

When he didn't say anything, Jaz said, "Good. Now move!" She pushed past him and walked straight to her bedroom, slamming the door and locking it in the process.

"What the fuck just happened?" Kyree asked himself.

After running herself a hot bubble bath, Jaz lit a few candles. Once in the warm water, she let the water relax and console her. She had no idea where her attitude with Kyree came from, but she knew for sure he wasn't going to let the shit die. She had to laugh at herself for keeping her cool. She had to let Kyree know this wasn't going to be an easy task. As always, he'd fucked up, except this time, Jaz wasn't going to be the one to piece shit back together.

CHAPTER 20

The smell of bacon awoke Jaz before her alarm clock. It made her mouth water and she wondered where the smell could've come from, then instantly remembered her conversation with Kyree the night before. She figured he must've never left.

"This nigga." Jaz shook her head. Getting up from the bed, she took out her clothes and proceeded to get ready for her busy day. Once out of the shower, her stomach growled as she got another whiff of whatever Kyree was cooking, but she tried to ignore it as she gave herself the final onceover in the mirror.

Adjusting the pink wife beater she wore, Jaz couldn't help but notice how good she looked. Although simply dressed, her breasts were practically spilling out of her shirt and her ass in her True Religion blue jeans was sitting up extra high. Her hair had also grown tremendously, and the soft curls she wore were now past her neck. Sliding on the new pair of pink rhinestone-studded Anne Klein sandals she'd bought in retail therapy and her new favorite gold Betsey Johnson floral bracelet, Jaz tossed her pink Michael Kors bag over her shoulders and was ready to go. She took a long deep breath, not really in the mood to deal with Kyree, and turned the knob to her room door.

Jaz walked out with confidence, as if she didn't have a care in the world. She was looking for her keys when Kyree looked up from the refrigerator. He'd be a fool not to have noticed the pregnancy glow on her face. Jaz was the only girl who Kyree knew could make even the most ordinary outfit look like it belonged on a runway. She was always beautiful in his eyes, even when she was mad at him. He stood with his arms folded, leaning against the kitchen counter, watching her search high and low for her keys. She hadn't uttered so much as a hello to him. It was almost as if he didn't exist. But Jaz saw him. How could she not? His presence alone in his T-shirt and balling shorts had her attention from the moment she walked in the living room. Finding her keys probably would've been an easier task had she not noticed the dick print so visible in his shorts, causing her to slightly lose focus.

"Well good morning to you too, Jazzy." He looked her up and down and she still ignored him.

But her heart almost stopped when she heard the nickname he called her. It was the first time he'd called her that in a while. It was comforting, but it wasn't enough.

"I see you're still mad. I made breakfast." Kyree motioned toward the pancakes, eggs, and bacon he'd been making for the past hour. He'd even set the table.

"Here they are," Jaz said aloud, picking up her keys from out of one of her decorative bowls. Rolling her eyes, she figured Kyree must have put them there.

"Do you hear me?" Kyree looked at her, but she refused to make eye contact with him.

"I'm not hungry," Jaz lied. Truth was, her stomach was roaring, and his food looked even better than it smelled. She wanted to dive right in, but her anger towards him was still very present.

"You gotta eat something," he said.

"Whatever. When are you leaving?" she asked, one hand on the doorknob.

"I'm not goin' nowhere. Didn't you hear me last night? I'll be here when you get home." He stuffed a piece of bacon in his mouth.

Jaz huffed, "Whatever, Kyree. Just make sure you clean my damn kitchen when you leave." She opened the door and slammed it on her way out.

Kyree shook his head. He knew he'd fucked up, but he couldn't for the life of him figure out how to get back right. Sighing heavily, he picked up his phone and dialed Monica's number.

"Hello," she answered like she was out of breath.

"Hell you doin', Big Head?"

"Fixing these light fixtures in the shop before we open. What you doing? And where you at anyway?" Monica asked.

"Shit. At Jaz's house."

"Y'all worked it out, huh?" Monica got excited.

"Naw," he admitted, sitting down to eat his food.

"Then how the hell you over there? Kyree, don't be worrying that girl," Monica warned.

"Chill out. I took yo' key yesterday and I've been over here since she came home."

"Say wha' nah?" Monica had to pull the phone away to look at it and make sure she was still talking to her brother and not an imposter.

"What was I supposed to do, Mo? She wasn't giving me a chance to explain myself."

Monica sucked her teeth. "Damn, Kyree, now she's gonna think I gave you her key. It's bad enough you took my phone the other day. What's up with you? You've been trippin' lately."

"Man, Mo, that's kinda why I called you." Monica listened intently as Kyree now sounded overwhelmed. "I've tried everything, and I don't think it's working. Mo, this girl has thrown me completely off my square. One minute she good, the next minute I feel like she wants to fuckin' kill me." He let out a slight chuckle, and so did Monica. "And the part that scares me the most is that I think I love her now more than I did before." Kyree just shook his head.

"Awwww," Monica cooed.

"Don't start that shit, yo," Kyree warned. He was never one to wear his heart on his sleeve, but Jaz seriously left him no choice. "I seriously just wanna say fuck it and leave her alone for good, but she's carrying my child now. I can't just leave her like that," he reasoned.

"Don't do that, Kyree. Jaz loves yo' stupid ass to death, but she's tired of you not putting in an effort. You give up too easily, and you're always pushing her away. Jaz just doesn't want to feel like she's the only one fighting for y'all's relationship for nothing."

209

"I fight for her - physically and emotionally," Kyree spoke up.

"Yeah, but look at how easy it is for you to give up on her! When you went to jail, you left her. When you got out, you wanted her back, but as soon as she told you she had someone else, instead of putting up a bigger fight for her, you gave up. And when she told you she was pregnant, you said she was lying." Monica let his silence inform her that he was in deep thought. "Now, do you think Jaz would have EVER given up on you that easily?"

"Damn," Kyree said.

Hours later, Jaz was coming home after a long day at the shop. Everyone was so excited to find out she was pregnant, but even more surprised to find out it wasn't by Michael. She also told everyone about Asia too. There was no sense in anybody around HER shop spreading rumors about HER. She left no room for wonder. If they wanted to know something, they could pretty much bet that it was coming from the horse's mouth.

Walking into the house, she tossed her keys down on the counter. Kyree was playing PlayStation 4 on the couch.

"How was your day?" he asked, placing his game on pause.

"Why are you still here?" She sighed heavily.

"Because I told you I ain't goin' nowhere. Now, how was your day?"

"It was fine, Kyree. Just leave me alone." She rolled her eyes at him and walked back toward her room. It was really baffling her why he was still there. She thought for sure by now he'd give up and say to hell with her, like always. But little did she know, Kyree had a plan. He wasn't going to walk out like he usually did. He was going to stay and prove his love to Jaz.

"You wanna come play the game with me?" he yelled back to her.

"No!" she shouted, reaching for her door to slam it. "What the fuck?" Jaz said aloud. She had to turn on her bedroom light to make sure she wasn't trippin', but her suspicions were confirmed. She made a brisk walk back into the

210

living room, where Kyree had resumed his game. She stood in front of the TV with her arms folded, giving him a look that could kill.

"Damn, girl, can't you see I'm trying to play the game?"

"Fuck yo' game!"

"What?"

"Nigga, you heard me. Kyree! Where is my damn door?"

Kyree had to try his best to keep his composure and prevent himself from laughing. It was true. He had taken her door completely off the hinges. "Yo, you slamming doors on me ain't gon' work, ma. I'm just tryna' talk to you, and you run in the room and slam the door. How are we gonna make it work for the baby if you keep doing childish shit like that?"

Jaz started to ask him if he was serious, but the look on his face pretty much said he was. She took a deep breath and massaged her temples. Saying something and arguing with him, would've only caused her already high blood pressure to rise even more. So instead, she walked back to her guest room thinking she could slam that door to prove a point. But he'd removed that door too. "Shit!" she cursed.

Kyree had to laugh at himself. He'd removed every door in the house. The only door left was the one leading outside, and that was only because it would draw too much attention from the neighbors. But he had to admit, watching her throw a tantrum was hilarious. And it pretty much went on like that for a whole week. He annoyed Jaz every chance he got. He was going to get her to talk to him, whether she liked it or not.

It got to be pretty routine too. She'd go to work, come home, watch TV, and then go to sleep. It was almost as if he were invisible. That was until one day she was lying on her living room sofa, on the phone with Ms. Ray, talking about the current episode of *Being Mary Jane*.

"Girlllllll," Ms. Ray expressed, "that damn Dre is too damn fine. And Mary Jane? Honeeee, what has her risking everything for a married man?"

"I don't know. Must be that nigga she got putting down that good..." Jaz paused as she looked up. She had to do a double take, and she immediately became hot all over.

"Good what, girl?" an impatient Ms. Ray wanted to know.

"Dickkkkk," Jaz seductively said, looking over at a naked Kyree and biting her bottom lip.

There he stood, in her kitchen, wearing nothing but a pair of socks and Nike flip-flops, drinking a glass of apple juice with the refrigerator door open. She didn't want to appear to have seen him, so as soon as he closed the refrigerator, she quickly turned her head. Ms. Ray was going on and on about the show, but Jaz had no idea what the hell he was saying. She couldn't concentrate to save her life.

Kyree looked over at her and smirked at her stealing glances. "You want something to drink?" he asked, taking a sip from his glass. He was really fucking with her now.

"Nah, I'm fine," she nervously uttered.

He walked over and stood right in front of the TV. "You sure? What about something to eat?"

Jaz had to control herself from jumping over and hopping on the ten inches of meat that stood between his thighs. His chocolate dick was begging to be touched, caressed, kissed, and ridden into the night. Kyree wasn't playing fair. Jaz knew their problems couldn't be fixed with just sex alone, but damn, did she wish it could. "No, I'm fine. Now, could you please get your ass from in front of the TV?" she snapped, trying to seem unfazed by the mouthwatering Snickers bar practically staring her in the face.

Kyree nodded his head and walked away. He made sure he walked close enough for her to get a good look at what she was missing. As soon as he was out of sight, Jaz instantly started tugging at her shirt. She was hot as hell. She told herself that she was doing the right thing, but her throbbing box disagreed. She was beating Jaz up for not giving her the chance to feel the warmth of her best friend. "Damn." Jaz shook her head and bit her bottom lip.

"Jaz!" Ms. Ray screamed, trying to get her attention.

"I'm here. Damn!" Jaz barked, frustrated.

"See, maybe you need some of that Dre Dick to help with that little attitude of yours," Ms. Ray pointed out.

"Fuck you!" Jaz said, but deep down, she knew he was right.

For days after that, Kyree did everything he could to get on Jaz's last nerve and she was really on the verge of killing him. But today was a new day, and Jaz felt great. She was now eight weeks pregnant and her two-month checkup was in a few hours. Wearing a yellow maxi dress with white accessories and a pair of studded white Vera Wang sandals, Jaz stood in the mirror and admired her stomach. She wasn't really showing, but the small pudge in her belly was all she needed to make her smile. She was so excited; nothing could spoil her day. Or so she thought.

Walking into her living room, she saw Kyree sitting at her kitchen table reading the newspaper with his elbows resting on his knees. He was dressed in a yellow polo V-neck, black cargo shorts, and a pair of black LeBron's. Jaz hadn't noticed before, but Kyree's goatee was now a neatly tapered beard. The man looked good enough to eat, but Jaz couldn't allow herself to indulge. For a second, she wondered where he was going all dressed up, considering he hadn't left her house in a week, but she didn't care enough to ask. She just hoped wherever he was going, he'd stay there.

"Good morning." He looked up from his paper.

"Hey," she spoke dryly. "You seen my keys?" she asked, frantically searching.

"You goin' to work?"

"Uhh...yeah," Jaz lied.

"On a Monday?" Kyree eyed her suspiciously.

Damn, Jaz cursed herself, realizing the shop was closed on Mondays. "I have to finish some last minute inventory."

"So that's the story you wanna stick with?" He eyed her and she looked away.

"Yeah, Kyree. Damn!" She rolled her eyes.

He let out a slight chuckle and rubbed his beard. "Jaz, please," he shook his head. "Your doctor called the house phone yesterday to confirm your appointment for today. So what, you weren't going to tell me?"

She sucked her teeth and rolled her eyes. Standing up, he picked up his Steelers Snapback, placed it on his head, and headed for the door. "I'll be in the car waiting. Don't worry about your keys; they're safe. And don't even think about looking for the spare. I found those too. Now you better hurry up before we're late," he said, shutting the door behind him.

Jaz stood dumbfounded. He'd really left her no choice. She couldn't say she expected anything less from him. She was carrying his child. She just hated that that meant she had to tolerate him. Grabbing her purse, she headed outside towards Kyree's car. The ride to the hospital was a quiet one, and Jaz was fine with that. The less she had to hear his voice, the better.

With matching yellow outfits, Jaz and Kyree walked into the doctor's office looking like a happy couple on the cover of *Essence* magazine. Unbeknownst to the rest of the world, Jaz hadn't even spoken to him in days. She signed herself in, and within minutes, they were calling her to the back. Jaz sat with her feet dangling from the exam table while Kyree looked around. He couldn't help himself. He just had to touch everything in sight.

"Yo, Jazzy, wait 'til you look like this," Kyree laughed, holding up a model pregnancy belly.

"You better put that down before you break something," Jaz warned.

"Man, ain't nobody gon' break shit. Oops!" he said, almost dropping it.

Jaz just had to shake her head.

"Yo, check me out," he said.

Jaz looked over at him and couldn't help but laugh. Kyree was wearing the pregnancy sympathy belly. He looked ridiculous, and Jaz couldn't control her laughter. The doctor came in, startling Kyree. He turned and knocked down all of the vagina models on the counter.

214

Jaz's eyes grew wide as she looked from the doctor to a shaken Kyree.

"Jazmine, is this the father?" Jaz's doctor, Dr. Gomez, asked.

Jaz nodded her head in shame.

"Well, could you tell him to stop playing with my vagina?" The doctor and Jaz both burst out laughing and Kyree shook his head as he fixed the models in embarrassment.

The doctor gave Jaz a once over, and then it was time for the part Jaz had been waiting for. She was finally going to get to hear her baby's heartbeat.

"Alright, Jazmine, now this is going to be a little cold on your stomach," the doctor warned. Jaz giggled at the coldness from the jelly. She watched the screen intently as the doctor showed her the ultrasound. "Hey, Dad, do you want to see your baby?" The doctor smiled. Kyree moved closer and stood beside Jaz. "Alright, there's your baby," the doctor said, pointing to the screen.

Jaz sat in awe. She couldn't keep her eyes off the screen. Kyree couldn't either. He felt closer to Jaz now, more than any time before. He grabbed her hand and held it in his as they listened to their baby's heartbeat, which matched their own. "Damn, ma, this shit crazy," he beamed.

Jaz looked up at him and returned his smile. It was the first time he'd seen her do so in a long time, and he wanted to do nothing but keep that smile there forever.

They left the doctor's office with a brand new feeling. Kyree drove back to the house, but he couldn't think straight. Jaz kept looking at the sonogram, and he couldn't help but think how stupid they both were acting. Pulling over to the emergency lane, he put the car in park.

"What the hell are you doing?" Jaz looked at him like he was crazy.

"Look, Jaz! I'm done playing with you. This shit is crazy. We got a baby on the way."

"Kyree, don't start." She put up her hand, and looked out the window.

"Naw, Jazzy, you listen. I ain't going no fuckin' where. That's a little piece of me inside of you," he pointed at her stomach. "I miss you, ma. I miss us."

Jaz shifted her gaze down, afraid that if she looked up, she would most certainly cry.

"I still love you, Jazzy, and I know you still love me."

"Pssh!" She rolled her eyes with her arms folded tightly.

"Yeah, you do. Say it," he challenged her. When she ignored him and continued to stare out the window, he lightly pushed her. She looked at him, convinced he had clearly lost his damn mind. "Say it!" He pushed her again.

With her brow furrowed, she turned to him and pushed him back, hard. "I fucking hate you, Kyree!" she seethed with clenched teeth.

"Naw, you don't mean that shit." Kyree refused to believe her. He could see right through her lies. They were made for each other, and she knew it.

"I hate you, Kyree! I hate that you left me! I hate that I lost our baby! I hate that you're out of jail! I hate that you're here right now! I hate every fucking thing about you!" she screamed, on the verge of tears.

Her words were like a knife through Kyree's heart. Maybe he was wrong and they couldn't go back to the way things were. He felt like such a fool. Feeling defeated, he sat speechless and then proceeded to start up the car.

Jaz put her hand on top of his to prevent him from putting the car in drive; she wasn't finished with him just yet. She grabbed his arm and forcefully turned him around so that he was facing her. "And you wanna know what I hate most, Kyree?" she asked, tears now freely falling down her face.

Kyree didn't think he could take anymore; she had hurt him like he'd never been hurt before. He wasn't sure he could continue to keep his composure. "What the fuck else you gotta say, Jaz, huh?"

"I hate that whenever I see you, my heart beats so fast and loud, I'm afraid you'll hear it. I hate that after being gone three years, you can come into my life and make me question everything I thought was right. I hate that carrying this child is the happiest I've been in a long time. I hate that I thought I was over you, and yet, I can't stop crying. I hate that being around you hurts so bad." She started to cry again. "And I really hate," she took a deep breath, and released it, "that I still love you," she finally admitted.

It was as though the mask that was suffocating her was finally removed as soon as she said it. Admitting it was one thing, but saying it to him was something totally different. He kissed her greedily on the lips. He'd been waiting to hear her say that again for years. He then proceeded to hug her tightly.

"Don't ever leave me again," she whispered in his ear.

"This shit is forever. I'll always come back to you," he promised.

A COUPLE OF FOREVERS

CHAPTER 21

After having lunch, Jaz and Kyree headed home. Kyree couldn't stop touching her stomach. He was so mesmerized. He followed behind her as they got out of the car with his chest pressed firmly against her back. Jaz was in heaven.

"Ky, can I get my key?" she giggled.

He handed her the key with one hand while the one that rested on her stomach, made its way between her legs, and massaged her slit through her dress. Jaz's eyes grew wide and she fumbled the keys. "Shit," she said, picking them up off the ground. He pulled her in close so that she could feel his erect penis on her ass. "Kyree, stop, somebody's gonna see us out here," she said, trying to control her breathing as he kissed her neck.

"Well then you better open that damn door, 'cause the way I'm feeling right now, I don't give a fuck."

Jaz couldn't open the door fast enough. The fluttering in her stomach and the wetness forming in her underwear was an all too well known sign that she was horny as hell. She pushed open the door and nearly fell in the house with Kyree pressed against her. He was like a dog in heat, he was so anxious. Turning around to close the door, Kyree turned her back around to where she was facing him. He planted kisses all over her face and neck while holding her hands above her head with one hand. The other worked its way up her dress. With his two fingers, Kyree inserted them into her vagina to test the waters, and as he expected, Jaz was soaking wet. She was in total bliss as he worked his way down, nibbling at her nipples through her dress. Before she knew it, he had completely removed her underwear and his head was buried underneath her dress. With one of her legs across his shoulder, Kyree sucked on the lips of her pussy, one at a time. He then proceeded to take his tongue and dip it in and out, in and out.

"Aahhhh," Jaz moaned. She thought she was going to lose her mind.

Kyree was teasing her in the worst way, and she was afraid that if she moved too suddenly, she'd most certainly fall. Balancing on one leg with nothing to hold on to, she grasped the doorknob with one hand while the other hand held onto Kyree's shoulder. Kyree loved every moment of it too. Besides the fact that she tasted like peaches, he loved seeing her so vulnerable. Jaz put on a hard exterior, but he now had her right where he wanted her: begging, crying, and screaming his name.

"Kyyyyyyyyyyyy," she helplessly whimpered.

He laughed to himself, knowing she had nowhere to go. As he flicked his tongue rapidly back and forth, Jaz bit her bottom lip so hard she could taste blood. Loving to see her get hers but also not wanting to miss out on getting his, Kyree decided it was time to take her to her highest point. Stiffening his long tongue, Kyree dug in deep as far as it could go and worked his tongue in a circular motion.

Jaz could no longer take any more. Her stomach began to convulse and she screamed for all her neighbors to hear. "Oh my...God! Ahhhhhhhhhhh...." She let out a long moan, her eyes rolled to the back of her head, and she beat the wall with the side of her fist.

Kyree cleaned her up with his tongue and then finally came up for air. When he removed Jaz's leg from across his shoulder, she couldn't even stand and she slid down to the floor. He smiled at the work he had done. Jaz sat on the floor, panting, too weak to even move. She was spent, and there was nothing she could even do about it.

Kyree removed his shirt in one quick motion. Looking up at him, Jaz thought she could just die. His abdomen revealed a flawless six pack, his arms were perfectly crafted, a full sleeve tattoo covered one arm, and a half sleeve covered the other. When he removed his shorts, she could see the slits in his lower stomach that led to the ten inches of steel he held between his legs. He removed his boxers and he was sticking straight out. Jaz shook her head. She could have sworn she heard it call out her name. *Jazzy, Jazzy,* she thought she heard it say.

Kyree gave a cocky smirk. "You ready for him?"

Jaz sucked on her bleeding bottom lip and innocently nodded her head yes.

"Then come get him," Kyree dared her, walking back to her bedroom.

Jaz was always up for a challenge, but she thought she was going to lose all sense of reality as she tried to get up. Her legs were weak, but hell, she'd crawl if she had to. Mustering up enough strength, Jaz used the doorknob to pull herself up. She stood against the wall for a second, trying to catch her breath. Hearing Chris Brown's "Beg For It" coming from her surround sound, Jaz had to laugh at Kyree's not so subliminal message. With wobbling knees, Jaz made her way to her bedroom, where Kyree was lying with his hands behind his head. Jaz completely removed her dress and tossed it to the other side of the room.

With precision, she gradually climbed on top of his torso, kissing his neck. Rolling her onto her back, Kyree wasted no time entering her slowly. She was too tight for him to dive in headfirst. He had to work his way inside. Jaz was up for anything. She arched her back, allowing him to fully enter. She could swear once he was fully inside, he was hitting all kinds of vital organs and probably the baby. Jaz's insides felt like the OJ glove on Kyree's dick.

"Uhnn," he grunted. Working her insides, he began to flick his tongue over the spot behind her ear.

"Ahhh!" Jaz cried out. He knew exactly what that spot did to her. Clawing at his back, she held on for dear life as she came for the second time. Jaz felt feeble; she didn't think she could take anymore.

But Kyree still wasn't ready to cum just yet. Rolling her onto her stomach, he entered her from behind and massaged her breasts while kissing all over her neck. "You miss me?" he whispered into her ear.

"Yessssssssssssss," she whined.

"You miss him too?" Kyree went in deeper.

"Ahhhh...yesssss," she groaned, her eyes rolling all over her head.

Feeling all the blood rush to

the tip of his dick, Kyree grabbed a hold of her waist, licked the spot behind her ear, and released his load along with her.

"Ahhhhhhhh..." they both moaned at the same time.

Kyree and Jaz lay there panting, until they finally drifted off to sleep. It was still pretty early in the day, so when they awoke, they watched TV, caught up on each other's lives, and then fucked all over again.

The next morning, Jaz awoke as giddy as a schoolgirl. With Kyree still asleep, she decided to go make breakfast. Hell, the way he worked her out last night, the man deserved a steak from Ruth Chris. She heard the shower running and figured he must've been up. Hearing her phone play "Flawless", Jaz answered.

"Hello?"

"Yeah, girl, what up?" Monica asked. "Wait, hold that thought. I got a beep." Monica clicked over to her other line.

Jaz continued to cook while she waited for Monica to return to the phone. While singing Monica's "Love all Over Me", Jaz flipped her pancakes. She was in total bliss, and hadn't even noticed Monica was back on the phone.

"The hell you so happy for?" Monica quizzed, noticing Jazz's less ratchet playlist.

Jaz couldn't do anything but smile. "Nothing, Mo."

"Um hmm," Monica said, not believing her at all.

"Hey, when you get to the shop, can you ask Ms. Ray if he could take my 11:00 and my 1:30 appointments and I'll give him an extra $50? I already told my clients, and they're cool with it."

"Hell, I'll take that," Monica stated matter-of-factly.

"Mo, you never take my clients when I ask you."

"Well, you never offer me $50 either." They both laughed. "What the hell you need us to take your clients for anyway?"

"Oh, I might be a little late today."

"That's every damn day. What makes today so different?"

"Nothing," Jaz lied.

"Ay, bae." Jaz heard Kyree coming and turned around. She quickly covered the mouthpiece to her phone with her hand, but inadvertently put it on speaker. "You got some more soap? This fruity shit ain't gon' work."

"Yeah, it's some Axe body wash at the bottom of the linen closet." Kyree gave her a look, knowing that it probably used to belong to Michael. "What? It's just soap." She shrugged.

"A'ight. Don't get fucked up," he warned.

Jaz rolled her eyes and Kyree planted a wet kiss on her lips. He walked away and Jaz smiled, almost forgetting Monica was on the phone. "Hello?"

"Soooo," Monica said, causing Jaz to jump from the loudness of the phone. She quickly realized she had the shit on speaker. "You still say you ain't got nothin' going on, huh?" Monica probed.

"Um," Jaz stammered.

Monica couldn't help but laugh. "Bitch, I heard everything!"

"Ugh!" Jaz rolled her eyes.

"So y'all worked it out?"

"Yeah."

"Good, cause y'all were being stupid."

"Whatever," Jaz dismissed her.

"Oh, I almost forgot why I called you in the first place. I'm supposed to meet up with La today around 5:00. He finally wants to meet his son." Monica rolled her eyes, not too thrilled with the whole situation.

"That's wassup. But you don't sound too thrilled." Jaz picked up on her standoffish demeanor.

"It's just that it's been two years, J. And now he wants to step up?" Monica shook her head.

"Well, it's better late than never," Jaz reminded her.

"I know, but never late is better. I just keep thinking, what if he hurts my baby? Whether it be physically, which I doubt, or emotionally, which I'm most afraid of, I don't know what I'll do."

"Well, you bet' not do shit 'cause I'm gonna fuck him up and we can't both be in jail. Then who's gonna take care of Kayden?"

Monica and Jaz both laughed, knowing they were both equally serious. "You're crazy. So why will you be later than usual today? What you doin'?"

"Yo' brother." Jaz laughed at Monica's silence, knowing how touchy she was about hearing anything sexual between the two of them.

"Jaz, don't start," Monica warned.

"What? You asked. So after I finish making my nigga breakfast, I'm gonna make my nigga scream." Jaz laughed, and then pulled the phone away, realizing Monica had hung up on her. She couldn't help but laugh again.

Jaz finished cooking and had to give herself a pat on the back. She'd outdone herself. She couldn't remember the last time she'd cooked. It kind of made her wonder why she stayed with Michael so long, and how long it took for her to realize that she never really loved him in the first place. She never really cooked for him, never took off work for him, and she most certainly wasn't as kinky with him in the bedroom. Kyree brought out a side of her that she didn't even know existed until she was with another man who couldn't compare. She had no idea how miserable she was in their relationship until now. Looking back on it, there were so many times where she questioned whether or not she was making the right decision by being with him and so many times she forced herself to believe it was love, when it was probably only infatuation. But what she had with Kyree was most certainly love, a love like no other. No matter what, they'd always come back to each other.

With a tray filled with pancakes, bacon, eggs, fresh fruit, and Kyree's favorite, apple juice, she proceeded to her bedroom. Kyree was texting on his phone, but put his phone down and gave a slight smirk when she walked in with the food. She didn't have to do much to get his undivided attention.

"What you got for me?"

She set the tray down on his lap and Kyree looked on with his mouth watering at the sight before him. He reached over and planted a thankful kiss on her lips and then immediately dug in. Jaz sat, flipping through channels on the TV, while Kyree ate his food.

After cleaning his plate and gulping down the apple juice, Kyree noticed Jaz hadn't eaten. "You ain't gon' eat nothin'?" he asked with confusion, putting his tray on the floor beside him.

"Naw, there was nothing in the kitchen I wanted," she shrugged.

"Well, what you want?" he asked, ready to give in to her pregnancy cravings.

"Sausage," she stated.

"Well, you want me to go to the store and get you some?"

Jaz smiled, happy that he was at her beck and call for once. She turned and kissed him lovingly. "No need to go to the store." She looked at him, seductively biting her bottom lip, and in one smooth motion, untied her bathrobe.

Kyree immediately took the hint as he lay back on the bed and cockily put his hands behind his head. Jaz nibbled at his bottom lip and then placed kisses all over his neck, working her way down to his chest. She used the tip of her tongue to write her name on his chest while clasping her right hand around his dick and rubbing it with the perfect touch. She trailed her letter 'z' all the way down to his penis curves until she was in perfect position with his groin. Kyree looked on in excitement as she started to lick his balls. She then took the shaft of his penis and licked all around it. She was tickling his dick with the tip of her tongue while massaging his balls.

When Jaz hit the vein, Kyree arched his back and grabbed ahold of the sheets. Jaz licked up from the shaft, inserting five inches of his ten-inch penis into her mouth. Her

225

warm jaws formed a vacuum-like suction around Kyree's dick as she bobbed her head up and down to the perfect rhythm. This was Jaz's show, and she had full control. She didn't need any guidance from Kyree as he tried his damndest to keep his hands at bay.

"Ah shittttt....oh my....fuck!" When his hand reached for Jaz's head, she grabbed ahold of it, tightly interlocking it with hers, then taking his other hand and doing the same. Kyree's mind was going insane as he watched her do her thing with no hands. She bobbed up and down, up and down, fast and slow, slurping, sucking, and smacking. Kyree's toes were curling, and he and Jaz both knew he was about to cum at any second now - but definitely not before she got hers.

Slowly lifting her head, she climbed on top of his dick, inserting him slowly into her canal. She clasped onto his hands and rode him like the black stallion he was. Moving his hips to match that of her rhythm, Kyree didn't think he could hold himself back any longer. Pulling himself up, he rocked her middle. Jaz thought she could hold out, but when he pulled up, he tickled her G-spot.

"Ky, I'm about to..." she moaned.

Kyree didn't have any more energy as he felt the blood rushing to the tip of his dick. He hit her spot one more time.

"Ahhhhhhh!" Jaz screamed out in pleasurable agony while biting down on his shoulder blade.

"Fuuuuuccccckkkkk!" he grunted immediately after her. Kyree held onto a weak and shaking Jaz as she leaned onto him like a rag doll while he continued to unleash his entire load inside of her. "Damn, I love you, girl." He kissed her greedily on the lips.

"I love you too, Ky," she managed to get out. "Hey, Ky?"

"Wassup?" he tiredly asked.

"You think I can get my doors back now?"

He opened his eyes to look down at her and burst out laughing. But Jaz didn't find it so funny. She was dead serious. She smacked him on the chest and rolled her eyes. Tucking one hand under his back, she rested her head onto his chest and dozed off. Kyree was still laughing even after she'd gone to sleep.

CHAPTER 22

5 months later

Dressed in a blue blazer, black leggings, and blue suede pumps, Monica sat on her couch with her legs crossed, pissed to the ultimate form of pisstivity. She was supposed to be going to the movies with Jaz, Ms. Ray, Kori, and Bri, but like always, they were running late. She'd already missed the 7:00 show they were originally scheduled to go to and now they'd rescheduled to go to the 10:00 show. She knew they all had their own lives, and she was trying to be considerate, but today was supposed to be her day. They were the ones who originally made plans to make her feel better about her current situation. Today was the first day she'd allowed Kayden to spend the entire weekend alone with Latrell.

Over the past few months, Monica had supervised all of their visits. Kayden really seemed to gravitate to him, so when Latrell asked if he could take him for the weekend, she reluctantly agreed. After Kayden was gone, she cried. She really had no idea why. She felt like she was probably being selfish because for so long, it had always been just the two of him. Jaz tried assuring her that no one could ever take her place, but Monica's emotions were taking over her logical thinking. Just sitting on the couch contemplating it all was making her all the more emotional.

"Fuck it," she said, shooting up from her seat. She sent them all text messages saying she was going to go to the movies by herself, grabbed her keys, and was headed out the door. Monica made up her mind that she was going to the movies without them, anything to get out of the damn house. When she got outside, she saw that she'd left her car lights on the whole night. "Shit!" she cursed. Getting into her car, she hoped and prayed that it started when she hit the automatic start button. When she heard it start up, she was so relieved, but her joy quickly diminished when she saw that she didn't have much gas. She shook her head, knowing she had no one to blame but herself. It wasn't like she didn't have the money; she just didn't like stopping to pump her gas.

Once at the gas station, Monica turned off her car and pulled her debit card out of her purse. While the gas was pumping, Monica zoned out. She could have sworn that in the distance, she saw Mario, but she wasn't too sure. She really didn't want to see him if it was. They hadn't talked in four months. It wasn't anyone's fault but her own. She really did like him, but she made up every excuse in the book, never allowing him to get fully close to her. She ended up just dismissing him and not responding to any of his messages or calls. She squinted a little and noticed that it was in fact him and he was walking towards her. She ducked her head, shook the pump real quick, put it back in its rightful position, and quickly got into her car.

"Ay yo, Monica!" Mario yelled.

Monica pretended not to see him as she went to start her car. She pressed the start button, but it wouldn't start. "Shit!" Monica tried desperately to get it to start. She kept hitting the brakes, hearing nothing. She jumped when she heard the knock at her window. She grabbed at her chest. She'd almost forgotten that Mario was coming towards her. She tried rolling down her window, but quickly remembered her battery was dead. She opened her car door and looked up at him. "Heeeeeey," she awkwardly said.

"You know you fucked up, right?" He stood with his arms folded tightly.

"Me? What I do?" she pretended not to know.

"Man, Monica, I ain't even tryna hear that bullshit you spittin' right now. The fuck is up with you not returning my calls?"

"I've just been busy," she lied.

"Yeah, right. Man, pop the hood," he said.

"Huh?" She looked at him confused.

"I know your car ain't startin'. Pop the hood."

Monica did as she was told and watched as Mario looked to see what was wrong. Taking a rubber band from around his wrist, he put his dreads up into a ponytail so that he could see more clearly. He was undeniably sexy. Wearing a pair of True Religion blue jeans, a white V-neck tee, and pair of clean wheat Timberlands, the man made Monica nervous.

"Start it now!" he yelled.

"It's still not working," she said.

"Let me bring my truck around to give you a jump."

Mario brought his all-black Infiniti truck around and parked it in front of Monica's Lexus. He hooked up the jumper cables and let it sit for a minute while he pretended to browse through his phone. He couldn't keep his eyes off of her though. From the moment he first laid eyes on her, he wanted her. She was beautiful, funny, smart, and independent. But she was obviously broken, and he wanted to be the one to fix her. She didn't need him at all, but he just wanted her to want him. Mario thought they shared something as they were getting to know one another, but when she stopped responding to him, he fell back. He wasn't going to chase someone who didn't want to be caught.

"Try it again," he said. Monica tried it, but it still wouldn't start. "Just as I thought," Mario said, closing her hood.

"What?" Monica grew weary at the thought of an expensive service bill.

"Your battery is fried. You're going to need a new one."

"Damn," Monica sighed.

"Well look, if you buy the parts, I'll do the labor for free on Monday."

Monica looked at him with admiration. "Really?"

"Yeah. Just call AAA and have them tow it to the shop."

"Thank you so much, Mario. This means everything to me right now." He nodded his head graciously. "Do you think you could take me home?"

Mario agreed to take her home. Monica couldn't help but notice the whole time he was trying to text and drive. Her mind wondered if he was talking to another girl. It wouldn't surprise her though. Mario probably had women lined up around the block. Only she would be the dummy to let him get away. But at the same time, Monica felt a hint of jealousy toward the person on the other end of the text message that had all of his attention.

"You checking in with your girlfriend?" Monica asked, immediately regretting it. She had no idea how those words even became audible. They weren't supposed to leave her consciousness, let alone her lips.

Mario gave a slight laugh. "Naw, ma, I ain't got no girl." He whipped his truck into the front of her townhouse.

Monica smiled inside. That was the best news she'd heard all day.

"That was just my homeboy. He's just making sure everything was in order for the fight party I'm having tonight." Monica nodded her head. "But before I go there, I gotta clean this oil and shit off my hands. You think I can use your bathroom?"

"Sure. It's the least I can do."

Monica sat at her kitchen table waiting on Mario to finish. When he returned from the bathroom, she couldn't help but admit how much she wanted and needed his company at the moment. She really didn't want to be alone. He stopped in the hallway to admire all of her pictures. "Where li'l dude at?" he asked.

"With his father." It felt so weird for her to say those words.

"That's wassup," he nodded.

Walking over to her, he stood directly in front of her. Invading her personal space, and making her nervous once again, he asked, "And what'chu 'bout to get into?" His deep voice sent chills up her spine.

"I was about to go out with my girls, but they seem to be bullshittin', soooo—"

Monica was cut off by Mario lifting her from the chair, and onto her feet. He picked her up off the ground and greedily kissed her lips while giving her the warmest, deepest hug she'd ever experienced. He released her, and Monica still had her eyes closed. She never wanted it to end.

"I've been waiting to do that since I first met you," he admitted.

Trying to steady her breathing, Monica said, "You wanna know what I've been waiting to do since the moment I met you?"

"What?"

She looked him up and down, gave him a devious grin, and then proceeded to her bedroom, making sure to put an extra switch in her walk as she made her way up the stairs.

"Dat ass though?" Mario said, just above a whisper. It was almost hypnotizing as he followed behind her to her bedroom.

Pulling her in close, he began to kiss her on the neck while simultaneously removing his boots. Monica tilted her head back as he allowed one hand to travel up her shirt and he began to massage her breasts. He removed her shirt from over her head, tossing it across the room. He picked her up and Monica wrapped her legs around his waist. Lying her down on the bed, he kissed her while Monica helped him to remove his shirt. He took her breasts into his mouth, sucking on each one, and then inserted two fingers inside of her, moving in a circular motion. He licked and blew at her breasts until her nipples were sticking straight out and he nibbled at them. Monica was loving the feeling all too much. Her stomach was fluttering and her box was soaking.

Mario worked his way down until his face was planted directly at her kitty. He used his tongue to lick up and down her center. "Ahhhh," Monica cooed. He stuck his tongue in as deep as it could go and rapidly flicked it. Monica grasped tightly to his head with her knees while her hands pulled at his dreads. "Oh...my..." Her stomach started to convulse and she let out a gut-wrenching orgasm.

Her legs fell as she lay there shaking, unable to move. Mario began to remove his pants and Monica closed her eyes, hoping she wouldn't be disappointed like her last encounter.

When she opened her eyes and saw him remove the gold wrapper from his pockets, she let out a sigh of relief. It was almost like seeing the winning ticket in a Wonka Chocolate Bar. She watched as he put the condom on and she finally got a chance to see his whole body. She had to admit, she was very impressed. His body was perfect. A slew of tattoos covered his perfectly ripped chest and in between his toned thighs rested what Monica predicted to be at least nine inches of the most beautiful penis she'd seen in a long time.

Kissing her collarbone and nibbling on her ear, Mario stuck the tip of his dick in and then pulled it out. "You want it?" he whispered into her ear.

"Yesssss," she hissed.

"No you don't," he continued to toy with her.

He had no idea how much she really did want it, and at that moment, she felt like she'd die without it. It had truly been too long for her. "Pleassseeee," she begged.

Satisfied with her response, Mario plunged in deep. Monica's eyes shot open and she clawed at his back. The warmth from her pussy was almost like magic to Mario. He started to work her middle as she found the perfect rhythm to match his. It was so fulfilling, and Monica felt like she could almost feel him moving in her chest. She was extra tight, and Mario wanted to go in even deeper. He lifted her up to arch her back and went in even deeper.

"Ahhhhhhhh!" she screamed out, on the verge of tears. Monica stopped breathing for what felt like forever. She thought was going to lose consciousness, and Mario wasn't even finished yet.

"Get up, Mo," he instructed, trying to pull her up by her limp arms.

Monica could barely move, but she managed to wrap her arms around him. Turning himself over onto his back, he grabbed at her hips, trying to get her to move. Quickly picking up the hint, Monica mustered up enough strength to work her hips. With her hands pressed against his chest, she rode his dick

233

like it was the last one she'd ever ride. Mario had to grab at her waist to stop himself from cumming too soon.

Grabbing both of his hands, Monica put them at his side. Putting one leg across his head and spinning around, Monica was now in reverse cowgirl position. Mario was in shock. She didn't even have to remove his dick to do it. He watched her back gyrate in a circular motion while her ass bounced up and down. Keeping up with her movements wasn't that hard, but then she turned the tables on him, grabbed a hold of her ankles, and bent all the way back onto his chest. He tried to thrust his hips, but she threw it back at him and he lost control. "Oh, God...girl...what the...shitttttt!" Mario couldn't hold it any longer and he held on to her stomach with both hands until he came.

They both lay there breathing heavily. Mario kissed her forehead and she nestled in the crook of his arm. "What time's your party?"

"Shit, it started about thirty minutes ago," he laughed. "But I'm gon' kick it with you for another half hour then make sure my boys don't fuck up my shit."

Monica smiled, feeling important in his arms. The two dozed off for over an hour, and then Monica started to stir in her sleep, causing Mario to wake up. He adjusted his eyes, and then asked her, "What time is it?"

Monica looked over at the clock on her dresser, "Um, 9:45."

"Oh shit!" He got up from the bed. "My niggas been at my place by themselves for too long. I know my shit is fucked up." He shook his head as he searched for his clothes. "You gon' get dressed and come out to the party?" He looked at her.

"Naw, I'm kind of tired," she spoke sincerely.

Mario was kind of disappointed, but he could live with her choice, knowing he'd worked her back out. "A'ight, bet. But you mind if I use your shower right quick?"

"Not at all. It's extra toothbrushes, washcloths, and towels in the closet in the bathroom."

Mario headed for the bathroom while Monica lay there trying to gather up enough energy to do the same. With her naked body wrapped around her sheets, she lay there basking in the moment. Not only did she put an end to her two-year drought, but the shit was awesome. She was also proud to know that she hadn't lost a step at all. She could still do all of the positions she could before, and if Mario played his cards right, he'd get to see a few more.

Hearing her phone vibrate, she reached over to retrieve it from the nightstand. Scrolling through, she saw that she had four missed calls from her friends. She figured they probably felt bad because she said she was going to the movies without them. Rolling her eyes, she went straight to their text messages.

>>> **8:32 PM, Kori: Don't go w/o us girl. We'll b there. Promise.**

>>> **8:47 PM, Ms. Ray: If u went 2 that movie w/o me, I'll kill u bitch...hear me bitch? *Ike Turner voice.***

>>> **8:52 PM, Bri: That's cool and everything. I saw the movie already anyway. (Shh...Don't tell Ko). But ya ass better b up 4 drinks l8r.**

>>> **9:02 PM, Jaz: Bitch...pleez!**

By the time she was done reading all of her messages, she was practically in tears. They had to be the silliest people on the planet, but they would just have to get over it. She wasn't going to the movie, and they would just have to live with the guilt of thinking she went alone. "Serves them right," she said.

She could hear Jaz in her head already. *"I'm sorry, MoMo."* She then thought she could really hear her, a little too well. She started to shake her head to get her thoughts together, because she could've sworn she heard Jaz say, *"I don't give a damn"*.

"I'm trippin," Monica reasoned with herself. But then she heard her again, followed by the sound of keys jingling and other muffled voices. "Oh shit!" Monica shot up with a new burst of energy. Quickly grabbing her bathrobe, she listened from the top of the steps.

"Damn, Jaz, how long it's gon' take you to find the key? Shit!" Ms. Ray rolled his eyes.

"Boy, if you don't shut up! And you know I gotta pee," Jaz warned, finally getting the door open.

"Y'all sure Mo at the movies?" Kori asked.

"I guess so, her car ain't outside," Bri informed.

"I don't give a damn where she's at, I gotta pee!" Jaz quickly wobbled past them to the downstairs bathroom.

"You've had to pee at every house we've been to!" Ms. Ray yelled out to her as Jaz threw up her hand to dismiss him.

But he was right. Jaz was now seven months pregnant and the baby was pushing down on her bladder. Ms. Ray hated that he picked her up first. When he blew for her to come outside, she was in the bathroom. When they went to pick up Kori and Bri, she had to use the bathroom. Their last stop was Monica's house. But when they noticed her car wasn't outside, Jaz insisted they couldn't leave because she had to use the bathroom.

"Boy, leave that girl alone," Kori said. "You just mad because you can't push a baby out ya ass." Kori and Bri both laughed and Ms. Ray gave them both the middle finger.

Jaz came walking real fast out of the bathroom. "Ain't no tissue in there!" Jaz huffed.

"Go upstairs," Bri suggested. Jaz had almost forgotten about the upstairs bathroom. She took to the stairs as an ear hustling Monica retreated to her bedroom. She had to think fast. She didn't want Jaz and the others to know about her rendezvous just yet, and she most certainly didn't want them to find out like this. Knowing Jaz was going to the bathroom, she had to beat her to it. Walking into the hallway, Monica met Jaz as soon as she hit the corner.

"Ahhh!" Jaz screamed, taken aback. "Damn, girl, you almost sent me into early labor!" Jaz grabbed at her chest.

"Hell you doin' here?" Monica griped, her arms folded.

"Look, Mo, I'm sorry for being late, but I gotta pee." Jaz desperately fidgeted.

It didn't take long for the rest of the crew to join them upstairs.

"Dang, Mo, we didn't know you were home. Where's your car?" Ms. Ray quizzed.

"I don't have time for all of that, I gotta pee!"

Monica stood in front of the door, blocking Jaz from entering.

"What the fuck, Mo?" Jaz barked.

"Go downstairs. If your lazy ass would've looked, you would've seen the tissue in the cabinet. And once you're done, exit the premises," Monica said.

"Naw, Mo. Do you know how long it took me to walk my big ass up these steps? Fuck that!" Jaz tried to push her out the way, but to no avail.

"Don't be like that, Mo, we're sorry. We can still make the movie if we leave out now," Kori suggested.

"Please let this damn girl go to the bathroom," Bri begged. She really didn't feel like hearing Jaz's mouth anymore. Hell, no one did.

"Damn, Mo! What, you blew it down in there and don't want nobody to smell yo' shit?" Ms. Ray laughed. "What the fuck is the big deal?"

Ms. Ray's, and everyone else's, questions were answered as the door to the bathroom flew open and they all jumped in fear. "Hey, y'all," Mario gave them a head nod. Monica dropped her head in embarrassment.

"Heeeeeey," they all awkwardly said in unison.

Mario smirked. Monica moved away from the door to allow him to pass.

"A'ight, Mo, I'll check you later," he said.

She nodded her head and he looked at her like she was crazy. Pulling her in close for a hug, he said, "Don't think I was gon' let you get off without showing me no love." He then lifted her, very embarrassed, face up with one finger, and kissed her sweetly on the lips. Everyone's eyes grew wide with surprise as they whispered amongst themselves. "A'ight, y'all," he said.

"Byyyyyyye." They all waved.

As soon as they heard the door shut downstairs, they all diverted their attention to Monica.

"Sooooo..." Jaz began.

"Ugh!" Monica huffed. "Don't start!" She put her hand over top her forehead. This was the main reason why she didn't want them to know. She really didn't feel like hearing them bombard her with questions and nonstop jokes.

"Oooooh, Mo," Ms. Ray shook his head, "you nassssssty!"

Monica simply rolled her eyes.

"Well, was it worth you missing the movie you cried to see?" Bri laughed.

"Fuck y'all!" Monica turned on her heels and proceeded back to her room.

"Y'all leave Monica alone," Kori interjected.

"Thanks, Kori," Monica took a sigh of relief.

"Besides, it's not her fault the dick makes her walk crazy," Kori sang as the rest of them burst out laughing at the slightly different pep in Monica's step.

Monica threw up her middle finger at them and slammed her door.

"Y'all better tell her to stop slammin' doors before Kyree's crazy ass come take her shit off the hinges too," Ms. Ray said. Bri and Kori were in tears. Jaz had stopped laughing and looked at them like they were crazy.

"That's not funny," Jaz said with seriousness, knowing in actuality, had it been one of them, she would've laughed just as hard, if not harder. "Y'all stop laughing! He put the doors back!" Her protests fell on deaf ears as they all continued to laugh. She could even hear Monica laughing from her bedroom. "Fuck y'all, I gotta piss!" She rolled her eyes and stormed into the bathroom.

"Ay, Jaz," Bri called out from outside the bathroom.

"What!" She barked.

"How it feel to piss with the door closed?" Bri burst out laughing and Ms. Ray, Kori, and even Monica were on the floor in tears. They couldn't breathe.

"Fuck y'all!" Jaz shouted.

CHAPTER 23

The girls all convinced Monica to come out with them to Applebee's. They were able to catch the end of the fight while kicking back and laughing over drinks. When they were done, Ms. Ray made sure to drop Jaz off first. She'd already gone to the bathroom before they left the restaurant, and he wanted to make sure the next house they stopped her at was her own. When Jaz was upstairs in her apartment, she sent Monica a text saying she was good. She did a quick look around the apartment while in a mad dash for the bathroom, but she didn't see Kyree anywhere in sight.

It may have gotten on everyone else's nerves, but it bothered no one like it bothered her. Jaz felt like she spent more time pissing than she did breathing. Deciding to run herself a nice hot shower, Jaz undressed and allowed the water to rinse all of the ache in her body away. Since being back with Kyree, she was in total bliss. She hadn't heard from Michael or Asia in months, and if she never saw them again, it would be too soon. That part of her life was over. Now, every day she woke up smiling. She felt like the luckiest woman in the world, covered in sunshine. But there was something at the back of her mind, a feeling in her soul - call it her own intuition - telling her a storm was soon to follow. She couldn't shake this feeling for the world. But everything in her life was going so right. She'd enjoy it while she could and prepare for the storm when it came. She'd survived hurricanes before, and she was confident she could weather whatever storm was up ahead. She just wished she knew what she was up against.

Turning off the water, she dried herself off and grabbed her bathrobe. Wrapping it around her waist, she picked up her ringing cell phone. "Hey, Mo," Jaz spoke.

"Hey, you seen Kyree?" Monica asked.

"Naw, but let me check my back pocket. Well will you look at that, he's not there," Jaz said.

"Don't get smart," Monica rolled her eyes. "I was just asking for my mama. She's been trying to call him."

"I don't know where that boy is, but I know he's getting on my nerves leaving the cap off the damn toothpaste," Jaz snarled, placing the cap back on the toothpaste.

Monica laughed. "Girl, I can't wait for yo' evil ass to have that baby."

"Whatever." Jaz rolled her eyes, walking towards the kitchen. "You over there fuckin' ol' boy, or nah?" Jaz gave a sinister laugh.

"Ugh! I can't stand you. That's why I didn't want yo' nosy ass to find out. I could've kicked yo' ass when I saw you come up those stairs." Monica slowly shook her head, regretting the day she gave her a key.

"Mo, you ain't gon' do shit," Jaz boasted, putting her phone on speaker and pouring herself a glass of apple juice.

"A'ight, we'll see how much shit you talk when Ky go upside yo' head for wearing them damn heels tonight," Monica laughed.

"Girl, please. Kyree ain't gon' do shit either. I'm grown." She took a big gulp from her glass.

"Um hmm, that's what ya smart ass mouth sayin' now."

Hearing a phone vibration, Jaz turned around and saw Kyree's phone sitting on the kitchen counter beside a white box. "This is why he's not answering the phone. His simple ass left it at the house and I bet he's still at the fight party." Jaz shook her head while trying to open the box.

"Don't try and act like you don't love that nigga." Monica disregarded her, knowing Jaz was all talk.

"Ahh!" Jaz screamed, practically on the verge of tears.

"What is it? What's wrong?" an alert Monica asked.

"He bought me a carrot cake." She smiled.

"Are you serious right now? That's why you were just screaming like your life was in danger or some shit?" Monica had to pull the phone away to make sure this shit was real.

Jaz had no desire for the dessert before, but since being pregnant with Kyree's baby, she suddenly had a craving for all of his favorite foods. It was the weirdest thing ever, and she hoped like hell her taste buds would return. But for now, she would relish in the moment of the mouthwatering cake that sat before her. "But Mo, it's my favorite," Jaz reasoned.

"You know what? This pregnancy has really got you trippin'. You're even more nuts now than you were before. I'll talk to you tomorrow. Bye." Monica ended the call before Jaz could even respond.

Cutting herself a huge slice of cake, Jaz giggled as the baby did somersaults in her stomach in anticipation. She brought the cake up to her mouth and chewed it slowly. It was almost like eating a piece of heaven. "Daddy loves us, huh, baby?" She smiled while rubbing her belly.

Taking her piece of cake with her, Jaz decided to finish up on the baby's room. Kyree had been saying he was going to finish it for weeks now and she was tired of waiting for him. Her dad had always taught her how to be independent, so she really didn't need him to help her set up the crib. But she did want him to do it, which was why they'd gotten into an argument before she left the house in the morning.

Jaz sighed heavily as she opened the door, expecting to see a mess of boxes and fabric samples everywhere. But what she actually saw almost made her drop her cake. What was once a room filled with baby junk was now complete. It was exactly how she wanted it. A white crib sat in the corner while a changing table sat up against the wall along with a beautiful armoire. There was also a white rocking chair in the corner beside the window. Jaz couldn't help but get emotional, realizing Kyree had listened to her when she said she wanted to sing to the baby at night with nothing but the moon to light the room. She didn't think he took her seriously because he laughed and called it corny, but obviously, he'd heard everything she said.

Bringing her hands up to her face, Jaz started to cry when she saw the name Kylee Simone written in white block letters on the pink walls. They'd come up with the name three months ago after finding out they were having a girl. Jaz suggested Kylee, after Kyree, and he'd suggested Simone, after her mother. Jaz was so excited; she just had to talk to Kyree. She picked up the phone to dial his number, but quickly remembered he'd left it at home, so she decided instead to call his business cell phone. Not many people had that number, but Jaz would be damned if he had another phone she didn't have access to. She was told on numerous occasions not to call him at that number unless it was an emergency, but she really didn't care.

It didn't stop him from answering right away. "Hell I tell you 'bout calling me on this line?" he playfully snapped.

"Boy, boo!" Jaz dismissed him. "You left your other phone at home. You still at the fight party?" she asked, picking up a pink dolphin from out of the crib.

"Naw...I'm minding my business."

"Stop playing, Ky," she whined. "Where you at, for real?"

"With Keyshia."

"Wha'?" Jaz rolled her neck and brought the phone away from her ear. She'd never heard of this Keyshia and Kyree had better been playing before she fucked him up. He started to laugh. "Boy, don't play with me. Where are you?"

"I told you, chillin' with this bitch named Keyshia."

Jaz was seconds away from losing her patience and cussing Kyree slam out when a potent, but delectable, smell tickled her nostrils. She gave a slight laugh with the phone still pressed to her ear and said, "Oh, really?"

"Yep," he said with confidence.

Jaz opened her balcony door just as Kyree was releasing a long drag from his perfectly rolled blunt. She walked over and pushed him in the arm. "Keyshia, huh? Nigga, if you weren't talkin' 'bout weed, you know I would've killed you, right?"

Kyree gave a lazy smile, knowing she was most surely telling the truth. Even when they broke up for short periods of time, Jaz made her position known. He'd never actually cheated on her, but he had come close one time. Although they were broken up at the time, Jaz didn't see it as such. She shut that shit down quick. Asia wasn't the first chick she had beaten into hiding. After Jaz had body slammed the girl Kyree was fooling around with, she slapped Kyree. It pretty much sent a message that no one fucked with Kyree. "That bitch Jaz is crazy," they'd all say. And they were right. She didn't play when it came to Kyree.

"How my favorite girl doin', huh?" he asked, hugging her tightly, and rocking her from side to side.

"Good, I'm just tired," she yawned.

He pulled her away. "I'm not talking to you. I'm talking 'bout my baby girl." He bent his head down and pressed his ear firmly against her belly. Jaz rolled her eyes. He'd made a habit out of rubbing her stomach and talking to it. She found it almost sickening. "How my baby doin'? Yo' mama been treating you right?"

"Fuck you, Kyree." She pushed him.

"I'm just playin'." He gave her a wet kiss on the cheek. "You know I can't forget about my big baby," he smirked. Jaz sucked her teeth. "But yo, go in the house. You don't need to be around all of this smoke and shit." He waved the smoke out of her face.

"Well, put it out then."

He ignored her and leaned over the banister. Jaz wrapped her arms around him and hugged him from behind, her head resting on his back. "Thanks for fixing the baby's room. I love it."

He nodded his head. "You have a good time tonight?"

"Yeah. It was fun. We haven't all chilled like that in a while."

"Cool," he said, spinning her around so that she was facing him. "So what you wear out?"

She looked at him skeptically. "My pink Nicole Miller maternity dress. Why?"

He took one more long drag, put his blunt out, and folded his arms. "And what shoes did you wear with this outfit?"

Jaz wouldn't dare tell him she wore heels tonight. He'd warned her about that too many times. "My flat white studded flip flops," she said with a straight face.

"Lies!" he called her out. Jaz stood with her mouth agape, totally appalled. "Jazzy, don't try to play me. I know you wore heels because I've been out here the whole time since you've been home and I heard you tell Mo I wasn't gon' do shit." Jaz had the complete stuck on stupid face. "Um hmm...keep fuckin' with me Jazzy. I told you if something happens to my baby, they're gonna need a doctor to remove my foot out yo' ass."

Jaz had been caught in a lie and there was no denying it, but that didn't mean she couldn't change the subject. "So you've been out here the whole time and you didn't say anything?" He sucked his teeth, knowing Jaz's game all too well. Looking at him seriously, she asked, "What's wrong with you?" Kyree didn't say anything, but Jaz knew something was up. He only smoked weed when something was on his mind. It helped him to put things into perspective. "Huh?"

"Nothing, Jazzy. Yo, go back in the house," he said, taking a seat in the chair.

"No, not until you tell me what's wrong with you," she stated. He took a long deep breath and overlooked her. He did have a lot on his mind, but he really didn't feel like discussing it with her just yet. "So you're just gonna ignore me, huh?" She stood in front of him and turned his head so that he was facing her. He pulled his head away and brushed her off. "Oh, I see." Jaz climbed on top of his lap, straddling him with her thighs. She knew the ways to get information out of her man. She kissed him all over his face while saying, "You still not gon' tell me?"

He shook his head no while simultaneously untying her bathrobe. Surprised, but still just as happy, to see her exposed naked body, he used his hand to rub her belly. He started to massage her breasts and then took them into his mouth.

"Kyree." she tried closing her robe. "What if someone sees us?" She looked around.

"It's two in the morning, and everybody's 'sleep. Besides, you owe me one out here. What, you scared?"

Jaz cocked her head to the side and looked at him like he was trying to challenge her. And he knew what he was doing too because Jaz never backed down from a challenge. She pulled his shirt above his head and moved his shorts down. Looking down at his very erect penis, Jaz eased her body down onto it. Since being pregnant, Jaz's pussy had completely changed, but most definitely for the better. Her walls were now fatter, she was wetter, and her shit practically had a death grip on his dick when he was working her middle.

"Ssssss...shit," he moaned.

She was working her hips, making him feel like he was losing his mind, but she still had some information to get out of him and she hadn't forgotten. "So you gon' tell me?" she asked, out of breath while nibbling on his ear.

Kyree continued to ignore her, bringing her in close and licking her spot.

"Ummm," she moaned, biting her lip.

He kissed her on the chin and then began sucking on her collarbone. He had to stay focused to prevent his dick from sliding all over the place, she was so wet.

"You love me?" he asked her.

"Yessss," she whined.

"Good." He licked her face. "I gotta..." he started.

"You gotta what, baby?" she whimpered, grabbing a hold of his neck while trying to work her big belly up and down.

He nibbled at her ear, pulled her in deeper, and finally said, "I gotta go back to New York."

Jaz's eyes grew big at what she thought she heard. She let go of his neck to look at him. She had to make sure she was hearing him right. "Say wha' nah?" She looked at him, her neck cocked to one side. "Kyree, answer me!" She punched him in the chest.

Kyree didn't even answer her; he couldn't even look at her. Instead, he grabbed her by the waist with one hand while

245

the other hand pushed her body all the way back and he hit her sweet spot with the death stroke.

"Kyreeeeeeeeeeeeeeeeeeeeeeeeeeeeeee!" she screamed out loud enough for all her neighbors to hear.

He ignored her screaming and came along with her. "Agghhhhh!"

When he was done, he lifted Jaz back up. They sat there, panting for dear life. Jaz felt so weak, she could barely move. Her legs were trembling and she couldn't breathe. He held her in his arms and Jaz lay over his shoulder like a wilted flower. After a minute of trying to regain her composure, Jaz sat herself up and stared at him. When he couldn't look her in the eye, it was all the confirmation she needed. She quickly tied her robe and maneuvered herself off his lap.

"Jazzy...wait!" He tried to grab her arm to stop her from leaving.

She quickly snatched her arm away from him and stormed inside the house. The disgusted look she gave him made Kyree's stomach churn. He wanted nothing more than to be the man she wanted him to be, but circumstances prevented that. He sat outside with his head in his hands, frustrated beyond words. He hated to do this to Jaz again, but he had to go. He couldn't leave the streets until he set up this last deal. He'd been working on this deal since he first went to Charlotte. But shit didn't go through as planned and he needed to distribute his product elsewhere. He'd kept the deal off for too long now because he wanted to be there for Jaz during her pregnancy, but he could no longer avoid the inevitable.

He loved Jaz. She was his queen and she treated him like a king. Their princess would only add to the royal family he had created. Although there had been a few before her, there were never any after her. No one could hold a candle to Jaz. He had plans to build a future with her, and she was just going to have to understand that he had to do what he had to do. Pulling up his shorts and putting his shirt back on, he took a deep breath, preparing himself for the war on the other side of the door.

When he walked into the house, Jaz was pacing back and forth in frustration. Upon seeing him, she turned up her nose and snarled. It hurt her too much to even look at him. She couldn't understand how he could be so stupid. He had a family, a booming business, and shit was finally going right in his life. Why he had to challenge his own happiness, Jaz had no idea.

"Jazzy, let me—"

"Don't even fucking speak to me right now, Kyree!" she snapped, throwing her hand up.

Kyree was at a loss for words. The look she had on her face hurt him to his core. He never thought he could feel as low as he felt at that moment. The look of disappointment plastered on her glowing face made him feel like absolute shit. He sat on the arm of the couch, looking down at the floor. "Jazzy...say something to me. Please," he begged.

She stopped pacing and looked at him as though he were the scum of the earth. Standing with her arms folded tight, she asked, "So you're back sellin'?"

"Not exactly." He tried to soften the blow.

"What the fuck is that supposed to mean, Kyree?"

"Jaz, now you know I can't tell you that." He looked at her.

"Nigga, I don't give a fuck! You better tell me something! What does 'not exactly' mean, Kyree?"

Kyree took a deep breath. "It means I've just been connecting people with my old connect, trying to find him someone new he can trust."

"And how long has this been going on?" He didn't answer her. "Since you got out, huh?" He still didn't say anything, but he didn't have to. Jaz had her suspicions a few months back, but she refused to allow herself to believe them. She wanted to trust and believe in Kyree, but when he did shit like this, it made it so hard. "What the fuck is wrong with you?" She punched him real hard in the arm. He jumped at the hit and had to stop himself from reacting too quickly. Jaz tried hard to control her emotions, but upon punching him, she instantly began to cry. She blamed her pregnancy for her not being able to hold everything together. "Kyree, why are you doing this to me again? Are you trying to drive me crazy?" She looked at him, tears in her eyes, desperately wanting to know.

He embraced her by the waist and rested his head on her stomach. "No, Jazzy, and I swear, this is the last time," he promised.

"Kyree, you said the last time was the last damn time!" She stomped her foot in frustration.

"I know, bae, but I'll be back before you know it. I promise." He kissed her stomach. "Trust me."

She pushed him off of her. "Fuck your promises, Kyree! You promised me the last time. You said you'd never leave me then and you promised me again." She started pacing the floor again. "Naw, fuck that!" She looked up at him. "When are you leaving?"

"At the end of the week," he said.

"Cool. I'm going with you," she said matter-of-factly.

Kyree jumped up. "No the hell you're not, Jaz!"

"Is it safe enough for you?" she asked with a stern face.

"Yeah, but—"

"Well, fine then. I guess it's safe enough for your unborn child and me too."

"Hell naw, Jazzy, you crazy as hell!" He waved her off.

"Kyree, this is not up for discussion. I'm going, and that's final." She looked at him, waiting for his rebuttal.

Kyree really didn't have one though. He didn't want to involve his family in his stupidity, but Jaz was so set in her ways. Once she got a notion in her head, it was final. "A'ight, man," he said in defeat.

"Coo. Now I'm going to bed." She turned and headed toward their bedroom, yelling obscenities about him the whole way there.

Kyree had no idea how things had turned. He couldn't allow Jaz to come with him. He had to think of something fast, but for now, he would just allow her to believe that she'd won. He needed time to think, and she had officially fucked up his high. Strolling into the bedroom, he noticed that Jaz was crying.

He secured her into his chest and allowed her to release all of her emotions until she cried herself to sleep.

CHAPTER 24

With her eyes still closed, Jaz stretched her arm across the bed, reaching for Kyree. When she didn't feel him there, she immediately popped her head up. Looking over to see that his spot was empty, Jaz picked up her phone to see the time. It was eight in the morning, and he wasn't at her side. She tossed the covers over her body and frantically sprang from the bed to the window. She took a huge sigh of relief seeing Kyree's 745 parked alongside his new black Audi Q7. Jaz just shook her head every time she looked at that car. She really had no idea why he even bought the damn thing.

Figuring he must've been on his morning run, Jaz went to pee for what felt like the umpteenth time in the past twenty-four hours. She had worried herself ragged the night before thinking about Kyree. She had no idea what she'd do if she ever lost him again. By going back to New York, he was risking his freedom and his life. Her nerves were already shot to shit, not to mention the growing baby inside of her stomach. She just didn't think she could handle any more bad news, and Kyree had another thing coming if he thought she was just going to stand idly by and watch him leave her again. She was going with him, whether he liked it or not.

After relieving her bladder, Jaz ran the water to brush her teeth. She brushed, rinsed, gargled, and then proceeded to wash her weary face. Taking a long look in the mirror as she worked the warm rag along her face, Jaz's heart stopped at the reflection staring back at her. With her brow furrowed, she brought her hand away from her face and did several blinks to make sure she wasn't losing her mind.

"What the hell?" she asked herself. Using her other hand to cover her mouth, Jaz stood in shock. She had to press her back against the wall to keep from passing out. She couldn't believe her eyes. Of all the things she'd ever owned in her life, from the least to the most expensive, nothing had ever been as beautiful as the two-toned rose gold and platinum split shank four-carat diamond ring that sat on her left ring finger. She had no idea how the beautiful stone got on her finger, but she definitely knew who'd placed it there.

Racing to her phone, she quickly dialed Kyree's number. Although he answered in two rings, it felt like forever. "What up?" he spoke coolly into the phone.

"Baby, please don't play with me. What is this?" Jaz asked on the brink of tears.

"Go make yourself look presentable right quick. But first, hold on a sec." He clicked over to his other line.

Jaz rolled her eyes to the ceiling and slipped on a pair of jeans and her favorite Mickey Mouse maternity shirt. He'd surely fucked up her mood by putting her on hold. While she waited for him to return to the phone, she admired the ring. She thought back to last night and immediately realized he must have slipped the ring on her left finger while she was asleep from the punishing he'd put on her insides.

Last night, while she lay crying in bed, Kyree pulled her in close and spooned her, inserting his dick from behind, hitting her with nice, slow, and long strokes. When he was finished, Jaz was done for and crying for other reasons. She drifted off into a deep sleep and that's when it must have happened. But she had no idea what he was trying to imply by slipping the ring on her finger, because that surely wasn't going to get him the answer to the question she hoped he was going to ask. He was going to have to come way harder than that.

"Yo, bae," Kyree got back on the line.

"Yeah, Ky, what is this? And where are you?" she wondered.

"Open up your computer and pull up Skype," he instructed.

Jaz quickly opened her computer and did as she was told. When she connected to Skype and joined Kyree's chat room, her mouth dropped in shock.

"Er'body say wassup," Kyree said.

Before Jaz knew it, a host of her closest friends and family were all saying hello to her in a group chat room. Her father, Jackie, Monica, Ms. Ray, Bri, Kori, and everyone from the shop were on her computer screen with smiling faces. Kyree had even put the camera on Fat Boy, who was sitting right beside him. Jaz was so overwhelmed with emotion that she had no idea what to say. All that she could manage to get out was an, "Oh my gosh!"

"Oh my gosh is right, honaaay. Look at that head," Ms. Ray said as everyone laughed at the bonnet that covered Jaz's head.

"Shut up, boy!" She let out an embarrassed laugh and slowly pulled off her scarf, revealing her hair in a perfect bun.

"Jazzy, I had to take care of some business, but I couldn't let this wait another second," he said.

Jaz shook her head and looked up to prevent herself from crying, knowing he was in fact already on his way to New York. He looked as though he were Skyping from his cell phone. But she wouldn't ruin his time to shine just yet, not in front of everyone, so she allowed him to continue.

Kyree took a deep breath and Jaz couldn't believe the nervousness evident on his face. She'd never seen him so tense. Kyree was always so calm and secure in everything he did and said. Kyree wiped a bead of sweat that was sliding down his forehead. Everyone listened intently as he finally began to speak.

"Jazzy, I've loved you from the moment I laid eyes on you. Letting you go was the hardest thing I've ever had to do, and when I realized that, it was too late. But I should have never let you go in the first place, because I know when shit got rough, you were there—"

"Ay now!" Jackie scolded him for cursing, and everyone laughed.

"My bad, ma," he chuckled. "But really, Jazzy, I've never cared for anyone like I care for you. Seeing you with another nigga made my insides hurt. And now you're pregnant with my princess. Girl, you don't how good that makes me feel. Every day you're glowing, looking more beautiful with time. Before you, there were many, but after you, there were none. No one could ever compare to the girl who always stands behind me, because you trust me to walk in front of you to lead the way. And I lead the way because I know you'll always have my back." Kyree paused and licked his lips, and aside from him and Calvin, there wasn't a dry eye on the screen. "I wanna do nothing more than provide for you. You look past all of the stupid things I do, and you see me for me. I would be an idiot to mess this up again. So..." Kyree took a long deep breath as everyone sat on the edge of their seats. "Jazmine Denise Elliott, will you –"

"Stop!" Jaz put her hand up, cutting him off.

Everyone was so in shock, whispering amongst themselves. "What?" Kyree looked at her, confused.

"Hey y'all, can I talk to Kyree alone, please?" Jaz said to everyone.

"What the fuck? Hell naw! We wanna see too," Monica whined.

"Monica!" Jackie chastised her. Monica looked like a deer caught in headlights. "Don't make me get off this computer and come over there to beat yo' ass," Jackie warned.

"Oh snap, time to go!" Bri logged off her computer and everyone else soon followed suit. Jaz closed her computer just as Monica began to apologize.

Jaz picked up her phone and called Kyree.

"Yo, Jaz, what the fuck, yo?" Kyree asked, trying to get a sense of where her head was at.

"Kyree, are you on your way to New York right now?"

"Baby, that ain't got shit to do with –"

"Just answer the damn question," Jaz said, fed up.

"Yeah, bae, but –"

"But nothing, Kyree. You said you would wait for me."

"Jazzy, you know I couldn't have you out in no shit like that. Shit ain't safe," he reasoned.

"Then why the hell are you going?" she seethed through clenched teeth.

Kyree ran his hand over his face. This was not going as he'd planned it, but he didn't want to waste any more time and he thought this would be something different and creative. He was quickly beginning to see it wasn't his best idea. He had to regain control of this situation, and fast. Sighing heavily, he said, "Bae, listen to me." Jaz sucked her teeth. "Look, cut that attitude out, shit! I got something to say. You listening?" When she didn't respond, he said, "Ay!"

"Ugh! What?" she barked.

"I can't have you mad at me, Jazzy. Bae, say we good, please," he begged. When he heard her sniffling, he blamed himself. No matter what he did, he could never get right. He was always the reason for the stress in her life, and he hated it. Not only was she pregnant, but she was also pregnant with high blood pressure, and he wasn't helping matters. "Jazzy, I know you hear me, so just listen. You don't have to say anything just yet." Kyree paused for a second to gather his thoughts while Jaz held the phone waiting for him to speak. "Remember back in the day when we broke up for the first time because you wanted me to stop running the streets?" Jaz listened intently as he spoke; she had to know the direction in which he was going. "And then you saw me out with Shayna in front of my mama house?"

Jaz's eyes damn near sliced the phone down the middle. Kyree had better been going somewhere with this blast from the past or else she was going to let his ass have it. Not only did she catch him out with Shayna after only two weeks of being broken up, but she'd also caught her in the front seat, deep throating Kyree's dick like there was no tomorrow. Kyree didn't even see Jaz coming, as he sat back with his eyes closed, enjoying the tantalizing feeling. Jaz knocked on the window and Kyree looked over, but he couldn't react fast enough. Jaz had already flung open the passenger side door and pulled the girl up by her sew-in, causing her teeth to scratch Kyree's dick, sending an excruciating pain to his erect penis. Jaz dragged the girl up and down the street while Monica came running out of the house trying to break it up. It was no secret that the two had

255

never liked each other, ever since Shayna had slept with the boyfriend of one of Jaz's close friends back when they were in high school. Kyree was in too much pain to even move. By the time Monica had broken it up, and Shayna limped up the street to her house, Kyree had finally regained his composure. The look Jaz gave him could kill the grim reaper himself. Now he was bringing the shit up again and Jaz was curious as to why.

"Kyree, if you say some shit I don't like, I swear I'm hangin' up on yo' ass. My blood pressure is already high. Ain't nobody got time for this." She rolled her eyes hard.

Kyree threw his head back and let out a slight laugh. "There is a point to this, I swear. Remember what you told me after I reminded you that we were broken up and I could do whatever the hell I pleased?"

"Before or after I slapped you?"

"Don't play," he warned.

Jaz sucked her teeth, remembering exactly what she'd said to him that fateful night - after slapping him of course.

"What'd you say to me, Jazzy?"

She took a deep breath. "No matter what, we'd always come back to each other –"

"This shit is forever," they said simultaneously.

They both laughed as a steady flow of tears now fell freely from Jaz's eyes.

"And Jazzy, baby, this shit *is* forever. Can't nothing keep me away from you. You don't know this, but when I went to New York the first time, I wasn't just going on business, baby. I went to see a jeweler, but I never got the chance to go. As soon as I was released, I went to see that jeweler, and when I got back to Virginia and heard you were engaged? Man, I was so mad!" Kyree bit his bottom lip just thinking about it. "But like a dumbass, I said fuck it and let you walk away from me. I gave up too easily, like I always do. But not this time. I told you I'm not running away from shit. So..." He took a deep breath. "Jazmine Denise Elliott...will you marry me?"

Jaz was breathing heavily as she took a seat on the edge of her bed. Her mind was racing with every thought imaginable.

For years, she'd been waiting on him to say those words to her, and for years, she'd imagined what she'd say and how she'd say it. In all those years, never before had she imagined that she'd say, "No".

Upon hearing her answer, Kyree immediately felt as though his heart were being ripped from his chest. It didn't help matters that he was sitting on the passenger side as Fat Boy drove, so he couldn't show his true emotions. All he could muster out was, "What?"

"You heard me, Kyree. No," she reiterated.

"Why not?" Kyree asked as Fat Boy tried to read what was going on through the expressions on his face.

"Because I said so," Jaz said.

Kyree sat on the phone speechless while Fat Boy nudged him in the arm, trying to get the scoop. He couldn't hear anything around him and his head began to spin. He was stuck in a trance until he just barely heard her say his name. "Yeah?" he answered.

"Kyree, I won't marry you...until you ask me in person." She beamed.

Kyree looked up. "What?"

The way he left so suddenly and with the abrupt proposal in his absence made Jaz feel like he didn't think he was going to make it home safely. She just needed his assurance that he would come back to her. "You heard me, nigga. You said you're coming home in a week. So in a week, I want your ass here, down on one knee, asking me to be your wife. You got that?" she asked him matter-of-factly.

Kyree's face turned from confusion into a satisfied grin. "Yeah, I got you," he nodded.

"Okay, good. Now bring us back something nice. Kylee misses you already," Jaz rubbed her belly.

"Oh yeah? Well tell my li'l mama Daddy will be home soon."

"You better. Promise me you'll come back to me," she said.

"I'll always come back to you. This shit is forever."

Kyree's words stuck with Jaz that whole week. She ran herself crazy with worry. She expected him to call her every six hours with updates on his whereabouts, and like clockwork, he did. If it weren't for her friends and family, Jaz didn't think she could make it. Every night she fell asleep in one of his T-shirts, just so she could feel closer to him. She hoped like hell that Kyree was right about leaving the streets alone this time. The stress from the worry was killing her. But she was sure that even if he stayed at his old ways, she wouldn't leave him alone. She couldn't. He was her rock. From the moment they met, he took her heart, and he had yet to give it back. With Tanya Stephens's "These Streets" on repeat, Jaz swayed her head to the music and sang along. Her neighbors had to be going crazy. It was 8:00 on a weeknight and the song had been on all day, but she didn't care. It fit her mood so perfectly. Hearing her phone ringing, Jaz answered it.

"Hello?" she said.

"Girl, if you don't turn off that damn song! I'm so sick of hearing you play that shit." Monica shook her head.

"Whatever, Mo."

"I'm just sayin'. Kyree is on his way home as we speak. Stop crying, you're depressing me."

Jaz sucked her teeth. "Girl, please. I'm surprised you even have time to talk. Finally hopped off the dick, huh?"

"Fuck you, Jaz!"

Jaz laughed just as a call was coming through. "I gotta let you go, Mo. This is your brother." Jaz didn't even wait for her to respond before she was clicking over to her other line. "Hello?" she said.

"Fuck you doin'?" he joked.

"Shit, waiting for you."

"We're on I-64 now. I'll be home in like fifteen minutes."

Jaz took a long sigh of relief. It was as though she were breathing for the first time in a week. Hearing him say that he was so close was reassuring, to say the least. She suddenly felt safe again knowing he was on his way home.

"So how did your doctor's appointment go?" he asked.

"I didn't go," she admitted.

"Why the hell not?" He got loud for a second.

Jaz sucked her teeth. "Because, Kyree. I looked in the mirror the other day and it looked like I had Buckwheat in a headlock between my thighs. I can't go to the doctor like that."

Kyree laughed at her. Jaz could be so shallow at times. "Baby, I understand, but you can't be missing your appointments. How 'bout when I get home, I trim you up?"

"You better, 'cause I'm not going back until it's done. Kyree, I can't see past my stomach," she whined.

Kyree was in tears with laughter, but Jaz didn't find it so funny. "Okay, Jazzy, when I get there, I'll –" Kyree paused.

"What's that noise?" Jaz asked.

Kyree looked at the flashing lights behind them and immediately knew he couldn't tell Jaz. "Nothing, bae. I'll see you in a minute."

"Kyree, what's going on?" Jaz looked at her phone, only to see that he'd already hung up. Instant panic set in and she began to pace the floor. There was no doubt in her mind that those were police sirens in his background. She couldn't believe that this was happening again. Running her fingers through her relaxed hair, Jaz didn't know what she was going to do. After trying to call Kyree back and not getting a response, she called Fat Boy's number, only to be greeted with the same operator on their voicemails. With her lips pursed, Jaz looked up at the ceiling to prevent herself from crying again. The only thing on her mind was how close they were to home.

"Fuck this!" Jaz threw on a pair of sweats, grabbed her coat and car keys, and headed for the door. She was going to drive down I-64 until she found her man. Opening her front door, Jaz's protruding belly bumped into what felt like a wall. "What the hell?" Jaz looked up only for her heart to drop down to her stomach. Everything around her went black, she couldn't breathe, and she felt like she was drowning. But she couldn't muster up the words to scream for help.

"Hey, Jaz. You miss me?"

The person staring back at her was one of the last people she wanted to see in the world.

"Aren't you going to invite me in?"

Jaz slowly shook her head no. With the uninvited guest revealing a black .9mm, Jaz quickly changed her mind and stepped back inside the house.

"Thought you'd change your tune," he said with a sinister smirk.

Jaz was completely stuck and speaking was damn near impossible, but she finally swallowed hard and slowly uttered the words, "What're you doing here?"

"Now is that any way to talk to your ex-fiancé?"

CHAPTER 25

Jaz sat on her couch, watching Michael as he paced back and forth. She hadn't seen him since that dreadful day she'd caught him with Asia. Although he tried calling her several times, she never returned his calls, or any of his messages. Even though she saw his ring as a new Hermes Birkin bag, Kyree saw it as nothing more than a burden and ordered her to send it back to him. She had the ring FedEx'ed along with a bunch of his other things. She thought she'd made it clear that it was pretty much over between the two of them. But now, as he wore out her carpet with a gun in his hand, she wondered what the hell he could possibly want from her. He was obviously out of his damn mind, and the last thing she wanted to do was provoke him. But being blessed with a smooth tongue was one of her strong suits, so she figured maybe she could talk her way out of it.

"Mike, what're you doing here?" Jaz shifted in her seat.

He quickly turned to look at her. He thought he'd heard her say something, but he was so lost in his own thoughts that he couldn't be sure. "What?"

His gaze made Jaz nervous. "I just asked what you were doing here."

He smirked. "You think you can just leave me for someone else, and I'm supposed to be cool with that?" He got in Jaz's face and she leaned away from him. "Send me my fuckin' ring in an envelope without so much as a phone call? Have a baby by this motherfucker and live happily ever after?" Jaz didn't know what to say. The dangerous look in his eyes made her regret ever opening her mouth in the first place. "Huh, Jaz? Huh!" He was now so close in her face that spittle from his mouth landed directly on Jaz's cheek.

Michael was beyond infuriated with Jaz's disposition. She'd not only left him for the next nigga, but she'd also embarrassed him beyond belief. He couldn't go a day without hearing his mother say, "I told you so" - and she had, on several occasions. Jaz's lifestyle and upbringing did not fit in with his family's plan for him. They lived for the day Jaz would break his heart, but Michael wouldn't allow it. He loved Jaz; he just didn't understand why she didn't feel the same way about him.

"So you're just going to start up a family with him, even though he broke your heart before?" He searched her face for an answer.

"But I love him, Michael," she said with desperation.

"And you don't love me?" he begged to know.

"Michael, I love you, yes. But when it all boils down to is that I'm *in* love with Kyree. And not even you with a gun in my face can make me say otherwise."

Michael watched as a single tear fell from her face. He instantly felt like shit. He brought his thumb closer to her face and Jaz flinched. The regret on his face said he meant her no harm as he brushed away her tear. Dropping his head into his hands, Michael said, "Fuck!"

Jaz instantly felt responsible for the whole situation. Had she been honest with herself, and everyone else, from the jump, she wouldn't have been in this position in the first place. Taking her hand, Jaz rubbed Michael's back to console him. This wasn't his fault. She'd left so much unsaid for so long, she just knew it would eventually come to bite her in the ass.

"It's okay, Michael. You'll find someone else," she assured him.

Taking a long sigh, Michael slowly raised his head. "Well, can you at least tell me this one thing?" He placed the gun down on the coffee table in front of them.

Jaz looked at him skeptically, but soon realized he just wanted to know the truth, and she did owe him that much. She slowly nodded her head yes, figuring they both had unanswered questions.

"How long were you fucking Kyree?"

Jaz bit her bottom lip in shame, but knowing she had to own up to her hand in this, she told him. "It only happened once while you and I were together right after he got out of jail. I regretted it every day, because I really did care about you, Michael. But I couldn't continue lying to myself," Jaz admitted.

"Damn," he shook his head. "Well then, is that the reason you didn't fuck me since I proposed?" He let out a half laugh.

Jaz looked at him and couldn't help but to laugh herself. "Naw, I planned on doing that from the jump. But I never thought I'd stick with it. Only reason I did it for so long was because I felt guilty about fucking Kyree."

Michael nodded his head, slightly relieved to get some confirmation. He always thought it was his sex game that turned her away. Little did he know, that was partially the reason why she strayed in the first place. But Jaz didn't bother going any further; she only nodded her head.

"Now that you've got that off your chest, I have a bone to pick with you as well," Jaz opened up, now more at ease to speak freely, knowing he didn't want to hurt her. "You and Asia?" Jaz gave him an arched eyebrow.

Michael looked at her and gave a slight smirk. "You don't remember how you got referred to me, do you?"

"Yeah. Ms. Maggie that comes into the shop referred me. Why?"

"Well, Ms. Maggie is good friends with my parents. She always refers people to me."

Jaz looked dumbfounded as he had yet to answer her question.

"Well, Ms. Maggie also referred Asia to me, about a few months before I met you."

Jaz's mouth dropped in shock. All she could think about were all the times the two pretended as though they didn't know each other. But before jumping down his throat, she decided it best she allow him to finish first. She heard her phone buzzing off in the distance, but she was too intrigued with what Michael had to say to answer it.

"Asia started off as my patient, but that quickly grew to much more, mainly sex. We would get it in whenever and wherever."

Jaz threw her hand up, asking him to spare her the details.

"But no. You need to hear this, Jaz." He looked at her with a serious face, which immediately caught Jaz's attention. "Look, Asia pursued me, and normally I like to do all the work. But after I gave her first exam, she locked the door and proceeded to remove my pants, and you can only guess what happened from there. It wasn't long before our little rendezvous turned into a frequent thing." Michael licked his lips and dropped his head in shame. "But then I met you and you changed my world. You were my perfect opposite, and yet I wanted to do nothing more than to make you my wife."

Jaz too looked at the floor, too ashamed of how she broke his heart to look him in the eye.

"As soon as I met you, I broke it off with Asia. At first she had no idea who you were until the day I came up to the salon to take you to lunch. We pretended not to know each other, and she later confronted me about it. I told her about my feelings for you and she seemed to be cool with it. It wasn't until I proposed that she lost her fucking mind." Michael shook his head and bit the inside of his jaw at just the thought. "She blackmailed me into sex. She threatened to tell you about her and me every chance she got. I thought about telling you so many times, but she said she'd tell you that we'd been fucking around, even after you and I had been together. It got so bad that I'd program her number in as The Hospital, and whenever she'd text, I'd meet her somewhere." He paused because Jaz's facial expressions looked as though she were finally putting together the missing pieces to a puzzle. "Listen, Jaz." He turned her body so that she was facing him. "I know I came here on some crazy lunatic shit at first." They both gave a brief laugh, knowing Michael really wasn't about that life. "But Asia really does not like you. This was actually all her idea. She really has it out for you. It's like she wants to be you or something."

Jaz waved him off. This was nothing new to her. She'd been saying it for years, only no one believed her. "I'm not at all worried about that crazy hoe."

"But you really should be. After she started blackmailing me, I began to dig more into her file and I found a bunch of different mandatory medications that she has to take."

Jaz looked at him as if to say, "And?"

"The medications that she's required to take are usually prescribed to paranoid schizophrenics and manic depressives. Jaz, she's literally certifiably crazy. Please do me a favor," he pleaded with his eyes. "Be careful. She's manipulative, dangerous, and just plain psycho. Promise me you'll be careful?"

Jaz nodded her head, "I promise."

"Good. I sent her a text saying you weren't home, so that should ward her off. I have no idea what she was planning on doing to you, and I don't even know why my dumb ass even agreed to it knowing how unstable she is." He shook his head in disgust.

"I might not like the way you went about it, but it's okay, Michael. I understand you were just a man with questions that needed answers."

He gave a warm smile and stood up. "I can't believe you're pregnant. You're glowing."

"Thanks," Jaz blushed.

"Do you have a good doctor?"

"Yeah, Dr. Gomez."

"Oh yeah? Dr. G is one of the best - next to me, of course," he grinned. "Alright, let me get up out of here. Give me a hug, girl."

Jaz stood up, realizing they'd both gotten the closure they so desperately needed. A hug would only solidify the deal and confirm one last final goodbye. Wrapping his arms around Jaz, Michael hugged her close. He wanted so badly to have her to himself, but seeing her happy meant so much more to him.

"You take care of yourself, Michael," she whispered.

"You too," he said.

Michael gently kissed her on the forehead just as the front door flew open. "What the fuck?"

Jaz gasped and backed away from Michael upon the initial shock. "Bitch, you got some fuckin' nerve!" Jaz said.

"I send yo' ass to do one fucking little thing, and you can't even do that!" Asia slammed the door behind her and made a brisk walk toward Michael.

"Asia, this isn't right," he tried to reason with her.

Picking up the gun off the table where Michael had left it, Asia said, "You know what they say: if you want something done right, you gotta do the shit ya'self."

"This bitch really is fucking crazy!" Jaz looked at her with disbelief.

Michael approached her slowly. "Asia, calm down. Don't you think you're being a little irrational?"

Asia looked at him real crazy like, and then, *whomp!* Out of nowhere, the butt of the gun came crushing Michael on the side of the head, knocking him out cold. "Ugh! You get on my fucking nerves always taking this bitch's side!"

Jaz was at a loss for words for the first time ever, because unlike so many other times, she was actually scared for her life. The look Asia gave her was like none she'd ever seen before in real life, although she could have sworn she'd seen it in a couple of Lifetime movies. It was now obvious to her that Asia wasn't dealing with a full deck.

"Now as for you..." Asia cocked her gun and aimed it at Jaz, a cocky grin on her face. "Sit yo' ass down!"

Jaz took a huge gulp and did as she was told. Normally she would've told her where the fuck she could go, or charged at her, even with the gun in her hands. But that was before she was pregnant. Now her life wasn't the only one hanging in the balance, and she had to consider that. With Michael, she wasn't as afraid. He really didn't scare her as much as Asia. Even her baby was afraid as it entered into its own little personal kickboxing contest with her stomach.

As Jaz sat on the couch, Asia looked her up and down. "I don't see what the fuck they all see in yo' ass anyway." She steadied the gun and kept it aimed at Jaz. "Do you know how many freaky things I did to that man? And for what? For him to leave ME, for YOU?"

Jaz pursed her lips, too afraid to speak.

"You know, when he told me he wanted to stop fucking with me, I was hurt, but I was cool with it after a while - until I found out it was yo' ass." Asia sucked her teeth. "So to try to compete with you, I changed my hair, the way I dressed, and even the way I acted. But he didn't notice. I loved that nigga so much. And then I saw the way you reacted when Kyree came back into town, and I just knew that was the way to get to you. So I started to fuck with him, just to make you as mad as you made me. But then I actually started to like him, and he told me he was leaving me. For YOU!" Asia seethed at the mouth.

Not really sure what else to say, Jaz said, "I'm sorry."

"You're sorry? Bitch, I gave my all to them niggas and all they wanted was you. I'm so sick and tired of hearing about JAZ! Jaz's shop! Jaz's man! Jaz's baby! Fuck Jaz!" Asia shook her head and quickly looked from her left to her right shoulder. "Shut the fuck up!" she screamed over her back. The voices in her head were growing louder by the second. Pulling on the sides of her hair, she shook her head frantically. It had been weeks since she'd stopped taking her medication. In her mind, she was cured and she no longer needed the drugs to live her life. They only stopped her from being herself.

Jaz rubbed her belly to calm the nerves of her and her unborn child. Asia was losing her mind more and more by the second. Jaz had no idea how she was going to get out of this, but she had to think of something fast. "Asia, it's not your fault. They just didn't see what kind of person you are."

Asia looked up and Jaz knew she had her attention.

"You know how these niggas act. They don't know a good thing when it's in front of their face. You gave your all to them, and in return, they left you. Niggas ain't shit, girl. You know that's the motto," Jaz forced a smile.

Asia dropped her head and nodded. All of her life, men had done nothing but disappoint her, from her father who abandoned her, to the uncle that robbed her of her childhood, to Michael and Kyree, who constantly chose Jaz over her. The thought of it all made her cry. Everything always seemed to go right for Jaz and wrong for her and she hated her for it. But without her medication, she didn't have very many lucid moments. Right now, she suddenly had a change of heart. Lowering the gun at her side, she dropped her head in shame.

"It's okay, Asia," Jaz assured her from the couch.

Asia stood in shame, sniffling and crying, just as the door flung open.

"Jaz!"

Asia gasped and Jaz turned around. *Boom!* Asia let off one shot from the .9mm into Kyree's chest.

"Nooooo!" Jaz frantically screamed, rushing to Kyree's aide.

Kyree grabbed at his chest, saw the blood, and instantly dropped to his knees.

"Oh my God! I didn't mean to!" Asia cried out.

Jaz couldn't hear, or see anyone for that matter. All she saw was Kyree. It was as though nothing else in the world existed, which was why she didn't notice when a frantic Asia made her way out the door.

"Kyree! Baby!" Jaz tried to lay him down, but he wouldn't move. She could feel him grab her arm tightly and try to say something. "What is it, baby?"

"I'm...on...my...knees, ma. You...gon'...marry...me?" he strained to say, his chest heaving with each breath.

With tear-filled eyes, Jaz slowly nodded her head yes. "Yes, Kyree. I will marry you, baby."

Kyree gave a slender smirk as he let go of Jaz's wrist and began to fall backward. Jaz held him in her grasp and gently laid him on the floor. "SOMEBODY HELP ME!" Jaz screamed.

Reaching for her phone on the table, with shaking hands she frantically dialed 911, gave them a quick rundown of what was going on, and then made her way back to his side. "Stay with me, baby!" Jaz ordered, holding on tightly to his hand.

Kyree could hear Jaz's voice, but as it became more distant, he felt he needed to muster up enough strength to tell her something. Jaz heard him struggling to speak and brought her face closer to his. "Yes, baby?"

"I...lu...lu...love you Jaz...zy," he let out one last breath and closed his eyes.

"WHAT? NO! KYREE! YOU PROMISED ME YOU WOULDN'T LEAVE ME! WAKE UP, BABY!" Jaz started to shake him and he wouldn't budge.

"NOOOOOOOOOOO!" Jaz let out a long, bloodcurdling scream and fell desperately on top of Kyree's lifeless body. "I love you too, Kyree. This shit is forever, baby. Forever!"

TO BE CONTINUED....

www.ingramcontent.com/pod-product-compliance
Lightning Source LLC
Chambersburg PA
CBHW070659280626
47159CB00022B/994